NOTHING VENTURED

ALSO BY JEFFREY ARCHER

THE CLIFTON CHRONICLES
Only Time Will Tell
The Sins of the Father
Best Kept Secret
Be Careful What You Wish For
Mightier than the Sword
Cometh the Hour
This Was a Man

NOVELS
Heads You Win
Not a Penny More, Not a Penny Less
Shall We Tell the President?
Kane & Abel
The Prodigal Daughter
First Among Equals
A Matter of Honor
As the Crow Flies
Honor Among Thieves
The Fourth Estate
The Eleventh Commandment
Sons of Fortune
False Impression
The Gospel According to Judas
(with the assistance of Professor Francis J. Moloney)
A Prisoner of Birth
Paths of Glory
Heads You Win

SHORT STORIES
A Quiver Full of Arrows
A Twist in the Tale
Twelve Red Herrings
The Collected Short Stories
To Cut a Long Story Short
Cat O' Nine Tales
And Thereby Hangs a Tale
Tell Tale

PLAYS
Beyond Reasonable Doubt
Exclusive
The Accused
Confession
Who Killed the Mayor?

PRISON DIARIES
Volume One—Belmarsh: Hell
Volume Two—Wayland: Purgatory
Volume Three—North Sea Camp: Heaven

SCREENPLAYS
Mallory: Walking Off the Map
False Impression

JEFFREY ARCHER

NOTHING VENTURED

St. Martin's Press ≋ New York

First published in the United States by St. Martin's Press, an imprint of St. Martin's Publishing Group

NOTHING VENTURED. Copyright © 2019 by Jeffrey Archer. All rights reserved. Printed in the United States of America. For information, address St. Martin's Publishing Group, 120 Broadway, New York, NY 10271.

www.stmartins.com

Library of Congress Cataloging-in-Publication Data

Names: Archer, Jeffrey, 1940– author.
Title: Nothing ventured / Jeffrey Archer.
Description: First U.S. Edition. | New York : St. Martin's Press, 2019. |
    Series: William Warwick novels; 1
Identifiers: LCCN 2019024269 | ISBN 9781250200761 (hardcover) |
    ISBN 9781250200778 (ebook)
Subjects: LCSH: Art thefts—Fiction. | GSAFD: Love stories. | Mystery fiction.
Classification: LCC PR6051.R285 N68 2019 | DDC 823/.914—dc23
LC record available at https://lccn.loc.gov/2019024269

Our books may be purchased in bulk for promotional, educational, or business use. Please contact your local bookseller or the Macmillan Corporate and Premium Sales Department at 1-800-221-7945, extension 5442, or by email at MacmillanSpecialMarkets@macmillan.com.

Originally published in Great Britain by Macmillan, an imprint of Pan Macmillan

First U.S. Edition: September 2019

10   9   8   7   6   5   4   3   2   1

To Commander William Hucklesby QPM

ACKNOWLEDGMENTS

My thanks for their invaluable advice and research to:

Simon Bainbridge; Jonathan Caplan QC; Gregory Edmund;
Colin Emson; Eric Franks; Vicki Mellor; Alison Prince;
Ellen Radley, Forensic Handwriting and
Document Examiner (Ret.); Catherine Richards;
Susan Watt and Johnny Van Haeften

Special thanks to Detective Sergeant Michelle Roycroft (Ret.)
and Chief Superintendent John Sutherland (Ret.)

Dear Reader,

After I finished writing the last of the Clifton Chronicles, several readers wrote to tell me they'd like to know more about William Warwick, the eponymous hero of Harry Clifton's novels.

I confess that I had already given the idea some thought before I began working on *Nothing Ventured*, the first in the William Warwick series.

Nothing Ventured opens when William leaves school and, much to his father's dismay, decides he wants to join the Metropolitan Police, rather than become a pupil in his father's chambers. William perseveres, and in this opening novel we follow his life on the beat with a cast of characters, some good, some not so good, who cross his path as he tries to become a detective and transfers to Scotland Yard.

During the series, you will follow William's fortunes as he progresses from detective constable to the commissioner of the Metropolitan Police.

I'm currently working on the second novel in the series which will focus on William's time as a young detective sergeant in the elite drugs unit.

Should he ever make it to commissioner will depend as much on William Warwick's determination and ability as my hopes for longevity—mine, not yours.

Jeffrey Archer
September 2019

This is not a detective story,
this is a story about a detective.

NOTHING VENTURED

1

July 14, 1979

"You can't be serious."

"I couldn't be more serious, Father, as you'd realize if you'd ever listened to anything I've been saying for the past ten years."

"But you've been offered a place at my old college at Oxford to read law, and after you graduate, you'll be able to join me in chambers. What more could a young man ask for?"

"To be allowed to pursue a career of his own choosing, and not just be expected to follow in his father's footsteps."

"Would that be such a bad thing? After all, I've enjoyed a fascinating and worthwhile career, and, dare I suggest, been moderately successful."

"Brilliantly successful, Father, but it isn't your career we're discussing, it's mine. And perhaps I don't want to be a leading criminal barrister who spends his whole life defending a bunch of villains he'd never consider inviting to lunch at his club."

"You seem to have forgotten that those same villains paid for your education, and the lifestyle you presently enjoy."

"I'm never allowed to forget it, Father, which is the reason I intend to spend my life making sure those same villains are locked up for long periods of time, and not allowed to go free and continue a life of crime thanks to your skillful advocacy."

William thought he'd finally silenced his father, but he was wrong.

"Perhaps we could agree on a compromise, dear boy?"

"Not a chance, Father," said William firmly. "You're sounding like a barrister who's pleading for a reduced sentence, when he knows he's defending a weak case. But for once, your eloquent words are falling on deaf ears."

"Won't you even allow me to put my case before you dismiss it out of hand?" responded his father.

"No, because I'm not guilty, and I don't have to prove to a jury that I'm innocent, just to please you."

"But would you be willing to do something to please me, my dear?"

In the heat of battle William had quite forgotten that his mother had been sitting silently at the other end of the table, closely following the jousting between her husband and son. William was well prepared to take on his father but knew he was no match for his mother. He fell silent once again. A silence that his father took advantage of.

"What do you have in mind, m'lud?" said Sir Julian, tugging at the lapels of his jacket, and addressing his wife as if she were a high court judge.

"William will be allowed to go to the university of his choice," said Marjorie, "select the subject he wishes to study, and once he's graduated, follow the career he wants to pursue. And more important, when he does, you will give in gracefully and never raise the subject again."

"I confess," said Sir Julian, "that while accepting your wise judgment, I might find the last part difficult."

Mother and son burst out laughing.

"Am I allowed a plea in mitigation?" asked Sir Julian innocently.

"No," said William, "because I will only agree to Mother's terms if in three years' time you unreservedly support my decision to join the Metropolitan Police Force."

Sir Julian Warwick QC rose from his place at the head of the table, gave his wife a slight bow, and reluctantly said, "If it so please Your Lordship."

—◦—

William Warwick had wanted to be a detective from the age of eight, when he'd solved "the case of the missing Mars bars." It was a simple paper trail, he explained to his housemaster, that didn't require a magnifying glass.

The evidence—sweet papers—had been found in the waste-paper basket of the guilty party's study, and the culprit wasn't able to prove he'd spent any of his pocket money in the tuck shop that term. And what made it worse for William was that Adrian Heath was one of his closest pals, and he'd assumed it would be a lifelong friendship. When he discussed it with his father at half term, the old man said, "We must hope that Adrian has learned from the experience, otherwise who knows what will became of the boy."

Despite William being mocked by his fellow pupils, who dreamed of becoming doctors, lawyers, teachers, even accountants, the careers master showed no surprise when William informed him that he was going to be a detective. After all, the other boys had nicknamed him Sherlock before the end of his first term.

William's father, Sir Julian Warwick Bt, had wanted his son to go up to Oxford and read law, just as he'd done thirty years before. But despite his father's best efforts, William had remained determined to join the police force the day he left school. The two stubborn men finally reached a compromise approved of by his mother. William would go to London University and read art history—a subject his father refused to take seriously—and if, after three years, his son still wanted to be a policeman, Sir Julian agreed to give in gracefully. William knew that would never happen.

William enjoyed every moment of his three years at King's College London, where he fell in love several times. First with Hannah and Rembrandt, followed by Judy and Turner, and finally Rachel and Hockney, before settling down with Caravaggio: an affair that would last a lifetime, even though his father had pointed out that the great Italian artist had been a murderer and should have been hanged. A good enough reason to abolish the death penalty, William suggested. Once again, father and son didn't agree.

During the summer holidays after he'd left school, William backpacked his way across Europe to Rome, Paris, Berlin, and on to St. Petersburg, to join long queues of other devotees who wished to worship the past masters. When he finally graduated, his professor suggested that he should consider a PhD on the darker side of Caravaggio. The darker side, replied William, was exactly what he intended to research, but he wanted to learn more about criminals in the twentieth century, rather than the sixteenth.

◄o►

At five minutes to three on the afternoon of Sunday, September 5, 1982, William reported to Hendon Police College in north London. He enjoyed almost every minute of the training course from the moment he swore allegiance to the Queen to his passing-out parade sixteen weeks later.

The following day, he was issued with a navy-blue serge uniform, helmet, and truncheon, and couldn't resist glancing at his reflection whenever he passed a window. A police uniform, he was warned by the commander on his first day on parade, could change a person's personality, and not always for the better.

Lessons at Hendon had begun on the second day and were divided between the classroom and the gym. William learned whole sections of the law until he could repeat them verbatim. He reveled in forensic and crime scene analysis, even though he quickly discovered when he was introduced to the skid pad that his driving skills were fairly rudimentary.

Having endured years of cut and thrust with his father across the breakfast table, William felt at ease in the mock courtroom, where instructing officers cross-examined him in the witness box, and he even held his own during self-defense classes, where he learned how to disarm, handcuff, and restrain someone who was far bigger than him. He was also taught about a constable's powers of arrest, search and entry, the use of reasonable force, and, most important of all, discretion. "Don't always stick to the rule book," his instructor advised him. "Sometimes you have to use common sense, which, when you're dealing with the public, you'll find isn't that common."

Exams were as regular as clockwork, compared to his days at university, and he wasn't surprised that several candidates fell by the wayside long before the course had ended.

After what felt like an interminable two-week break following his passing-out parade, William finally received a letter instructing him to report to Lambeth police station at 8 a.m. the following Monday. An area of London he had never visited before.

◄○►

Police Constable 565LD had joined the Metropolitan Police Force as a graduate but decided not to take advantage of the accelerated promotion scheme that would have allowed him to progress more quickly up the ladder, as he wanted to line up on his first day with every other new recruit on equal terms. He accepted that, as a probationer, he would have to spend at least two years on the beat before he could hope to become a detective, and in truth, he couldn't wait to be thrown in at the deep end.

From his first day as a probationer William was guided by his mentor, Constable Fred Yates, who had twenty-eight years of police service under his belt, and had been told by the nick's chief inspector to "look after the boy." The two men had little in common other than that they'd both wanted to be coppers from an early age, and their fathers had done everything in their power to prevent them pursuing their chosen career.

"ABC," was the first thing Fred said when he was introduced to the wet-behind-the-ears young sprog. He didn't wait for William to ask.

"Accept nothing, Believe no one, Challenge everything. It's the only law I live by."

During the next few months, Fred introduced William to the world of burglars, drug dealers, and pimps, as well as his first dead body. With the zeal of Sir Galahad, William wanted to lock up every offender and make the world a better place; Fred was more realistic, but he never once attempted to douse the flames of William's youthful enthusiasm. The young probationer quickly found out that the public don't know if a policeman has been in uniform for a couple of days or a couple of years on William's second day on the beat.

"Time to stop your first car," said Fred, coming to a halt by a set of traffic lights. "We'll hang about until someone runs a red, and then you can step out into the road and flag them down." William looked apprehensive. "Leave the rest to me. See that tree about a hundred yards away? Go and hide behind it, and wait until I give you the signal."

William could hear his heart pounding as he stood behind the tree. He didn't have long to wait before Fred raised a hand and shouted, "The blue Hillman! Grab him!"

William stepped out into the road, put his arm up, and directed the car to pull over to the curb.

"Say nothing," said Fred as he joined the raw recruit. "Watch carefully and take note." They both walked up to the car as the driver wound down his window.

"Good morning, sir," said Fred. "Are you aware that you drove through a red light?"

The driver nodded but didn't speak.

"Could I see your driving license?"

The driver opened his glove box, extracted his license, and handed it to Fred. After studying the document for a few moments, Fred said, "It's particularly dangerous at this time in the morning, sir, as there are two schools nearby."

"I'm sorry," said the driver. "It won't happen again."

Fred handed him back his license. "It will just be a warning this time," he said, while William wrote down the car's number plate in his notebook. "But perhaps you could be a little more careful in future, sir."

"Thank you, officer," said the driver.

"Why just a caution," asked William as the car drove slowly away, "when you could have booked him?"

"Attitude," said Fred. "The gentleman was polite, acknowledged his mistake, and apologized. Why piss off a normally law-abiding member of the public?"

"So what would have made you book him?"

"If he'd said, 'Haven't you got anything better to do, officer?' Or worse, 'Shouldn't you be chasing some real criminals?' Or my favorite, 'Don't you realize I pay your wages?' Any of those and I would have booked him without hesitation. Mind you, there was one blighter I had to cart off to the station and lock up for a couple of hours."

"Did he get violent?"

"No, far worse. Told me he was a close friend of the commissioner, and I'd be hearing from him. So I told him he could phone him from the station." William burst out laughing. "Right," said Fred, "get back behind the tree. Next time you can conduct the interview and I'll observe."

◄○►

Sir Julian Warwick QC sat at one end of the table, his head buried in *The Daily Telegraph*. He muttered the occasional tut-tut, while his wife, seated at the other end, continued her daily battle with *The Times* crossword. On a good day, Marjorie would have filled in the final clue before her husband rose from the table to leave for Lincoln's Inn. On a bad day, she would have to seek his advice, a service for which he usually charged a hundred pounds an hour. He regularly reminded her that to date, she owed him over twenty thousand pounds. Ten across and four down were holding her up.

Sir Julian had reached the leaders by the time his wife was

wrestling with the final clue. He still wasn't convinced that the death penalty should have been abolished, particularly when a police officer or a public servant was the victim, but then neither was the *Telegraph*. He turned to the back page to find out how Blackheath rugby club had fared against Richmond in their annual derby. After reading the match report he abandoned the sports pages, as he considered the paper gave far too much coverage to soccer. Yet another sign that the nation was going to the dogs.

"Delightful picture of Charles and Diana in *The Times*," said Marjorie.

"It will never last," said Julian as he rose from his place and walked to the other end of the table and, as he did every morning, kissed his wife on the forehead. They exchanged newspapers, so he could study the law reports on the train journey to London.

"Don't forget the children are coming down for lunch on Sunday," Marjorie reminded him.

"Has William passed his detective's exam yet?" he asked.

"As you well know, my dear, he isn't allowed to take the exam until he's completed two years on the beat, which won't be for at least another six months."

"If he'd listened to me, he would have been a qualified barrister by now."

"And if you'd listened to him, you'd know he's far more interested in locking up criminals than finding ways of getting them off."

"I haven't given up yet," said Sir Julian.

"Just be thankful that at least our daughter has followed in your footsteps."

"Grace has done nothing of the sort," snorted Sir Julian. "That girl will defend any penniless no-hoper she comes across."

"She has a heart of gold."

"Then she takes after you," said Sir Julian, studying the one clue his wife had failed to fill in: *Slender private man who ended up with a baton*. Five, seven, and four.

"Field Marshal Slim," said Sir Julian triumphantly. "The only man to join the army as a private soldier and end up as a field marshal."

"Sounds like William," said Marjorie. But not until the door had closed.

2

William and Fred left the nick just after eight to set out on their morning patrol. "Not much crime at this time of day," Fred assured the young probationer. "Criminals are like the rich, they don't get up much before ten." Over the past eighteen months William had become used to Fred's oft-repeated pearls of wisdom, which had proved far more useful than anything to be found in the Met's handbook on the duties of a police officer.

"When do you take your detective's exam?" asked Fred as they ambled down Lambeth Walk.

"In a few weeks' time," replied William. "But I don't think you'll be getting rid of me quite yet," he added as they approached the local newsagent. He glanced at the headline: "PC Yvonne Fletcher killed outside the Libyan Embassy."

"Murdered, more like," said Fred. "Poor lass." He didn't speak again for some time. "I've been a constable all my life," he eventually managed, "which suits me just fine. But you—"

"If I make it," said William, "I'll have you to thank."

"I'm not like you, Choirboy," said Fred. William feared that he would be stuck with that nickname for the rest of his career. He preferred Sherlock. He had never admitted to any of his mates at the station that he had been a choirboy, and always wished he looked older, although his mother had once told him, "The moment you do, you'll want to look younger." *Is no one ever satisfied with the age they are?* he wondered. "By the time you become commissioner," continued Fred, "I'll be shacked up in an old people's home, and you'll have forgotten my name."

It had never crossed William's mind that he might end up as commissioner, although he felt sure he would never forget Constable Fred Yates.

Fred spotted the young lad as he came running out of the newsagent's. Mr. Patel followed a moment later, but he was never going to catch him. William set off in pursuit, with Fred only a yard behind. They both overtook Mr. Patel as the boy turned the corner. But it was another hundred yards before William was able to grab him. The two of them led the young lad back to the shop, where he handed over a packet of Capstan to Mr. Patel.

"Will you be pressing charges, sir?" asked William, who already had his notebook open, pencil poised.

"What's the point?" said the shopkeeper, placing the cigarette packet back on the shelf. "If you lock him up, his younger brother will only take his place."

"It's your lucky day, Tomkins," said Fred, clipping the boy around the ear. "Just make sure you're in school by the time we turn up, otherwise I might tell your old man what you were up to. Mind you," he added, turning to William, "the fags were probably for his old man."

Tomkins bolted. When he reached the end of the street he stopped, turned around and shouted, "Police scum!" and gave them both a 'V' sign.

"Perhaps you should have pinned his ears back."

"What are you talking about?" asked Fred.

"In the sixteenth century, when a boy was caught stealing, he would be nailed to a post by one of his ears, and the only way he could escape was to tear himself free."

"Not a bad idea," said Fred. "Because I have to admit I can't get to grips with modern police practice. By the time you retire, you'll probably have to call the criminals 'sir.' Still, I've only got another eighteen months to go before I collect my pension, and by then you'll be at Scotland Yard. Although," Fred added, about to dispense his daily dose of wisdom, "when I joined the force nearly thirty years ago, we used to handcuff lads like that to a radiator, turn the heat full on, and not release them until they'd confessed."

William burst out laughing.

"I wasn't joking," said Fred.

"How long do you think it will be before Tomkins ends up in jail?"

"A spell in borstal before he goes to prison, would be my bet. The really maddening thing is that once he's locked up he'll have his own cell, three meals a day, and be surrounded by career criminals who'll be only too happy to teach him his trade before he graduates from the University of Crime."

Every day William was reminded how lucky he'd been to be born in a middle-class cot, with loving parents and an older sister who doted on him. Although he never admitted to any of his colleagues that he'd been educated at one of England's leading public schools before taking an art history degree at King's College London. And he certainly never mentioned that his father regularly received large payments from some of the nation's most notorious criminals.

As they continued on their round, several local people acknowledged Fred, and some even said good morning to William.

When they returned to the nick a couple of hours later, Fred didn't bother to report young Tomkins to the desk sergeant, as he felt the same way about paperwork as he did about modern police practice.

"Feel like a cuppa?" said Fred, heading toward the canteen.

"Warwick!" shouted a voice from behind them.

William turned round to see the custody sergeant pointing at him. "A prisoner's collapsed in his cell. Take this prescription to the nearest chemist and have it made up. And be quick about it."

"Yes, Sarge," said William. He grabbed the envelope, and ran all the way to Boots on the high street, where he found a small queue waiting patiently at the dispensary counter. He apologized to the woman at the front of the queue before handing the envelope to the pharmacist. "It's an emergency," he said.

The young woman opened the envelope and carefully read the instructions before saying, "That will be one pound sixty, constable."

William fumbled for some change, which he gave to the pharmacist. She rang up the sale, turned around, took a packet of condoms off the shelf, and handed it to him. William's mouth opened, but no words came out. He was painfully aware that several people in the queue were grinning. He was about to slip away when the pharmacist said, "Don't forget your prescription, constable." She passed the envelope back to William.

Several amused pairs of eyes followed him as he slipped out into the street. He waited until he was out of sight before he opened the envelope and read the enclosed note.

Dear Sir or Madam,

I am a shy young constable, who's finally got a girl to come out with me, and I'm hoping to get lucky tonight. But as I don't want to get her pregnant, can you help?

William burst out laughing, put the packet of condoms in his pocket, and made his way back to the station; his first thought: *I only wish I did have a girlfriend.*

3

Constable Warwick screwed the top back onto his fountain pen, confident he had passed his detective's exam with what his father would have called flying colors.

When he returned to his single room in Trenchard House that evening, the flying colors had been lowered to half mast, and by the time he switched off his bedside lamp, he was sure he would remain in uniform and be on the beat for at least another year.

"How did you do?" the station officer asked when he reported back on duty the following morning.

"Failed hopelessly," said William, as he checked the parade book. He and Fred were down to patrol the Barton estate, if only to remind the local criminals that London still had a few bobbies on the beat.

"Then you'll have to try again next year," said the sergeant, unwilling to indulge the young man. If Constable Warwick wanted to wallow in self-doubt, he had no intention of rescuing the lad.

◄○►

Sir Julian continued sharpening the carving knife until he was confident blood would run.

"Two slices or one, my boy?" he asked his son.

"Two please, Father."

Sir Julian sliced the roast with the skill of a seasoned carver.

"So did you pass your detective's exam?" he asked William as he handed him his plate.

"I won't know for at least another couple of weeks," said William, passing his mother a bowl of brussel sprouts. "But I'm not optimistic. However, you'll be pleased to hear I'm in the final of the station's snooker championship."

"Snooker?" said his father, as if it were a game he was unfamiliar with.

"Yes, something else I've learned in the last two years."

"But will you win?" demanded his father.

"Unlikely. I'm up against the favorite, who's won the cup for the past six years."

"So you've failed your detective's exam and are about to be runner-up in the—"

"I've always wondered why they're called brussel sprouts, and not just sprouts, like carrots or potatoes," said Marjorie, trying to head off another duel between father and son.

"They started life as Brussels sprouts," said Grace, "and over the years the 'B' became small, and the 's' disappeared, until finally everyone has come to accept brussel as a word, except the more pedantic among us."

"Like the *OED*," suggested Marjorie, smiling at her daughter.

"And if you have passed," said Sir Julian, refusing to be distracted by the etymology of the brussel sprout, "how long will it be before you become a detective?"

"Six months, possibly a year. I'll have to wait for a vacancy to arise in another patch."

"Perhaps you'll go straight to Scotland Yard?" said his father, raising an eyebrow.

"That's not possible. You have to prove yourself in another division before you can even apply for a job at the holy grail. Although I will be visiting the Yard tomorrow for the first time."

Sir Julian stopped carving. "Why?" he demanded.

"I'm not sure myself," admitted William. "The super called me in on Friday and told me to report to a Commander Hawksby at nine on Monday morning, but he didn't give any clue why."

"Hawksby . . . Hawksby . . ." said Sir Julian, the lines on his forehead growing more pronounced. "Why do I know that name? Ah yes, we once crossed swords on a fraud case when he was a chief inspector. An impressive witness. He'd done his homework and was so well prepared I couldn't lay a glove on him. Not a man to be underestimated."

"Tell me more," said William.

"Unusually short for a policeman. Beware of them; they often have bigger brains. He's known as the Hawk. Hovers over you before swooping down and carrying all before him."

"You included, it would seem," said Marjorie.

"What makes you say that?" asked Sir Julian, as he poured himself a glass of wine.

"You only ever remember witnesses who get the better of you."

"Touché," said Sir Julian, raising his glass as Grace and William burst into spontaneous applause.

"Please give Commander Hawksby my best wishes," added Sir Julian, ignoring the outburst.

"That's the last thing I'm going to do," said William. "I'm hoping to make a good impression, not an enemy for life."

"Is my reputation that bad?" said Sir Julian, with an exasperated sigh worthy of a rejected lover.

"I'm afraid your reputation is that good," said William. "The mere mention of your name in the nick evokes groans of despair, with the realization that yet another criminal who should be locked up for life will be set free."

"Who am I to disagree with twelve good men and true?"

"It may have slipped your notice, Father," said Grace, "but women have been sitting on juries since 1920."

"More's the pity," said Sir Julian. "I would never have given them the vote."

"Don't rise, Grace," said her mother. "He's only trying to provoke you."

"So what is the next hopeless cause you will be championing?" Sir Julian asked his daughter, thrusting the knife in deeper.

"Hereditary rights," said Grace, as she took a sip of wine.

"Whose in particular, dare I ask?"

"Mine. You may well be Sir Julian Warwick Bt, but when you die—"

"Not for some time, I hope," said Marjorie.

"William will inherit your title," continued Grace, ignoring the interruption, "despite the fact that I was the firstborn."

"A disgraceful state of affairs," mocked Sir Julian.

"It's no laughing matter, Father, and I predict that you'll see the law changed in your lifetime."

"I can't imagine their lordships will readily fall in with your proposal."

"And that's why they'll be next in line, because once the Commons realizes there are votes in it, another sacred citadel will collapse under the weight of its own absurdity."

"How will you go about it?" asked Marjorie.

"We'll start at the top, with the Royal Family. We already have a life peer willing to present a primogeniture bill to the House, which would allow a woman to succeed as monarch if she was the first born, and not be pushed aside by a younger brother. No one has ever suggested that Princess Anne wouldn't do as good a job as Prince Charles. And we'll cite Queen Elizabeth I, Queen Victoria, and Queen Elizabeth II to prove our case."

"It will never happen."

"In your lifetime, Dad," Grace repeated.

"But I thought you disapproved of titles, Grace," said William.

"I do. But in this case it's a matter of principle."

"Well, I'll support you. I've never wanted to be Sir William."

"What if you became commissioner, and earned it in your own right?" said his father. William hesitated for long enough for his father to shrug his shoulders.

"Did that poor young woman you were defending last week manage to get off?" Marjorie asked Grace, hoping for a break in hostilities.

"No, she got six months."

"And will be out in three," said her father, "when she will no doubt go straight back on the street."

"Don't get me onto that subject, Dad."

"What about her pimp?" asked William. "He's the one who should be locked up."

"I'd happily boil him in oil," said Grace, "but he wasn't even charged."

"In oil?" said her father. "We'll have you voting Conservative yet."

"Never," Grace responded.

Sir Julian picked up the carving knife. "Anyone for seconds?"

"Dare I ask if you've met anyone recently?" asked Marjorie, turning to her son.

"Several people, Mama," said William, amused by his mother's euphemism.

"You know exactly what I meant," she chided.

"Fat chance. I've been working on the roster for the past month, seven nights in a row, finishing up at six in the morning, by which time all you want to do is sleep. Then you're expected to report back for duty two days later, to start an early shift. So let's face it, Mum, PC Warwick isn't much of a catch."

"Whereas if you'd taken my advice," said his father, "by now you'd be an eligible barrister, and I can assure you there are several attractive young women in chambers."

"I've met someone," said Grace, which silenced her father for the first time. He put down his knife and fork and listened intently. "She's a solicitor in the City, but I'm afraid Dad wouldn't approve of her as she specializes in divorce."

"I can't wait to meet her," said Marjorie.

"Whenever you like, Mama, but be warned, I haven't told her who my father is."

"Am I a cross between Rasputin and Judge Jeffreys?" asked Sir Julian, placing the tip of the carving knife next to his heart.

"You're not that nice," said his wife, "but you do have your uses."

"Name one," said Grace.

"There's a clue in yesterday's crossword that is still baffling me."

"I'm available to be consulted," said Sir Julian.

"*Out of sorts family?* Thirteen letters. Third letter is 's,' tenth letter 'o.'"

"Dysfunctional!" the other three cried in unison, and burst out laughing.

"Anyone for humble pie?" said Sir Julian.

—◄o►—

William had told his father that he was unlikely to win, but now it was in the bag, or to be more accurate, in the corner pocket. He was about to pot the last ball on the table and win the Lambeth station snooker championship, and end a run of six victories for Fred Yates.

Somewhat ironic, William thought, as it was Fred who'd taught him to play the game. In fact, William wouldn't have ventured into the snooker room if Fred hadn't suggested it might help him get to know some of the lads who weren't too sure about the choirboy.

Fred had taught his charge to play snooker with the same zeal he had applied to introducing the lad to life on the beat, and now, for the first time, William was going to beat his mentor at his own game.

At school, William had excelled on the rugby pitch in the winter as a wing three-quarter, and during the summer as a sprinter on the track. In his final year at London University, he'd been awarded the coveted Purple after winning the Intercollegiate Championship. Even his father managed a wry smile whenever William broke the tape in the 100-yard dash, as he called it, although William suspected that "re-rack," "maximum break," and "in off" weren't yet part of his father's vocabulary.

William checked the scoreboard. Three games all. It now rested on the final frame. He had started well with a break of 42, but Fred had taken his time, eating away at the lead until the game was finely poised. Although William was still leading by 26 points, all the colors were on their spots, so that when Fred returned to the table, all he had to do was clear the last seven balls to capture the trophy.

The basement room was packed with officers of every rank; some were perched on the radiators while others sat on the stairs. A silence fell on the gathering as Fred leaned across the table to address the yellow. William resigned himself to having lost his chance of becoming champion, as he watched the yellow, green, brown, and blue disappear into the pockets, leaving Fred with just the pink and black to clear the table and win the match.

Fred lined up the object ball before setting the cue ball on its way. But he'd struck it a little too firmly, and although the pink shot toward the middle pocket and disappeared down the hole, the white ended up on a side cushion, leaving a difficult cue, even for a pro.

The crowd held its breath as Fred bent down. He took his time lining up the final ball which, if he potted, would take him over the line: 73–72, making him the first person to win the title seven years in a row.

He stood back up, clearly nervous, and chalked his cue once again as he tried to compose himself before returning to the table. He bent down, fingers splayed, and concentrated before he struck the cue ball. He watched anxiously as the black headed toward the corner pocket; several of his supporters willed it on its way, but to their dismay, it came to a halt just inches from the edge. There was an exasperated sigh from the crowd, who were aware William had been left with a shot even a novice could have pocketed, and they accepted that a new name was about to be added to the honors board.

The contender took a deep breath before glancing at the honors board, to be reminded that Fred's name was printed in gold for 1977, 1978, 1979, 1980, 1981, and 1982. *But not 1983*, thought William, as he chalked his cue. He felt like Steve Davis moments before he became world champion.

He was about to sink the final black when he spotted Fred standing on the other side of the table, looking resigned and dejected.

William leaned over the table, lined up the two balls, and hit the cue ball perfectly. He watched as the black touched the rim of the pocket, wobbled precariously over the hole, but remained tantalizingly balanced on the lip, and failed to drop. The stunned crowd gasped in disbelief. The lad had buckled under pressure.

Fred didn't squander a second chance, and the room erupted when he sank the final ball to win the frame, and the championship, 73–72.

The two men shook hands while several officers surrounded them, patting both men on the back, with "Well done," "Couldn't have been closer," and "Bad luck, William." William stood to one side when the super presented Fred with the cup, which the champion raised high in the air to even louder cheers.

An older man, dressed in a smart double-breasted suit, whom neither of the gladiators had noticed, slipped quietly out of the room, left the station, and instructed his driver to take him home.

Everything he'd been told about the lad had turned out to be true, and he couldn't wait for Constable Warwick to join his team at Scotland Yard.

4

When Constable Warwick emerged from St. James's Park tube station, the first thing he saw on the far side of the road was the iconic revolving triangular sign announcing NEW SCOTLAND YARD. He gazed across with awe and apprehension, as an aspiring actor might approaching the National Theatre, or an artist entering the courtyard of the Royal Academy for the first time. He pulled up his collar to protect himself from the biting wind, and joined the stampede of early morning lemmings on their way to work.

William crossed Broadway and continued walking toward the headquarters of the Metropolitan Police Force, a nineteen-story building covered in decades of grime and crime. He presented his warrant card to the policeman on the door, and headed for the reception desk. A young woman smiled up at him.

"My name is Constable Warwick. I have an appointment with Commander Hawksby."

She ran a finger down the morning schedule.

"Ah, yes. You'll find the commander's office on the fifth floor, at the far end of the corridor."

William thanked her and headed toward a bank of lifts, but when he saw how many people were waiting, he decided to take the stairs. When he reached the first floor, DRUGS, he continued climbing. He passed FRAUD on the second floor, and MURDER on the third, before finally reaching the fifth floor, where he was greeted by MONEY LAUNDERING, ART AND ANTIQUES.

He pushed open a door that led into a long, brightly lit corridor.

He walked slowly, aware that he still had a little time to spare. Better to be a few minutes early than a minute late, according to the gospel of St. Julian. Lights were blazing in every room he passed. The fight against crime knew no hours. One door was ajar, and William caught his breath when he spotted a painting that was propped up against the far wall.

Two men and a young woman were examining the picture carefully.

"Well done, Jackie," said the older man, in a distinct Scottish accent. "A personal triumph."

"Thank you, guv," she replied.

"Let's hope," said the younger man, pointing at the picture, "this will put Faulkner behind bars for at least six years. God knows we've waited long enough to nail the bastard."

"Agreed, DC Hogan," said the older man, who turned and spotted William standing in the doorway. "Can I help you?" he asked sharply.

"No, thank you, sir."

While you're still a constable, Fred had warned him, call anything that moves "sir." That way you can't go far wrong. "I was just admiring the painting." The older man was about to close the door when William added, "I've seen the original."

The three officers turned to take a closer look at the intruder.

"This is the original," said the young woman, sounding irritated.

"That's not possible," said William.

"What makes you so sure?" demanded her colleague.

"The original used to hang in the Fitzmolean Museum in Kensington until it was stolen some years ago. A crime that still hasn't been solved."

"We've just solved it," said the woman with conviction.

"I don't think so," responded William. "The original was signed by Rembrandt in the bottom right-hand corner with his initials, RvR."

The three officers peered at the right-hand corner of the canvas, but there was no sign of any initials.

"Tim Knox, the director of the Fitzmolean, will be joining us in a few minutes' time, laddie," said the older man. "I think I'll rely on his judgment rather than yours."

"Of course, sir," said William.

"Do you have any idea how much this painting is worth?" asked the young woman.

William stepped into the room and took a closer look. He thought it best not to remind her of Oscar Wilde's comment on the difference between value and price.

"I'm not an expert," he said, "but I would think somewhere between two and three hundred pounds."

"And the original?" asked the young woman, no longer sounding quite as confident.

"No idea, but every major gallery on earth would want to add such a masterpiece to its collection, not to mention several leading collectors, for whom money wouldn't be an object."

"So you haven't got a clue what it's worth?" said the younger officer.

"No, sir. A Rembrandt of this quality is rarely seen on the open market. The last one to come under the hammer was at Sotheby Parke Bernet in New York."

"We know where Sotheby Parke Bernet is," said the older man, making no attempt to hide his sarcasm.

"Then you'll know it went for twenty-three million dollars," said William, immediately regretting his words.

"We are all grateful for your opinion, laddie, but don't let us hold you up any longer, as I am sure you have more important things to do," he said, nodding toward the door.

William tried to retreat gracefully as he stepped back into the corridor only to hear the door close firmly behind him. He checked his watch 7:57. He hurried on toward the far end of the corridor, not wanting to be late for his appointment.

He knocked on a door that announced in gold lettering, COMMANDER JACK HAWKSBY OBE, and walked in to find a secretary seated behind a desk. She stopped typing, looked up and said, "PC Warwick?"

"Yes," said William nervously.

"The commander is expecting you. Please go straight through," she said, pointing to another door.

William knocked a second time, and waited until he heard the word, "Come."

A smartly dressed, middle-aged man with penetrating blue eyes and a lined forehead, making him look older than his years, rose from behind his desk. Hawksby shook William's outstretched hand and pointed to a chair on the other side of the desk. He opened a file and studied it for a few moments before he spoke. "Let me begin by asking you if you are by any chance related to Sir Julian Warwick QC?"

William's heart sank. "He's my father," he said, presuming that the interview was about to come to a premature end.

"A man I greatly admire," said Hawksby. "Never breaks the rules, never bends the law, but still defends even the most dubious charlatans as if they were saints, and I don't suppose he's come across many of those in his professional capacity." William laughed nervously.

"I wanted to see you personally," continued Hawksby, clearly not a man who wasted time on small talk, "as you passed out top in your detective's exam, and by a considerable margin."

William hadn't even realized he'd passed.

"Congratulations," the commander added. "I also noted that you're a graduate, but chose not to take advantage of our accelerated promotion scheme."

"No, sir. I wanted to—"

"Prove yourself. As I did myself. Now, as you know, Warwick, if you are to become a detective, you will have to be transferred to another patch. With that in mind, I've decided to send you to Peckham to learn the ropes. If you're any good, I'll be seeing you again in a couple of years' time, and then I'll decide if you're ready to join us here at Scotland Yard, and take on the first division criminals, or if you should remain in the outer reaches and continue your apprenticeship."

William allowed himself a smile, and settled back in his chair only to be shocked by the commander's next question.

"Are you absolutely sure you want to be a detective?"

"Yes, sir. From the age of eight."

"It's not the white-collar criminals your father comes across that you'll be dealing with, but the worst scum on earth. You'll be expected to cope with everything from the suicide of a pregnant mother who can't take being abused by her partner any longer, to finding a young drug addict with a needle sticking out of his arm who's not much older than you. Frankly, you won't always be able to sleep at night. And you'll get paid less than a manager at Tesco."

"You sound like my father, sir, and he couldn't put me off."

The commander stood up. "Then so be it, Warwick. See you in two years' time." They shook hands again; the obligatory interview over.

"Thank you, sir," said William. After closing the door quietly behind him he wanted to leap in the air and cry Hallelujah, until he saw three figures standing in the outer office looking directly at him.

"Name and rank?" said the older man he'd seen earlier.

"Warwick, sir. Constable William Warwick."

"Make sure Constable Warwick doesn't move, sergeant," said the older man to the young woman, before knocking on the commander's door and going in.

"Good morning, Bruce," said Hawksby. "I hear you're about to arrest Miles Faulkner. Not a moment too soon."

"I'm afraid not, sir. But that wasn't why I wanted to see you . . ." was all William heard before the door closed.

"Who's he?" William asked the young woman.

"Detective Chief Inspector Lamont. He heads up the Art and Antiques unit and reports directly to Commander Hawksby."

"Do you also work for the art squad?"

"Yes. I'm DS Roycroft, and the chief's my gaffer."

"Am I in trouble?"

"Up to your neck, constable. Let's just say I'm glad I'm not in your shoes."

"But I was only trying to help . . ."

"And thanks to your help, you've single-handedly managed to scupper a six-month undercover operation."

"But how?"

"I suspect you're about to find out," said DS Roycroft as the door swung open and Detective Chief Inspector Lamont reappeared, glaring at William.

"Come in, Warwick," he said. "The commander wants another word with you."

William walked tentatively into Hawksby's office, assuming he was about to be told that he was back on the beat. The commander's smile had been replaced by a grim look, and this time he didn't bother to shake hands with PC 565LD.

"You're a nuisance, Warwick," he said, "and I can tell you now, you won't be going to Peckham."

5

"Your last day in uniform," said Fred as they left the nick and set out on their evening patrol.

"Unless I'm not cut out to be a detective," said William. "In which case, I'll be back on the beat in no time."

"Balls. You'll make a name for yourself, and everyone knows it."

"Only thanks to you, Fred. You've taught me more about the real world than I ever learned at university."

"Only because you've led such a sheltered life, Choirboy. Unlike me. So which unit will you be attached to?"

"Art and Antiques."

"I thought that was just a hobby for people with too much time and money on their hands, not a crime."

"It can be a very lucrative crime for those who've worked out how to find a way around the law."

"Enlighten me."

"There's a scam going on at the moment," said William, "where professional criminals steal paintings without any intention of selling them."

"You've lost me," said Fred. "Why steal something you don't intend to sell or pass on to a fence?"

"Insurance companies are sometimes willing to make a deal with a go-between rather than pay out the full amount on a policy."

"A fence in an Armani suit?" said Fred. "So how do you nick 'em?"

"You have to wait until they get too greedy, and the insurance company refuses to pay up."

"Sounds like a lot of paperwork to me, so I'd never have made a detective."

"Where are we patrolling tonight?" asked William, well aware that Fred didn't always follow daily orders to the letter.

"Saturday night. Better check the Barton estate and make sure the Suttons and Tuckers aren't spoiling for a fight. Then we'll head back to Luscombe Road before the pubs close. Might even find a drunk and disorderly for you to arrest on your last night on the beat."

Although William had spent two years on probation with Fred, he knew almost nothing about his private life. He could hardly complain, because he himself was just as secretive, but as it would be their final patrol together, he decided to ask Fred something that had often puzzled him.

"What made you join the force in the first place?"

Fred didn't answer for some time, almost as if he was ignoring the question. "As I'm never going to see you again, Choirboy," he eventually replied, "I'll tell you. To start with, it wasn't in the first place. And was more by accident than design."

William remained silent as they turned into an alley that led to the back of the Barton estate.

"I was born in a tenement block in Glasgow. My father spent most of his life on the dole, so my mother was our only source of income."

"What did she do?"

"She was a barmaid, who learned soon enough that she could earn a damn sight more doing favors on the side. Trouble is, I'm still not sure if I was the result of one of those favors."

William didn't comment.

"But the cash dried up when she began to lose her looks, and it didn't help that my father gave her a regular black eye if she didn't come home on a Saturday night with enough cash to pay for his next bottle of whiskey and the chance to back another fourth-place nag."

Fred fell silent, while William thought about his own parents, who usually went out to dinner and the theater on a Saturday night. He still found it difficult to comprehend the tyranny of domestic violence. He'd never once heard his father raise his voice in front of his mother.

"London's a long way from Glasgow," prompted William, hoping to learn more.

"It wasn't far enough for me," said Fred, flashing his torch down an alley and grinning when a young couple scurried away. "I was fourteen when I left home. I jumped on the first tramp steamer that would have me. I'd seen half the world by the time I was eighteen and landed up in London."

"Is that when you joined the force?"

"No. I still looked on them as the enemy. I spent a few months stacking supermarket shelves before becoming a bus conductor. Soon got bored with that, so decided to join either the army or the police. If the police hadn't interviewed me first, I might be a general by now."

"Or dead," said William, as they walked onto the estate.

"You're just as likely to be killed in this job as you are in the modern army," said Fred. "I've lost seven colleagues in the past twenty years, and far too many others, injured and invalided out of the force. And at least in the army you know who the enemy is, and you're allowed to kill them. We're expected to handle drug dealers, knife crime, and gang warfare, while most of the public prefer not to know."

"So why did you stick at it when you could have chosen a far easier life?"

"We may have come from opposite sides of the tracks, Choirboy," said Fred, "but we do have one thing in common—we're both a bit bonkers, but at least we're doing the job we were destined for. And let's face it, I've never had a job that's half as exciting or rewarding as being a Met copper."

"Rewarding?"

"I don't mean financially, although if you put in the overtime, the pay's not too bad. *Deprehendo Deprehensio Vitum*," said Fred. "Overtime Solves Crime."

William couldn't stop laughing, and Fred added, "Don't worry, it's the only Latin I know. What I enjoy most about the job is that no two days are ever the same. And, more importantly, this is my manor, and I know almost everyone who lives here. They may not always be one big happy family, but they're my family, and although I'd never admit it in the canteen, I like to kid myself that I've made a difference."

"And you've got two commendations to prove it."

"Not to mention three suspensions, but as I've only got a few months left before I hang up my truncheon, I won't be stepping out of line again. Wouldn't want to do anything that would affect my pension," he added as they strolled off the Barton estate.

"It's quiet tonight," said William.

"They saw us coming, and like rats, they disappeared down the nearest drain. They'll reappear the minute we're out of sight. But then, we wouldn't want any trouble on your last night on the beat, would we, detective?"

William laughed, and was about to ask another question, when Fred glanced across the road and said, "Silly old moo. But I don't suppose she knows any better."

William suspected that another piece of homespun philosophy was about to be dispensed, although he couldn't see what Fred was going on about.

"Number twenty-three," said Fred. "Mrs. Perkins."

"Burgled a couple of weeks ago," said William. "A TV and a VCR, if I remember correctly."

"Five out of ten," said Fred. "Now earn the other five."

William stared at number 23 but was none the wiser.

"What do you see, Choirboy?"

"Two empty cardboard boxes."

"And what does that tell you?

William tried to think like a thief catcher, an accolade only given to those who, like Fred, could smell a crime even before it took place.

Fred let out an exaggerated sigh. "Mrs. Perkins's insurance company must have paid up, so she's now the proud owner of a new television and VCR. But what she doesn't know is that a burglar often returns to the scene of the crime a few weeks later, well aware there will probably be a brand-new TV set for them to steal. And in her case, she's actually advertising the fact. All the villain has to do is wait until she goes out one evening to visit her friend Mrs. Cassidy at number ninety-one, then pop back in and rob her a second time."

"So what should we do?" asked William.

"Have a quiet word with her, and suggest she destroys the evidence," said Fred as he knocked on the door of number 23. Mrs. Perkins answered almost immediately, and once Fred had explained why two policemen were standing on her doorstep, she hastily removed the boxes, thanked him, and offered them a cup of tea.

"That's good of you, Mrs. Perkins, but I'd better get on." He touched the rim of his helmet before they continued on their round.

"When do you start your new job?" Fred asked after they'd walked a few more yards.

"I'm taking a couple of weeks' holiday in Italy before reporting to Scotland Yard on the first of October."

"Lots of pretty girls in Italy, I'm told."

"Most of them framed."

"Framed?"

"In gold."

Fred laughed. "I've never been to Italy, or even Scotland Yard for that matter, but I'm told they've got the finest snooker room in the Met."

"I'll come back and tell you what it's like . . ."

"You'll never come back, Choirboy. Lambeth has just been the first rung on what I expect will be a very long ladder. But be warned, on your way up you'll come across plenty of snakes who'll be only too happy to send you back down a ladder, and some of them will be wearing blue uniforms," he said, rattling a shop door to make sure it was locked.

William chuckled. Never a shift went by when he didn't learn something from Fred.

"Evenin', Jacob."

"Hello, Fred."

William looked down at a man who was sitting cross-legged on the pavement, nursing a half-empty bottle of whiskey. When he was first on the beat, Fred had taught him that there were four types of drunks: the sleepers, who fall into a drunken stupor, and when they eventually wake up, go home; the harmless, who are usually drowning their sorrows and are rarely any trouble; the lovers, who want to take you home and try on your uniform; and the aggressive ones, who are looking for a fight and consider a policeman fair game. Fred could identify each category at a dozen paces, especially those looking for a fight, who regularly ended up spending the night in a cell, and were often a completely different person the following morning. William had come across all four types over the past couple of years, and thanks to Fred's common sense and strong right arm, he only had one or two bruises to show for it.

"Which category?" asked William.

"Drowning his sorrows. Spurs must have lost this afternoon."

"How do you know that?"

"Jacob's as good as gold when they win, but if they lose, he's a lost cause."

They turned into Luscombe Road to see a few locals making their way home from the Marlborough Arms.

"Disappointing," said Fred. "Luscombe Road isn't what it used to be since the council cleaned it up. I was hoping we might come across a drug dealer, or even Lenny the Snitch, so you'd have something to remember from your last night on the beat."

"We could always arrest her," said William, pointing to a girl in a short black leather skirt who was chatting to a man through an open car window.

"What's the point? She'll only spend the night in a cell, pay a fine in the morning, and be back on the game tomorrow evening. It's not the girls I'd like to nick, but the pimps who live off them. And one in particular," Fred added.

The car sped away when the driver spotted two policemen in his rearview mirror. They ambled on toward the town center, Fred regaling William with stories, some of which he'd heard before but were worth a second outing, and others that he wasn't sure hadn't been embellished with the passing of the years.

William was going to ask Fred about his retirement plans when his mentor grabbed his arm and pulled him into the nearest doorway, suddenly no longer the friendly neighborhood bobby but transformed into a policeman who'd spotted a real criminal.

"It's our lucky night," said Fred, nodding in the direction of a giant of a man clutching a terrified girl by the neck. "I've been after that bastard for years. Don't bother reading him his rights. That can wait until he's banged up in a cell."

Fred drew his truncheon, leaped out from the shadows, and began running toward the assailant, causing several other girls to scatter like pigeons in every direction the moment they saw him. William followed and quickly overtook the old-timer, who was not only thirty years older, but hadn't won the 100 yards in his last year at school.

The thug looked around and, seeing William heading toward him, let go of the girl, who fell on her knees, whimpering. That was when William saw the knife, but he was only a couple of strides away and committed to the tackle. He dived low, hitting the man just below the knees, causing them both to crash onto the pavement. By the time William had recovered, the man was already back on his feet. William instinctively raised an arm to protect himself as the knife was thrust down. The last thing he remembered was the shock of the blade entering his chest.

"Officer down, officer down! Urgent assistance required in

Luscombe Road!" shouted Fred over his radio, as he leaped on the assailant.

◄o►

His eyes opened. He blinked and looked around the unfamiliar room. His parents and sister were standing by the side of the bed, and a senior officer he didn't recognize was stationed by the door. Three pips on each epaulette indicated that he was a chief inspector.

William gave his family a weak smile as he tried to sit up, but he could only manage a few inches, suddenly aware that his chest was heavily bandaged. He slumped back down.

"How's Fred?" were his first faltering words.

None of them seemed willing to answer the question. Finally the police officer stepped forward and said, "I'm Chief Inspector Cuthbert, and I'm sorry about this Constable Warwick, but I have to ask you some questions about what happened on Saturday night, because as you well know, we can't hold a suspect for more than twenty-four hours unless we have enough evidence to charge them."

"Of course, sir," said William, once again trying to sit up.

The chief inspector opened a large brown envelope and extracted several black-and-white photos of different men, one of whom William would never forget.

"Is that the man you attempted to arrest on Saturday night?" asked Cuthbert.

William nodded. "But why do you need to ask me, when Fred could identify him in person?"

Chief Inspector Cuthbert remained silent as he placed the photographs back in the envelope.

◄o►

The parish church of St. Michael and St. George was rarely full, even for the mayor's annual carol concert, but on this occasion the pews were packed long before the choir had entered the nave. PC Fred Yates QGM had been granted a full police service funeral, while a uniformed guard of honor lined the approach to the church.

The funeral cortege was escorted by mounted officers, and Fred's coffin was draped in the blue and silver colors of the Metropolitan Police, along with the Queen's Gallantry Medal and a silver trophy resting on top. Inside the church, senior officers were seated at the front, while those who couldn't find a seat had to be satisfied with standing at the back. William, seated in a wheelchair, was pushed down the aisle by his father, and the congregation rose to acknowledge him. A church warden guided them to reserved places in the front row.

He who would valiant be . . .

William held up well, until the coffin, borne on the shoulders of eight serving officers, made its slow progress down the aisle toward the chancel, when he was unable to hold back the tears. The parish priest looked down from the altar steps and offered prayers for the locals from Fred's patch, many of whom rarely, if ever, attended a church service. They had come to pay their respects, even though some of them didn't know Fred's second name. William looked around and spotted Mrs. Perkins among the mourners.

To be a pilgrim . . .

When the congregation knelt to pray, William bowed his head and recalled Fred's words: *I like to kid myself that I've made a difference.* He only wished that Fred could have been there to witness what a difference he'd made.

The hymns were sung lustily by Fred's colleagues and friends, which William knew Fred would have appreciated, although he would have described the eulogy delivered by the station's chief superintendent as way over the top. William could hear Fred chuckling away when the super talked about his commendations. *What about my suspensions?* he could hear him saying.

After the priest had given the final blessing, the congregation stood and the pallbearers resumed their duties, bearing the coffin back down the aisle and out of the church to the burial plot.

William tried to stand as it passed by, but he couldn't quite manage it until the desk sergeant and the super came to his aid.

When they got home that night, his father suggested that it wouldn't be a disgrace if William felt he had to leave the force. He was sure his colleagues would understand. "You could go to night school, study law, and then join me in chambers, where you could still fight criminals, but in the safety of a courtroom by day, rather than on the streets at night."

William knew his father was right. But it was Fred who had the last word.

We may have come from opposite sides of the tracks, Choirboy, but we do have one thing in common—we're both a bit bonkers, but at least we're doing the job we were destined for.

6

Commander Hawksby sat at the head of the table, as befitted the chairman of the board. The other three directors waited for him to open the meeting.

"I would like to begin by welcoming a new recruit to our team. Although DC Warwick doesn't have a great deal of experience as a detective—" *that's putting it mildly,* thought William—"he has considerable expertise in the field of art, which was his chosen subject at university. In fact he turned down the chance to do a PhD so he could join the Met. So I'm rather hoping that his specialized knowledge will make a difference when it comes to finally nailing Miles Faulkner. Bruce," he said, turning to the senior officer on the case, "perhaps you can bring us up to date."

Detective Chief Inspector Lamont had several files in front of him, but he didn't need to open any of them as most of the contents were indelibly lodged in his mind. He looked directly at Detective Constable Warwick, as he didn't have anything new to tell his two colleagues.

"For the past seven years we've been trying to catch a thief who by any standards is a master criminal, and to date he's been running rings around us. Miles Faulkner has developed an almost infallible system that allows him to steal major works of art and make a fortune without appearing to break the law." Several questions had already occurred to William, but he decided not to interrupt his new boss.

"First, you'll need to realize, Bill—"

"William, sir."

Lamont frowned. "You'll need to realize that if you've ever seen the film *The Thomas Crown Affair,* you should dismiss it for what it is. Pure fiction. Entertaining, I accept, but nevertheless, fiction. Miles Faulkner is no Steve McQueen. He doesn't steal masterpieces for the sheer pleasure of it and then hide them in his basement where he alone can spend hours admiring them. That's for filmgoers who want to enjoy a couple of hours imagining what it would be like to fool our colleagues in Boston, while sleeping with a beautiful woman who just happens to be the insurance broker working on the case. Although that's the one person in the film who does bear some similarity to the real world: the insurance broker—except in our case he's more likely to be a middle-aged, middle-management pen pusher who goes home at six every evening to his wife and two children. And more important, he won't be in Faulkner's league."

"Still with us, Warwick?" asked Hawksby.

"Yes, sir."

"Then you'll be able to tell us what DCI Lamont is going to say next."

"That Faulkner steals valuable pictures from galleries or collectors with the intention of making a deal with the relevant insurance company, which is willing to settle for considerably less than the sum insured."

"Usually about half," said Lamont. "But Faulkner still ends up making a handsome profit."

"Clever as he may be," said William, "he can't be carrying out such a complex operation on his own."

"No, he isn't. He has a small, highly professional team working alongside him, but whenever we've caught any of his associates, they've kept their mouths firmly shut."

"On one occasion," said Detective Sergeant Roycroft, "we even caught two of the thieves red-handed. But Faulkner was in Monte Carlo at the time of the robbery, sleeping peacefully in bed with a wife to confirm his alibi."

"And do we think his wife is also one of his most trusted associates?" asked William.

"She's covered for him several times in the past," said Hawksby, "but we've recently discovered that Faulkner has a mistress."

"That's not yet a crime," said William.

"True. But if she were to find out . . ."

"Weren't you able to turn either of the gang you arrested, and make a plea bargain?" was William's next question.

"Not a chance," said Lamont. "Faulkner had an unsigned contract with both of them, with no get-out clause."

"They were both sentenced to six years," said Hawksby, picking up the thread, "and their families on the outside were well looked after, although we've never been able to connect the crime to Faulkner. A third villain, who was involved in the Fitzmolean break-in, had his lips sewn together just to remind him what would happen if he decided to turn Queen's evidence."

"But if Faulkner is the fence . . ."

"Faulkner, according to his tax return," said Lamont, "is a farmer. He lives in a nine-bedroom mansion in Hampshire surrounded by three hundred acres on which a few cows graze, but never go to market."

"But presumably someone has to carry out the negotiations with the insurance companies?"

"Faulkner leaves that to another of his acolytes," said Lamont. "Mr. Booth Watson QC. A barrister who always acts on behalf of an unnamed client. However hard we press him, he simply reminds us about lawyer-client confidentiality."

"But if Booth Watson knows he's dealing directly with a criminal, isn't it his professional responsibility to report—"

"We aren't dealing with your father in this case, Warwick," said Hawksby, "but a man who has twice appeared before the Bar Council for conduct unworthy of his profession. On both occasions, he narrowly escaped being disbarred."

"But he still practices," said William.

"Yes, but he rarely appears in court nowadays," said Hawksby, "having discovered a way of charging exorbitant fees without ever having to leave his chambers. Whenever a major work of art is stolen, it's no coincidence that the first call the insurance company makes is to Mr. Booth Watson, who they ask to act as an intermediary. Surprise, surprise, the picture reappears a few days later in perfect condition, and the insurance company settles, often without even bothering to inform us."

"I find it hard to believe," said William, "that Faulkner's enjoyed a seamless record of success. This sounds as much like the stuff of fiction as *The Thomas Crown Affair.*"

"Quite right," said Hawksby. "At least one of the more established insurance companies has refused to pay the piper, and if the gallery concerned doesn't have the resources to offer a reward, then Faulkner can find himself stuck with the picture."

"If that's the case," said William, "the Rembrandt stolen from the Fitzmolean could still be out there."

"Unless Faulkner has destroyed it, to make sure the theft can never be traced back to him."

"Surely no one would destroy a Rembrandt?"

"I'd wait until you meet the man before you jump to that conclusion. We're not dealing with an art lover here, but someone who would shop his own mother, if it meant he would get off."

"What else do we know about Faulkner?" asked William, chastened.

This time it was DS Roycroft who opened a file. "Born in Sevenoaks in 1942, the only child of an estate agent and a hairdresser. Although that isn't what he tells his friends at the golf club. Awarded an open scholarship to Harrow at the age of eleven, and in his final year he won the school's art prize. After leaving Harrow, he took up a place at the Slade School of Art, but soon realized that although he was one of the brightest students of his year, he was, to quote the principal's graduation report, 'never going to make a living as an artist.' They recommended that he consider a career in teaching. He ignored their advice."

"By the time he left the Slade," said Lamont, taking over, "he'd worked out exactly what role he was going to play in the art world. But he needed to gain some experience before he could branch out on his own. He joined a leading West End gallery as a trainee, where he learned in the art world how much money could be made, especially if you were unscrupulous. He was sacked after a couple of years in circumstances that we're not altogether sure about, although we do know that no other gallery would employ him. For some time he disappeared off the scene, until a Salvador Dalí went missing from the Courtauld, long before the Art and Antiques squad had been set up."

"What makes you think he was involved in that theft?" asked William.

"We picked him up on a surveillance camera taking a photograph of the painting a month before it was stolen. A mistake he hasn't made since," said Hawksby.

"And he must have made a good enough profit from that deal, among others, because once again he disappeared off our radar until the Rembrandt was stolen from the Fitzmolean some seven years ago. But on that occasion Mr. Booth Watson was unable to reach a deal with the insurers, which looks like his only failure to date. Although the manner in which he carried out the theft would have impressed even Thomas Crown."

William didn't interrupt.

"A squad car turned up outside the Fitzmolean on a Saturday afternoon just after the gallery had closed. Two men dressed as policemen entered the museum claiming an alarm had gone off, coshed the door-man, and tied him up. Ten minutes later, they walked out of the front door with the Rembrandt tucked under their arms."

"Where were the security guards?"

"They said they were patrolling the top floor and didn't report back to the ground floor until half an hour later, at four forty-eight p.m."

"Is four forty-eight relevant?" asked William.

"He's sharp," said Lamont.

"Manchester United were playing Liverpool in the FA Cup that afternoon, and the match was being shown live on BBC One. The final whistle went at four forty-six."

"Where was the television?" asked William.

"In the staff canteen in the basement," said Lamont, "which I suspect Faulkner was well aware of, because the thieves arrived just after the whistle blew for the start of the second half, and we later discovered that both guards were Manchester United supporters, which I've no doubt Faulkner knew only too well."

"If the devil's in the details, he's the devil," added Hawsky.

"So now you know what we're up against," said DS Roycroft. "A highly professional, well-organized criminal, who only has to steal one major painting every few years to live the life of Riley, and can carry out the whole operation in a matter of minutes."

"I must have missed something," said William. "Why didn't Booth Watson make a deal with the insurers and settle the claim soon after Faulkner had stolen the Rembrandt?"

"The Fitzmolean were lamentably underinsured. A problem several leading galleries face at the moment. Their paintings and sculptures have soared in value over the years, and they simply can't afford to insure them for realistic sums."

"However," chipped in Lamont, "the setback will have taught Faulkner one lesson. Don't steal from galleries that aren't fully insured or don't have sufficient resources to offer a reward."

"Any questions, Warwick?" said Hawksby.

"Yes, sir," said William. "We now know that the Rembrandt you thought was the original is in fact a copy."

"What's your point?" said Jackie, still smarting from her mistake.

"Someone must have painted that copy."

"Faulkner perhaps?" suggested Lamont. "After all, he began life as an art student."

"Not if the Slade's opinion of his talent is to be believed. But that doesn't mean he wouldn't know an artist who was capable of doing the job. They might well have been contemporaries at the Slade."

"If that's the case," said Lamont, "you're the obvious man to find out who that person is."

"Agreed," said Commander Hawksby, checking his watch. "Do you have any more questions, DC Warwick?"

"Just one, sir. How did you get hold of the copy?"

"We were able to convince a local magistrate that we had reason to believe Faulkner might be in possession of an important work of art that had been stolen from the Fitzmolean. He signed a search warrant, and we raided Faulkner's home later that night. Until you appeared, we thought we'd hit the jackpot."

"Did you get a chance to study the rest of his collection while you were in his home?"

"Yes," said Lamont, "and not one of them was on our list of missing pictures, and he was also able to produce receipts for all his other paintings."

"So he reinvests his ill-gotten gains in artwork, which makes me even more convinced he won't have destroyed the Rembrandt."

"Don't bet your pensions on it," said Hawksby as he closed his file. "That brings us up to date, and I don't need to remind you that this is not the only case we are currently investigating. So don't neglect the others gathering dust on your desks. I'm finding it difficult enough to justify any further expense to the commissioner, and a few convictions, however minor, would assist our cause. This government seems to be more interested in the numbers game than in catching real criminals. So let's get back to work."

Everyone around the table gathered up their files and headed for the door. But before William could leave the room, Hawksby said, "I'd like a word, Warwick."

The commander waited until the door had been closed before he spoke again.

"William, I know you're bright, your colleagues also know

you're bright, so you don't have to continually remind them you turned what they had thought was a triumph into a disaster. If you want to end up in this chair one day, don't spend any more time pissing off the people you'll be working with. I suggest you occasionally seek advice, and don't just dispense it. Perhaps you should spend a little more time in the snooker room, as it didn't seem to do you any harm in Lambeth."

William recalled his father's words. *Not a man to be underestimated.*

Quietly he left the room, his head bowed. He thought about the commander's words as he walked slowly down the corridor. He hadn't yet visited the snooker room at Scotland Yard. When he returned to the office he shared with his colleagues, he found two case files had been dumped on his desk. He was halfway through one labeled CHURCHILL, when DS Roycroft appeared by his side.

"Which one do you think I should start on, sarge?" he asked her.

"Remind me," said Jackie.

"Winston Churchill, or moon dust?"

"Moon dust should be pretty easy to deal with. The professor is clearly not a criminal, and frankly, Mr. Underwood, the undersecretary at the American Embassy, is overreacting. But we don't want a diplomatic incident, so make sure you tread carefully."

"And Churchill?"

"Churchill will be more of a challenge, but as the Hawk reminded us, nowadays it's all about numbers, so make sure you apprehend the culprit and charge him, even though I suspect he'll only get a six-month suspended sentence. At least it will be one more for the record. More importantly, I'm sure you haven't forgotten that you're single-handedly going to find the Rembrandt forger in the hope he'll lead us to Faulkner. One piece of advice, Bill," she said pointedly. "Don't even think about going home before the light under the Hawk's door has been switched off."

"Thanks for the advice," said William, as he reopened the moon dust file. After reading all the details of the case, he had to agree with Jackie that the professor may have been naive, even culpable, but he certainly wasn't a criminal.

When Big Ben struck six times, William decided it was too late to phone the undersecretary at the American Embassy, as Mr. Underwood wouldn't have to wait until the light in the Hawk's office had been switched off before he could go home.

7

"Can you put me through to Mr. Chuck Underwood?"

"Who's calling?"

"Detective Constable William Warwick, from Scotland Yard."

"I'll see if the undersecretary is available."

William had to wait so long, he wondered if the line had gone dead. Finally a voice came on the line.

"Warwick?"

"Yes, sir."

"What's happened to DS Roycroft?"

"I've taken over the case, sir."

"Is there anything lower than a detective constable?"

"Only a probationer, sir, and I was one of those not so long ago."

"And you will be again if I don't get my moon dust back."

"I'm working on it, sir, but I need to ask you a few questions."

"Not again!"

"Did the American government originally give the phial of moon dust to Professor Francis Denning of Manchester University as a gift?"

"Yes, we did. But there were conditions attached. We made it clear it was never to be passed on to anyone else, and that under no circumstances was it to be sold to a third party."

"And was that put in writing at the time?"

"It most certainly was, and we have the documentation to prove it. And now, as I'm sure you are aware, a Dr. Keith Talbot has put the phial up for sale at Sotheby's."

"Yes, I did know, sir. I have the catalog in front of me."

"Then you will see on page thirty-one, lot nineteen, a phial of moon dust, rare, brought back from the Apollo 11 mission by Mr. Neil Armstrong."

"However," said William, "the late Professor Denning left the phial to Dr. Talbot in his will."

"It wasn't his to leave, Detective Constable Warwick, as I made clear to DS Roycroft."

"You did indeed, sir. But I am sure you understand that we must follow the letter of the law."

"At a snail's pace, it would seem, despite the fact that our legal team is at your disposal."

"That's good to know, sir, because we wouldn't want to do anything to harm the special relationship between our two countries, would we?"

"Cut out the sarcasm, Warwick, and just get my moon dust back."

The phone went dead. William swiveled around in his chair to see Jackie grinning at him.

"He grows on you," she said, "but Underwood's one of those Americans who considers Britain to be one of their smaller states. It won't be long before he reminds you that Texas is almost three times the size of the United Kingdom. So if you want to avoid a major diplomatic incident, I suggest you get his moon dust back."

"I hear you," said William. "But equally important, how do I get a train ticket to Manchester?"

"You report to Mavis in Travel on the ground floor. But I warn you, if you think Mr. Underwood is tough, compared to Mavis, he's a softie. If it was up to her, the Queen would travel second class, and the likes of us would be shoveling coal into the engine's furnace."

"Thanks for the warning."

◄○►

"Mavis—"

"Mrs. Walters to you, young man. You can't call me Mavis until you're at least a chief inspector. Start again."

"I'm sorry," said William. "Mrs. Walters, I need—"

"Name, rank, and department?"

"Warwick, DC, Art and Antiques."

"So what were you hoping for?"

"To be the commissioner."

"Try again," said Mrs. Walters, but she did at least manage a smile.

"A return train ticket to Manchester."

"What is the purpose of your trip, and how long will you be in Manchester?"

"I'll be visiting the university, and hope to go there and back on the same day."

"Then you'll have to catch the seven forty-two from Euston, and the last train back on a weekday is the ten forty-three. If you miss it, you'll be spending the night on a bench on platform twelve. You are entitled to one meal, at a cost of no more than two pounds eighty, which you can claim on your duty sheet 232, but I'll require a receipt." Mrs. Walters began to write out a train warrant for Manchester Piccadilly. "If you're going to the university, you'll have to catch the 147 bus. You'll also need an umbrella."

"An umbrella?"

"You've obviously never been to Manchester before."

◄o►

"Good morning, Mr. Warwick," said the young woman who met him at the front desk. "I'm Melanie Clore. How can I help you?"

"You have a sale coming up on July the seventeenth—"

"Which lot number do you want us to withdraw?"

"How could you possibly know—"

"The police don't visit Sotheby's to put something up for sale."

William smiled. "Lot number nineteen. A phial of moon dust brought back on the Apollo 11 mission by Neil Armstrong."

Miss Clore checked the catalog. "Offered to us by a Dr. Keith Talbot, who produced a will to confirm that the moon dust had been left to him."

"The American Embassy is claiming ownership and say they will sue everybody in sight if you go ahead with the sale."

"And we wouldn't want that, would we, Mr. Warwick?"

"It wouldn't worry me," said William, "if I thought Dr. Talbot had the law on his side."

"Even if he does, the legal battle could last for years."

"My boss is expecting me to solve this one in a couple of days."

"Is he? Well, if Dr. Talbot is willing to sign a standard release form, we will be happy to hand over the phial, and leave you to return it to the Americans. Let's just hope Dr. Talbot isn't another Mr. Finlay Isles."

"Dare I ask who Mr. Finlay Isles is?"

"He sued us in 1949 over a watercolor worth a hundred pounds, and we're still waiting for the courts to decide who the rightful owner is."

"How come?" asked William.

"It's a Turner which is now worth over a million."

◄○►

As the train rattled over the points on its progress to Manchester the following morning, William studied the moon dust file yet again, but learned nothing new.

He allowed his thoughts to return to the missing Rembrandt and how he could possibly find out the name of the artist who'd made the copy. He was convinced that in order to create such a convincing reproduction, the painter must have worked from the original. William still had difficulty believing that anyone who had been educated at the Slade would be capable of destroying a national treasure, but then he recalled the Hawk's words—"Wait until you meet the man before you jump to that conclusion."

William had read Faulkner's file from cover to cover, and although he didn't appear in public very often, one event he never missed was the opening night of a new James Bond film, and he was also a collector of first editions of Ian Fleming's books. William had recently read a diary piece in *The Daily Mail* reporting that *A View to a Kill* would be opening at the Odeon Leicester Square in a month's time. But how could he possibly get hold of a ticket? And even if he did, he couldn't see Mrs. Walters sanctioning it as a legitimate expense.

His mind returned to Dr. Talbot. One phone call had elicited the information that the professor would be delivering a talk in the geology department's lecture theater at eleven o'clock. William wondered what sort of man Talbot was, amused by the thought of the American empire bearing down on an innocent geology lecturer from the north of England. He knew where his sympathies lay. He placed the file back in his briefcase and picked up the latest edition of *RA Magazine,* but after flicking through a few pages decided it would have to wait until the return journey.

When the train pulled into Manchester Piccadilly at 10:49, William was among the first to hand over his ticket at the barrier. He jogged past a row of taxis to the nearest bus stop and joined a queue. A few minutes later he climbed onto the 147, which dropped him outside the main entrance to the university. How could Mrs. Walters possibly have known that? He smiled when he saw a group of students ambling through the gates and onto the campus at a leisurely pace he'd quite forgotten since joining the Met. He asked one of them for directions to the geology department, and arrived a few minutes late, but then he wasn't there to attend the lecture. He climbed the steps to the first floor, entered the theater by the back door, and joined the dozen or so students who were listening intently to Dr. Talbot.

From his seat in the back row, William studied the lecturer carefully. Dr. Talbot couldn't have been an inch over five foot, and had a shock of curly black hair that didn't look as if it regularly came into contact with a brush or comb. He wore a corduroy jacket, a check shirt, and a bootlace tie. His long black gown was covered in chalk dust. He spoke in a clear, authoritative voice, only occasionally glancing down at his notes.

William became so engrossed in Talbot's account of how the discovery of a previously unknown fossil in the early seventies had finally disproved the single species theory that he was disappointed when a buzzer sounded at twelve o'clock to indicate that the lecture was over. He waited until all the students had left and Dr. Talbot was gathering up his notes before walking casually down the center aisle to confront the master criminal.

Talbot looked up and peered at William through his National Health spectacles.

"Do I know you?" he asked. William produced his warrant card, and Talbot gripped the edge of the long wooden desk in front of him. "But I thought I'd paid that parking fine."

"I'm sure you did, sir. But I still need to ask you a few questions."

"Of course," said Talbot, fidgeting with his gown.

"Can I begin by asking how you came into possession of a phial of moon dust?"

"Is that what this is all about?" said Talbot in disbelief.

"It is, sir."

"It was a gift from the late Professor Denning, who left it to me in his will. The Americans presented it to him after he'd published his findings on the structure of the moon's surface."

"And why would he leave such an important historic artifact to you?"

"I was his research assistant at the time he wrote his dissertation, and after he retired, I took his place as head of department."

"Well I'm sorry to have to inform you, Dr. Talbot, that the Americans want their moon dust back."

"What makes them think it's theirs? They don't own the moon."

"True, but they did bring the dust back on Apollo 11, and Professor Denning must have forgotten that he'd signed a binding agreement not to sell it or pass it on to a third party."

"And if I refuse to give it back?" said Talbot, sounding a little more confident.

"The Americans will instigate legal proceedings, and I have a feeling their pockets might be deeper than yours."

"Why don't they just buy the damn phial when it comes up for auction at Sotheby's?"

"I admit that would be the easy solution," said William. "But they're in no doubt that the moon dust now belongs to them, and Sotheby's have already withdrawn the lot from their catalog. And, can you believe it, the phial is now locked in a high-security vault?"

Talbot burst out laughing, pointed a crooked forefinger at William, and in a feeble attempt to imitate Clint Eastwood, said, "Go ahead, make my day!"

"If you would be willing to sign a release form, sir, I could pick up the phial from Sotheby's and return it to the American Embassy, which would solve both our problems."

"You know, Mr. Warwick, if I were a millionaire I'd take on the Yanks, even though the moon dust will probably only fetch a couple of thousand pounds."

"And I'd be on your side, but I suspect we'd still lose."

"You're probably right. So, where do I sign?"

William opened his briefcase, extracted three identical forms, and placed them on the desk.

"Here, here, and here."

Talbot read the document carefully before adding his signature on three dotted lines.

"Thank you, sir," said William, placing two of the forms back in his briefcase and handing the third to Talbot.

"Do you have time to join me for lunch?" asked Talbot, taking off his gown, accompanied by a cloud of chalk.

"Only if you know a pub with a two pound eighty upper limit."

"I think we can do better than that."

◄○►

On the journey back to Euston, William checked Dr. Talbot's signatures. He'd enjoyed an excellent lunch in the faculty dining room with the professor, who turned out to be a fellow art junkie and a keen follower of a local artist whom he'd met as an under-graduate. Dr. Talbot had purchased a drawing by L.S. Lowry of a back street in Salford for fifty pounds, which he couldn't afford at the time, and certainly wouldn't be able to afford to buy now, although he admitted to William that he'd never sell it.

"So which artists should I be looking out for now, remembering my salary?" William asked.

"Diana Armfield, Craigie Aitchison, and Sydney Harpley. You'll find them all in the RA's Summer Exhibition."

William made a note of the names.

Over lunch William had jokingly suggested that they substitute a few grains of sand from Blackpool beach for the moon dust, as he was confident that the American undersecretary wouldn't know the difference. Talbot had laughed, but pointed out that his opposite number at the Smithsonian certainly would, even though he'd probably never been to Blackpool.

William finally opened his *RA Magazine* to check which exhibitions were coming up that he couldn't afford to miss. He selected three, circled them, and put the dates in his diary: Picasso, the early years; Hockney's California or bust; and the annual Summer Exhibition at the RA, where he would check out the three artists Dr. Talbot had recommended. But they were all quickly forgotten when he turned the page to find that Dr. Tim Knox, the director of the Fitzmolean, would be giving a lecture on the history of the museum, followed by a guided tour, in a couple of weeks' time. Tickets were five pounds, and only fifty people would be admitted. He wondered if Mrs. Walters would consider that a legitimate expense. Either way, he wasn't going to miss it.

William didn't sleep that night, although his only companion was a locked briefcase. He would have liked to tear up both copies of the release form, but he accepted that the Americans would get their way in the end.

◄o►

William didn't go straight to Scotland Yard the following morning, but took the tube to Green Park, before walking across to New Bond Street. He was standing outside the auction house long before a porter opened the doors at nine o'clock.

Melanie Clore studied Dr. Talbot's signature carefully, and compared it to the one on the sale document, before she was willing to part with Lot 19. She then disappeared to collect the phial from its safe, returning a few minutes later.

William couldn't believe it when he saw the phial for the first time. It was smaller than his little finger. He wrapped it in a tissue before putting it back in the box. More forms to sign before he could leave and make his way to Grosvenor Square. He climbed the steps of the American Embassy fifteen minutes later and reported to a marine sergeant on the front desk. He asked to see Mr. Underwood.

"Do you have an appointment, sir?"

"No," he said, producing his warrant card.

The marine pressed three buttons on his phone, and when a voice came on the line he repeated William's request.

"I'm afraid the undersecretary is in a meeting at the moment, but he could fit Mr. Warwick in at four this afternoon."

"Tell him I've got his moon dust," said William.

He could hear a voice saying, "Send him up."

William took the lift to the fourth floor, to find the undersecretary standing in the corridor waiting for him. They shook hands before Underwood said, "Good morning, detective," but didn't speak again until he'd closed the door of his office. "You move quite quickly for an Englishman."

William didn't respond, but opened his briefcase and took out the little box. He opened it, unwrapped the tissue slowly, and like a conjurer, revealed the phial of moon dust.

"That's it?" said Underwood in disbelief.

"Yes, sir," said William as he handed over the cause of so much trouble.

"Thank you," said Underwood, placing the box on his desk. "I'll be sure to get in touch with you again should any other problems arise."

"Not unless someone's stolen one of your nuclear warheads," said William.

8

"Can I claim five pounds on expenses to attend an art lecture at the Fitzmolean?"

"Is it directly connected to a crime you're investigating?" asked Mrs. Walters.

"Yes and no."

"Make up your mind."

"Yes, it is connected to a crime I'm investigating, but I must admit I would have gone anyway."

"Then the answer is no. Anything else?"

"Can you get me a ticket for the opening night of the new James Bond film?" William waited for the explosion.

"Is it directly connected to a crime you are working on?"

"Yes."

"Which row would you like to sit in?"

"You're joking?"

"I don't joke, detective constable. Which row?"

"In the row behind Miles Faulkner. He's—"

"We all know who Mr. Faulkner is. I'll see what I can do."

"But how—"

"Don't ask. And if you don't have any more requests, move on."

<o>

William arrived at the Fitzmolean a few minutes early. He paused on the pavement of Prince Albert Crescent to admire the Palladian mansion that nestled behind Imperial College. He was well aware that, for security reasons, since the theft of the Rembrandt only fifty people could now visit the gallery at any one time. He had managed to get ticket number forty-seven for the evening lecture. Half an hour later and they would have been sold out.

He presented his ticket to the uniformed guard on the door and was directed to the second floor, where he joined a small gathering of chattering enthusiasts who were waiting impatiently for Dr. Knox, the nation's leading authority on the Renaissance period, to make his entrance.

William was looking forward to the lecture, and hoped the director might even have a theory about what had happened to the missing Rembrandt.

At one minute to seven, a young woman made her way to the front of the group and clapped her hands a couple of times, before saying, "Good evening, ladies and gentlemen. My name is Beth Rainsford, and I am one of the gallery's research assistants." She waited for complete silence before continuing. "I'm sorry to have to inform you that Dr. Knox is suffering from laryngitis and is barely able to speak. He sends his apologies."

An audible groan went up, and one or two patrons began heading toward the exit.

"However, the director is confident that he will be fully recovered in a few days, so if you are able to return next Thursday evening, he will deliver his lecture then. For those unable to come back next week, your entrance fee will be refunded. Should anyone wish to remain, I will be happy to show you around the collection. But don't worry," she added, "your money will still be refunded even if you stay." This caused a ripple of laughter.

What had begun as a gathering of fifty was quickly reduced to a dozen, William among them. But then he hadn't been able to take his eyes off the director's replacement. Her neatly cropped auburn hair framed an oval face that didn't rely on makeup to make you look a second time. But it wasn't that, or her slim figure, that he found so captivating. It was her infectious enthusiasm as she talked about the Dutch men who surrounded her, adorned in their black pantaloons and ruffled collars. William glanced at her left hand as she pointed to the first picture, delighted to see that there were no rings on that finger. Even so, he thought, this vision must surely have a boyfriend. But how could he find out?

"The Fitzmolean," Beth was saying, her deep brown eyes sparkling as she spoke, "was the brainchild of Mrs. van Haasen, the wife of the distinguished economist Jacob van Haasen. A remarkable woman, who after her husband's death built up a Dutch and Flemish collection that is considered second only to those of the Rijksmuseum and the Hermitage. In her will, she bequeathed the entire collection to the nation in memory of her husband, to be displayed in the house they had shared during their forty-three years of married life." Beth turned and led her little band into the next gallery. She came to a halt in front of a portrait of a young man.

"Frans Hals," she began, "was born in Antwerp around 1582. His most accomplished work is considered to be *The Laughing Cavalier*, which you can see in the Wallace Collection."

William tried to concentrate on Hals, but decided he would have to come back the following Thursday, when he was sure Dr. Knox wouldn't have quite the same distracting effect on him. He continued to follow Beth until she stopped in front of a large empty gilded frame, with the legend REMBRANDT, 1606–1669 painted on a small plaque below it.

"This," she said reverently, "is where Rembrandt's masterpiece *The Syndics of the Clothmakers' Guild* once hung, before it was stolen from the gallery seven years ago. Sadly, it has never been recovered."

"Did the gallery offer a reward for its return?" asked a voice that sounded as if it hailed from Boston.

"No. Unfortunately it had never crossed Mrs. van Haasen's mind that anyone would steal one of her masterpieces, possibly because she only paid six thousand dollars for the picture at the time."

"How much would it be worth today?" asked a younger voice.

"The painting is priceless," said Beth, "and irreplaceable. The more romantic among us believe it's still out there somewhere, and that *The Syndics* will one day return to their rightful home."

A smattering of applause followed this statement before Beth continued. "Rembrandt was an ambitious man, and at one time the most sought-after artist of the Dutch Golden Age. Sadly, he lived beyond his means and ended up having to auction off most of his possessions, including several major canvases, in order to clear his debts. He only just avoided bankruptcy and ending his days in prison. After his death in 1669 he was buried in a pauper's grave, and his work fell out of fashion for over a century. But Mrs. van Haasen was in no doubt about his genius, and did much to revive his reputation as the greatest of the Dutch masters. Art connoisseurs would travel from all over the world to view *The Syndics,* which is considered to be one of his greatest works, and Mrs. van Haasen never made a secret of the fact that it was her favorite painting in the collection."

Beth and her little troupe moved on to the next picture, and she continued to answer all their questions well beyond the appointed hour. She finally came to an end with Jan Steen's *The Marriage at Cana,* describing him as "the storyteller of artists." "Are there any more questions?" she asked.

William decided not to ask his question until the rest of the group had departed. "What a fantastic talk," he said.

"Thank you," said Beth. "Did you have a question?"

"Yes. Are you free for dinner?"

She didn't respond immediately, but eventually managed, "I'm afraid not. I already have a date."

William smiled. "Well, it's been a memorable evening. Thank you, Beth."

As he turned to leave he heard a voice behind him say, "But I am free tomorrow night."

When William arrived at the office the following morning, he found a yellow Post-it note stuck to the top of his case files.

URGENT—Call Liz, 01 735 3000.

"What's this about?" he asked Jackie.

"All I know is that the Hawk said it was urgent. You're to record exactly what Liz has to say and send him a written report."

"Will do," said William as he dialed the number. A moment later a woman's voice came on the line.

"How can I help you?"

"This is Detective Constable Warwick calling from Scotland Yard. I'm returning Liz's call."

"Do you know Liz's surname, or which department she works in?"

"No, just that it's urgent I speak to her. She's expecting my call."

"This is the Buckingham Palace switchboard, sir. We only have one Liz, and I don't think she's available at the moment."

William turned bright red. "I'm so sorry," he said. "I must have got the wrong number." The moment he put the phone down, Jackie and DCI Lamont burst out laughing.

"I'm sure she'll call back," said Jackie.

"And by the way," said Lamont, "the Hawk's had a call from the American ambassador thanking us for returning the moon dust. Well done, laddie, now perhaps it's time for you to sort out Winston Churchill."

William opened the file marked CHURCHILL and tried to concentrate, but he couldn't put the previous evening out of his mind. He couldn't recall the last time a young woman had so preoccupied his thoughts. Tonight he would definitely leave the office before seven, even if the light was still shining under the commander's door.

He gathered his thoughts as he read about an ingenious scheme a petty forger had come up with to supplement his income. By the time he'd reached the last page, William realized he was going to have to visit a number of bookshops in the West End if he hoped to catch the thief red-handed. He warned DCI Lamont, who was preoccupied with the hunt for an international jewel thief, that he was about to do some good old-fashioned leather-bashing and might not be back by close of play.

William decided to start at Hatchards on Piccadilly, where the manager—he checked the name again—Peter Giddy, had made the original complaint.

He left Scotland Yard, and headed for the Mall—as he passed Buckingham Palace he couldn't help feeling chastened at his attempt to call Liz—then on up St. James's to Piccadilly, where he passed through a doorway under which three royal warrants were proudly displayed. William asked a woman on the front counter if he could see Mr. Giddy.

Once the manager had checked William's warrant card, he took him up to his office on the fourth floor and offered him a cup of coffee.

"What made you suspicious in the first place?" asked William, as he sat down and opened his notebook.

"I wasn't suspicious to begin with," admitted Giddy. "After all, Churchill was a politician, so would have signed a great number of his books. However, it's quite rare to come across a complete set of his *The Second World War* with all six volumes signed. But when I spotted a set in Heywood Hill, and then just a week later another set in Maggs, I began to have my doubts."

"Can you recall anything in particular about the man who offered to sell you the books?" asked William.

"Fairly nondescript. Sixty, sixty-five, gray hair, slightly stooped, average height and with an accent you could cut with a knife. In fact, a typical Hatchards customer."

William smiled. "I assume he didn't tell you his name."

"No. Said he didn't want the children to find out he was selling a family heirloom."

"But you would have had to make out a check?"

"In normal circumstances, yes, but he insisted on cash. He

turned up a few minutes before we closed, well aware that the till would be full."

"How much would an unsigned set of the books sell for?"

"A hundred pounds if they all had their original dust jackets."

"And a signed set?"

"Three hundred, possibly three-fifty if they were in mint condition."

"May I ask how much you paid for them?"

"Two hundred and fifty pounds."

"So our man could have picked up an unsigned set for about a hundred pounds, added the six signatures, and made a profit of a hundred and fifty. Not exactly the great train robbery," said William.

"I agree," said Giddy, clearly not amused. "But if one of our customers were to find out that we'd sold them a forgery, and the press got hold of it, we could lose our Royal Warrant."

William nodded. "Do you think he'll come back?"

"Not a chance. He won't risk trying to pull off the scam a second time in the same bookshop. And frankly, there are enough of us out there to keep him going for years."

"So where do you think I should begin?"

"I can give you a list of bookshops that specialize in signed first editions," said Giddy, opening a drawer in his desk and handing over a slim pamphlet.

"Thank you," said William, flicking through the pages.

"Don't worry, there are at least a dozen within a mile of here," said the manager, as he accompanied William to the lift.

Detective Constable Warwick spent the rest of the day tramping from bookshop to bookshop, and soon discovered that the Churchill forger was an industrious individual. When he wasn't buying, he was selling. The kind of cottage industry the government was so keen to encourage.

Every one of the managers promised to let him know if a man fitting that description offered them a signed set of Churchill's

The Second World War, but they all agreed with Giddy that it was unlikely he would appear in the same shop a second time.

"If he does show up, please call me at Scotland Yard, 230 1212. I'm on extension 2150," said William, before moving on to the next shop.

William didn't stop his inquiries until the last door closed behind him at six o'clock. He took the tube to Victoria, then jogged all the way back to Trenchard House. He had a quick shower and changed his clothes, taking an unusually long time to decide what to wear. He eventually settled on a blue blazer, an open-neck white shirt, and a pair of gray trousers, but decided against wearing his old school tie.

As he closed the front door behind him, he realized he would have to take a taxi if he wasn't going to be late; an expense Mrs. Walters wouldn't have approved of. The cab dropped him off outside Elena 1 in the Fulham Road, with seven minutes to spare.

"This is a very special date for me, Gino," said William after the head waiter had introduced himself. "A first in fact. So I may need your help."

"Leave it all to me, Mr. Warwick. I'll put you in a quiet alcove."

"Oh help, there she is," whispered William.

"Ah, signorina," said Gino, bowing slightly before taking her hand. "Mr. Warwick has arrived and is sitting at his usual table."

William leaped up, trying not to stare. She was wearing a simple off-the-shoulder yellow dress that fell just below the knee, with a pale green silk scarf, and a jade necklace to complement the outfit.

Gino pulled back the chair for her, while William waited for Beth to be seated.

"This must be one of your usual haunts," said Beth as she settled in her chair.

"No, first time. It was recommended by a friend."

"But the waiter said—"

"I met him five minutes ago," admitted William as Gino reappeared, and handed them both a menu. Beth laughed.

"Now, Mr. Warwick, will you have your usual drink?"

"And what is my usual drink?" asked William. Gino looked puzzled until William added, "Beth knows I've never been here before. What do you recommend?"

"For the beautiful signorina . . ."

"Gino, don't overdo it."

"You do not think she is beautiful?"

"Yes, but I don't want her to run away before we've had the first course."

Beth looked up from her menu. "Don't worry, I'm not going to run away. Well, not until after the second course."

"And what can I get you to drink, signorina?"

"A glass of white wine, please."

"We'll have a bottle of Frascati," said William, recalling a wine his father often ordered, though he had no idea how much it would cost.

Once Gino had taken their orders, Beth asked, "Is it William or Bill?"

"William."

"Do you work in the art world or are you a gallery groupie?"

"Both. I became a gallery groupie at an early age, but now I work with the Art and Antiques unit at Scotland Yard."

Beth seemed to hesitate for a moment, before she said, "So your visit to the Fitzmolean was just part of your job."

"It was until I saw you."

"You're worse than Gino."

"And you?" asked William.

"No, I'm not worse than Gino."

"No, I didn't mean . . ." began William, painfully aware how long it had been since his last date.

"I know what you meant," teased Beth. "I read art history at Durham."

"I knew I'd gone to the wrong university."

"So where did you go?" she asked as Gino reappeared with two piping hot bowls of stracciatella.

"King's. Also history of art. And after Durham?"

"I went up to Cambridge and did a DPhil on Rubens the diplomat."

"I nearly did a PhD on Caravaggio the criminal."

"Which would explain why you ended up joining the police force."

"And did you go straight to the Fitzmolean after that?"

"Yes, it was my first job after Cambridge. And it must have been painfully obvious that last night was my first attempt at giving a discourse."

"You were brilliant."

"I just about got by, which will become only too obvious if you attend Tim Knox's lecture next week."

"I can't imagine what it must have been like to stand in for your boss at the last moment."

"It was terrifying. So, dare I ask if you're any nearer to finding my missing Rembrandt?"

"Your Rembrandt?"

"Yes. But then everyone who works at the Fitzmolean is possessive about *The Syndics*."

"I can understand why. But after seven years, I'm afraid the trail has gone cold."

"But you can't have been working on the case for the past seven years?"

"Less than seven weeks," admitted William. "But I'm confident the Rembrandt will be back in its place by the end of next month."

Beth didn't laugh. "I still want to believe it's out there somewhere and will eventually be returned to the gallery."

"I'd like to agree with you," said William, as Gino whisked away their empty bowls. "But no one else in the department agrees with me."

"Do they think it's been destroyed?" asked Beth. "I just can't believe anyone could be that much of a philistine."

"Not even if it meant they avoided ending up in jail for several years?"

"Does that mean you know who stole it?"

William didn't reply, and was relieved when Gino reappeared with their main courses.

"I'm sorry," said Beth. "I shouldn't have asked. But if there's ever anything I can do to help, please let me know."

"There is something you might be able to advise me on. We've recently come across an outstanding copy of *The Syndics*, and I wondered if you knew anyone who specializes in that kind of work?"

"Not my field," admitted Beth. "I deal with dead artists, and then only if they're Dutch or Flemish. But I assume you've already visited the Fake Gallery in Notting Hill?"

"Never heard of it," said William, as he touched his jacket pocket, searching for a notebook, quite forgetting that he wasn't on duty.

"They have a number of artists working for them who can knock up a fake of any master you require, living or dead."

"Is that legal?"

"I've no idea. That's your department," Beth said with a grin. "But if you're not spending every waking hour trying to find my Rembrandt, you must be attempting to solve some even bigger crimes."

"The theft of a small phial of moon dust, and several signed copies of Winston Churchill's *The Second World War*."

"Are you allowed to tell me more?"

Beth couldn't stop laughing when William told her about Dr. Talbot and the American undersecretary. She even came up with a suggestion when he mentioned the fake Winston Churchill signed editions.

"Perhaps you should be looking for an unsigned set, so you'll be one step ahead of your forger."

"Good idea," said William, deciding not to tell her that was exactly what he'd been doing all day. "Perhaps we should meet regularly, as you should have been a detective."

"And you should clearly be giving lectures at the Fitzmolean."

They both laughed.

"How awkward first dates are," said William.

"Is this a first date?" asked Beth, giving him a warm smile.

"I hope so."

"Coffee?" asked Gino.

William didn't notice the time slip by until Beth whispered, "I think the staff want to go home."

He looked around to see that they were the last two customers in the restaurant, and quickly called for the bill.

"Do you live nearby?" he asked.

"In Fulham. I share a flat with a friend. But don't worry, I can catch a bus from here."

"I can't afford the bus fare," said William after looking at the bill. "So can I walk you home?"

"I hope we'll see you again soon, signorina," said Gino as he opened the door for them.

"I haven't decided yet," said Beth, returning his grin.

William took her hand as they crossed the road, and they didn't stop chatting about nothing, about everything, until they reached Beth's front door, when he leaned down and kissed her on the cheek. As she put her key in the lock he asked, "Would you like to come to the Fake Gallery with me?"

"Are you ever off duty, Detective Constable Warwick?" she asked.

"Not while there's an outside chance I'll find your Rembrandt, Miss Rainsford."

9

The rule was simple. If the phone rang, you took the call, like the next cab on the rank. You wrote down the details before briefing DCI Lamont, who would decide which one of them would take on the case, assuming there was a case to take on.

Quite often the call came from a member of the public who'd had a family keepsake stolen and wanted to know what the police intended to do about it. You had to explain that most burglaries were a matter for their local constabulary, as the Art and Antiques unit only had four officers, so it couldn't follow up every inquiry. However, Commander Hawksby never stopped reminding them that to an old lady who'd lost her Victorian brooch it was the Crown Jewels, and for many callers, this was their only direct contact with the police.

"When you put the phone down," he told William, "be sure you have a happy, satisfied customer, rather than someone who believes the police aren't on their side."

William picked up the phone.

"Sorry to bother you," said a well-spoken voice. "I just hope I'm not wasting your time."

"You won't be wasting my time," said William, "if you believe a crime has been committed."

"That's the problem. I'm not altogether sure a crime's been committed, but it looks a bit fishy."

William smiled at the quaint expression. "Can I start by taking your name, sir?" he asked, picking up a pen, aware that half the time the caller put the phone down after that question.

"Jeremy Webb. I work at the London Silver Vaults in the City. You might not have heard of us."

"My father took me there one half-term when he was buying a gift for my mother's birthday. I've never forgotten it. There must have been at least a couple of dozen different stalls, all hugger-mugger—"

"Thirty-seven shops," said Webb. "I'm president of the London Silver Vaults Association this year, which is the reason I'm calling. Several of our members have raised a problem with me."

"What kind of problem?" asked William. "Take your time, Mr. Webb, and don't hesitate to mention any detail, however insignificant it may seem."

"Thank you," said Webb. "The LSVA is comprised of a group of associated members whose principal activity is to buy and sell silver. It can be anything from a Victorian teaspoon to a large centerpiece for a dining room table. Now silver, as I'm sure you know, has to be hallmarked and accepted by the assayer's office before it can be described as sterling. No serious collector would ever consider purchasing an item unless it was properly hallmarked."

William remained pen poised, aware that Mr. Webb would get there in his own time.

"Over the past month, the vaults have regularly been visited by a gentleman whose only interest is in buying silver that is at least a hundred years old. He doesn't seem to care if it's a George V coronation medal, or a school trophy for the long jump. One of the four hallmarks indicates the year of manufacture, and several of my colleagues have noted that this particular gentleman always checks the age of a piece using a loupe, before taking any interest in the object itself."

"A loupe?"

"I'm sorry," said Webb. "It's a small magnifying glass, often used by jewelers and watchmakers."

"I see," said William, although he still wasn't sure where this was leading.

"The other thing that made my colleagues suspicious is that he always pays in cash."

"Large-denomination notes?"

"No. We're always on the lookout for that, following the Treasury's recent directives on money laundering. Am I making any sense, officer?"

"You are, Mr. Webb. Do you know the gentleman's name?"

"That's the thing," said Webb. "We always take the name and address of every customer, but this man has given us several different names, and never the same address."

William was suddenly more interested. "Do any of your stallholders have any idea who he might be?"

"One of our dealers says he recognizes him, but can't be sure from where. He claims he doesn't recall his name."

"You say 'claims.' That suggests you're not convinced."

"A few years ago, the stallholder in question was sentenced to six months in prison for handling stolen goods. The probation service asked us to give him a second chance, which we did—reluctantly. But we warned him that if he put a foot out of line again, he would be expelled from the society."

"What's his name?"

"Ken Appleyard."

William wrote down the name. "And given your experience in the field, Mr. Webb, do you have a theory as to why our mystery man is buying so much old silver?"

"To begin with, I assumed it might be money laundering, but he kept coming back. So, unless he's stupid, that didn't make any sense. Then I wondered if he was melting the silver down, but that also didn't add up, because the price of silver has fallen recently. So I confess I'm completely flummoxed. However, my board of trustees felt I should let you know, to be on the safe side."

"I'm most grateful, Mr. Webb. I'll brief my boss about your concerns, and may well get back to you."

The first thing William did after he'd hung up wasn't to brief Lamont, but to take the lift down to minus one, where the police national computer was housed. A PC who looked even younger than him tapped in the name Ken Appleyard, and in a matter of moments a record of his previous convictions was printed out. It confirmed that Appleyard had been sentenced to six months for receiving stolen goods. William was pleased to see that he had no other convictions, and since his release hadn't received so much as a parking ticket.

William returned to his office bearing the charge sheet. Lamont was on the phone, but waved William to the chair by his side. William knew that the boss was assisting an Interpol inquiry into a diamond smuggling ring that worked out of Ghana and Dubai. Once Lamont put the phone down he switched his attention to what William had to say.

"What do you think he's up to, boss?" asked William, when he had come to the end of his report.

"I've no idea. But the first thing you have to do is find out who the mystery man is, because until we know that, we're just floundering around in the dark."

"Where do I start?"

"Follow up your only lead. Go to the Silver Vaults and talk to Appleyard. But tread cautiously. He'll be sensitive about his prison sentence, especially with his colleagues working close by. Try to look like a customer, not a copper."

"Understood, sir."

"And, William, why haven't you arrested the Churchill forger yet?"

"He's gone to ground, sir. But if he resurfaces, I'll nab him and happily apply the thumbscrews."

Lamont smiled and returned to his diamond smugglers.

◄○►

William knew exactly where the Silver Vaults were, but before leaving he called his father to ask if he was free for lunch, as he needed to seek his advice.

"I can spare you an hour," replied Sir Julian, "but no more."

"That's all I'm allowed, Dad. Oh, and I can only give you two pounds and eighty pence toward the bill."

"I accept your pittance, although it's considerably less than I usually charge for an hour's con. Let's meet outside the entrance to Lincoln's Inn at one o'clock. You can tell me afterward if your canteen is any better than ours."

William left the Yard and caught a bus to the City. After a short walk up Chancery Lane, he entered the London Silver Vaults. A list of all the stallholders was displayed on a wall in the reception area. Mr. K. Appleyard's shop was number 23.

William took the wide staircase to the basement, where he found a long room with stalls huddled together on both sides. He would have liked to stop and look more closely at several exquisite pieces that caught his eye, but didn't allow himself to be distracted from his search for number 23.

Appleyard was showing a customer a sugar bowl when William spotted the name above his stall. He stopped at the dealer opposite, picked up a silver pepper pot in the form of a suffragette, and studied it closely. The ideal Christmas present for Grace, he thought. He was about to ask the price when Appleyard's customer drifted away, so he strolled across to join him.

"Good morning, sir. Were you looking for something in particular?"

"Someone," said William quietly, and produced his warrant card.

"I haven't done anything wrong," said Appleyard defiantly.

"No one's suggesting you have. I just want to ask you a couple of questions."

"Is this about that guy who's been buying old silver?"

"Got it in one."

"There's not a lot I can tell you. I came across him in Pentonville, but I can't remember his name. I've spent years trying to forget that period of my life, not revisit it."

"I quite understand," said William. "But it would be a great help if you could remember anything at all about the man—age, height, any distinguishing features."

Appleyard looked into space as if trying to conjure him up. "Shaved head, fifty, fifty-five, over six foot."

"Do you know what he was in for?"

"No idea. Golden rule in jail, never ask what crime another prisoner's committed, and never volunteer what you're in for." William added this piece of information to his memory bank. Appleyard was silent for a few moments before adding, "He had a small tattoo on his right forearm, a heart with 'Angie' scrolled across it."

"That's really helpful, Mr. Appleyard," said William, handing him his card. "If you think of anything else, please give me a call."

"No need to mention your visit to any of my colleagues?"

"Just another customer," said William, as he strolled across to the stall opposite, and asked how much the suffragette pepper pot was. A week's wages.

There were enough clocks chiming all around William to remind him that he was due to meet his father in fifteen minutes, and he knew the old man would have begun his first course if he wasn't on time.

He ran up the stairs and out onto the street, turned right, and kept running. He reached the entrance gate of Lincoln's Inn at 12:56, to see his father on the far side of the square, striding toward the main hall.

"What brings you to this neck of the woods?" Sir Julian asked as he led his son down a long corridor lined with portraits of pre-eminent judges.

"Business and pleasure. I'll explain over lunch. But first, how's Mum?"

"She's well, and sends her love."

"And Grace?"

"As dotty as ever. She's defending a Rastafarian who has five wives and fourteen children, and is trying to claim he's a Mormon

74

and therefore not bound by the laws of polygamy. She'll lose of course, but then she always does."

"Perhaps she'll surprise you one day," said William as they entered the dining room.

"It's self-service, so grab a tray," said his father, as if he hadn't heard him. "Avoid the meat at all costs. The salads are usually safe."

William selected a plate of sausage and mash and a treacle tart before they walked over to a table on the far side of the room.

"Is this a social call, or are you seeking my advice?" asked Sir Julian as he picked up a salt cellar. "Because I charge one hundred pounds an hour, and the clock is already ticking."

"Then you'll have to deduct it from my pocket money, because there are a couple of things I'd like your opinion on."

"Go."

William spent some time describing why he'd spent his morning just down the road in the Silver Vaults.

"Fascinating," said his father, when William came to the end of the story. "So you now need to find out who the mystery buyer is, and why he's melting down silver that's over a hundred years old."

"But we can't even be sure that's what he's up to."

"Then what's in it for him, unless he's a rich eccentric collector? And if he was, he wouldn't have given different names and addresses."

"Got any other ideas, Father?"

Sir Julian didn't speak again until he had finished his soup. "Coins," he said. "It has to be coins."

"Why coins?"

"It has to be something worth considerably more than the original silver, otherwise it doesn't make any sense." Sir Julian pushed his empty soup bowl to one side and began to attack his salad. "What's your other problem?"

"Have you come across a QC called Booth Watson? And if so, what's your opinion of him?"

"Not a name to be mentioned in polite society," said Sir Julian, sounding serious for the first time. "He'll happily bend the law to the point of breaking. Why do you ask?"

"I'm investigating one of his clients—" began William.

"Then this conversation must cease, as I have no desire to appear in court with that particular man."

"That's not like you, Dad. You rarely speak ill of your colleagues."

"Booth Watson is not a colleague. We just happen to be in the same profession."

"Why do you feel so strongly?"

"It all began when we were up at Oxford and he stood for president of the Law Society. Frankly, I was only too willing to support any candidate who opposed him. After the man I proposed was elected, Booth Watson blamed me, and we haven't passed a civil word since. In fact, that's him over there, on the far side of the room. Eating alone, which is all you need to know about him. Don't look, because he'd sue you for trespass."

"Who are you defending at the moment?" asked William, changing the subject, while unable to resist glancing across the room.

"A Nigerian chief who chopped up his wife and then posted various body parts to his mother-in-law."

"So you won't be getting him off?"

"Not a chance, thank God. In fact I'm thinking of giving up murder altogether. Agatha Christie got out just in time."

"What do you mean?"

"Poirot never had to contend with DNA, which is about to make it almost impossible to put up a reasonable defense for one's client. No, in future I'm going to concentrate on fraud and libel. Longer trials, and better refreshers, and you're still in with a fifty-fifty chance of winning," he said before wiping his mouth with a napkin.

William looked at his watch. "I ought to be going."

"Understood, but first, tell me how your social life is, because your mother's bound to ask."

"A little more promising. I've met someone who I think's a bit special. In fact I'm seeing her again tonight."

"Can I tell your mother?"

"Please don't say a word, otherwise she'll want to invite us both to lunch on Sunday, and I haven't prepared Beth for that particular ordeal yet."

"Mum's the word," said Sir Julian, laughing at his own feeble pun.

As they left the dining room, William couldn't resist taking another glance at Booth Watson, who was digging into the treacle tart.

"Good to see you, my boy," said Sir Julian as they stepped out into the courtyard.

"You too, Father." William smiled as he watched his father striding away. How much he owed him.

10

The first thing William did when he arrived back at the Yard was to brief the boss on his meeting with Appleyard.

"There was only one piece of information he supplied that just might prove useful," said Lamont. "Did you spot it?"

"The tattoo?"

"In one. Because if you find Angie, she could lead us to the mystery buyer."

"But all we've got to go on is a tattoo."

"Which may be enough."

"Why?"

"Think like a criminal, laddie, and not like a choirboy," said Lamont, leaning back in his chair.

"Pentonville," said William after a brief silence.

"You're on the right track. But who do you need to speak to at Pentonville?"

"The governor?"

"No. Too senior for what we need."

William looked lost, and once again had to wait for Lamont to come to his rescue.

"You told me Appleyard was only in Pentonville for three weeks before being transferred to Ford Open."

"Yes, sir."

"During that time he would have been entitled to three prison visits. So you need to find out if anyone called Angie visited someone at Pentonville while Appleyard was there. If she did, they'll have her details on file."

"We've also got to hope that she's still his girlfriend."

"That shouldn't be a problem. A tattoo to a con is like a ring to you and me. It's a commitment, and, let's face it, it's all we've got to go on. Have a word with the senior officer in charge of visits. His name is Leslie Rose. Sir to you. Make sure you pass on my best wishes."

William returned to his desk and looked up the number for the visits officer at HMP Pentonville. When the phone was answered, a stentorian voice barked, "Rose."

"Good afternoon, sir. My name is DC Warwick, and I'm ringing at the suggestion of my boss, Detective Chief Inspector Lamont."

"A complete wanker."

"I beg your pardon, sir?"

"Any idiot who believes Arsenal can win the Cup is a complete wanker. What can I do for you, detective constable?"

"In 1981, you had a prisoner called Appleyard at Pentonville. Ken Appleyard. He was only with you for three weeks, between April the ninth and the thirtieth, before he was shipped out to Ford."

"What about him?"

"During his stay, another prisoner, whose name he can't remember—"

"Or doesn't want to."

"—may have had a visit from his girlfriend, who we know was called Angie."

"What makes you so sure of that?"

"Appleyard recalls seeing a tattoo on the man's right arm. A red heart with the name Angie scrolled across it."

"A nice piece of detective work, young man. The odds aren't great, but I'll get back to you."

"Thank you, sir."

"Pass on my regards to Bruce. Tell him he has no hope on Saturday."

"No hope of what, sir?"

"Arsenal beating Spurs."

"So presumably you support Tottenham Hotspur?"

"I see the Yard is still only recruiting the brightest and the best. So who do you support?"

"Fulham, sir. And I should point out that you haven't beaten us recently."

"And I should point out, constable, that that might just be because we haven't played you for several years, and we're unlikely to do so while you languish in the second division." The phone began to purr.

William spent the rest of the afternoon writing up his report on the meeting with Appleyard and his telephone conversation with SO Rose at Pentonville. He decided to leave out the expletives and the Arsenal references, before he dropped a sanitized version on DCI Lamont's desk just after 5:30.

William planned on slipping away just before six, so he wouldn't be late for Tim Knox's postponed lecture at the Fitzmolean, and supper afterward with Beth.

He was just about to leave when the phone rang. Jackie picked it up.

"It's for you, Bill," she said, transferring the call to William's desk. He smiled, expecting to hear SO Rose's cheerful voice on the other end of the line.

"Detective Constable Warwick?" said a voice he could barely make out.

"Yes. Who's this?"

"My name's Martin. I work at John Sandoe Books in Chelsea, and you visited our shop last week. Your man is back, but this time he's looking at a Dickens first edition."

William raised a hand in the air, a sign that every other available officer should pick up their extension and listen to the conversation.

"Remind me of your address?"

"Blacklands Terrace, off the King's Road."

"Keep him talking," said William. "I'm on my way."

"There's a squad car waiting for you outside," said Lamont as he put down his phone. "Get moving."

William ran out of the office, bounded down the stairs two at a time, and shot out of the front door to find a waiting car, its engine running and passenger door open. The driver took off, siren blaring, lights flashing, before William had even closed the door.

"Danny Ives," the driver said, thrusting out his left hand, the other hand remaining firmly on the wheel as he accelerated away. He clearly didn't need to be told where to go.

"William Warwick," said William, who accepted that if a fellow officer didn't declare his rank he was probably a constable. Though in truth, most of the Met's drivers considered themselves to be in a class of their own, and that the capital was nothing more than a Formula One racetrack, with the added challenge of pedestrians.

Ives nipped into Victoria Street, dodging in and out of the early evening traffic as he made his way toward Parliament Square. He ran a red light as he passed the Houses of Parliament. Although William had been on a couple of blue light runs in the past, he still felt like a schoolboy fulfilling his wildest dream as cars, vans, lorries, and buses all moved aside to allow them through. As they approached the traffic lights at Chelsea Bridge, Ives slowed down and ignored the no-right-turn sign, cutting down his journey by several minutes. He accelerated along Chelsea Bridge Road toward Sloane Street, always particularly busy during the rush hour. He reached the traffic lights in Sloane Square just as they turned red and slipped into the bus lane without stopping. As they swung left past Peter Jones and continued on down the King's Road, Ives turned off the siren but kept his lights flashing.

"Wouldn't want to let him know we're on our way, would we?" he said. "A mistake they often make in films."

He turned into Blacklands Terrace, where William spotted a

young man standing outside the bookshop, waving his arms. He leaped out of the car and ran across to join him.

"You just missed the man. I couldn't stall him any longer. That's him, in the beige raincoat, heading toward Sloane Square."

William looked in the direction the bookseller was pointing but only caught a glimpse of the man as he turned the corner.

"Thanks!" William shouted as he took up the chase on foot. His eyes continually searching the crowd ahead, but he had to dodge between pedestrians, as he no longer had the help of a siren. And then he spotted a man in a beige raincoat. He was just about to grab him, when William noticed he was pushing a stroller with one hand and holding a small child's hand with the other.

William charged on, becoming less and less confident with each step, but then he caught sight of another beige raincoat disappearing into Sloane Square tube station. When he reached the ticket barrier he took out his ID card but didn't give the inspector a chance to check it as he raced past. He saw the man near the bottom of the escalator, but then he disappeared again. William dashed down the escalator, brushing aside the early evening commuters, and had nearly caught up with the man when he turned right and headed for the eastbound District line.

William emerged onto the crowded platform as a train screeched to a halt. He looked left and right before he spotted the man boarding the train about five carriages away. William leaped into the nearest carriage as the doors began to close, grabbed a handrail to steady himself, and caught his breath. When the train came to a halt at the next station, he jumped off, but a beige raincoat didn't appear. So, like the king on a chessboard, he advanced one square at a time, slipping into the next carriage at each stop.

The passenger in the raincoat didn't get off, and four stops later William was in the adjoining carriage. He took a seat near the front and glanced through the window of the dividing door to take a closer look at his quarry. The man was turning a page of *The Evening Standard,* and when they stopped at the next station he didn't even look up. This was going to be a long journey.

By the time the man folded his newspaper, they had stopped twenty-one times, which had given William more than enough time to be sure he was following the right man. Sixty, sixty-five, graying hair, slight stoop. He didn't need to hear his accent to know this was the same customer the manager of Hatchards had described to him.

The man finally got off at Dagenham East. William kept his distance as he left the station. To begin with he was able to lose himself in the crowd, but as the passengers thinned out he had to hang farther and farther back. He considered arresting the man there and then, but first he needed to find out where he lived, so he would know where the evidence was hidden.

The man turned down a side street, and stopped at a little wicket gate. William kept on walking, and noted the number, 43, as the man unlocked his front door and disappeared inside. When William reached the end of the street, he added Monkside Drive to his memory bank and reluctantly decided it might be wiser not to attempt to enter the house until he'd reported back to DCI Lamont and obtained a search warrant. He felt confident that the man in the beige raincoat wasn't going anywhere soon.

William turned back and headed for the station, feeling triumphant, but a few moments later his mood changed. He checked his watch: 7:21. Beth must be wondering where he was.

He ran all the way back to the station, but knew as he stood alone on the cold, windy platform waiting for the next train to appear that he had no chance of being in Kensington in time for Dr. Knox's lecture. The jolting progress between each stop, which William hadn't noticed during the journey to Dagenham when his adrenaline was pumping and he was having to concentrate every second, seemed interminable. The train finally pulled into South Kensington at 8:15. William ran up the escalator and out onto Thurloe Place, but by the time he reached the entrance to the Fitzmolean, the building was in darkness.

As he walked slowly in the direction of Beth's home, he began to prepare a speech explaining why he hadn't turned up in time for the lecture. He was almost word perfect by the time he reached her front door.

He stood there for some time before giving two gentle taps on the knocker. A few moments later, the door opened and a tall, handsome young man asked, "Can I help you?"

William felt sick.

"I was hoping to see Beth," he blurted out as a figure in a dressing gown appeared, a towel wrapped around her hair.

"Come in, William," said Beth. "I can't wait to find out why you stood me up. Can I assume you've found the Rembrandt? While I'm drying my hair, Jez," she said to the young man, "would you take William into the sitting room and give him a drink? Not that he deserves one."

11

"Did you get to the bookshop in time?" asked Lamont when William walked into the office the following morning.

"Yes, sir."

"So you arrested him?"

"No, sir."

"Why not?"

"By the time I caught up with him he was on a tube train to Dagenham East. I decided to first find out where he lived, then return with a search warrant this morning."

"Cretin," said Lamont. "You should have arrested him there and then, and immediately searched his house. Let's hope you won't have to explain to the Hawk why he's disappeared overnight."

"He's not going anywhere, sir."

"How can you possibly know that, detective constable? You're a policeman, not a fortune teller. Did he see you following him?"

"I don't think so, sir."

"Let's hope not, because you've certainly given him more than enough time to destroy the evidence, and even make a bolt for it."

William felt like an errant schoolboy receiving a dressing down from the headmaster because he hadn't done his homework properly.

"And can I also ask, laddie, why you're still dressed in the same clothes you were wearing yesterday?"

"I overslept, sir, and threw on the first things I could find, as I didn't want to be late."

"And is that also why you didn't shave?" William bowed his head. "Well, I hope she was worth it," said Lamont, "because you're in enough trouble as it is. I'll tell you what's going to happen next. You'll go home, take a shower, have a shave and a change of clothes, and be back here within the hour, by which time I will have obtained a warrant to search the suspect's premises. You and DS Roycroft will travel to Dagenham, arrest the suspect, charge him, and gather every scrap of evidence you can to ensure we nail the bastard when the case comes to court. You'll then escort him to the local nick, where he can stay put until he comes up in front of the magistrate tomorrow morning. And Warwick, if he's bolted, or destroyed the evidence, you'll be up in front of the commander, and I might have to recommend that a longer spell on the beat wouldn't do you any harm. Now get moving, before he dies of old age."

During his journey back to Victoria, William couldn't stop thinking about what had happened the previous evening. He and Jez, Beth's flatmate, had shared a beer, when Jez had done most of the talking. He'd explained that he and Beth had been at uni together, and their relationship was platonic. William didn't need him to explain why.

When Beth joined them, still wearing her dressing gown, Jez quickly disappeared.

"You didn't have to wash your hair just for me," said William.

"Don't try and get off the hook," said Beth, as she sat down next to him on the couch. "I still want to know why you stood me up."

William didn't get as far as Dagenham before he kissed her for the first time, and he would have finished the story of his pursuit of the Churchill forger over breakfast, if Beth hadn't reminded him what time it was.

"I'm going to visit the Fake Gallery tomorrow," he said as he headed for the door. "Would you like to join me?"

"Yes, assuming you're not held up by the Boston Strangler."

When William turned up at Scotland Yard later that morning he'd spent a few minutes in the washroom, doing his best to make himself presentable. But his feeble efforts hadn't fooled Lamont.

The moment he'd returned to his little room in Trenchard House, he showered, shaved, and put on some fresh clothes. He was back at his desk within the hour, by which time Lamont had identified the suspect from his address in Dagenham—a Mr. Cyril Amhurst. He'd also secured a search warrant from a local magistrate.

"Jackie will be accompanying you," he told William, "as you clearly need a nanny to hold your hand. Let's hope for your sake that Mr. Amhurst hasn't scarpered."

William picked up a car from the pool and headed east along the Embankment toward Dagenham, with nanny seated in the passenger seat. It was their first extended time together, other than the occasional team bonding session in the Tank, the popular watering hole on the ground floor of Scotland Yard. He still hadn't found the snooker room.

As they traveled through the East End, William discovered that Jackie was divorced with one daughter, called Michelle, and an understanding mother who made it possible for her to do the job she loved.

William didn't mention his parents or his sister, but he did tell Jackie that he intended to visit the Fake Gallery in Notting Hill the next day, with a research assistant from the Fitzmolean.

"Is she the reason you were late this morning?"

"Yes," said William, turning to look out of the window.

"Then let's hope she's understanding."

"What do you mean?"

"There are more breakups in the police force than any other profession. I still adore my ex-husband, but he got fed up with never knowing when I'd be home, even if I would be home, so he found someone else who was always back in time for supper, not breakfast. By the way, it might be wise to let the boss know you plan to visit the Fake Gallery tomorrow."

"Why? It's my day off."

"Even so, he doesn't like to find out things second-hand."

"Thanks for the advice," said William, as they drove into Dagenham.

William had learned more about Jackie in the past forty minutes than he had during the previous month.

"What do we do if he isn't in?" he asked as they pulled up outside 43 Monkside Drive.

"We wait until he shows up. A lot of police work consists of just hanging around."

"You or me?" asked William as they walked up the path.

"You. You're the case officer."

William felt nervous when he rapped on the door, and as the seconds passed, began to fear the worst. He was just about to go back to the car when the door opened.

"Mr. Cyril Amhurst?"

"Yes," the man said, giving them a warm smile. "How can I help you?"

"My name is Detective Constable Warwick, and this is my colleague, Detective Sergeant Roycroft." They produced their warrant cards, causing Amhurst's smile to evaporate. "May we come in, sir?"

"Yes, of course," he said, less warmly. He led them through to the front room, but didn't sit down. "So what's all this about?" he asked.

"We have received complaints from several London bookshops that you've been selling them signed copies of Winston Churchill's *The Second World War.*"

"I didn't realize that was a crime."

"It is if the signature's yours, and not Sir Winston's," said Jackie firmly.

"I also have to inform you," said William, "that I am in possession of a warrant to search these premises."

The blood drained out of Amhurst's face, and he collapsed onto the sofa. For a moment, William thought he was going to faint.

William and Jackie spent the next two hours going about their task, one of them always remaining in the living room, where Amhurst sat meekly on the sofa. It quickly became clear to William that DS Roycroft had carried out the procedure many times before.

"Would you like a cup of tea?" Amhurst asked as a molehill of books grew into a mountain in the middle of the room.

"No, thank you," said William, placing two bottles of Waterman's black ink next to several sheets of lined paper covered with row upon row of Winston S. Churchill signatures.

By the time Jackie considered the job had been done to her satisfaction, they had between them unearthed several gems, including a complete six-volume set of Churchill's *The Second World War*, of which three of the volumes were signed, as well as books by Lewis Carroll, Field Marshal Montgomery, and President Eisenhower, unsigned. But the ultimate prize was a first edition of *A Christmas Carol*, signed by Charles Dickens.

After Jackie had placed each item in separate exhibit bags and labeled them, William arrested Mr. Amhurst and cautioned him.

"Am I going to jail?" Amhurst asked anxiously.

"Not for the moment. But you'll have to accompany us to Dagenham police station where you will be interviewed and possibly charged. The custody sergeant will then decide if you should be granted bail. To be on the safe side, I'd recommend you pack an overnight bag."

Amhurst couldn't stop shaking.

William and Jackie escorted him to the local nick, booked him in, and handed over the evidential exhibits to the sergeant on duty. When Amhurst was charged, he made no comment, other than to ask if he might phone his solicitor. He was being fingerprinted and photographed when William and Jackie signed off to make their way back to Scotland Yard.

Once William had deposited the car keys in the pound, he joined Jackie in reception and they took the lift up to the fifth floor. When they stepped out into the corridor, William noticed that a light was still on under the commander's door.

"Do you think he leaves it on, even when he's not there?"

"It wouldn't surprise me," said Jackie. "But there's no way we're ever going to find out."

When they walked into their office they found Lamont on the phone, but once he'd finished his call, he sat back and listened to their report.

"You got lucky, William," he said when they came to the end. "Just be sure you don't make such a damn stupid mistake again. And remember that your responsibilities in this case aren't over yet. If Amhurst pleads not guilty, you'll be called upon to give evidence."

"Surely he'll plead guilty," said William. "The evidence is overwhelming."

"You can never count on it. I haven't got the time to tell you how many slam-dunk cases I've lost. But I admit this one looks pretty solid. By the way, SO Rose called from Pentonville. He wants you to give him a buzz."

After William had returned to his desk he sat in silence for a few moments, so many different thoughts whirling around in his head. Amhurst, followed by Beth, squeezed out by Rose. He picked up the phone, dialed HMP Pentonville, and asked to be put through to the SO.

"Rose."

"Warwick, sir, returning your call."

"You're in luck, DC Warwick." William flicked open his notebook. "Three women named Angie visited Pentonville to see prisoners between April the ninth and April the thirtieth 1981. A Mrs. Angie Oldbury, Angela Ibrahim, and Angie Carter."

"If I could take down the details of all three, sir."

"No need," said Rose, "because one of the prisoners who was visited by an Angie is still in Pentonville, and one was black, which I have a feeling Appleyard might have noticed. The third was released just over a year ago."

"What's his name?"

"Patience, young man. The one you might be interested in is

a right little villain called Kevin Carter, who lives in Barnstaple. That's in Devon, in case you don't know. He's an engraver by day, and a burglar by night. So now it's your turn to prove you're worthy of the prefix in front of your name."

"I'll get on to it straight away, sir."

"And did you pass on my salutations to your boss?"

"I did indeed, sir."

"And what was his response?"

"I think you'd better ask him yourself, sir."

"That bad," said Rose before he put the phone down.

William wrote a detailed memo of his conversation with SO Rose before handing it to the boss.

"And what is the one word that leaps off the page?" said Lamont after he'd read the report.

"Engraver."

"You're learning fast," said Lamont. "Though Carter and Barnstaple would be a close second and third." He swiveled his chair around. "Jackie, you'd better join us."

Once DS Roycroft had settled, the inevitable biro in hand, notebook open, Lamont continued.

"The two of you are going to have to spend at least a couple of days in the West Country keeping a close eye on Carter. I need you to find out what he's up to, and exactly what he's engraving on the silver he purchased from the vaults. And why he's suddenly a buyer, when he usually nicks the stuff. He doesn't have that sort of money, so someone must be bankrolling him. But who?"

"When do you want us to leave, sir?" asked Jackie.

"As soon as possible. Unless either of you have anything more important to keep you in London?"

"I may have," said William. "I recently met a researcher at the Fitzmolean, and although I didn't learn a great deal more about the theft of the Rembrandt, she suggested I visit the Fake Gallery in Notting Hill, which I had intended to do tomorrow morning."

"Why?" barked Lamont.

"On the off chance I might spot a similar work by the artist who produced the copy of the Rembrandt."

"Worth a try," said Lamont. "And take the young lady along with you, especially if she was the reason you were late this morning."

Jackie suppressed a smile.

"So that's settled," said Lamont. "You and Jackie can drive down to Barnstaple first thing on Monday morning."

"Can I ask how the diamond smuggling is going, sir?" asked William.

"Don't get cheeky with me, detective constable, or you might just find yourself back in Lambeth in time for the night shift."

◄○►

"I have an interesting case that might just appeal to you," said Clare as she handed over a file marked PRIVATE.

Grace took her time studying her instructing solicitor's appraisal of the case before saying, "But surely the presiding judge wouldn't allow the trial to proceed, given the circumstances?"

"There's a precedent," said Clare. "Mr. Justice Havers allowed his son and daughter to appear before him, with one of them representing the Crown while the other appeared for the defense. But not before the defendant had agreed to the arrangement."

"Not my usual fare," admitted Grace as she read the charge sheet for a second time. "But I confess I find the challenge irresistible. And I bet my father wouldn't put up any objection."

"Have you told him about us?" inquired Clare, trying not to sound anxious.

"I haven't found the right opportunity yet."

"Will you ever?" sighed Clare, before adding, "I looked up the word 'reactionary' in my *OED*, and your father's name appeared in the footnotes."

Grace laughed. "I've told my mother all about you, and she couldn't have been more supportive. She asked if you'd like to join us for lunch on Sunday, and let Dad work it out for himself?"

"Who do you think your father would be more happy to propose as a member of the Garrick—a mass murderer or a lesbian?"

"Mass, I couldn't be sure about," said Grace as she placed the folder on the bedside table and turned out the light.

12

They sat together on the top deck of a bus heading for Notting Hill.

"Do you have a plan, Detective Constable Warwick," asked Beth, "or are we just winging it?"

"We're winging it," admitted William. "But I'm hoping that by the time we get back on the bus I'll know who painted the copy of the missing Rembrandt."

"Did you manage to dig up anything interesting about the gallery?"

"It was founded twelve years ago by two brothers, Malcolm and Zac Knight. It started out as a portrait gallery, but they soon found there wasn't a profit in that and moved on to producing unsigned copies of famous paintings for customers who couldn't afford the real thing, but want a masterpiece on their wall for a thousandth of the price. That was when the business really took off. How about you?"

"I asked around my arty friends. A lot of them don't approve of the gallery, although one or two did admit that it's given some struggling artists a reasonable living they wouldn't otherwise have had. Apparently some of the copies are of exceptional quality. But I'd still rather have an original."

"Then you're going to have to steal one. Or marry a very rich man."

"Neither will be necessary," said Beth. "I already live with some of the finest artists on earth, and my latest boyfriend is practically penniless, so that doesn't look too promising."

"But most of those artists are dead Dutch men, so your boy-friend must be in with a chance."

"Not unless he finds my Rembrandt."

"Is that why you tried to pick me up?"

"It was you who tried to pick *me* up, in case you've forgotten. And on our second date, you didn't even show up."

"I'd already heard the lecture," said William, taking her hand.

"Well, I hope you're not thinking of leaving the Art and An-tiques squad before you've found my Rembrandt."

"I won't be moving for some time yet. But if I pass my ser-geant's exam, in a couple of years' time they'll probably move me to another department."

"You're not going anywhere until my Rembrandt is back in its frame, otherwise I shall transfer my affections to whoever takes your place."

"Lucky man. But if we find out who copied *The Syndics,* we'll be one step nearer to discovering what happened to the original."

The bus came to a halt, and William stood aside to allow Beth to go ahead of him.

"Not many men bother to do that nowadays," Beth commented as she made her way down the stairs. "I can't wait to meet your father. He must be an old-fashioned gentleman."

"That's something I've always taken for granted," admitted Wil-liam, "and have only begun to appreciate recently."

"You'll remember Mark Twain's comment about his father," said Beth as they stepped off the bus. "'When I was a boy of fourteen, my father was so ignorant I could hardly stand to have the old man around. But when I got to be twenty-one, I was astonished at how much he'd learned in seven years.'" William laughed, and Beth asked, "Do you have any idea where you're going?"

"No," said William, "but I've seen someone who might." He

stopped a passing bobby and asked him if he knew where Abbots Road was.

"Second on the right, sir."

"Thank you," said William.

"Were you ever in uniform?" asked Beth.

"I spent a couple of years on the beat in Lambeth."

"And are the public always as appreciative and polite as you?"

"Not always," said William quietly, before bowing his head.

"What did I say?" asked Beth, suddenly anxious.

"You brought back the memory of an old friend who should have been out on the beat this morning," said William as they turned the corner.

"I'm sorry," said Beth. She took his hand, aware that they still had so much to learn about each other.

"You weren't to know," said William.

As they strolled into Abbots Road, William spotted a colourful sign swinging in the breeze.

"Try not to sound like a policeman," whispered Beth as they entered the gallery.

A man dressed in an open-neck pink shirt, blazer, and jeans stepped forward to greet them. "Good morning," he said. "Zac Knight. I'm the proprietor of the gallery. May I ask if you were looking for anything in particular?"

Yes, thought William, but said nothing.

"No," said Beth. "We were just passing, and thought we'd take a look around."

"Of course," he said, giving her a warm smile. "The gallery is on two floors. Here on the ground floor are some remarkable paintings in the style of the modern masters."

"I'm surprised that's legal," said William.

Beth frowned as Knight gave William a closer look. He then lifted a picture off the wall and turned it around to reveal the word FAKE daubed on the back of the canvas in large black letters. "I can assure you, sir, that if you tried to remove the words, you would damage the painting beyond repair."

William nodded, but as Beth was still scowling at him, he didn't ask another question.

"And in the basement," continued Knight, placing the picture back on the wall, "you'll find copies of well-known masterpieces by some extremely talented artists."

"Is 'fake' printed on the back of those as well?"

"No, madam. However, the paintings are always unsigned, and are all either one inch smaller, or one inch larger than the original, so that no serious collector would be fooled. Please, enjoy both exhibitions, and don't hesitate to ask if you have any questions."

"Thank you, Zac," said Beth, returning his smile.

As they strolled around the ground floor, William was surprised by how convincing some of the fakes were. If you wanted to own a Picasso, a Matisse, or a Van Gogh, it could be yours for under a thousand pounds. Even Hockney's *A Bigger Splash* was on display, a print of which hung on his bedroom wall. But as they stood in front of a Rothko that might even have fooled an expert, he told Beth that he'd still rather have a Mary Fedden, a Ken Howard, or an Anthony Green for about the same price.

"Have you spotted your man?" whispered Beth.

"No. But he's far more likely to be downstairs."

"Why don't you pop down and take a look? If Mr. Knight reappears, I'll keep him occupied."

"Good thinking," said William and disappeared downstairs to find another large gallery filled with paintings, many of which he recognized. Turner's *The Fighting Temeraire* for two thousand pounds, and van Eyck's *Arnolfini Portrait*, which hung alongside a familiar nude by Goya.

But it was when he saw *A Dance to the Music of Time* by Poussin that he had to catch his breath. He had seen the original in the Wallace Collection, and could only marvel at how the artist had created such a likeness. A rare talent that shone in the presence of rude mechanicals. Some of the other copies were excellent, but none of them in this class. William wasn't in any doubt that he'd found his man, but there was no clue to the identity of the artist on the accompanying label.

After standing in front of the canvas for some time, he reluctantly returned upstairs, where he found Beth deep in conversation with the proprietor.

"I think you'll find Renoir's *The Umbrellas* rather proves my point," Knight was saying when William joined them. He gave Beth a nod.

"Perhaps you'd be kind enough to show me, Zac," she purred.

"Follow me," said Knight, ignoring William.

As Beth passed him, William whispered "Poussin," before she followed the proprietor downstairs. He walked slowly around the upstairs gallery for a second time, but his mind was elsewhere.

Jez had gone off to Shropshire for the weekend, and William had wanted to tell Beth how he felt about her, but he was worried that she might not be ready to consider a commitment after such a short time, though when his father had proposed to his mother after only three weeks, she was famously reported as replying, "What took you so long?"

Beth and Knight had been downstairs for about twenty minutes when William began to wonder if he should join them, but he somehow restrained himself. Twenty-five minutes. Thirty minutes. Just as he was heading for the stairs, Beth reappeared with the proprietor following closely behind.

"Thank you, Zac," she said. "That was fascinating, and I look forward to attending the private view on Wednesday. By the way, this is my brother, Peter."

Zac shook hands with William.

"Well, we ought to get moving, Sis," said William, "if we're not going to be late for lunch with Mother."

"I must admit," said Beth, "that I've been enjoying myself so much, I'd quite forgotten about dear mama."

"You have my number, Barbara," said Zac. "Give me a call any time."

William pretended not to notice as Knight opened the door and gave her a flirtatious smile.

"See you on Wednesday, Zac," said Beth.

Once they were back on the street, William said, "Keep walking, and try to look like my sister, not my girlfriend, because Zac's staring at us through the window."

Beth kept a sisterly distance, and didn't say a word until they'd turned the corner. When they reached a coffee shop she walked in and headed straight for a booth in the far corner, well hidden from the street.

"Nell Gwynne," said William, as he took the seat opposite her.

"More like Catherine the Great," suggested Beth, as she turned her back to the window.

"Reveal all."

"Zac is also a fake," she began, "who imagines that he's irresistible to women. I played along, until his hands began to wander."

"I'll kill him," said William, rising from his place.

"Not after what I have to tell you, you won't. Once I told him you were my brother, he couldn't resist making a move."

"Peter?"

"No, Peter Paul. Our mother named you after Rubens and me after Hepworth, which I felt was appropriate."

"You're a wicked woman."

"Cunning, I admit."

"So what did you find out?"

"All in good time," said Beth as a waiter appeared by their side.

"A cappuccino, please."

"Me too," said William.

"When I asked Zac who'd painted *A Dance to the Music of Time* he was cagey at first. Told me the gallery was careful not to reveal the identity of its artists, otherwise customers might try to deal with the artist direct, and cut them out."

"So how did you get over that hurdle?"

"I told him I was an impoverished secretary, and couldn't afford any of his wonderful paintings even if they were half the price. He then let slip that the artist wasn't available at the moment. 'Oh, I'm so sorry, has he left you for another gallery?' I asked, looking sympathetic. He told me it was a little more complicated than that."

"You're enjoying yourself, you hussy."

"Any more remarks like that, Detective Constable Warwick, and I might just forget what else my new friend Zac told me. Now, where was I before you interrupted me?"

"It's more complicated than that . . ."

"Ah yes. 'I'm not sure I know what you mean,' I said. 'But if you can't tell me, I quite understand.' He then admitted, 'I shouldn't be telling you this, but he's in jail.'"

"I adore you."

"Shh."

"What's he in jail for?"

"It seems he tried to sell a West End art dealer a long-lost Vermeer and got caught red-handed. 'How?' I asked. Apparently he didn't ask for enough money, which made the dealer suspicious, so he reported it to the police."

"What's his name?"

"I didn't ask."

"Why not?"

"Zac was beginning to sound suspicious, so I moved on to the Renoir, which is why it took so long to escape. In any case, it shouldn't be too difficult for one of the nation's leading detectives to track down someone who's in jail for faking a Vermeer."

"True, but Zac still thinks you're going to his opening on Wednesday?"

"Sadly Barbara won't be able to make it, or take up his kind offer to join him for the after-dinner party at the Mirabelle."

"But you gave him your number."

"01 730 1234."

"What's that?"

"Harrods Food Hall."

"I adore you."

13

They didn't sit down for breakfast on Sunday morning until just after ten.

Beth wanted to go for a run in Hyde Park, claiming she needed to lose a couple of pounds. William couldn't work out from where, but he agreed to join her.

"We won't need lunch," he said as he buttered another slice of toast. "This counts as brunch. But I'll have to call my mother and let her know I won't be joining them."

"You could still make it if you left now," teased Beth.

William ignored her as he helped himself to a dollop of marmalade.

"Jez and I usually go to the cinema on a Sunday evening," said Beth. "So we can be tucked up in bed at a sensible hour."

"Suits me. I've got a commander's meeting first thing in the morning."

"Sounds impressive."

"He is impressive, and responsible for four departments. A and A is his favorite, although it's the least important." William took a bite of toast before adding, "The team meet on the first Monday of every month to bring him up to date on the cases we've been investigating."

"Then you'll have rather a lot to tell him, won't you, Detective Constable Warwick?"

"You can be sure that if our artist is banged up, the Hawk will know his name, which prison he's in, and how long his sentence is."

"You'd like his job one day, wouldn't you?" said Beth, pouring herself another cup of coffee.

"Yes, but I'm not in any hurry. How about you? Do you want Tim Knox's job?"

"I love what I'm doing, and am quite happy to stay put until I get a better offer."

"My bet is you'll be director of the Tate before I sit in the commander's chair."

"I can't imagine the Tate will ever appoint a woman as its director."

"Even if she'd been captain of the school and captain of hockey?"

"Who told you that?"

"A policeman never reveals his sources."

"I'll kill Jez."

"Pity. I rather like him."

"He's the ideal flatmate," said Beth. "Clean, tidy, and considerate, and his rent helps to supplement the derisory salary the Fitzmolean pay me."

"I didn't realize you owned the flat."

"I don't. It belongs to my parents. Dad works for HSBC and he's been posted to Hong Kong for the next three years. The moment they return, Jez will have to go and I'll be moving back into his room."

Or mine, William wanted to say.

"You'd better call your mother while I do the washing up. The phone's in the study."

"Once a head girl, always a head girl," said William as he left her and made his way to the study. He picked up the phone and dialed the first number he'd ever known. He was hoping his father would pick up the phone, but a female voice came on the line.

"Nettleford 4163."

"Hi, Grace, it's William. I won't be able to make lunch today.

Something's come up. Would you apologize to Mum and Dad for me?"

"Something or someone?"

"It's a work thing."

"You're such a lousy liar, William. But I won't say anything, even though I was hoping you'd be around today."

"Why, is there a problem?"

"Dad will be meeting Clare for the first time, so I was relying on you for moral support."

"I've never really cared much for blood sports."

"Thanks a lot. Will you be around next week? I can't wait to meet the girl who would go on a second date with you."

"And I can't wait to meet the girl who would go on a second date with you."

"Touché. But I still wish you were here."

"You'll be fine, Grace. Just remember, when Dad snorts, only hot air comes out, no flames."

"That's easy for you to say from a safe distance."

"And in any case, you'll have Mum on your side."

"Two against one will make it a close-run thing. Three might have tipped the balance in my favor."

"I'll be there in spirit," said William, before he wished her luck and put the phone down. He was just about to leave the room when he spotted a row of postcards of the Hong Kong skyline displayed on the mantelpiece. The policeman in him wanted to look on the other side, but he resisted the temptation. He returned to the kitchen to find Beth doing the washing up.

"Jez usually does the drying."

"Subtle," said William, picking up a tea towel. "When we're finished, I'll go home, put on a tracksuit, and join you in the park."

"No need. You'll find everything you want in Jez's room."

"I've always wondered what a ménage à trois would be like."

A run in the park, followed by *My Beautiful Laundrette*, and then a Pizza Margherita—half each—before returning to

Beth's flat and disappearing under the blankets, to end an idyllic weekend.

◄○►

When William woke the following morning, he had to untangle himself before he could check his watch.

"Help!" he said as he leaped out of bed and charged into the bathroom. This was one meeting he couldn't afford to be late for. It would start at nine, with or without him.

Once he returned to the bedroom, he threw on his clothes and kissed a half-awake Beth.

"Hoping to escape before I woke, were you?"

"I have to go back to my place and get changed. I can't afford to be late again."

Beth sat up and stretched her arms. "Now you've had your way with me, Detective Constable Warwick, will I ever see you again?" She sighed and draped a languishing arm across her forehead.

"I could come back straight after work if that's OK. In which case, I'd be with you around seven."

"Suits me, then we can all have supper together. Jez can do the cooking, and you can do the washing up."

William sat on the bed and held her in his arms. "And what will you do?"

"Read Proust."

"By the way," said William, as he rose to leave, "my sister can't wait to meet you."

"Why?"

"It's quite complicated, but I'll reveal all this evening."

"Make sure you find my painting, DC Warwick!" were the last words William heard before he closed the bedroom door.

As he stepped out into the street William spotted a number 22 bus approaching the stop, and just managed to leap on board as it pulled away.

104

"Bugger," he said.

"I beg your pardon, young man," said the conductor. "There's no need for that sort of language on my bus."

"Sorry. I forgot to tell my girlfriend that I'm going to Barnstaple today."

"Then you're definitely on the wrong bus."

◄○►

"I'm sorry I haven't been able to spare you much time during the past month," said Hawksby as he took his seat at the top of the table. "No doubt you've all read about the drugs haul in Southampton last week. Two hundred pounds of cocaine and six arrests."

They all banged on the table with the palms of their hands.

"It's hardly worth that," said Hawksby. "The six we arrested were just minnows. The big fish are still sunning themselves on a beach in the south of France, and the biggest shark of all never leaves his estate in Colombia, where even the police are on his payroll. All we can do is try to intercept the next shipment and net another shoal of minnows, while we still have no idea how much is getting through. Be thankful none of you are attached to the drug squad."

The Hawk sat back, turned to his right, and said, "So what have you been up to in my absence, Bruce?"

"I've had much the same problem as you, sir," said Lamont. "Just exchange drugs for diamonds. The uncut stones are coming out of Ghana and being shipped to Dubai, before being sent on to Bombay where they're sold for cash. That way they avoid import and export tax, while at the same time pushing up house prices in Mayfair."

"Criminals always want to live in a law-abiding country," said Hawksby. "It makes it easier for them to carry on with their business."

"And like you, sir," continued Lamont, "we only catch some

minnows, who regard a few years in jail as no more than part of the deal."

"No wonder crime is currently fifteen percent of the world's economy, and growing," commented Hawksby. "Anything else, Bruce?"

"Yes, sir. I think it's just possible that DC Warwick might have made a breakthrough in the missing Rembrandt case, but I'll leave him to fill in the details."

"After further investigation, we—" began William.

"We?" interrupted Hawksby.

"Thanks to the help of a research assistant at the Fitzmolean, we've identified an artist who I think may have painted the copy of the Rembrandt."

"Name?"

"Eddie Leigh," said Lamont. "He tried to sell a fake Vermeer to a West End gallery. I was in charge of that case, and he's been banged up in Pentonville for the past two years."

"What makes you think that Leigh was responsible for the copy of the Rembrandt, DC Warwick?" asked Hawksby.

"I saw an example of his work at the Fake Gallery in Notting Hill, sir. He has a rare talent, but even so, I don't think he could have produced something of that quality unless he'd seen the original."

"But he could have bought a print of *The Syndics* from the Fitzmolean for five pounds," said Hawksby.

"That's true, but if he only had a print to work from, he wouldn't have been able to capture the vivid color, vibrancy, and flair of the original in the way he has, which makes me think it's just possible the original hasn't been destroyed."

"But that's still damned unlikely," said Lamont, without the trace of a smile.

"How long does Leigh have left to serve?" asked Hawksby.

"Just over four years, sir," said Lamont. "And I think he let slip where Faulkner is going to strike next."

"Enlighten me," said Hawksby.

"SO Langley called me from Pentonville yesterday to tell me that he's been regularly listening in on Eddie Leigh's weekly phone conversations with his wife, but there hasn't been anything worth reporting until last Friday."

"You have us on the edge of our seats, Bruce," said the commander.

Lamont read out the exact words Leigh had said to his wife.

"'How's the painting coming along?' 'You can tell him I've finished *Woman on a Beach*.' 'In the nick of time.'"

"That's from Picasso's Blue Period," said William.

"I don't give a damn what period it's from," said Hawksby. "Who owns the original?"

"A Mr. and Mrs. Brookes," said Lamont. "It's currently hanging in their country home in Surrey."

"Not for much longer, I suspect, and now we know where Faulkner intends to strike next, we need to find out when."

"I think I might have the answer to that," said Jackie, looking rather pleased with herself. She allowed herself a moment before continuing. "'In the nick of time' is the clue, sir, because the Brookes are going on holiday in two weeks, and although they'll be away for a fortnight, there is only one evening when the house will be empty." She allowed herself an even longer pause.

"Get on with it, sergeant," said Lamont.

"The Brookes have a driver, David Crann, and a cook, Elsie. Both live in, but the cook always goes on holiday when they're away."

"And the driver?"

"Crann will be on the premises night and day during that fortnight, except for the evening of Monday the twenty-third when Chelsea are playing Liverpool at home."

"I'm halfway there," said Hawksby, "but fill in the details."

"Crann has a season ticket, and never misses a Chelsea home game. The match kicks off at seven, so he'll leave the house around five and won't be back much before midnight."

"Are the premises fully alarmed?" asked Lamont.

"State of the art, sir. However, the nearest police station is about twenty minutes away, which would give the villains more than enough time to steal the picture and be back on the motorway before the local police could get there."

"That's an outstanding piece of policework, sergeant."

"Thank you, sir," said Jackie.

"For a change," said Lamont, "I think we may be one step ahead of Faulkner."

"Let's just hope he's not two steps ahead of us," said Hawksby. "However, prepare an outline plan for the twenty-third, Bruce, with the aim of catching them red-handed this time. But we also need some concrete results to keep the commissioner off my back. So before you leave, Warwick, what's the latest on Churchill and old silver?"

"Cyril Amhurst, the forger of the Churchill signatures, is coming up in front of the bench at Snaresbrook Crown Court later this week," said William. "We're expecting him to be granted bail, and to appear in court sometime in the next couple of months. I'm assuming he'll plead guilty."

"Never assume anything," said Lamont.

"And the silver?" asked Hawksby.

"Turns out to be one of our regulars," said Lamont, taking over. "Kevin Carter. In and out of jail like a cuckoo in a Swiss clock. But we're not sure what he's up to this time, although one thing's certain—it can't be his own money he's using to buy that amount of silver. Way out of his league. DS Roycroft and DC Warwick will be going down to Barnstaple later today to keep an eye on Carter and try to find out what he's up to."

Bugger, William wanted to say for a second time that morning. He'd have to call Beth at the gallery, which he knew her boss wouldn't approve of.

"Keep me briefed," said Hawksby.

"And, Bruce, I suggest you and DC Warwick pay a visit to Pentonville as soon as William gets back from Barnstaple. Now, returning to the Rembrandt for a moment: Mr. Booth Watson QC has been calling my office daily, demanding we return his client's copy of the painting."

"Not just yet," said Lamont.

"Why not?" asked Hawksby.

"Because if Jackie or I were to turn up at Faulkner's house, we wouldn't get past the front gate. But if we were to send an inexperienced, wet-behind-the-ears young constable to deliver the painting, there's just a possibility he might get a foot in the door."

"Fair point," said Hawksby. "But why not just yet?"

"Faulkner is booked onto a BA flight to Monte Carlo next Monday, and he won't be back for at least a month."

"How can you be sure of that?"

"He's a creature of habit. Every December he leaves for his home in Monte Carlo, and rarely returns before the end of January."

"And how do you know which flight he's booked on?"

"BA security is run by a former Met officer, who keeps me well informed, sir."

"Something else that might be of interest, sir," said Jackie. "He won't be traveling with his wife this time. Sitting next to him, her ticket paid for with the same American Express card, will be a Miss Cheryl Bates."

"She could be his secretary," said Hawksby.

"I don't think typing is her speciality, sir," said Jackie as she passed a photo of Miss Bates in a bikini across to the commander.

A ripple of laughter broke out among the team, but order was quickly restored when Hawksby said, "So when Warwick turns up with the copy of the Rembrandt at Faulkner's home in Hampshire, he will already be in Monte Carlo."

"Correct, sir, but his wife will still be in Hampshire," said Lamont.

"Good, because I have a feeling that Mrs. Faulkner might turn out to be a little more accommodating than her husband," said the commander after taking a second look at the photograph of Miss Bates.

14

"I'm in real trouble," said William as he turned on the ignition.

"With the Hawk or Lamont?" asked Jackie, as she fastened her seatbelt.

"Far worse. With Beth. I told her I'd be back in time for supper this evening, and now I'm on my way to Barnstaple with another woman."

"I think this calls for a dozen roses," said Jackie. "And I know just the person to solve your problem."

As they passed through Earls Court, Jackie said, "Pull over."

"But it's a double yellow," said William, "and we're always fair game for traffic wardens."

"We'll only be a couple of minutes. And in any case, it's official police business."

Jackie got out of the car and William reluctantly followed her into a flower shop.

"A dozen roses," said Jackie, "and make sure they're fresh or I'll arrest you for impersonating a florist. And we need them delivered."

The florist took his time selecting each rose before asking for a name and address.

"Beth Rainsford, the Fitzmolean Museum, Prince Albert Crescent," said William.

"Rainsford . . . Rainsford . . . Why does that name ring a bell?" said Jackie.

"Do you want to add a message?" asked the florist, handing William a card and a biro.

Sorry, something came up. Can't make this evening. William x

"I thought you liked this girl," said Jackie, tearing up the card. "Sounds as if you're writing to your sister to let her know you've got the mumps. Try again."

Miss you. Will call this evening and explain. Love William xx

"Not a lot better, but I've just spotted a traffic warden, so we'd better get moving."

"That will be two pounds," said the florist.

William handed over a couple of pound notes.

"Thank you, Mike."

"My pleasure, Jackie," said the florist as they ran back to the car.

"So what's the plan once we get to Barnstaple?" asked William, when they joined the traffic on the motorway heading west.

"First, we find out where Carter lives, then check into a one-star hotel or guesthouse nearby."

"And what are we looking for?" asked William, as he'd never taken part in a stakeout before.

"Visitors, especially those who obviously aren't locals. Not that I think Mr. Big is likely to come down to Barnstaple just to please us. But we'll need to take photos of everyone who goes in or out of the house, and when we get back to the Yard we'll check to see if they match up with anyone in our rogues' gallery."

"Anything else?"

"Number plates of every car parked near the house, or any suspicious-looking vehicles. We can check them out on the police national computer later. And don't assume the person we're looking for will park right outside Carter's front door. Police work isn't that convenient."

"Do we split up or work as a pair?"

"That will depend on whether we can watch the house from the car without being spotted. Either way, it will be hours of patient surveillance, with no certainty of anything to show for it."

"Do you think we'll find out what he's up to?"

"Unlikely," said Jackie. "But you can bet there'll be a surprise or two, when we'll have to think on our feet."

"Who decides when we go back to London?"

"Lamont."

"Then we could be stuck down there forever."

Jackie laughed. "I don't think so. Don't forget he expects you to accompany him when he visits Pentonville to interview Eddie Leigh. And you've also got to take the copy of the Rembrandt back to Faulkner's home in the country."

They drove on for some time in companionable silence.

"Does Lamont have any family?"

"He's a triple disaster," said Jackie. "Three ex-wives, and five children. His first three marriages lasted six years, three years, and one year, and I'm not sure the latest will survive for much longer. God knows how he can afford the alimony. It would be cheaper to take the occasional lover, like the rest of us."

William laughed. "What about the Hawk?"

"Married to Josephine for over thirty years. Three grown-up daughters, who've got him wound around their little fingers."

"I'd like to see that," said William. "But then you have a daughter," he said, hoping Jackie was feeling relaxed enough to exchange confidences, but she didn't respond. He glanced to his left to see that she had fallen asleep. Always catch some kip whenever possible, wherever possible, she'd advised him often enough.

Jackie hadn't wanted to answer any more questions, so she closed her eyes. She had known within days of William joining the team that he was destined for higher things. Far higher than she could ever hope for.

Reporting an inspector who'd placed a hand on her thigh when she was a young constable hadn't improved her chances of promotion. And taking six months off after her daughter was born only ensured that when she returned to work she found herself once again back on the beat. It hadn't deterred her.

However, when Ms. Roycroft was named as co-respondent in a

senior officer's divorce, the local commander suggested that perhaps the time had come for her to consider early retirement. She didn't point out that she was only thirty-four, and had no intention of giving up the job she loved, well aware they couldn't sack her. She clung on, but accepted that detective sergeant was probably the highest rank she was likely to attain.

William was different. He may have been naive and a little too smooth, but after she'd introduced him to the real world, where criminals didn't say please and thank you, she was sure he would progress quickly through the ranks. But she'd still have to watch his back whenever he came across less capable colleagues who would be only too happy to let him carry the can for their mistakes and, being a public schoolboy, he wouldn't sneak.

When William eventually became the commissioner, Jackie wondered if he would even remember her name.

William stuck to the middle lane and kept a steady speed so as not to wake her. It wasn't long before his mind drifted back to Beth. How long would she tolerate a boyfriend who was so unreliable? He would call her the moment they arrived in Barnstaple and explain why he wouldn't be joining her for supper.

Old silver, a missing Rembrandt, and how to get into Faulkner's house and meet his wife continued to occupy his mind, although Beth was continually trying to butt in.

The moment William turned off the motorway, Jackie woke up and immediately began to check the map on her lap. "Head for the town center," she said, as if she'd never been asleep. "It will be a left turn for the street Carter lives in. I'll warn you in good time."

After a couple more miles Jackie said, "Take the next turning on the left, and slow down when you pass number ninety-one. Then first right, and make sure you park well out of sight."

Jackie took a close look at the modern semidetached house with its pocket-handkerchief garden as they passed number 91 Mulberry Avenue, but it wasn't the house that caught her attention. William turned right and parked behind a large van.

Jackie got out of the car, stretched her arms, and scanned the horizon. "Do you see what I see?" she said.

William looked in the direction she was pointing. "Do you mean that large house up on the hill?"

"The Romans would have occupied that position and built a fortress so they could keep a close eye on their enemies."

"But it's a long way away."

"True, but it has a panoramic view of the town, including Carter's house. But as we're not Romans let's hope it's a hotel," Jackie said as she climbed back into the car.

William kept the building in sight as he wound his way slowly up the hill until he spotted a sign announcing SEA VIEW HOTEL, with an arrow pointing up a long drive.

"All we need now is for the room with that big bay window at the front to be available for the next few days," said Jackie. "You do the talking. I'll try and look meek."

"That will be a first," muttered William as he parked the car.

"Good afternoon," said the young woman at the reception desk. "How can I help you?"

"We were wondering if the room overlooking the bay was free," said William.

"The Queen Anne suite? Let me check, sir." She took a moment to look at the register, before saying, "Yes, but only for a couple of nights. The room's already booked for Wednesday."

"How much?" asked William.

"Thirty pounds a night, breakfast included."

William hesitated. "We'll take it," said Jackie, and whispered, "Mr. and Mrs. Smith," before he signed the register.

"The porter will take the bags up to your room, Mr. Smith," the receptionist said, handing him a key.

William wondered how many Mr. and Mrs. Smiths had occupied the Queen Anne suite over the years. Certainly none to do what he and Jackie had in mind.

They took the lift to the top floor, where they found the porter already standing by an open door carrying their bags.

115

"Will there be anything else, sir?" he asked after showing them the room.

"No, thank you," said William, handing him 50p that he was certain Mrs. Walters wouldn't be reimbursing.

By the time the porter had closed the door, Jackie was already looking out of the window through a pair of binoculars.

"A professional hitman couldn't ask for a better sight line," she said as she focused in on Carter's front room.

"Isn't Lamont going to kick up a fuss about the cost of a suite?"

"Only if we go back to London empty-handed."

"I'll sleep on the couch," said William, looking enviously at the double bed.

"No one's going to sleep on the couch," said Jackie. "We'll work in shifts, night and day, so we can both get some kip, while never letting Carter out of our sight. Now, you keep your eye on the house while I go and report to the local nick and let them know what we're up to. And don't eat all the biscuits, because we won't be ordering room service."

William settled into a comfortable chair and focused the binoculars on Carter's house. He could just make out the number plate of a Volvo parked in the drive, and made a note of it. He shifted his attention to a large shed in the corner of the garden, then back to the house, where he spotted someone in the front room. A solitary figure, whom he assumed must be Carter, was sitting by the fire reading a newspaper. A woman entered the room and began vacuuming. Was she Angie? After he'd read the back page, Carter folded the newspaper, stood up, poked the fire, and left the room. A few moments later the front door opened, and he crossed the lawn, unlocked the shed door, and went inside. Once again, William lost sight of him.

William swung quickly around when the door behind him opened. He knew it couldn't be Jackie.

"I'm so sorry, sir," said a maid. "Would you like me to make up the room?"

"No, thank you," said William, who quickly stood up, making sure the binoculars were out of sight. When the door closed, he disobeyed Jackie's orders and began to nibble on a biscuit, before returning to his post. He turned his attention back to the shed and could just make out what looked like a workbench, and a crouched figure working on something, but on what?

About an hour later, Carter emerged from the shed and made his way back into the house. He'd only been inside for a few moments before he reappeared in the front room and once again settled down in the armchair.

William was beginning to understand what Jackie had meant when she'd said there would be endless hours of tedium, with little to show for it. He'd only spent a couple of hours keeping an eye on Carter and he was already bored. When Carter dozed off in his armchair, William felt like doing the same.

The door behind him opened a second time and he turned round to see Jackie, holding a carrier bag.

"Seen anything worth reporting?" she asked, as she stared at a plate of biscuit crumbs.

"Carter left the house to go into his shed, and spent an hour there. I think he was working on something, but I couldn't make out what it was."

"Then it will be our job to find out tomorrow. I've briefed the local intelligence officer on what we're up to. Good lad, if a little sensitive about the Met straying onto his patch without warning. He's well aware of Carter's past record in fact, he's a pro now. But to date he's given him no trouble. A model citizen in fact. He does a bit of engraving for one or two of the local schools and sports clubs, although he claims he's retired."

"'Criminals never retire,'" said William, "'they just get more cunning.'"

"The Hawk?"

"No, Fred Yates. So, are you going to take over up here, while I go down and have a closer look?"

"Sure. If Carter comes out of the house, follow him. But if he drops into his local, don't join him. You'll stick out like a sore thumb."

"And when do you want me to come back?"

"Around midnight, then you can catch some sleep while I do the night shift. I left some sandwiches in the car for you, but now I wish I'd eaten them," said Jackie, once again glaring at the biscuit crumbs.

"Sorry," said William. "I'm sure there must be something in the fridge."

"Which will only be added to our bill, and I don't have to remind you, detective constable, that we're not on holiday."

William slipped out of the room, drove back into town, and parked between two cars on the far side of Mulberry Avenue, from where he had a clear view of the house. Just after eleven, he saw the light on the ground floor go off and moments later an upstairs light was switched on. Twenty minutes later the house was in complete darkness.

He took his time munching the sandwiches, feeling more guilty with every bite. Fearing he would fall asleep, he tried various ways of staying awake, including reciting Tennyson's *Morte d'Arthur*, singing "Nessun Dorma" out of tune, and recalling the top ten Test batting averages of all time—Bradman 99.94, Pollock 60.97, Headley . . .

At midnight, he drove back to the hotel to find Jackie already up and ready to take his place.

"Anything of interest?" she asked.

"He watched television, had supper, watched some more TV, and went upstairs to bed just after eleven. Twenty minutes later the lights went out."

"It doesn't get much better than that," said Jackie. "And the midnight shift is by far the worst one. It's so easy to fall asleep, and if you do, you can be sure that Volvo won't be in the drive when you wake up."

"Doing nothing is exhausting," said William as he handed over the car keys.

"You'll be on the midnight shift tomorrow, so make sure you get a good night's sleep," were Jackie's final words before leaving.

William got undressed, took a shower, and climbed into a warm bed. It made him think about Beth. Hell, he hadn't called her, and now it was too late. Moments later he was fast asleep.

15

William woke just after seven the next morning, took a shower, shaved, and was dressed by the time Jackie returned following her night vigil. They sat in the bay window enjoying a large breakfast of bacon and eggs, while still keeping an eye on the house. Carter didn't come downstairs until after nine, and they had no way of knowing what he had for breakfast, as his kitchen was at the back of the house.

"So what now?"

"We'll return to Mulberry Avenue and hope he leaves the house at some point. If it's by car, we'll follow him. If it's on foot, I'll stay in the car while you try to find out what he's been up to in that shed. Perhaps it's totally innocent, but Lamont will still want to know."

Twenty minutes later they were parked on the other side of the road from Carter's house, some thirty yards from his front gate, their eyes never leaving the front door.

"This is pointless," said William after another futile hour spent discussing everything from Princess Diana's proposed visit to Scotland Yard, to who would be the next commissioner.

"Is the Hawk in with a chance?" asked William.

"Not this time around," said Jackie. "But possibly at some time in the future, although he has his enemies."

Another hour slunk by, before William said, "What happened to that guy who was with you when I first saw the copy of—"

"Ross Hogan." Jackie paused before adding, "The Hawk sent him back to Peckham."

"Where I was meant to go!"

"And you still may if we don't find the Rembrandt. Because Ross has disappeared off the face of the earth."

"Probably resigned after being sent to Peckham."

"Or working undercover."

"I thought about going undercover."

"You'd be useless," said Jackie. "You look, sound and smell like a choirboy."

"No, Ross would be perfect for undercover work. Even criminals think he's a criminal."

"And keep concentrating, because you can never tell when everything will change in a split second."

"But when's that second ever going to happen?" asked William at the end of the third hour. Then the front door opened and they both fell silent.

Carter appeared carrying an empty shopping bag. He walked down the path, opened the gate, and headed off in the opposite direction.

"Right, now's our chance," said Jackie. "Take the camera and see if you can get some pictures of what's inside that shed."

"Can we justify that?"

"Just about. We'd plead reason to suspect." Jackie didn't sound at all convincing. "The moment he reappears, I'll honk the horn once. Just be sure to stay hidden behind the shed until well after he's gone back into the house. And don't forget the three-minute rule."

"What about Angie?"

"If she comes out, I'll honk twice. Three times if she spots you, in which case start running, because we'll have to get out of town sharpish. Sometimes you only get one chance."

"No pressure," said William as he grabbed the camera from the back seat, got out of the car, and crossed the road, eyes darting in every direction. He walked cautiously toward number 91. No sign of anyone, and Carter had left the gate open. He nipped in behind the Volvo, and moved deftly toward the shed. He couldn't have been visible from the front window for more than a few seconds. He tried the door but it was locked, then he heard a car coming down the road and ducked behind the shed until it had turned the corner.

Looking through the small window of the shed, he could make out a wooden bench and a chair. Some silver filings were scattered over the surface of the bench but it was so dark he could hardly make out anything else. Could he risk using the flash? He pressed the camera up against the window and fired off a whole roll of film, but he couldn't be sure if any of the pictures would come out.

He removed the film and was reloading the camera when he heard a car horn honk once. Carter, not Angie. He looked up to see Jackie driving past, and quickly dropped down behind the shed just as Carter reached the gate clutching a Sainsbury's bag. William heard the front door open and close. A man returning home almost always goes straight to the lavatory, a process that takes at least three minutes. William waited for thirty seconds before making his move: twenty-seven, twenty-eight, twenty-nine, thirty. He stood up, moved swiftly across the lawn, around the far side of the Volvo, and out of the front gate. He didn't run, and he didn't look back.

A hundred yards down the road he could see Jackie waiting for him in the car, engine running. No sooner had he closed the passenger door than she drove off.

"Do you think he saw me?" asked William, as they headed back to the hotel.

"No. I kept an eye on the front door, and there was no sign of either of them. So, did you find out what he gets up to in that shed?"

"It was so dark in there I could hardly see anything, but I took a roll of photos, so we'll just have to wait and see how they come out."

◄O►

"We'll have to move out of here tomorrow," William reminded her as they drove into the hotel car park.

"I haven't forgotten," said Jackie. "I've spotted a B and B that's quite nearby, but unfortunately it has no view of the house so we'll be spending most of our time in the car."

Once they were back in their room, Jackie called Lamont and brought him up to date. William sat by the window, peering through the binoculars while munching the latest supply of ginger biscuits. Carter had returned to the shed, where William could just see an arm moving up and down, working on something . . . but what?

"What did Lamont have to say?" he asked when Jackie eventually came off the phone.

"To stay put for now. Meanwhile, you keep an eye on the house while I go and get the film developed."

William waited for her to leave before he sat down on the end of the bed and rang Beth's flat. No reply. She couldn't be back from work. He wondered if he should risk calling her at the gallery, but decided against it.

He returned to the window and once again focused in on the shed. Carter was bent over the table, arm still pumping away. He didn't return to the house until it was dark, when William lost sight of him. It was almost six o'clock before Jackie bounced in, a look of triumph on her face.

"He's stamping out coins from a mold, just as your father suggested."

"What type of coins?"

"Other than they're silver, I've no idea. You're going to have to get hold of one tomorrow. Do you know how to pick a lock?"

"No, that must have been one of the induction courses I missed."

"Then I'll have to do it."

"Without a search warrant?"

"Lamont's determined to find out who Carter's backer is, and what they're up to. The last thing he said before he put the phone down was, 'I'm sick of catching minnows.'"

"That's all very well," said William, "but how do we go about it?"

"That's tomorrow's problem," said Jackie. "For now, you go down and carry out the night shift while I get some kip. Whatever you do, don't fall asleep."

William reluctantly left the hotel, but not before grabbing a couple of Mars bars and a bottle of water from the fridge. Surely Mrs. Walters couldn't object to that. He could hear her saying, "Tap water in future, constable." He drove back into town, turned into Mulberry Avenue, and parked behind a van, from where he had a clear view of Carter's front door.

He noticed a red telephone box at the other end of the street and cursed. He still hadn't spoken to Beth. He should have been taking her to the James Bond film this evening and keeping an eye on Faulkner, instead of freezing in an uncomfortable car and staring at a house that was in pitch darkness. 007 somehow managed to save the world from a notorious criminal in a couple of hours, while William tried to stay awake keeping an eye on a local villain. He turned on the radio. The General Synod of the Church of England had been debating whether women should be ordained. The thin end of the wedge, he could hear his father saying. "They'll want to be bishops next." The news was followed by a program about the recent proliferation of the tsetse fly in sub-Saharan Africa. He fell asleep, only waking up when he heard the pips announcing the five o'clock news.

"Good morning, this is the BBC. The prime minister . . ."

William blinked, rubbed his eyes, and looked across at the house to see a light beaming from the top floor. Instantly he was wide awake, his heart beating furiously. A few moments later the light on the top floor went off, and a light on the ground floor came on. William opened his bottle of water, took a swig, and was splashing a few drops on his face when the front door opened and Carter appeared carrying a bulky leather holdall, which he placed in the boot of his car before climbing into the driver's seat. It took him three attempts before the engine spluttered into life.

The Volvo pulled out of the drive. William eased his car across the road, leaving the lights off. Carter turned right at the end of the road and William followed, keeping his distance as there were few vehicles on the road at that time in the morning. Carter turned left at a roundabout and joined the early morning traffic heading out of town.

"Please, please, please," murmured William, as Carter continued on toward the motorway.

At the next roundabout, William's prayers were answered when he took the third exit and joined a stream of motorists heading toward London.

Carter remained in the inside lane, and never once exceeded the speed limit. This was clearly a man who didn't want to be stopped by the police, which made William wonder what could possibly be in the holdall. As each mile passed, William became more confident that Carter was heading for the capital, possibly to meet up with the man Lamont was so keen to identify. But then, without indicating, Carter swung off the motorway and began to follow the signs for Heathrow, where he pulled into the short-term car park.

William parked on the floor above, before following Carter into terminal two, where he watched him head for the BA desk. William hung back as Carter checked in and was handed a boarding pass. He took the escalator to the first floor, leather holdall firmly in hand, and headed for Departures.

William moved swiftly over to the check-in counter and showed the woman on the desk his warrant card. "I need to know which flight a Mr. Kevin Carter is booked on."

She hesitated for a moment before pressing a button under her desk. Moments later a tall, heavily built man appeared by her side. William produced his warrant card again and repeated his request.

"Who's your boss?" was all the man said.

"DCI Lamont, head of the Art and Antiques unit at Scotland Yard."

The security man picked up a phone. "What number?"

"01 735 2916." William prayed Lamont was at his desk.

"Lamont," said a voice.

The security man handed the phone to William, who explained to Lamont why he was at Heathrow.

"Put him back on, laddie," said Lamont. William passed the phone back and listened to a one-sided conversation which ended with the words, "Yes, sir."

The security man nodded, and the booking clerk checked her computer before saying, "Mr. Carter is on flight 028 to Rome. The gate closes in twenty minutes."

"I've got two problems," said William, turning back to the security man. "I need a seat on that flight, and I don't have a passport."

"Make out a boarding pass for Detective Constable Warwick," said the security man, "and if possible, seat him a couple of rows behind Carter."

"I can do three rows behind him," she said, tapping away on her computer.

"Couldn't be better," said William.

She printed out the boarding pass and gave it to him.

"My name's Jim Travers," said William's new minder. "Follow me. We've no time to waste."

William was taken backstage, and accompanied Jim down a gloomy gray brick corridor, where there were no passengers, just airport staff. After a long swift walk, Jim pushed open a door that led William out of the terminal, to where an unmarked car was parked by the runway. Jim jumped in and drove him to the side of a waiting aircraft.

"Good luck," he said, before William ran up the steps and onto an empty plane.

He took his seat near the back and didn't have to wait long before the first passengers appeared. Carter was among the last. Still clutching on to his holdall, he took a window seat three rows in front of William.

After the plane had taken off, William had his first proper meal for the past couple of days, before taking the opportunity to lean back and close his eyes. After all, Carter wouldn't be getting off before they landed in Rome.

The plane touched down at Da Vinci two hours later and taxied to the gate. There were only a couple of passengers between William and Carter when they entered the terminal and headed for passport control. Help, thought William, when he remembered that he didn't have a passport. But he had only walked a few more yards when a smartly dressed young woman appeared by his side and linked her arm in his.

"Just stay with me, Detective Constable Warwick."

"But I could lose the man I'm following."

"Two of our officers are already tailing Carter. You'll catch up with him on the other side."

They headed toward a gate marked CREW, and were clearly expected, as they passed through passport control without even breaking stride. William felt like royalty as he was whisked out of the terminal, where a car was waiting for him, back door open.

He thanked the young woman before climbing in to find a man in a smart beige uniform seated in the back, who was obviously expecting him.

"Good morning," he said. "My name is Lieutenant Antonio Monti. I'm here to give you whatever assistance you require."

"*Grazie*," replied William as they shook hands.

"*Parla l'italiano?*"

"Enough to get by," said William. "*Ma poi Roma è la mia città preferita.*"

They had to wait for another thirty minutes before Carter sauntered out of the building, bag in hand, and joined a taxi queue, by which time the lieutenant knew almost as much about Carter as William did.

The Italian police driver turned out to be far more adept than

William when it came to tailing a suspect, which allowed him to enjoy some familiar sights: the Colosseum, St. Peter's Basilica, Trajan's Column, all of which he remembered from his student days when he'd sat at the back of an overcrowded bus with no air conditioning, heading for a youth hostel not exactly in the center of town.

When Carter's taxi finally came to a halt, it was not outside a hotel as William had expected, but a large municipal building with an Italian flag fluttering from a mast on the roof.

"Stay put and leave this to me," said the lieutenant. "We don't want him to spot you." He got out of the car and followed Carter inside.

William also got out, but only to stretch his legs, then suddenly took a step back and hid behind a fountain when he spotted a familiar figure entering the building. His eyes never left the front door for more than a few seconds, but it was almost an hour before the lieutenant reappeared and joined him in the back of the car.

Carter came out a few moments later, and hailed a taxi, but Monti didn't instruct the driver to follow them.

"He's on his way back to the airport," said Monti. "The bag is now empty," he added without explanation. "They've booked on the three ten to Heathrow."

"Then I should be on the same plane," said William.

"Not necessary. DS Roycroft will be at Heathrow waiting for them. In any case, we have more important things to do."

"Like what?"

"First, you must experience a little Italian hospitality. We will have lunch at Casina Valadier before dropping into the Borghese, and you will still be in time to catch the five twenty to London."

"But my expenses won't—"

"You're in Italy, *mi amico*," said the lieutenant, "and have just performed a great service for the Italian people. You must therefore be rewarded. In any case, we don't get quite so worked up in Italy about expenses as you English."

Clearly they didn't have a Mrs. Walter to contend with, thought William.

"Perhaps you might care to take a look at this," said Monti, as he handed William an official-looking document.

William glanced at the front page. "My Italian isn't that good," he admitted.

"Then I will have to take you through it, line by line over lunch, because I need to know if you wish us to grant Mr. Carter's application for the license, or whether Scotland Yard would prefer us to turn his request down."

◄о►

William knocked on the front door, and when Beth opened it he was greeted with, "Hello, stranger, what's your excuse this time?"

"I've been to Rome."

"To visit another woman?"

"Napoleon's sister."

"She's quite cold, I'm told."

"As marble," said William, bending down to kiss her, but he only brushed her lips, as she turned away.

"Not until I've heard Pauline's side of the story," Beth said, as she led him through to the kitchen.

Over dinner he told her everything that had happened since he'd last seen her, including a memorable meal at Casina Valadier and an afternoon spent with Antonio Monti at the Borghese.

"You should have joined the Italian police, William, they obviously have superior galleries, finer food, and—"

"But not more adorable women," he said, taking her in his arms.

She pushed him playfully aside and said firmly, "Not until you tell me what Carter needed a license for."

16

"I called this meeting at short notice," said Hawksby, "as I understand there has been a development in the Carter case."

"There has indeed, sir," said Lamont. "Carter left Barnstaple early on Wednesday morning. DC Warwick followed him to Heathrow, where he checked in for a flight to Rome. DC Warwick phoned me from the airport, and I told him to keep following Carter, who only had a holdall with him, so he clearly wasn't going on holiday. I'll hand over to DC Warwick who can brief you on what happened next."

"I sat three rows behind Carter on the flight," said William. "At Da Vinci, I was met by a Lieutenant Monti of the Italian Special Investigation Team, who could not have been more cooperative. Carter got a taxi, and we tailed him to a government building in the center of Rome. Monti followed him inside, and informed me afterward that Carter had an appointment at the Naval Division office, where he applied for a diving and recovery license to explore a shipwreck off the coast of Elba."

· "What's he looking for?" Asked Hawksby.

"Seven hundred eighteenth-century Spanish silver cob coins," said William. "In 1741, during a particularly violent storm, a vessel called the *Patrice* sank off Elba, drowning all fifty-two passengers, along with nine crew and a cargo that included the coins and other valuables. I have the records of the Italian Receiver of Wrecks from the time," he continued, "which read, 'This claim has been confirmed by Lloyd's of London who insured the vessel and cargo for ten thousand guineas, and paid the amount in full.'"

"I'm halfway there," said Hawksby.

"Over the years, several attempts have been made to locate the wreck and recover the coins, but without success."

"And Carter thinks he might get lucky, despite the odds?"

"I don't believe he's relying on luck, sir," said Jackie. "While DC Warwick was swanning around Rome, I returned to London and had the photographs he took of Carter's shed enlarged by our specialists here in Scotland Yard. They confirmed one thing without question: DC Warwick is no David Bailey."

They all laughed.

"However, after one of our experts had studied the photographs more closely, she came up with a very interesting suggestion." Jackie handed each member of the team an enlarged photo of the workbench in Carter's shed.

"What are we looking for?" asked Hawksby, as he studied the image.

"You'll notice all the usual equipment required by any engraver—chisels of various sizes, wire brushes, even a nail file. But if you look more closely, you can also see what Carter is working on." She handed around three enlargements showing the top of the workbench for the team to consider.

"It looks like a half crown to me," said Hawksby.

"Same size, same shape, different value," said William, "as I discovered when I visited a numismatist at the British Museum, who told me he's fairly sure it's a Spanish cob, which as you can see is dated 1649."

"No doubt you asked him its value?"

"He had no idea, sir, but recommended I visit Dix Noonan Webb in Mayfair, who are specialists in the field. Mr. Noonan showed me a similar example of a Spanish cob coin from one of his recent catalogs which sold for just over a thousand pounds."

"Multiply that by seven hundred," said Lamont, "and Carter would end up with more than seven hundred thousand."

"I think I know what he's up to," said William.

"Spit it out, Warwick," said Hawksby.

"I suspect that all the old silver he's been buying recently has been melted down, and he's spent the last few months stamping seven hundred newly minted Spanish cob coins."

"If you look at the photographs more closely," said Jackie, "you'll see something we might have missed in normal circumstances." She pointed to the bottom left-hand corner of one of the pictures.

"It looks like a bucket of water to me," said Hawksby.

"That was my first thought," said William, "until I think I've worked out Carter's next move."

"Don't keep us all in suspense," said Hawksby.

"I suspect he intends to return to Rome as soon as possible, collect his license, and then be seen sailing off into the sunset in search of seabed treasure. A few days later he'll sail back into port bearing a wooden casket full of silver coins. And if you look more closely at photo 2B, you'll even see the casket that will be raised from the bottom of the sea."

It was a few moments before Lamont said, "And the bucket of water?"

"Seawater," said William.

"Of course," said Hawksby.

"But I thought seabed treasure was the property of the government in whose waters it's found," said Lamont.

"That's correct, sir," said William. "But the recovery team would typically receive a fifty percent finder's fee, which is probably why Booth Watson turned up."

"Did I hear you correctly?" said Hawksby.

"You did, sir. Booth Watson entered the building a few minutes after we arrived."

"You certainly save the best for last, William," said the commander. "Do you have any idea why he was there?"

"Monti said he checked all the paperwork meticulously, before he let Carter sign anything."

"So this could be just another of Faulkner's many enterprises," said Jackie.

"Booth Watson does have other clients," said the commander. "But I agree, the odds must be on Faulkner, who can expect to get around three hundred and fifty thousand pounds once Carter's retrieved the coins."

"I suspect Carter won't get much more than a few thousand," said Lamont, "now we know who's behind this scam."

"Why do you say that, Bruce?"

"I've banged him up three times in the past ten years, but never for anything on this scale. And as Lieutenant Monti discovered, when Carter applied for the license to search for sunken treasure he handed over five thousand pounds in cash to the Italian Naval Office in Rome, although the standard fee is less than half that amount."

"That explains why he never let the holdall out of his sight," said William. "And why, according to Monti, it was empty when he left the building."

"No doubt he was hoping that his application would mysteriously find its way to the top of the pile," suggested Jackie.

"In one," said Lamont.

"That may well be the case," said William, "but Lieutenant Monti made it clear that if we want Carter's application to be held up indefinitely, or even rejected, all we have to do is ask."

"Bruce?"

"Carter hasn't committed any crime on British soil that we're aware of, and the only way we're going to find out what he's up to is to tell the Italians we have no objection to him being granted a license. In fact, the sooner the better."

"If that's the case," said Jackie, "why not arrest Carter even before he reaches the airport and confiscate the coins?"

"And charge him with what?" said Hawksby. "With Booth Watson on his side, he'd claim the coins were just reproductions that he intended to sell for a small profit. Besides, if we want to nail whoever's bankrolling Carter, we have to let him carry out the whole operation. Because whoever is the brains behind it has to be someone with imagination, nerve, and enough capital to see the whole operation through, which I agree is looking more and more like Faulkner."

"So with your permission, sir," said Lamont, "I'll call Lieutenant Monti and ask him to rubber stamp the application, and keep us fully informed. Meanwhile, I'll ask my contact at BA to call me the moment Carter books another flight to Rome."

"Where you, Lieutenant Monti, and DC Warwick will be sitting on the dockside waiting for him," said Hawksby.

"Not me, sir," said Lamont. "Carter knows me far too well."

Jackie looked hopeful.

"Then I'll have to make the sacrifice and accompany DC Warwick myself," said Hawksby. "Anything else?"

"Just one thing, sir. DC Warwick and I are going to Pentonville tomorrow morning to interview Eddie Leigh."

"The man Warwick is convinced copied the Rembrandt?"

"Yes, sir. But I can't pretend I'm hopeful that we'll get much out of him. People who've worked for Miles Faulkner in the past don't open their mouths if they hope to stay alive."

"Just get him talking," said Hawksby. "He might let something slip he later regrets. And when will Warwick be returning the copy of *The Syndics* to Faulkner's home? I ask only because Mr. Booth Watson keeps threatening me with fire and brimstone."

"Faulkner leaves for Monte Carlo on Monday morning," said Lamont. "So any time next week."

"You've got another busy week ahead of you, DC Warwick," said the commander, "so I won't hold you up."

17

"Good cop, bad cop has become a bit of a cliché," said Lamont as he and William were driven out of Scotland Yard on their way to Pentonville. "And in our case, a five-year-old could work out which was which. Nevertheless, we need to decide what we're trying to achieve at this meeting."

"Surely our first priority," said William as the traffic came to a halt in Trafalgar Square, "should be to find out whether or not *The Syndics* has been destroyed, and if it hasn't, where it is now."

"That wouldn't be my first priority, laddie," said Lamont, his Scottish accent even more pronounced than usual. "I want to prove the link between Leigh and Miles Faulkner, because I'd sacrifice half my pension to put that man behind bars."

I'd give up my entire pension to have been born with Eddie Leigh's talent, thought William, as the car drove onto Kingsway, but he didn't express his opinion.

"So let's discuss tactics," said Lamont. "I'll lead the interrogation, and if I sit back, it means you should take over. But don't interrupt me before then, because I know the exact line of inquiry I want to pursue."

"What happens if he goes off in a direction neither of us had anticipated?"

"That's unlikely. Don't forget, we're dealing with a con who will have worked out exactly what he's going to say long before he sees us."

Once again, William didn't offer an opinion.

"And if I start to bargain with him, keep schtum. The Hawk has made it clear just how far I can go."

"What's the worst-case scenario?" William asked as the car turned left into Grays Inn Road.

"That he refuses to answer any of our questions, in which case the interview will be over in a few minutes, and we'll have wasted our time."

"This will be my first prison visit," William volunteered, after neither of them had spoken for some time.

Lamont smiled. "Mine was a jolly Irishman who made me laugh with his stories of the Emerald Isle."

"What was he in for?"

"Robbing a post office, which turned out to be quite hard to prove, because he never even made it to the counter, and his only weapon was a cucumber. Luckily he pleaded guilty."

"More, more," demanded William.

"Another time," said Lamont as they drew up outside HMP Pentonville.

"You couldn't blame Her Majesty," mused William, "if she decided she could do without prisons in her portfolio."

"If she did, she might have to do without Buckingham Palace in that same portfolio," said Lamont as the car swung into the Caledonian Road.

William stared beyond the high wall at a forbidding brick building that dominated the landscape.

The car came to a halt at the barrier, and a uniformed officer stepped forward. Lamont wound down his window and produced his warrant card.

"Mr. Langley is expecting you, sir," said the man, after inspecting the card. "If you'll park over there, I'll let him know you've arrived."

The driver slipped into the first available space and turned off the engine.

"I can't be sure how long we'll be, Matt," said Lamont to the driver, who was taking a paperback out of the glove compartment.

"But when we get back, you can let me know if the latest Len Deighton is worth taking on holiday this year."

"It's the third in a trilogy, sir, so I recommend you start with the first, *Berlin Game*."

As they got out of the car, they were approached by a senior prison officer whose name tag on the pocket of his uniform read "SO Langley."

"How are you, Bruce?"

"Can't complain, Reg. This is DC Warwick. Keep your eye on him. He's after my job."

"Good morning, sir," said William, as they shook hands.

"Follow me," said Langley. "I apologize for the excessive security procedures, but they're standard in any Cat. B prison."

They both signed the register at the gatehouse, before being issued with visitors' passes. William counted five sets of barred gates that were locked and unlocked before they came across their first prisoner.

"Leigh's waiting for you in the interview room, but let me warn you, Bruce, he's been particularly uncooperative this morning. As you've nicked him on three occasions in the past, I don't suppose you're his favorite uncle."

William noticed as they walked down a long green brick corridor that the cons either turned their backs on them, usually accompanied by an expletive, or simply ignored them. But there was one exception, a middle-aged man who stopped mopping the floor to take a closer look at the man. William thought there was something familiar about him, and wondered if he'd arrested him at some time when he was on the beat in Lambeth.

William couldn't hide his surprise when they came to a halt outside a large glass cube that looked more like a modern sculpture than an interview room. Inside he could see a prisoner sitting at a table, head bowed, who he assumed must be Eddie Leigh.

"Before you ask," said Lamont, pointing at the glass cube, "that's as much for your protection as his. When I was a young sergeant, I was once accused of punching a prisoner during an interrogation.

It's true that I wanted to punch him, but I didn't," he paused, "on that occasion."

"Coffee and biscuits?" said Langley.

"Give us a few minutes with him first, Reg," said Lamont.

William and Lamont entered the room and sat down opposite Leigh. No suggestion of handcuffs or an officer sanding behind him. A privilege afforded only to those with no record of violence. Leigh must have waived his right to have a solicitor present.

William looked carefully at the prisoner seated on the other side of the table. At first glance, the forty-seven-year-old forger looked like any other con, dressed in the regulation prison garb of blue striped shirt and well-worn jeans. He was unshaven, with dark hair and brown eyes, but what surprised William was his hands. How could a man with bricklayers' hands produce such delicate brushwork? And then he spoke, revealing that he hailed from the same part of the world as Lamont.

"Can you spare us a fag, guv?" he asked politely.

Lamont placed a packet of cigarettes on the table, extracted one and handed it to the prisoner. He even lit it for him. The first bribe had been offered and accepted.

"My name is Detective Chief Inspector Lamont," he said as if they'd never met before, "and this is my colleague, Detective Constable Warwick." Leigh didn't even glance at William. "We'd like to ask you a few questions."

Leigh didn't respond, other than to exhale a large cloud of gray smoke.

"We are investigating the theft of a Rembrandt painting from the Fitzmolean Museum in Kensington, some seven years ago. We have recently come across a copy which we have reason to believe was painted by you."

Leigh took another drag on his cigarette, but said nothing.

"Did you paint that picture?" asked Lamont.

Leigh still made no attempt to respond, almost as if he hadn't heard the question.

"If you cooperate with us," said Lamont, "we might be willing to make a favorable recommendation to the Parole Board when you come up in front of them in a couple of months' time."

Still nothing. William began to realize, as he looked into Leigh's sullen eyes, just how far Miles Faulkner's tentacles stretched.

"On the other hand, if you don't cooperate, we can also report that to the Board. The choice is yours."

Even this didn't appear to move Leigh. A few seconds later the door opened and a trusty prisoner entered carrying a tray of coffee and biscuits, which he placed on the table before leaving quickly. Leigh grabbed a mug of black coffee, dropped in four sugar lumps, and began to stir. Lamont sat back in his chair.

"Mr. Leigh," said William, aware that no prison officer would have addressed him as Mr. during the past four years, "as it's clear that you have no intention of answering any of our questions, I'd just like to say something before we leave." Lamont added another lump of sugar to his coffee. "I'm an art nut, a groupie, call it what you will, but more important, I'm a huge admirer of your work." Leigh turned to look at William for the first time, as a large piece of ash fell off the end of his cigarette and onto the table. "Your Vermeer, *Girl at a Virginal,* was certainly accomplished, although I wasn't surprised it didn't fool the leading Dutch scholars, particularly Mr. Ernst van de Wetering. But the copy of *The Syndics* is unquestionably a work of genius. It's currently in our office at Scotland Yard, and I'm reluctant to return it to Miles Faulkner, who claims it's his. It's just a pity you weren't born in Amsterdam three hundred years ago, when you could have been a pupil of the master, even a master yourself. If I had a fraction of your talent, I wouldn't have bothered to join the police force."

Leigh continued to stare at William, no longer smoking.

"May I ask you a question that has nothing to do with our inquiry?"

Leigh nodded.

"I can't work out how you managed the yellow effect on the Syndics' sashes."

It was some time before Leigh said, "Egg yolk."

"Yes, of course, how stupid of me," said William, well aware that Rembrandt had experimented with the yolks of gulls' eggs when mixing his pigments.

"But why didn't you add Rembrandt's familiar RvR? That was the one thing that made me realize it wasn't the original."

Leigh took another drag on his cigarette, but this time he didn't respond, probably fearing he'd already gone too far. William waited for a few more moments, before he accepted that Leigh wasn't going to answer any more questions.

"Thank you. I'd just like to say what an honor it's been to meet you."

Leigh ignored him, looked at Lamont, and said, "Can I have another fag?"

"Keep the packet," said Lamont, before he turned and nodded to SO Langley, to indicate that the interview was over.

Langley joined them in the glass box. "Back to your cell, Leigh, and be sharp about it."

Leigh rose slowly from his place, put the packet of cigarettes in his pocket, then leaned across the table and shook hands with William. Lamont couldn't hide his surprise. Nobody spoke until Leigh had left the room.

"There can't be any doubt he painted the copy," said Lamont, "which makes me all the more convinced it was Faulkner who was responsible for the theft. Did you notice that Leigh's hands trembled at just the mention of his name? Congratulations, William."

"Thank you, sir."

"And Reg, are you still listening in on Leigh's telephone conversations?"

"Yes. Every Thursday evening, six o'clock, and always to his wife."

"Any further mention of the Picasso?" asked William.

"Not a dicky bird," said Reg.

"Of course not," said Lamont. "Leigh wouldn't risk repeating the message twice, so the Hawk will have to decide if that is enough for us to mount a full operation."

"I would," said William.

"You haven't got his job yet, laddie."

◄○►

The first thing William did after they'd returned to Scotland Yard was to look up a number in the S–Z telephone directory.

"This is Detective Constable Warwick," he told the girl who answered the phone. "Can you tell me if an Edward Leigh was ever a student at the Slade? It would probably have been around the early 1960s."

"Give me a moment, Mr. Warwick, and I'll look up the name." A few minutes later she came back on the line. "Yes, he graduated with honors in 1962. In fact, he won the founder's prize that year, and his one-man show was a sellout."

"Thank you, that's most helpful." William put the phone down, and smiled after he checked another file that confirmed Faulkner had attended the Slade between 1960 and 1963. Fred Yates had taught him never to believe in coincidences.

William spent the next hour writing up his report on the visit to Pentonville. After putting it on Lamont's desk, he checked his watch. Although it was only 5:30, he felt he could leave before the light under the Hawk's door was switched off.

He grabbed his coat and was about to slink out when Jackie said, "Have a good weekend. You've earned it."

"Thanks," said William, who couldn't wait to see Beth, and tell her there was just a possibility she might be reunited with the other man in her life.

Back at his room in Trenchard House, he showered and changed into more casual clothes. He was looking forward to a weekend of debauchery. Well, his idea of debauchery—a meal at Elena's, a couple of glasses of red wine, a run around Hyde Park in the morning, and the latest film in the evening—anything that didn't have cops in it—and tucked up in bed with Beth by eleven.

He decided to walk to Beth's so he could pick up some flowers on the way. By the time he reached her front door, he could feel

141

his heartbeat quickening. He knocked twice and a moment later Jez appeared, looked at the flowers, and said, "Are those for me?"

"You wish."

"But Beth's gone away for the weekend."

"What? I thought that—"

"She asked me to apologize. Something came up at the last minute. She'll call you as soon as she gets back."

"Then they are for you," said William, thrusting the flowers into his hands.

Jez watched as the forlorn suitor turned around and walked slowly away, shoulders slumped. He closed the door and returned to the sitting room, where he handed the flowers to Beth and said, "Don't you think it's time you told him the truth?"

18

Beth phoned William at home on Sunday night to apologize, explaining that she'd had to visit a friend in hospital, and she'd been nervous about calling him at work.

"Of course you can ring if it's something important enough to deprive me of sleep," said William.

"Can you come to supper tomorrow?"

"As long as something else doesn't come up," said William, regretting how harsh his words must have sounded the moment he put down the phone.

William was the first to arrive at the office on Monday morning. He sat down at his desk and was about to open one of his case files when the phone rang. He immediately recognized the voice on the other end of the line.

"William, you asked me to let you know as soon as Carter had been granted a license to search for the *Patrice*," said Lieutenant Monti. "It was rubber stamped this morning, and posted to his home address. So he should have it by the end of the week."

"Thank you, Toni. I'll tell the boss immediately."

"Tell me what?" said Lamont, who had just walked into the room.

"Carter's been granted his exploration license, so he could be on the move within days."

"I'll call the Devon Constabulary and ask them to keep an eye on him. I'll also warn Jim Travers at BA to keep an eye open, so he can let us know when a booking comes up in Carter's name. Shouldn't you be on your way?"

"On my way, sir?"

"You're meant to be at Snaresbrook Crown Court this morning giving evidence. We got a call after you swanned off on Friday afternoon to say that, to everyone's surprise, Cyril Amhurst put in a plea of not guilty, and the case would be heard this morning. You'd better get going if you don't want to lose your first case before the judge even opens proceedings."

William quickly retrieved the Amhurst–Churchill file from his desk drawer, and put his jacket back on.

"Make sure he goes down for twenty years," said Lamont.

"At least," said Jackie, who appeared just as he was heading for the door.

The long tube journey to Snaresbrook gave William a chance to reacquaint himself with the details of the case, but when he reached the last page of the file, he still couldn't understand why Amhurst was pleading not guilty.

The train pulled into the station just after 9:45, and once William was out on the street he asked a news vendor the way to the Crown Court. He followed the man's directions and it wasn't long before he spotted an imposing building looming up in front of him. He sprinted up the steps and pushed his way through the door just before ten o'clock. Checking the court timetable, he saw that *The Crown v. Amhurst* was scheduled for 10:00 in court five. He ran up another flight of steps to the first floor, where he found a young man dressed in a long black gown and holding a wig pacing around, looking anxious.

"Are you Mr. Hayes?" asked William.

"I am, and I'm hoping you're Detective Constable Warwick." William nodded.

"The first thing I should tell you," said Hayes, "is that because Amhurst's case has come up at such short notice, I could apply for a postponement and get the trial set for a later date."

"No, let's get on with it," said William. "The damn man hasn't got a leg to stand on."

"I agree, but your evidence may still prove crucial, so I'll quickly take you through what I consider to be the salient points."

"When do you think we'll be called?" asked William as they sat down on a bench outside court five.

"There are a couple of bail applications to be heard, and a request for a liquor license to be dealt with before us, so we should be on around ten thirty."

By the time Hayes had finished briefing William, he felt even more confident that Amhurst was whistling in the wind, although he did admit to Hayes that this would be the first time he'd given evidence in a trial.

"I'm sure you'll be fine," said Hayes. "I have to leave you now and set up my stall in the court. Just hang about until your name is called."

William didn't hang about. He paced up and down the corridor, becoming more nervous as each minute passed. Finally, the court usher appeared from within and announced, "Detective Constable Warwick."

William nervously followed him into the courtroom. He passed the defendant in the dock, and without looking at him, headed straight for the witness box.

The clerk of the court handed William a Bible and he delivered the oath, relieved to hear that his voice sounded more assured than he felt. But when Mr. Hayes rose from his place, what little confidence William possessed had evaporated.

"Detective Constable Warwick, would you please tell the court how you became involved in this case."

William began by describing his meeting with Mr. Giddy, the manager of Hatchards, and his concern that he might have been sold a set of Winston Churchill's *The Second World War* with fake signatures. He went on to tell the court about his visits to other bookshops, a number of which had been offered, and some had purchased, a total of twenty-two volumes of Churchill's memoirs purportedly signed by the former prime minister.

"And what happened next?" asked Hayes.

"I had a call from an assistant at John Sandoe Books in Chelsea, to tell me that the suspect had returned so I went straight to the shop. But he had just left."

"So you lost him?"

"No. The assistant was able to point the man out as he was walking toward Sloane Square. I chased after him, and had nearly caught up with him when he disappeared into Sloane Square tube station. I continued to pursue him, and just managed to jump on the train he'd got onto as the doors were closing."

"And then what happened?"

"The suspect got off at Dagenham East, when I followed him to a house in Monkside Drive. I made a note of the address, and then took the tube back to Scotland Yard. The following day I obtained a search warrant for the defendant's home, where I found a number of signed books, including a complete set of Sir Winston Churchill's *The Second World War*, three of which had been signed, and several sheets of paper with rows of handwritten Churchill signatures."

"These are all in the list of exhibits, Your Honor," said Hayes, before turning back to the witness. "And did you discover anything else of particular interest?"

"Yes, sir. I found a first edition of *A Christmas Carol*, signed by Charles Dickens."

"Your Honor," said Hayes, "that is also in the court bundle. Perhaps you and the jury would care to examine the exhibits."

The judge nodded, and the jury took their time studying the books, as well as the pages of Churchill signatures, before they were handed back to the clerk of the court.

"What did you do next, Detective Constable Warwick?"

"I arrested Mr. Amhurst, and escorted him to Dagenham police station, where he was later charged with three counts of fraud, deception, and forgery."

"Thank you, Detective Constable Warwick. I have no more questions for this witness, Your Honor," said Hayes, before sitting down.

William was relieved that the ordeal was over. Not as bad as he'd feared. He was about to leave the witness box when Hayes leaped back up and said, "Please remain there, Detective Constable, as I suspect my learned friend may have a question or two for you."

"I most certainly do," said defense counsel, as she rose from her place at the other end of the bench. William stared at her in disbelief.

"Before I begin my cross-examination, Your Honor, I should point out to the court that this witness is my brother."

The judge leaned forward and took a closer look first at Grace, and then at William, but made no comment.

"I can assure Your Honor that neither my instructing solicitor nor my client is at all concerned about this unusual situation. But it is of course possible that my learned friend, or indeed the witness himself, may be. In which case I will withdraw and allow my junior to conduct the cross-examination."

Mr. Hayes was quickly on his feet. "I believe that would be the simplest solution, Your Honor."

"Possibly," said the judge. "But I'm more interested to hear Detective Constable Warwick's opinion."

William recalled his father's words: *Grace only takes on hopeless cases, and never wins.* "Bring her on," he muttered staring defiantly at his sister.

"I beg your pardon?" said the judge.

"I'm quite happy for my sister to conduct the cross-examination, Your Honor."

"Then you may proceed, Ms. Warwick."

Grace bowed, straightened her gown, and turned to the witness. She gave him a warm smile, which he didn't return.

"Constable Warwick, may I begin by saying how much I enjoyed your colorful description of how you chased my client halfway across London and then failed to arrest him, but returned the following morning to make a second attempt. It all sounded rather like an episode from the Keystone Cops, which may make the jury wonder just how long you have been a detective." William hesitated. "Don't be shy, constable. Are we talking about weeks, months, or years?"

"Three months," said William.

"And was this your first arrest as a detective constable?"

"Yes," admitted William reluctantly.

"Would you speak up, constable. I'm not sure the jury heard your reply."

"Yes, it was," said William, as he gripped the sides of the witness box.

"Now, I'm curious to understand, constable, why, having pursued my client from Chelsea to Dagenham, you didn't arrest him long before he reached the safety of his home?"

"I needed to obtain a warrant before I could search his house."

"Curiouser and curiouser," said Grace. "Because surely you could have arrested Mr. Amhurst the moment he'd stepped off the train at Dagenham East, taken him to the local police station, and obtained a section eighteen authority from the senior officer on duty, and then searched his home that same day."

William knew she was right, but couldn't admit he'd made such a basic mistake, so he remained silent.

"Can I presume, constable, that you have read section eighteen of the 1984 Police and Criminal Evidence Act, which grants you the power to search a suspect's address following an arrest?"

Several times, William wanted to tell her, but still said nothing.

"As you seem unwilling to answer my question, constable, can I assume that you had no fear that my client might destroy any evidence or absent himself before you returned the following morning?"

"But I was confident he hadn't seen me," said William, trying to fight back.

"Were you indeed, constable? Can you remember what Mr.

Amhurst said when you and a colleague arrived the following day with a warrant to search his home?" Grace held on to the lapels of her gown, readjusted her wig, and stared at her brother, giving him the same disarming smile, before saying, "Would it help if I reminded you?" She prolonged William's embarrassment by waiting a little longer, before turning to face the jury. "He said, 'Would you like a cup of tea?'"

A few people in the well of the court began to laugh. The judge frowned at them.

"Wouldn't you agree that doesn't sound like the response of a guilty man, fearful of being arrested and thrown in jail?" said Grace.

"Yes, but—"

"If you could stick to answering my questions, constable, and not offering personal opinions, it would be much more helpful."

William was stunned by the ferocity of her attack, and certainly wasn't prepared for her next question.

"Are you an expert in recognizing forged signatures, or did you just take it for granted that my client was guilty?"

"No, I didn't. I had written statements from nine booksellers to whom Mr. Amhurst had offered complete signed editions of Churchill's history of the Second World War."

"None of whom, sadly, including the manager of Hatchards who made the original complaint, were able to find the time to come to court and give evidence today. Were you by any chance in Hatchards on Saturday morning?"

"No," said William, puzzled by the question.

"If you had been, Constable Warwick, you could have obtained a copy of Graham Greene's latest novel *The Tenth Man*, because the author signed over a hundred copies before going on to sign even more books at several other bookshops in the West End. Now, as Sir Winston was a politician, I don't suppose he was shy about signing the odd copy of his works."

One or two of the jury nodded.

"But we found several other books," spluttered William, still trying to fight back. "Don't forget the first edition of *A Christmas Carol,* signed by Charles Dickens, for example."

"I'm glad you raised the subject of the Dickens," said Grace, "because my client has long treasured that particular family heirloom, left to him by his late father, so he would never have considered selling it. Indeed, the court may be interested to know that my client is in possession of the original receipt for the sale of the book, dated December nineteenth, 1843, price five shillings."

Mr. Hayes was quickly on his feet. "My Lord, I must protest. This document has not been offered in evidence by the defence."

"There's a simple explanation for that, Your Honor," said Grace. "My client has been searching for the receipt since the day he was arrested, but Constable Warwick and his colleague left his home in such a mess that he only came across it this morning."

"How convenient," said Hayes, loud enough for the jury to hear. The judge scowled but didn't rebuke him.

Once again, the jury took their time studying the receipt.

"I hope, Constable Warwick," said Grace after William had looked briefly at the receipt, "that you're not going to suggest my client forged that as well?"

Several members of the jury began to chat among themselves, while Hayes made a note on his pad.

Grace smiled up at her brother and said, "I have no more questions for this witness, Your Honour."

"Thank you, Ms. Warwick," said the judge. "Perhaps this might be a convenient time to adjourn for lunch."

◄○►

"We're not beaten yet," said Hayes, enjoying a Caesar salad in the canteen.

"But I didn't exactly help our cause," said William, unable to eat. "I should have reminded my sister about the pages of Churchill signatures we found in Amhurst's house."

"Fear not," said Hayes. "Once Amhurst steps into the witness box, I will remind the jury about the fake signatures again and again."

"And I'm puzzled about that receipt," said William. "Why didn't we find it when we searched the house?"

"Because I suspect it wasn't there. Amhurst probably bought it quite recently to cover himself. A point I shall put to him under oath."

William glanced across at his sister, who was having lunch on the other side of the canteen with her instructing solicitor, who he suspected was Clare. But neither of them once looked in his direction.

◄○►

When the court reconvened, Mr. Justice Gray asked defending counsel if she would like to call her first witness. Ms. Warwick rose from her place and said, "I shall not be calling any witnesses, Your Honor."

A murmur went up around the court. William leaned forward and whispered in Hayes' ear, "So if Amhurst isn't going to testify, won't that make the jury assume he's guilty?"

"Possibly. But don't forget your sister will have the last word. And if I'd been representing Amhurst, I would have given him the same advice."

The judge turned his attention to prosecuting counsel.

"Are you ready, Mr. Hayes, to sum up on behalf of the Crown?"

"I am indeed, Your Honor," said Hayes, who rose and placed his summation on the little stand in front of him. He coughed, adjusted his wig, and turned to face the jury. "Members of the jury, what a fascinating case this has turned out to be—although perhaps you might feel that you are attending a performance of *Hamlet* without the prince. Let me begin by asking you, why defending counsel never once in her cross-examination of Detective Constable Warwick mentioned the pages of Winston Churchill signatures that were found in the defendant's home, written on pages torn from a 49p WHSmith lined pad. I think we can assume that they weren't signed by the great war leader, and not least because he died before decimalization.

"We also know that DC Warwick found a complete set of Churchill's *The Second World War* in the defendant's home, of which three of the six volumes were signed and three unsigned. So I'm bound to ask why the other three weren't signed." Hayes paused. "Perhaps they were next on his list?"

One or two members of the jury rewarded Hayes with a smile.

"And next, you must consider the signed copy of *A Christmas Carol* by Charles Dickens. Defending counsel would have you believe that it is a family heirloom, passed down from generation to generation. Did you not find that a little too convenient? Isn't it more likely that Mr. Amhurst bought an unsigned copy of *A Christmas Carol*, along with its original receipt, on one of his many visits to bookshops all over London? You might also ask yourselves why two Scotland Yard detectives, having carried out a comprehensive search of Mr. Amhurst's residence, didn't come across that receipt.

"I am quite happy for you to decide," continued Hayes, his eyes never leaving the jury, "if you prefer to believe the more romantic version, as suggested by my learned friend, or the more likely version, as supported by the facts. I feel confident that common sense will prevail."

When Hayes resumed his place on the bench, William wanted to applaud, and felt they were back in with a chance. The judge looked across at defending counsel and asked if she was ready to put the case for the defence.

"More than ready, Your Honor," replied Grace, as she rose from her place. She looked directly at the jury for some time before she spoke.

She began by reminding them that in English law, it was the defendant's privilege not to enter the witness box, which might have proved quite an ordeal for "this frail old gentleman."

"He's only sixty-two," muttered Hayes, but Grace sailed on, ignoring the ill wind.

"Let us now consider what is undoubtedly the crucial piece of evidence in this case. If Mr. Amhurst is guilty as charged, and was in possession of an autographed first edition of *A Christmas Carol*, why didn't he offer it for sale, as it would have fetched ten times as much as a signed set of Churchill's history of the Second World War? I'll tell you why, because he wasn't willing to part with a family heirloom, which he will in time pass on to the next generation."

"He doesn't have any children," William whispered in Hayes's ear.

"You should have told me that earlier."

"Last night, members of the jury," continued Grace, "while I was preparing this case, I spent a little time calculating how much Mr. Amhurst would have made had he sold the three volumes of Churchill's memoirs that Constable Warwick produced in evidence and claimed had been falsely signed. It comes to just over a hundred pounds. So, ladies and gentlemen of the jury, I would suggest this is hardly the crime of the century. Yet for reasons best known to itself, Scotland Yard has chosen to come down on Mr. Amhurst with the full force of the law. If you believe beyond reasonable doubt," she emphasized, "the Crown has proved that Cyril Amhurst is a master forger and an accomplished fraudster, then he should spend his Christmas in prison. If, however, you find, as I believe you will, that the Crown has not proved its case, you will surely release him from this ordeal and allow him, like Tiny Tim's father, to spend Christmas in the bosom of his family."

When Grace sat down, Mr. Hayes turned and whispered to William, "What a pro. She's a chip off the old block. Your father would have been proud of her."

"But not of his son," hissed William, who could quite happily have murdered Grace.

The judge's summing-up was fair and unbiased. He presented the facts without trying to influence the jury in either direction. He placed considerable emphasis on the unexplained sheets of Churchill signatures, but he also stressed that the Crown had produced no evidence to prove that *A Christmas Carol* was not a family heirloom. After he had completed his summation, he instructed the jury to retire and consider their verdict.

Just over two hours later the seven men and five women filed back into the jury box. Once they were settled, the clerk of the court asked the foreman to rise. A stout, steely-looking woman in a smart, tightly fitting check suit rose from her place at the end of the front row.

"Foreman of the jury, have you been able to reach a verdict on which you are all agreed?"

"Yes we have, Your Honor."

"On the first charge, of forgery, namely of the signature of Sir Winston Churchill on eighteen books, with the intention of deceiving the public and making a profit. Do you find the prisoner guilty or not guilty?"

"Not guilty," she replied firmly.

"And on the second charge, of being in possession of a book bearing the forged signature of Charles Dickens with the intention of deceiving the public and making a profit. Do you find the defendant guilty or not guilty?"

"Not guilty."

"And on the third charge, of possessing three volumes from Winston Churchill's *The Second World War* bearing the forged signature of Sir Winston Churchill, do you find the prisoner guilty or not guilty?"

"Guilty."

While some in the courtroom gasped, William breathed a sigh of relief. He would be able to return to work the next day, if not in triumph, then at least not having to admit to being a complete failure.

"Will the prisoner please rise," said the clerk of the court.

Amhurst rose, his head slightly bowed.

"Cyril Amhurst, you have been found guilty of a serious crime, for which I sentence you to one year in prison."

William tried not to smile.

"However, as you have up until now had an unblemished record, and this is your first offense, the sentence will be suspended for two years, during which time I would recommend you do not visit too many bookshops. You are free to leave the court."

"Thank you, Your Honor," said Amhurst, before stepping down from the dock and giving his counsel a long hug.

William shook Hayes's hand, and thanked him for his gallant effort.

"Your sister was quite brilliant," admitted Hayes. "With almost nothing to play with, she beat us two–one, and in the end she even had the referee coming down in her favor. I won't make the same mistake if I come across her again."

"Nor will I," said William, before slipping quietly out of the courtroom. He found Grace standing in the corridor, waiting for him.

She gave him that grin he knew so well. "Got time for a drink, bruv?"

◄◦►

Over dinner that evening, William told Beth exactly what had happened in court. She burst out laughing and said, "You're a complete idiot."

"I agree. I'm dreading going into work tomorrow. If I'm not back on the beat, I'll certainly be put in the stocks."

"The laughing stocks would be my bet," said Beth. "I only wish I'd been there to see the look on your face when the judge decided to suspend the sentence."

"Thank God you weren't. But if I ever come up against my sister again, I'll make sure I'm better prepared."

"So will she."

"Whose side are you on?"

"I haven't decided yet, because you still haven't told me how you got on when you visited Eddie Leigh in Pentonville."

William put down his knife and fork and described the meeting in great detail. When he came to the end, all Beth said was, "Egg yolk. That more than makes up for your feeble effort in the witness box this morning. But do you think Leigh knows where the Rembrandt is?"

"I'm fairly sure he does, because it turns out that he and Faulkner were at the Slade at the same time. But we're the last people he's going to tell. In fact I expect he regrets going as far as he did."

"Maybe you'll learn more when you take the copy back to Faulkner's home tomorrow."

"Maybe I won't get past the front gate."

19

William sat at his desk nervously awaiting his fate. He was reading about the latest development in the Blue Period Picasso case when Lamont came barging into the room.

"What was the outcome yesterday?" were the DCI's first words.

William took a deep breath. "Amhurst was sentenced to a year, but the judge suspended it for two."

"Couldn't have worked out better," said Lamont, rubbing his hands gleefully.

"What do you mean?" asked William.

"I won the squad sweepstake. One year suspended," he said as Jackie walked in.

"Who won the jackpot?" Jackie asked, even before she'd taken off her coat.

"I did," said Lamont.

"Damn."

"And what did you predict?" William asked her.

"Six months suspended. So not only did I lose, but you also beat me, jammy bastard."

"What do you mean?"

"The judge threw my first case out of court, and me with it. I left a crucial piece of evidence in my car, so the defendant was released before he even made it to the witness box."

William burst out laughing.

"Right," said Lamont. "Let's all get back to work. Jackie, I need you to take me through the details for tomorrow night's operation before I can finally give it the green light."

Jackie went quickly across to her desk and grabbed the relevant file.

"And, William, the copy of the Rembrandt has been placed in a locked van that you'll find in the car park. Collect the keys from reception and be on your way. Not that anyone's betting on you getting past the front gate."

"Did Faulkner fly to Monte Carlo yesterday?" William asked.

"Yes, he landed in Nice around midday, and isn't expected back for at least another month."

Commander Hawksby poked his head round the door. "So, what was the verdict?"

"One year suspended," said Lamont.

"Damn."

"Dare I ask, sir?" said William.

"Fifty hours community service."

"Can DS Roycroft and I come and see you, sir, once I've finalized the details for Operation Blue Period?" said Lamont.

"Yes, of course, Bruce. And good luck with Mrs. Faulkner, William."

William reported to reception and collected the keys for the van, before heading down to the underground car park. He checked that the crate containing the painting was safely stored in the back of the van before driving out of the Yard and onto Broadway. During the journey to Limpton, he went over parts A, B, and C of his plan, aware that he could be on his way back to the Yard within an hour if he didn't get past the front door.

When he left Beth that morning, he'd promised to be back in time for supper.

"With all six Syndics safely in the back of the van," she teased.

Conscious of the painting in the back, William never exceeded the speed limit. He'd been warned by Lamont that if it wasn't returned in perfect condition, Mr. Booth Watson QC would be demanding compensation for his client before the end of the week.

When he reached the picturesque village of Limpton in Hampshire, it wasn't difficult to work out where the Faulkners lived. Limpton Hall stood proudly on a hill that dominated the landscape. William followed a sign that took him along a winding country lane for another couple of miles, before he came to a halt outside a pair of iron gates, stone pillars surmounted by crouching lions on either side.

He got out of the car and walked up to the gates to find two buzzers nestled in the wall. One had a brass plaque reading LIMPTON HALL, and another below, TRADESMEN. He pressed the top button and immediately regretted his decision, as he might have had a better chance of getting inside the house if he'd pressed Tradesmen. A voice on the intercom demanded, "Who is it?"

"I have a special delivery for Mr. Faulkner."

William held his breath, and to his surprise the gates swung open.

He drove slowly, admiring the centuries-old oaks that lined the long drive as he considered the next part of his plan. Eventually he pulled up in front of a house that wouldn't have looked out of place on the cover of *Country Life*.

The front door was opened by a tall slim man dressed in a black tailcoat and pinstriped trousers. He looked at William as if he'd come to the wrong entrance. Two younger men came scurrying down the steps and quickly made their way to the back of the van. Time to consider Plan B.

William opened the back door of the van, and picked up a clipboard, while the two young men lifted the crate carefully out, carried the painting up the steps, and propped it against a wall in the hall. The butler was closing the door, when William said in an authoritative voice that he hoped sounded like his father's, "I need a signature before I can release the package."

He wouldn't have been surprised if the door had been slammed in his face. But the butler reluctantly took a pen from an inside pocket of his jacket. Time for plan C.

"I'm sorry, but the release form has to be signed by Mr. Faulkner," said William, placing a foot inside the door like a door-to-door salesman. If the butler had said *take it or leave it*, he would have had to take it and leave without another word.

"Will Mrs. Faulkner do?" asked a voice in the background.

An elegant, middle-aged woman appeared in the hallway. She was wearing a red silk dressing gown that emphasized her graceful figure. Did the rich, as Fred Yates had often suggested, not get up before ten in the morning? However, it was her raven-black hair, tanned skin, and air of quiet authority that left him in no doubt she was the mistress of the house.

She signed the form, and William was about to leave when she said, "Thank you, Mr.—"

"Warwick, William Warwick," he replied, breaking his rule of trying not to sound like a public schoolboy.

"I'm Christina Faulkner. Do you have time to join me for a coffee, Mr. Warwick?"

William didn't hesitate, although it wasn't part A, B, or C of his plan. "Thank you," he said.

"Coffee in the drawing room, Makins," said Mrs. Faulkner. "And when the painting has been unpacked, I'd like it rehung."

"Yes, of course, madam."

"Miles will be so pleased to see the picture back in place when he eventually returns," said Mrs. Faulkner, emphasizing the word "eventually," as she led William into the drawing room.

William couldn't take his eyes off the magnificent paintings that adorned every wall. Miles Faulkner may have been a crook, but he was without question a crook with taste. The Sisley, Sickert, Matisse, and Pissarro would have graced any collection, but William's gaze settled on a small still life of oranges in a bowl, by an artist he hadn't come across before.

"Fernando Botero," said Mrs. Faulkner. "A fellow countryman, who, like myself, escaped from Colombia at a young age," she added as the butler appeared carrying a tray of coffee and a selection of biscuits.

William sat down and looked at a large empty space above the mantelpiece where the copy of the Rembrandt must have hung. The butler placed the tray on an antique coffee table William thought he recognized, but was distracted when the two young men entered the room carrying the painting.

The butler took charge of the hanging, and once the picture was back in place, he gave Mrs. Faulkner a slight bow before discreetly leaving.

"Am I right in thinking," said Mrs. Faulkner as she poured her guest a coffee, "that you are a detective, Mr. Warwick?"

"Yes, I am," William replied, without adding, but not a very experienced one.

"Then I wonder if I might seek your advice on a personal matter?" she said, crossing her legs.

William stopped staring at *The Syndics* and turned to face his hostess. "Yes, of course," he managed.

"But before I do, I need to be sure I can rely on your discretion."

"Of course," he repeated.

"I need the services of a private detective. Someone who's discreet, professional, and more important, can be trusted."

"A number of retired Met officers act as private detectives," said William, "and I'm sure my boss would be happy to recommend one of them. Unofficially," he added.

"That's good to know, Mr. Warwick. However, I can't stress how important it is that my husband doesn't find out. He's away at the moment and won't be back for at least a month."

"I'm sure I'll be able to find the right person for you, Mrs. Faulkner, long before your husband returns." He stole a final glance at a picture he doubted he would ever see again.

"You really like that painting, don't you?"

"Yes, I do," admitted William without guile.

"It's also one of Miles's favorites, which may be the reason we have one just like it in our drawing room in Monte Carlo. In fact I can never tell the difference between the two."

William's hand began shaking so much he spilled some coffee on the carpet. "I'm so sorry," he said. "How clumsy of me."

"Don't worry, Mr. Warwick, it's not important."

If you only knew how important it is, thought William, his mind still racing with the implications of what she'd just revealed.

"Can I tempt you to stay for lunch?" asked Mrs. Faulkner. "It would give me a chance to show you the rest of the collection."

"That's kind of you, but my boss will be wondering where I am. So I ought to be getting back."

"Another time, perhaps."

William nodded nervously, as Mrs. Faulkner accompanied him back into the hall, to find the butler standing by the front door.

"It was nice to meet you, Mr. Warwick," she said as they shook hands.

"You too, Mrs. Faulkner," said William, aware that the butler was watching him closely.

William couldn't wait to get back to the Yard and let the team know that Mrs. Faulkner had accidentally let slip that the original of *The Syndics* was hanging in Faulkner's villa in Monte Carlo. He could already see Beth jumping up and down with joy when he told her the news. But as the gates closed behind him, he put his head in his hands and shouted, "You're an idiot!" Why hadn't he accepted her invitation to lunch? He could have seen the entire collection and possibly identified other paintings that were unaccounted for.

"Idiot!" he repeated even louder. Perhaps he wouldn't mention the missed opportunity to Lamont when he wrote his report.

◄○►

William reluctantly left Limpton Hall, but not before repeating the word "idiot" several more times before he reached the motorway.

On his arrival back at the Yard, he parked the van, returned the keys, and went straight up to the office. He found Lamont and Jackie poring over a map covered in little red flags, as they put the finishing touches to Operation Blue Period, which he knew was planned for the following evening. They both looked up as he entered the room.

"Did you get past the front gates?" asked Lamont.

"I not only got past the front gates, I can tell you where the Rembrandt is."

The little red flags were abandoned while Lamont and Jackie listened to William's report. After he had fully briefed them—well, almost fully—all Lamont had to say was, "We should inform the commander immediately."

As William and Jackie assumed he wasn't using the royal "We," they followed him out of the room and down the corridor to Hawksby's office.

"Angela, I need to see the commander urgently," Lamont told Hawksby's secretary as he entered the room.

"Chief Inspector Mullins is with him at the moment," she said, "but I don't expect them to be too much longer."

"Mullins?" whispered William to Jackie.

"Drugs. Pray you don't get transferred to his section. Few survive, and the ones that do are never the same again."

After a few more minutes the door opened and the chief inspector came out, accompanied by Commander Hawksby.

"Good morning, Bruce," said Mullins, not breaking his stride as he left the room.

"I hope you have some good news for me," said Hawksby. "Because so far, it's been one lousy day."

"A possible breakthrough in the missing Rembrandt case, sir."

"Then you'd better come in."

Once they had all settled around the table in Hawksby's office, William went over his meeting with Mrs. Faulkner in great detail. He was surprised by the Hawk's immediate response.

"I don't think that 'we have one just like it in our drawing room in Monte Carlo. In fact I can never tell the difference between the two' was a slip of the tongue. I think Mrs. Faulkner knew exactly what she was telling the young detective she'd invited to join her for coffee."

"I agree," said Lamont. "And coupled with that, she asked for the name of a private detective who can be trusted. It's no wonder the gates were opened."

"So what's she up to?" asked William.

"At the risk of stating the obvious," said Jackie, "it's my bet she needs a private detective because she's planning to divorce her husband, and getting her hands on a large settlement won't be enough. She's looking for revenge, and what better way than telling us where the Rembrandt is?"

"That's a risky game she's playing," said Hawksby, "considering who she's up against."

"She's had seven years to think about it," said William.

"It still may not be enough," said Lamont.

"Got anyone in mind for the job, Bruce?" said Hawksby.

"Mike Harrison would be my first choice. Capable, reliable, and trustworthy. And if she gives him the job, we'd have someone on the inside."

"Set up a meeting," said Hawksby, "and if he's agreeable, William can introduce him to Mrs. Faulkner."

"I'll get on it right away, sir," said Lamont.

"And well done, William, although it won't be easy to get the Rembrandt out of Monte Carlo while Faulkner's in residence. But if his wife is on our side, it might just be possible for us to take him by surprise for a change. Now to more immediate problems. Jackie, are you all set for Operation Blue Period?"

"It's green lit for tomorrow night, sir. We'll have the property so well surrounded even a mole wouldn't be able to burrow its way out without us knowing about it."

"Are you sure you've got all the necessary backup, Bruce?"

"The Surrey Constabulary couldn't have been more cooperative, sir. They're supplying us with around twenty officers, who'll be stationed in two buses at the entry and exit points. We'll be sitting waiting for the villains the moment they come out of the house."

"And the owners?"

"They're away on holiday in the Seychelles, as Faulkner must know, so safely out of harm's way."

"Once the thieves are in custody, be sure to call me, whatever time it is."

"It's likely to be around two or three in the morning, sir," said Jackie.

"Whatever time it is," repeated Hawksby.

Lamont, Jackie, and William stood up, aware that the meeting was over.

"Warwick," said Hawksby, as they turned to leave, "could you stay behind for a moment? I'd like a private word."

William was amused by the word "could," although he assumed he was about to receive a bollocking for his lack of preparation in the Amhurst case.

"William," said Hawksby once Lamont and Jackie had left, "I make a point of never involving myself in the private lives of my officers unless it's likely to affect an ongoing inquiry."

William sat tensely on the edge of his seat.

"However, it has come to my attention that you have developed a friendship with a young woman who works at the Fitzmolean Museum, and is therefore an interested party in the missing Rembrandt case."

"It's more than a friendship, sir," admitted William. "I'm all but living with her."

"All the more reason to be cautious. And what I'm about to say is an order, not a request. Do I make myself clear?"

"Yes, sir."

"You will not, under any circumstances, reveal to anyone outside of this office that we might know where the missing Rembrandt is. In fact, it would be wise not to tell Miss Rainsford anything further concerning our investigation, and I mean anything."

"I understand, sir."

"I don't have to remind you that as a police officer, you have signed the Official Secrets Act, and if you were responsible for undermining this, or any other operation you were involved in, you could find yourself in front of a disciplinary board, which would undoubtedly set your career back, if not derail it. Do you have any questions?"

"No, sir."

"Then you will return to your unit and not discuss this conversation with anyone, even your colleagues. Is that clear?"

"Yes, sir."

Back at his desk, William looked at the pile of pending cases in front of him, but couldn't get the commander's words out of his mind. This morning he had been dreading coming into the office. This evening he was dreading going home.

◄○►

When Beth heard the front door open she immediately ran out of the kitchen and into the hallway.

"So how did your meeting with Mrs. Faulkner go?" she asked, before William had a chance to take his jacket off.

"I didn't get past the front gates."

"You're a dear sweet man," she said, draping her arms around his neck, "but such an unconvincing liar."

"No, it's the truth," protested William.

She stood back and looked at him more closely. "What have they told you about me?" she asked, her tone suddenly changing.

"Nothing, I swear. Nothing." And then he recalled Hawksby's words: *You will not, under any circumstances . . . tell Miss Rainsford anything further concerning our investigation, and I mean anything.*

What circumstances? thought William. And then he remembered Jackie's words when he'd bought Beth some flowers before going to Barnstaple: *Rainsford? Why does that name ring a bell?*

◄○►

The first thing William did when he arrived at work the following morning was to write up a detailed report of his visit to Limpton

Hall. Once he'd handed it in to Lamont, he called Mrs. Faulkner on her private line.

"I think I may have found the right person to help you, Mrs. Faulkner. When would you like to meet him?"

"I'm driving up to London next Monday. Why don't you join me for lunch? I can't risk you coming down here again."

"Why not?" William asked, sounding disappointed.

"Makins would be on the phone to my husband before you reached the front gate. In fact, Miles called me last night to ask why I'd even let you into the house."

"What did you tell him?"

"That when you returned the picture, you let slip that the Rembrandt investigation had been dropped and relegated to the unsolved cases file."

"Do you think he believed you?"

"You can never tell with Miles. I don't think even he knows when he's telling the truth. Shall we say the Ritz, one o'clock? My treat."

Well, it certainly wasn't going to be Mrs. Walters's treat, thought William as he put down the phone.

Later that morning he joined Lamont for a different type of lunch. A pork pie, a packet of crisps, and a pint of bitter in the Sherlock Holmes pub, and a chance to meet Mike Harrison. A policeman's policeman, was how Lamont had described him, and William could immediately see why. He was uncomplicated, forthright, and treated William as an equal from the moment they met. More importantly, he was just as keen to unearth the missing Rembrandt as the rest of the team. He'd been a member of the unit when it had been stolen seven years ago, so he considered it unfinished business.

On his way home that night, William picked up a bunch of flowers as a peace offering for Beth. But the moment he turned the key in the lock, he knew she wasn't there. And then he remembered—Tuesday was Friends' Night at the Fitzmolean. Smoked salmon sandwiches, bowls of nuts, and sparkling wine to loosen the wallets of the museum's loyal supporters. She wouldn't be back much before eleven. He returned to Trenchard House for the second night in a row, called her at 10:30, and again at eleven, but she didn't answer the phone, so he went to bed.

20

William was woken by the phone ringing. He grabbed it, wondering who could possibly be calling him at that hour of the morning. He hoped it was Beth.

"Carter's on the move," said a voice he recognized immediately. "Meet me at Heathrow, terminal two. There's a car on its way. Should be with you in a few minutes. Bring an overnight bag, and don't forget your passport this time."

William put the phone down and headed straight for the bathroom. He took a quick shower, followed by an even quicker shave, with two nicks to prove it, then returned to the bedroom to pack an overnight bag. A couple of shirts, plus pants, socks, and a toothbrush, before finally picking up his passport from a desk drawer. The car was waiting outside, its engine running. He immediately recognized the driver who'd whisked him to Chelsea.

"Good morning, Danny," he said.

06:37 GMT

Jackie didn't need a wake-up call that morning. She was already on her way to Waterloo station by the time William was speeding down the M4.

Lamont was waiting for her on platform 11, and they boarded the 7:29 to Guildford, second class. On arrival they were met by Superintendent Wall, the only man from the Surrey Constabulary

169

who'd been fully briefed on what they had planned for the rest of the day.

"You don't have a driver?" said Lamont, as Wall climbed behind the wheel and switched on the ignition.

"Cutbacks," he growled.

07:14 GMT

William spotted him the moment he entered the terminal. A dark blue double-breasted blazer, white shirt, and striped tie. The commander probably slept in double-breasted pajamas.

"Good morning, sir."

"Good morning, William. Carter's booked on BA flight 003 to Rome, departing in an hour and a half, and we're on an Alitalia plane which takes off in forty minutes. Lieutenant Monti will meet us at the airport before driving to Civitavecchia. We'll hang about here for a few more minutes to make sure Carter checks in. If he suspects someone might be following him, he could abort his whole trip, in which case we'll be heading back to Scotland Yard, not Rome." The commander was still speaking when he grabbed William by the arm and nodded in the direction of the BA desks. Carter was striding toward the check-in counter, accompanied by a man William didn't recognize, who was carrying a bulky holdall and pushing a trolley with two small suitcases.

"I have a feeling I know what's in that holdall," said Hawksby. "But there's not a lot we can do about it."

"We could have them searched by security before he boards the plane."

"That's the last thing we want."

"Why?"

"For two reasons," said Hawksby as Carter was issued with his boarding pass. "First, we'd need to have reasonable suspicion that he'd committed a crime before we could consider checking his luggage, and secondly, if we didn't find anything suspicious, we would have warned them off and blown our cover."

"Do you recognize the other man?" asked William as they headed towards passport control.

"Damien Grant, GBH, former weightlifter, and more recently club bouncer. He's only there to make sure that holdall reaches its destination."

"Last call for Alitalia, flight number . . ."

10:07 GMT

Once they had settled in Superintendent Wall's office, the three police officers checked and double-checked every detail of Operation Blue Period. When Lamont had answered his final question, Wall checked his watch. "Time to go down to the basement car park and brief the troops. It's the only space we've got that's big enough to accommodate your private army."

Lamont and Jackie followed the superintendent out of his office and down a flight of well-worn steps into the car park, where a couple of dozen policemen and two policewomen were chatting as they waited to find out why they were there. They fell silent the moment the superintendent appeared.

"Good morning," he said, tapping his swagger stick against his leg. "We are joined today by two officers from the Met. We are here to assist them with a special operation that will be taking place on our patch. I'll hand over to DCI Lamont, who will brief you on the details."

Lamont waited until Jackie had set up an easel and placed an aerial photograph of a large country estate on it.

"Ladies and gentlemen," said Lamont, "the Met have been preparing this operation for several months, but we have always known that its outcome will depend on the professionalism of the officers on the ground." He pointed at them. "That's you!"

Laughter and a smattering of applause broke out.

"We have reason to believe," continued Wall, "that a well-organized gang of criminals will be raiding this property tonight." Jackie pointed to the photograph of a large Lutyens mansion surrounded by several acres of parkland.

"The gang's purpose is to steal a Picasso worth several millions, and be out of harm's way long before the police arrive. But we'll be waiting for them. You may ask why we need such a large force for this operation, when there will only be three or possibly four thieves involved. That's because we know who's behind this scam, and he's beaten us once too often in the past. So this time we're going to cut off his balls before he thinks about doing it again."

A second, louder round of applause followed.

"For this particular well-planned operation, I can assure you the villains have done their homework," continued Lamont. "They know the owners are on holiday, and they also know that the nearest police station is twenty minutes away, which they believe will give them more than enough time to vanish into thin air long before the police turn up. My second in command, DS Roycroft, will now take you through the details of Operation Blue Period, and the role you'll be playing. DS Roycroft."

Jackie took a pace forward, delighted to be greeted by so many enthusiastic faces who were clearly looking forward to catching some real villains, and nailing one in particular.

12:45 Central European Time

The Alitalia flight landed at Da Vinci airport a few minutes behind schedule. The first thing William saw as he descended the aircraft steps was Lieutenant Monti waiting by the side of an unmarked car.

William introduced Hawksby to Monti, who saluted, opened the back door, and waited for them both to climb in. Hawksby was surprised that the lieutenant was unshaven and his breath stank of garlic, but he didn't comment.

"No passport control, no customs?" asked William.

"If it had been just you, William," said Monti, "I would have met you in the arrivals hall, but when my comandante heard that Commander Hawksby would be accompanying you, he ordered me to pull out all the stops. I hope that's the appropriate English expression?"

"Spot on," said William. "The meaning derives from an organist pulling out the stops of his instrument to increase the volume."

"Thank you, constable," said Hawksby. "Most interesting."

"It's not a long journey to Civitavecchia," said Monti, as they sped off. "But we need to be there well ahead of Carter and Grant. They're booked into the Grand Hotel—grand in name only."

"And where are *we* staying?" asked Hawksby.

"I'm afraid your hotel is even less grand. But it does have the advantage of being on the quayside, so I've booked you a room overlooking the port."

"And William?"

"He will be with me at all times. The harbormaster informed me that Carter has chartered a small, fully equipped shallow search and recovery vessel for seven days. It's ideally suited for expeditions in search of seabed treasure."

"Why seven days," asked William, "when they will be taking on board what they're looking for?"

"It's just for show," Monti explained, "although we can't be sure how many of the crew are in on the scam. But we assume the captain and the two divers must be."

"So do we just sit in Civitavecchia and wait for them to return before we arrest them?"

"Certainly not," said Monti. "I've signed us both on as deckhands. They clearly want as many innocent onlookers as possible to witness their remarkable discovery."

"But my Italian isn't that good," William reminded him.

"I know," said Monti, "so once we're on board, leave the talking to me. And I ought to warn you, these can be choppy waters."

"And I ought to warn you," said William, "I'm not a good sailor."

12:21 GMT

"Any questions?" asked Jackie when she'd come to the end of her briefing.

A hand shot up. "Which of the two teams is more likely to be needed?"

"We won't know until the last moment. There are two exits from the house, here and here, where the buses will be hidden," said Jackie, pointing to the map. "But we have no way of knowing which one they'll take. If for any reason we don't manage to intercept them, we've got a helicopter on standby."

"I should stress," interjected Lamont, "that while you're waiting, you can't listen to the radio, or even chat among yourselves, because the slightest sound will alert them. Just be sure you're not the idiot who frightens them off."

"What sort of vehicle are you expecting them to be in, sir?"

"Because of the size of the painting they plan to steal," said Lamont, "it's likely to be a large van. They know exactly what they're looking for, and you can be sure they'll have worked out their escape route to the inch. Which is why we need so many of you surrounding the target."

"Are they likely to be armed?"

"We think that's unlikely," said Lamont. "You can get life for armed robbery, while for burglary you rarely get more than six years. But just to be on the safe side, we'll have a small squad of armed police in place, but well hidden."

"Any intel on when they might strike?" asked a young constable.

"Not before six, and it won't be after midnight," said Lamont without further explanation. A long silence followed.

"If there are no more questions," said Jackie, "let's adjourn for lunch. Try and get some kip this afternoon, and make sure you go to the toilet before you get on the bus. The first bus will leave at four ten p.m. The second will follow twenty minutes later, so we avoid looking like a convoy."

"And once you're in place," said Lamont, "don't forget that silence is our most effective weapon."

14:08 CET

Monti drove William and Hawksby straight to the commander's dockside hotel in Civitavecchia, and they all went to the room reserved by Monti on the third floor. The first thing Hawksby did was to check the sight lines from the window. He had a clear view of the port, and wouldn't need binoculars to keep an eye on the vessel Carter had chartered. Monti had even supplied a copy of the company's brochure in English, with a photograph of a shipwreck on the cover to tempt potential customers. What it didn't record was their failure rate over the years. But then the crew were pirates at best, while the customers who chartered the ship were often romantics, chasing a dream. But not on this occasion.

William was about to take a shower, until Monti said, "Don't bother. Try not to forget you're a deckhand. We don't want you smelling like a lily."

Hawksby now understood why the lieutenant hadn't shaved for some days, and stank of garlic.

Monti opened a large trunk that he'd left in the room earlier and produced outfits for the role they were about to play: two pairs of well-worn jeans; two unmarked T-shirts; two sweaters, one blue, one gray; and two pairs of trainers without a brand logo. Everything looked and was second-hand.

"Let's hope I've got your size right," said Monti, as William began to pull on a pair of jeans.

"And what about me?" asked Hawksby.

"You'll be just fine, sir," said Monti. "If you stroll along the dock dressed as you are, everyone will assume you're the owner of a large yacht, not that you're keeping a lookout for a couple of villains."

"I wish."

"We'll have to leave you now, sir. We should be on board before Carter arrives."

"Do I have any backup should their plans suddenly change?"

"You'll only see them if you need them," said Monti. "But I can assure you this isn't the only room that we've booked."

"Chapeau," said Hawksby, touching his forehead.

After Monti and William had left, the commander returned to his lookout point and watched the two young officers as they walked along the quayside and boarded the ship before reporting to the chief deckhand. How he wished he was twenty years younger.

13:08 GMT

Lamont and Jackie had joined the team in the canteen for lunch, where the babble of expectant chatter revealed how eager they all were to get on with the job.

At four o'clock, after a final briefing from DS Roycroft, Lamont divided the young officers into two groups, before they began to board the two buses. At the same time, a squad of the special firearms division was setting out from Scotland Yard with orders to contact DCI Lamont the moment they had reached the target.

At eleven minutes past four, the first bus left the car park, drove up the ramp, and out onto the high street. It kept a steady pace, always remaining on the inside lane, and never once breaking the speed limit. At 4:33, the second bus maneuvered its way onto the main thoroughfare, where they were held up by early commuters on their way home from work, while they were on their way to work.

Lamont had been taken by surprise when Superintendent Wall

told him that he would be accompanying them on the mission. Lamont accepted that if Wall was hoping to add the prefix chief to his rank, "Operation Blue Period" would look good on his service record. Lamont had to admit, if only to himself, that the thought of promotion had also crossed his mind.

The superintendent, Lamont, and Jackie were the last to leave Guildford police station in an unmarked car. By the time they reached the target, both buses were in place, engines idle, with their lights off. Twenty-six men and three women sat and waited in silence.

16:23 CET

After stowing their bags in the sleeping quarters below, the two new itinerant deckhands reported for duty on the main deck.

"How long will it take to reach the site?" Monti asked the chief deckhand.

"It's about forty nautical miles away, so a little over five hours. We'll be casting off as soon as our customers and the divers come aboard. Meanwhile, you two can help with the loading."

William and Monti made sure they pulled their weight, loading everything from crates of apples to a new winch, as clearly the skipper wanted to make it look as if they would be at sea for at least seven days.

William only stopped working when a Mercedes drew up alongside the gangway and two men stepped out onto the dockside. He recognized them immediately. A couple of deckhands took their luggage—not a lot, thought William, considering they'd booked the vessel for a week. Grant was still clutching on to the bulky holdall, and made sure the two deckhands didn't get anywhere near it.

William and Monti remained in the shadows, to avoid coming in contact with the two passengers as they boarded the ship.

"I can't imagine much will happen until we reach the salvage site," whispered Monti, "but it's still a risk we can't afford to take. So we'll have to remain on deck until eight bells."

18:22 GMT

"The firearms squad is in place, sir," said a lone voice over the intercom, sounding like a crack of thunder, after a couple of hours of silence.

"Welcome aboard," said Lamont. "Maintain radio silence until you see the robbers entering the house."

"Roger that, sir."

21

William settled down on his bunk just after ten, but he didn't sleep. Some of the deckhands were playing cards, while others told unlikely tales of treasure they had recovered from the bottom of the ocean. It soon became clear they had no idea how successful this trip was going to be, and not many of them sounded optimistic.

While William rested, Monti continued working and keeping watch on deck. He was back by William's bunk just after midnight, and as it was a little quieter, was able to brief his colleague without being overheard.

"Nothing much is happening on deck," he said. "Carter and Grant haven't left their cabins since we set sail. I doubt if we'll see either of them before first light. But we can't afford to take any chances, so you'd better take my place. When you go up on deck, you'll see a lifeboat on the starboard side."

"Which is the starboard side?" asked William.

"The right, idiot. I thought you came from a nation of sailors. Climb in under the tarpaulin, so if anyone comes out on deck during your watch, they won't see you. Just make sure you don't fall asleep. Wake me at four and I'll take your place."

William made his way up a spiral staircase and out onto the deck. He spotted the lifeboat, gently swaying in the breeze, and crept cautiously toward it, stopping at the slightest unfamiliar sound.

One last check to make sure no one was watching him. He steadied the lifeboat, pulled himself up, and slithered underneath

179

the tarpaulin. He soon realized there was no danger of falling asleep. He was far more likely to be sick.

He tried to master the technique of swinging with the boat, and however many times he kept looking at his watch, the minute hand didn't move any faster. And then, without warning, he heard heavy footsteps approaching, followed by a voice speaking in English.

22:19 GMT

Jackie decided that this was even worse than a stakeout, because they were waiting for someone who wasn't there, rather than for someone who was there and must eventually show up.

00:58 CET

"Everything's in place. Now all we have to do is . . ."

William didn't move a muscle until the voice faded away. More words, but they were scattered in the wind. He raised the tarpaulin an inch, and his eyes settled on a group of four men standing only a few yards from the lifeboat.

Grant unzipped the holdall and lifted out the old wooden casket William had first seen in Carter's workshop. He placed it carefully on the deck. The chief deckhand deftly tied a rope around it as if he were wrapping a large Christmas present. Once he was satisfied that it was secure, he walked across and attached the rope to a winch that William and Monti had helped carry on board. The deckhand took the handle and turned it slowly until the rope's slack had been taken up. An older man with a weatherbeaten face and a dark unkempt beard, who was wearing a cap with braid on it, steadied the casket as it was raised inch by inch, slowly off the deck.

When it was about three feet in the air, the captain guided it gently over the ship's railing, then nodded. The chief deckhand started to turn the winch in the opposite direction. The casket began its slow downward journey toward the water. William didn't lose sight of the box until it disappeared beneath the waves. It was several more minutes before the wincher had done his job, and the casket came to rest on the seabed, some 130 feet below them. The captain and the chief deckhand then lowered a small anchor overboard. It was attached to a flashing buoy, marking the exact location of the drop.

Carter gave the captain a mock salute. Grant picked up the empty holdall and they made their way across the deck. William slipped back under the tarpaulin, but could not make out what they were saying until they passed the lifeboat.

"I hope they can be trusted."

"They're being paid well enough, and if . . ."

William didn't move a muscle, deciding to wait until he was sure they must be back in their cabins.

00:00 GMT

The superintendent crossed his legs. He badly needed a pee, but he wasn't going to be the first to admit it. Lamont continued to stare hopefully down the long drive that led up to the house as he listened attentively for the sound of an engine.

For the past three hours Jackie had been repeatedly checking her watch, becoming more anxious by the minute.

02:00 CET

William raised the tarpaulin half an inch, and peered in every direction. No sign of anyone. He checked his watch, before crawling out of the swaying lifeboat and lowering himself uneasily over the side, nearly losing his grip. He landed head first on the slippery deck.

He tried to steady himself and stand up, but he was so weak and giddy that he had to grasp the ship's rail. Finally he gave in, leaned over the side, and was violently sick. When he looked up, he noticed that the ship was now circling the bobbing buoy.

It was some time before he had recovered enough to clamber back down the spiral staircase and collapse on his bunk, where he lay still, willing himself not to be sick again.

He decided not to wake Monti, as there was little point in his spending the next two hours in that lifeboat, when nothing was going to happen before first light. William still didn't sleep.

01:07 GMT

Lamont could hear the sound of a car coming from behind him. Moments later a green Jaguar drove past and proceeded along the driveway, lights full on. It came to a halt outside the house.

The driver climbed out, opened the front door, and disappeared inside. Moments later the hall lights came on.

Lamont cursed several times, before he broke radio silence and issued an order he'd been dreading.

"Operation Blue Period aborted. Return to base."

Perhaps it was a good thing he couldn't hear the chorus of groans and expletives emanating from the two buses in which his loyal foot soldiers had remained silent for more than five hours. Several of them jumped off the bus and began to pee in unison.

06:09 CET

"Why didn't you wake me at four?" demanded Monti. He glared down at William, who was the same color as his soaking sheet, and still sweating. William placed a finger to his lips and indicated that they should go up on deck.

Squawking gulls hovered above them as William pointed to the flashing marker buoy bobbing up and down in the waves, before he explained to Monti why he hadn't bothered to wake him.

"Good thinking," said Monti.

They looked up at the bridge, where the captain was steering the vessel in ever-decreasing circles around the buoy. There was no sign of Carter or Grant, but William doubted they were asleep.

For the next forty minutes Monti and William carried out whatever orders the chief deckhand gave them, but their eyes continually returned to the entrance of the private quarters as they waited for the main actors to make their entrance.

Just after seven, Carter, accompanied by two divers in wetsuits, walked out onto the deck. The divers put on their masks and flippers, sat on the rail, and adjusted their breathing apparatus. They then fell backward into the water and disappeared below the waves.

05:20 GMT

Superintendent Wall drove Lamont and Jackie back into Guildford, and dropped them off in the town center. "I feel sure you'll be able to find your way to the station," he said, before driving off.

"You can hardly blame him," said Jackie twenty minutes later, as they stood on a cold, gray platform waiting for the first train to Waterloo.

"By the time we get back to the Yard," said Lamont, "we'll probably find that Chief Inspector Warwick is the new head of the Art and Antiques squad, and I've been demoted to detective sergeant and have to call him sir."

"Which means I'll be back on the beat doing traffic duty," said Jackie.

08:30 CET

The two divers reappeared on the surface four times during the next hour, and on each occasion gave a thumbs-down sign, before returning to their task. After a couple more hours they clambered back on board looking exhausted, and lay flat on the deck recovering. William suspected that they had never been more than a few feet below the surface.

Carter and Grant looked suitably disappointed, and the crew were already beginning to lose interest in their efforts. But William knew they were only witnessing the first act in this pantomime, and that the curtain was about to rise again following the interval.

Once the divers had recovered, they returned to their task. Three more thumbs-down signs were clear for all to see during the next couple of hours. It was Monti who noticed that the marker buoy and its flashing light were no longer to be seen. "They must have located the casket," he whispered.

"But they're not ready to admit it yet," said William.

The divers disappeared below the waves once again, but this time when they resurfaced one of them was waving frantically while the other gave a thumbs-up sign. The crew ran over to the starboard side and began cheering, although William noticed that the captain remained remarkably calm. But, then, he'd already read the second act.

The chief deckhand quickly returned to the winch, and began to take up the slack. Carter and Grant joined the crew, who were leaning over the side in expectation, and when the casket reappeared on the surface a few minutes later, barnacles in place, they looked just as surprised and delighted as the rest of the men.

The chief deckhand slowed down his efforts so the precious cargo could be raised safely over the railing and back onto the deck. He fell on his knees and began to untie the rope as the captain came down from the bridge. Everyone else hung around, waiting impatiently to discover what was in the box. Well, not quite everyone.

Once the rope had been removed, the chief deckhand stood aside to allow Carter to perform the opening ceremony, but he still pretended to need Grant's assistance to force open the rusty old lock. William could only wonder in what antiques shop Carter had come across such a convincing prop. When the lid was finally lifted, there followed a moment of total silence, as everyone on deck stared down in disbelief at the 712 silver cob coins. Only Carter knew the exact number.

The ship's company cheered as Grant picked up the casket and cradled it in his arms as if it were an only child who had been rescued from the sea. He then walked slowly toward the private quarters, a smiling Carter following a pace behind.

The captain announced to the crew that they would be returning to port immediately, but every deckhand would still receive a full week's pay. This elicited an even louder cheer.

10:54 GMT

"Commander Hawksby's office."

"It's Bruce Lamont, Angela. Can you put me through to the boss?"

"He's still in Italy, Bruce. I'm not expecting him back until Monday."

"Any hope of him staying there?"

"I beg your pardon, chief inspector?"

"You never heard me say that, Angela."

"Can it wait until Monday?"

"It will have to. But, then, I'm getting rather used to waiting around only to find that no one's there."

12:36 CET

Once the ship had docked, William and Monti leaned over the railing and watched as Grant lugged the casket down the gangway. He was still clutching it as he climbed into the back seat of a waiting car.

William recognized the driver. Funny, he thought, that he knew exactly what time he would be needed to pick up his two passengers although they had no way of communicating with each other. Carter shook hands with the captain, the chief deckhand, and the two divers, revealing who was in on the plot. He then walked down the gangway and joined Grant in the back of the car.

As the car drove off, and before William could ask, Monti said, "Don't worry, they're being tailed. In any case, we know exactly where they're going."

"But if they were to change their plans?" said William.

"We'll arrest them, steal the box, and retire."

William laughed as a smartly dressed man in a double-breasted blazer strolled past the ship and headed back to his hotel, looking like a wealthy tourist.

William and Monti stood in line with the rest of the crew to receive a full week's pay. Not cheap, thought William, but then Carter needed the bit-part players to repeat a plausible version of what they had witnessed to their families and friends, and anyone else who cared to listen.

When they had both signed off, they made their way back to Hawksby's hotel, where he was waiting for them. This time William was allowed to take a shower, and Monti shaved and brushed his teeth for the first time in days.

Once they'd changed back into their own clothes, they joined Hawksby for lunch. Not that William was hungry. They were just finishing the main course when a waiter approached their table and told Lieutenant Monti there was a call for him, which he could take at the desk.

"Good man, Monti," said Hawksby, raising a glass after he'd left the table.

"He certainly is," said William, as he poured himself another glass of wine. "I wonder how Operation Blue Period went?"

Hawksby checked his watch. "It will be over by now, one way or the other," he said as the lieutenant reappeared and took his seat.

"I can confirm that a wooden casket containing over seven hundred silver cob coins has been handed in to the Italian Naval Office in Rome. A Mr. Carter has produced his authorized stamped license, and is claiming the find as a treasure trove, a Mr. Booth Watson by his side."

The Hawk and William banged the table with the palms of their hands.

"Mr. Carter was last seen having his photograph taken while chatting to journalists about his remarkable find," said Monti, as William refilled his glass. "How do you want to take it from here, sir?"

"I'm in no hurry," replied Hawksby. "The wheels of government always grind slowly, so why not allow the villains to enjoy a few days spending their unearned profits before we let the world know their amazing find is not, after all, worth over seven hundred thousand pounds, but a few thousand at best."

"And they won't even get their hands on that," said Monti, "because we'll have to confiscate the casket and its contents as evidence in their forthcoming trial, which won't take place for at least a year."

13:25 GMT

William and the commander parted company at Heathrow.

"I'll see you in my office at nine on Monday morning for a debriefing," said Hawksby. "Have a good weekend."

For the first time, William felt he was a fully paid-up member of the team.

As he boarded the tube into London, he wondered if Lamont and Jackie had experienced similar success with Operation Blue Period. He considered calling her at home but decided it could wait until the Hawk's meeting on Monday.

He left South Kensington tube station and headed in the direction of home. But was it home any longer? Would Beth have forgiven him, and already forgotten their first quarrel, or would she have locked him out? And if she had, who could blame her? He was feeling apprehensive as he walked up to the front door, but when he put his key in the lock, it not only opened, but his flowers were in a vase on the hall stand.

Beth came running out of the kitchen and threw her arms around him.

"I'm so sorry," she said. "I acted like a fool. Of course I realize you can't talk about your work, especially if it concerns the Rembrandt. But, please, next time you steal away in the middle of the night, at least phone me and give me a clue when you'll be coming home. I've spent the last three days wondering if you'd left me, and when you didn't call . . ."

"I was on a job."

"I don't need to know," said Beth, leading him through to the kitchen. The table was already laid with only the candles waiting to be lit.

"I've cooked a special lovers' tiff meal in an attempt to make up for my appalling behavior. It will be ready in about half an hour, and then I can tell you my news."

William pulled her into his arms and kissed her. "I've missed you."

"Missed you too. In fact I thought I'd lost you."

He took her by the hand and led her out of the kitchen.

"But we haven't had dinner yet!" she said as he dragged her up the stairs.

"People have been known to have sex before dinner."

"Caveman," Beth said as he began to unbutton her dress.

‹o›

William was reading an article in *The Guardian*—a newspaper he'd never considered taking before he met Beth. He checked the report from their Rome correspondent a second time before handing Beth the paper and waiting for her reaction.

"Wow, over seven hundred thousand pounds," she said. "What a coup. Is that why you had to leave in such a hurry? Sorry, I shouldn't have asked."

William nodded. "The real story should come out fairly soon, and it won't be on page twelve, but the front page, but until then I can't say anything."

"I understand," said Beth as she sliced the top off her egg.

"Last night," said William, "you hinted that you also had some interesting news."

"That was before you interrupted me, caveman."

"So are you going to tell me?"

"I've got a new job."

"You're leaving the Fitzmolean?"

"No, not until you've returned the picture I'm not allowed to ask about."

"Then what?"

"I've been promoted to assistant keeper of paintings."

"I rather fancy living with an assistant keeper of paintings, even if I'm not sure what they do."

"I'll be responsible for organizing special events, like the Van Eyck exhibition next month, and I'll report directly to Mark Cranston, the keeper."

"With a rise in salary?"

"Not so you'd notice. But to be fair, I didn't even know I was being considered for the position."

"Your parents will be so proud of you," said William.

"I phoned my father last night to tell him the good news."

William was surprised, but didn't comment.

"And I have another piece of news: Jez is leaving me."

"For another man?"

"Yes, he's moving in with his friend Drew, so I'll be looking for a new lodger. And before you ask, the answer is no."

22

William and Beth left the house together on Monday morning. The new assistant keeper of paintings wanted to be early on her first day, and William needed to write his report on the trip to Italy.

They parted company outside South Kensington tube station, before Beth went on to the museum by foot. William thought about the weekend they had spent together. It couldn't have gone better, and he was now more keen than ever for Beth to meet his parents. He had asked her if she could join them for lunch on Sunday but she had once again put him off, explaining that she had already promised to visit a friend in hospital that afternoon, and didn't feel she could cancel at such short notice. Perhaps next Sunday, William had suggested. And then something flashed into his mind that should have worried a detective long before now. He would double-check the postcards from Hong Kong when he got back to the flat tonight.

When William walked into the office he was surprised to find no sign of either Lamont or Jackie. He sat down at his desk and began to write his report, thinking he must remember to call Monti and thank him, because without his backup and assistance, Carter would have cashed in his chips and now be living off his ill-gotten gains.

At 8:55, William picked up the Carter file, walked down the corridor, and knocked on the commander's door. Angela waved him through to the inner sanctum, where he found Lamont and

Jackie already seated at the table, listening intently to the commander.

Hawksby nodded at William as he took his usual place next to Jackie.

"I spent most of my weekend taking calls from the chief constable of Surrey, and a Superintendent Wall of the Guildford Police," said Hawksby. "And I can tell you, neither of them minced their words. Incompetent, unprofessional, amateur were among the kinder ones. The chief constable warned me that if I didn't brief the assistant commissioner by midday, then he would. And I can't say I blame him."

"I'm the one to blame, sir," said Jackie quietly. "I was convinced my contact was on the level, and ended up being the one who was taken for a ride."

"Along with twenty-six police officers, not to mention an elite firearms squad, a helicopter crew on standby, and an irate superintendent whose job is now on the line."

Neither Lamont nor Jackie attempted to defend themselves.

"And if that wasn't enough," Hawksby continued, "it turned out to be nothing more than an elaborate decoy, because while you were sitting waiting for the villains to appear, they were breaking into another house just a few miles away, where they stole a Renoir worth several million. Leigh knew only too well you were listening in on his phone conversations, and simply sent you to the wrong house, where you thought they were going to steal a Picasso. Don't be surprised when Booth Watson settles another large insurance claim for his unknown client."

William could see that Jackie was struggling to control her emotions.

"There's no one else to blame," she repeated, looking directly at Hawksby.

The commander closed his file, and William assumed he would move on, but then he said, "Why didn't you follow the basic rule every copper learns on their first day on the beat? Accept nothing, believe no one, and challenge everything." William would always remember the person who'd first told him that. "Perhaps your recent promotion was a step too far, DS Roycroft," Hawksby continued. "A few weeks on traffic duty might not do you any harm." At least she'd got that right.

A long silence followed, which was finally broken when Lamont said, "I understand your fishing trip to Italy couldn't have gone better, sir."

"Except as the commissioner pointed out that when Carter is eventually arrested, it will be the Italian police, and not the Met, who end up getting the credit for an operation we masterminded."

"But if we were to find the missing Rembrandt, and return it to the Fitzmolean—" said William, trying to rescue his colleagues.

"Let's hope that's not another false alarm," said Hawksby. "Are you still having lunch with Mrs. Faulkner today?"

"Yes, sir. I'll report back to DCI Lamont as soon as I return this afternoon."

"Is Mike Harrison going with you?" asked the commander, sounding a little calmer.

"No, sir. She has an appointment with him in his office at four o'clock this afternoon."

"That woman's up to something," said Lamont. "We should assume she's every bit as devious as her husband, and quite capable of dangling the bait of a Rembrandt in front of us, especially if she knows William's girlfriend works at the Fitzmolean."

"How could she possibly know that?" said William.

"Try to think like a criminal, for a change," barked Lamont.

"I agree," said Hawksby. "And if it turns out that she's taking you for a ride too, it won't only be DS Roycroft who's on traffic duty. Now, let's all get back to work, and I don't want to see any of you unless you've got something positive to report."

Back in the office the atmosphere felt like a prison cell, while the condemned woman waited for the priest to come and read her the Last Rites.

William was relieved to escape just after 12:30 for his lunch with Mrs. Faulkner.

He walked briskly across the park and into St. James's, arriving well in time for his lunch date. As he entered the Ritz, a liveried doorman saluted as if he were a regular. William had to stop at the reception desk and ask where the dining room was.

"Far end of the corridor, sir. You can't miss it."

He strolled down the thick carpeted corridor, past little alcoves filled with people chattering away while ordering exotic cocktails. He had to agree with F. Scott Fitzgerald, the rich are different.

"Good morning, sir," said the maître d' when he reached the entrance to the restaurant. "Do you have a reservation?"

"I'm a guest of Mrs. Faulkner."

The maître d' checked his list. "Madam hasn't arrived yet, but allow me to take you to her table."

William followed him across the large, ornately decorated dining room to a window table overlooking Green Park. While he waited, he took a discreet look at the other diners. The first thing that struck him was that it could have been a gathering of the United Nations.

He rose the moment he saw Mrs. Faulkner enter the room. She was wearing an elegant green dress that fell just below the knee with a matching scarf and carrying a tan leather handbag Beth would have coveted. She sailed across the room, leaving William in no doubt that, unlike his, this wasn't her first visit to the Ritz. Despite the Hawk's warning, even he couldn't have denied her style and class.

While one waiter held back her chair, another one approached.

"Can I get you a drink, madam?"

"Just a glass of champagne, while I decide what I'm going to eat."

"Of course, madam," he said before melting away.

"I'm so glad you were able to join me for lunch, William," she said as the waiter reappeared and poured her a glass of champagne. "I was afraid you might cancel at the last minute."

"Why would I do that, Mrs. Faulkner?"

"Christina, please. Because Commander Hawksby might have felt it was inappropriate, considering how much is at stake."

"You know the commander?" asked a surprised William.

"I only know my husband's opinion of him, which is why I want him in my corner," she said as the head waiter handed them both a menu.

"I'll just have the smoked salmon, Charles," she said, not even bothering to open the menu. "And perhaps another glass of champagne."

"Yes, of course, madam."

William studied the rows of dishes that gave no hint of their price.

"And for you, sir?"

"I'll just have fish and chips, Charles." He couldn't resist adding, "And a half pint of bitter."

Christina stifled a laugh.

"Yes, of course, sir."

"Are you sure it isn't Mike Harrison you should be having this lunch with?" asked William once the waiter had left them.

"Quite sure. If anything were to go wrong, I need to know the cavalry are on my side, not just a former foot soldier."

"Then perhaps you should have asked Commander Hawksby to lunch."

"If I had," said Christina, "Miles would have known about it before they'd served coffee, and then I would have had no chance of pulling off my little coup."

"But why me?"

"If Miles is told I was seen having lunch with a good-looking young man, he'll assume we're having an affair, because that's how his mind works. And as long as you can convince your boss I'm not Mata Hari, there's a good chance the Fitzmolean will get their Rembrandt back, and I don't mean a copy."

William wanted to believe her, but Lamont's words, *That woman's up to something*, lingered in his mind. "And what would you expect in return?" he asked.

"As I'm sure you know, my husband flew off to Monte Carlo last week with his latest tart, and I'll be instructing Mr. Harrison to gather enough evidence to initiate divorce proceedings."

So Jackie saw that coming, thought William.

"I also need to know where he is night and day during the next month."

"Why is that so important?" asked William, as a plate of wafer-thin smoked salmon was placed in front of her, while he was served with cod and chips, not in a newspaper.

"I'll come to that in a moment," said Christina, as another waiter refilled her glass with champagne, and poured half a pint of bitter into a crystal tumbler for her guest.

"But first I have to let you know what I have in mind for Miles, whom I assume you despise as much as I do."

William tried to concentrate, knowing that the commander would expect a verbatim account of what Mrs. Faulkner had said from the moment she'd arrived to the moment she left.

"Do you know the great Shakespearean actor Dominic Kingston?"

"I saw his Lear at the National last year," said William. "Quite magnificent."

"Not as magnificent as his wife's recent performance."

"I didn't know she was an actress."

"She isn't," said Christina, "but she does give the occasional performance that brings the house down." William stopped eating. "It turns out that Mrs. Kingston knew her husband's theatrical routine whenever he was performing, down to the last minute, and took advantage of it. I intend to do the same. When Kingston was playing here at the National, he followed a routine that never varied. He would leave his home in Notting Hill around five in the afternoon, and be in his dressing room at the theater by six, giving him more than enough time to transform himself into the aging king before the curtain rose at seven thirty.

"The first half of the show ran for just over an hour, and the curtain came down on the second half around ten twenty. After taking his bow, Kingston would return to his dressing room, remove his makeup, shower, and change before being driven back home to Notting Hill, where he was dropped off around eleven thirty. So, from the moment he left the house, to the moment he got back home was over six hours. More than enough time."

"More than enough time for what?" asked William.

"One Thursday evening, just after six," continued Christina, "three removal vans turned up outside Mr. Kingston's home and left five hours later, by which time every stick of furniture and, more importantly, his celebrated art collection, had been removed. So when Mr. Kingston arrived home at eleven thirty, he found the cupboard was literally bare."

"Would you care for another drink, sir?" asked the wine waiter.

"No, thank you," said William, not wanting her to stop.

"I'm grateful to Mr. Kingston," continued Christina, "because I intend to create even more devastation for Miles, and, more importantly, I'll have seven days, not seven hours, in which to carry out my little subterfuge."

"Why do you need seven days?" asked William.

"Because like Mrs. Kingston, I know exactly what he has planned for the next month. On December twenty-third, he intends to dump the tart and give her a one-way ticket back to Stansted, before he flies on to Melbourne to spend Christmas with some of his more dubious friends. On December twenty-sixth, he'll be sitting in a box watching the opening day of the second Test match, so the earliest he could possibly return to Monte Carlo or England is December thirty-first. While he's engrossed in a cricket match on the other side of the world, I'll be packing up all of his most valuable paintings in Monte Carlo and shipping them to Southampton. I'll then return to England and carry out the same exercise at Limpton Hall. By the time he gets home, his treasured art collection will consist of just one picture: the copy of the Rembrandt."

The head waiter whisked away their plates while the wine waiter poured Mrs. Faulkner another glass of champagne.

"But what about Makins? He won't just sit back and watch while you pack up all your husband's paintings."

"Makins is spending Christmas with his daughter and son-in-law in the Lake District, and won't be returning until January second, by which time I'll be in New York, removing the paintings from our apartment on Fifth Avenue. A couple of Rothkos, a Warhol, and a magnificent Rauschenberg among them."

"But he'll come after you."

"I don't think so, because my final destination will be a country where he is *persona non grata,* and would be arrested even before he reached passport control. I must admit, I had several to choose from."

"You do realize that everything you've just told me will be repeated word for word to Commander Hawksby?"

"I was rather hoping you'd say that." She touched William's hand gently, before adding, "I don't know about you, darling, but I'm ready to look at the dessert menu."

◄○►

"Do you think there's any chance that she might be on the level?" asked Lamont after William had delivered a blow-by-blow account of his lunch with Mrs. Faulkner.

"Possibly," said Hawksby, "although I wouldn't bet on it. But as long as Mike Harrison's down under keeping an eye on Faulkner, there's not a lot we can do about it until she invites William to join her in Monte Carlo."

"What makes you think she'll do that?" asked William.

"Because the Rembrandt's too hot for her to handle, and she also realizes it's her one chance of keeping us on side. My bet is she won't be in touch with you again for at least a couple of weeks, by which time Carter should have been arrested and the memory of that disastrous night in Surrey might just have faded a little."

The phone on the commander's desk rang. "Commander Hawksby."

"Good afternoon, sir. It's Lieutenant Monti. I thought I'd give you a call and bring you up to date on what's been happening at our end."

198

"I appreciate that, lieutenant," said Hawksby, switching on the intercom so William could hear the conversation.

"As you know, Carter has submitted a claim to the Italian Naval Office for fifty percent of the value of the cob coins, which he's telling the press are worth around seven hundred thousand pounds."

"Which would be a fair price if they had originated from Madrid around 1649, rather than Barnstaple in 1985."

"A specimen coin has been sent to the Museum of Ancient Artifacts in Florence to be examined by their professor of numismatics. I expect to have his report on my desk in a few days' time."

"He's certain to dismiss the coin as bogus," said Hawksby.

"Bogus?"

"Not the real thing."

"I agree, sir," said Monti. "And the moment he does, all I will need is an extradition order so you can arrest Carter and Grant when they set foot back in England."

"What are those two up to at the moment?"

"They're staying at the Albergo Del Senato hotel, waiting to hear the expert's opinion."

"That'll cost them an arm and a leg," said Hawksby.

"How appropriate," added William.

"I'm not sure I understand," said Monti.

"In the sixteenth century, Italian portrait painters would paint your head and shoulders for an agreed sum, but if you wanted a full-length portrait, it would cost you an arm and a leg."

"Fascinating," said Monti.

Hawksby didn't look fascinated. "Call me the moment the professor's report lands on your desk."

"Will do, sir."

"Thank you, lieutenant."

"Actually, sir, when I next call, I may well be a captain."

"Congratulations," said Hawksby. "You've certainly earned it."

William returned to his office and stared at the pile of case files on his desk that never seemed to diminish. A tough week ahead, but at least a quiet weekend to look forward to. Just a doctor's appointment for his annual checkup on Saturday, and lunch with his parents on Sunday. Beth had promised to be back from visiting her sick friend in time for them to go to the cinema that evening, but he was disappointed that she still hadn't met his family, because he felt he couldn't propose to her before she did. "Call me old-fashioned," he could hear his father saying.

23

William arrived a few minutes early for his appointment at 31A Wimpole Street, and pressed the bell marked Dr. Ashton. He felt confident he would tick every box. After all, he ran two or three times a week, played squash regularly, and his new mantra of walking five miles a day had usually been achieved by the time he'd walked back to Fulham in the evening.

"All you'll have to do, laddie," Lamont had told him, "is touch your toes, do twenty press-ups, and cough when he grabs your balls, and you'll be clear for another year."

A buzzer sounded. William pushed the door open, walked up to the second floor, and gave the receptionist his name.

"The doctor is with another patient at the moment, Mr. Warwick, but he'll see you shortly. Please take a seat."

William sat down in an ancient leather chair and examined the limited choice of reading material neatly laid out on the coffee table. Out-of-date copies of *Punch* and *Country Life* seemed to be obligatory in every doctor's waiting room. The only other periodical on offer was a large selection of the Metropolitan Police's fortnightly newspaper, *The Job*.

After he'd exhausted the wit and wisdom of Mr. Punch and admired the photos of several country houses he would never be able to afford, William gave in and turned to copies of the Met's frayed newspapers. He flicked through several editions, only stopping when he came across a photograph of Fred Yates on an old cover. Turning to the editorial, the heroism of the mentor constable who'd saved his life stretched to four pages; William offered up another silent prayer in Fred's memory. He was just about to put the copy back on the table when the front page headline from an earlier issue caused him to catch his breath: RAINSFORD SENTENCED TO LIFE FOR MURDERING BUSINESS PARTNER. TWO MET OFFICERS PRAISED FOR THEIR HANDLING OF THE CASE.

"The doctor will see you now, Detective Constable Warwick," said the receptionist, before he'd had a chance to finish the article.

As predicted by Lamont, the examination was fairly cursory, although Dr. Ashton did check William's resting heart rate a second time, as he thought it was quite high for a man of his age.

After a page of little boxes had been filled in with ticks, William was given a clean bill of health. "See you next year," said Ashton.

"Thank you," said William as he zipped up his trousers.

Back in the waiting room, he picked up the Met newspaper and continued to read the article. If the murderer had been named Smith or Brown, he wouldn't have given the coincidence a second thought, but Rainsford was not a common name. He dropped the newspaper back on the table and tried to dismiss the thought from his mind. But he couldn't.

"You're an idiot," he said. The receptionist looked offended. "Sorry," said William. "Me, not you." But as he made his way toward the tube station, he couldn't remove the possibility from his mind, and he knew the one person who could dismiss his fears.

William got off the tube at St. James's Park and crossed the road as if it was a normal workday. He went straight to his desk and looked up the number. He was well aware that he shouldn't be making a personal call from the office, but he had no choice.

"SO Rose," said a voice.

"Good morning, sir," said William. "It's DC Warwick calling from Scotland Yard. You might not remember me. I—"

"How could I forget you, constable. The sad man who supports Fulham. What can I do for you this time?"

"I'm inquiring about one of your inmates, Arthur Rainsford, who's in for murder."

"If Rainsford's a murderer," said Rose, "I'm Jack the Ripper. Do you want to see him?"

"No, sir. But I did wonder if Rainsford is expecting a visitor today."

"Hold on a jiff, and I'll check." William could feel his heart pounding, and was only glad Dr. Ashton wasn't checking his resting pulse at that moment. "Yes, Rainsford does have a visitor this afternoon. His daughter. She's a regular. Adores her father, and of course she's absolutely convinced of his innocence. But then they always are."

"And her name?" asked William, his voice faltering.

Another pause. "Elizabeth Rainsford."

"Do you by any chance know where she works?"

"Everyone who visits an A-cat has to register where they work." After another pause Rose added, "She works at the Fitzmolean Museum. And before you ask, I'd bet my pension she had nothing to do with stealing that Rembrandt."

"It's not the Rembrandt I'm worried about."

"I'm glad to hear it."

"Thank you for your help, sir," said William, before putting down the phone.

He must have sat there for over an hour, trying to make some sense of it. He now understood why there were no photographs of Beth's father in the flat. And when she had told him that she'd called her parents in Hong Kong just after he'd arrived back from Rome, she'd obviously forgotten that it would have been the middle of the night in the Far East. He now wished he'd looked at the back of those postcards. His thoughts were interrupted when the door opened and Hawksby looked in.

"I saw a light under the door," he said, "and thought I'd just check."

William looked up at his boss, tears streaming down his face.

"What's wrong, William?" asked Hawksby, sitting down next to him.

"How long have you known?"

Hawksby didn't reply immediately. "Since the theft of the Rembrandt, we've done regular background checks on everyone who works at the Fitzmolean, and her father's name popped up. I discussed the problem with Bruce after you started seeing her, and we both assumed she must have told you about her father."

"I've only just found out."

"I'm very sorry," said Hawksby, placing a hand on his shoulder. "We all know how you feel about her, and Jackie warned us that it could be serious."

"I've just discovered how serious," said William. "Now I don't know what to do."

"If I were advising you, I'd suggest you tell your father everything. He's a shrewd and thoughtful man, and one thing's for sure, he won't just give you the answer you want to hear."

"Do you remember the case, sir?"

"Not well, but I do recall the two officers involved, Stern and Clarkson. DI Stern retired soon after the trial ended, and frankly it wasn't a day too soon. But now you know, what are you going to do about it?"

"Go home and wait for Beth to get back from Pentonville."

"Why not go straight to the prison? Be there when she comes out, so you can take her home."

William didn't answer, just sat staring into the distance as if he hadn't heard him.

"And if you're going to make it in time," added Hawksby, looking at his watch, "you'd better get a move on."

"Of course you're right, sir," said William. He jumped up, grabbed his coat, and dashed toward the door, only turning back to say, "Thank you."

Once he was out on the street, William hailed the first taxi he spotted.

"Where to, guv?"

"Pentonville prison."

"That's all I need," mumbled the cabbie as William climbed in the back.

"What's the problem?"

"There couldn't be a worse journey for a cab driver."

"How come?"

"If you take someone to Pentonville, you never get a return fare, because most of them are in for life!" William laughed, which he wouldn't have thought possible only a few minutes ago. "Are you checkin' in or just visitin'?"

"Picking up my girlfriend."

"I didn't know there were women prisoners at Pentonville."

"There aren't. She's visiting her father."

"Nothing serious, I hope."

"Murder."

The long silence that followed allowed William to compose his thoughts, and plan what he would say when Beth saw him standing outside the prison. She would be shocked at first, possibly unable to believe he wanted to share her problems, and not walk away.

The cab swung off the main road and headed down a side street toward a high brick wall that almost blocked out the sun. They came to a halt at a barrier, when the driver said, "This is as far as I'm allowed to go."

William stared up at a vast wooden gate. A sign outside read HMP PENTONVILLE.

"Will you be going in, guv?"

"No, I'll wait outside."

"Do you want me to drive you both back into town?"

"Not possible, I'm afraid," said William after he'd checked the meter and handed over his last couple of pounds. "I've barely got enough to cover the bus ride back."

"Have this one on me, guv. I've got to go back in any case."

"That's very generous of you, but it could be some time be-fore—"

"Not a problem. And it might make up for me not minding my own business."

"Thank you," said William, as a side door opened that allowed only one person at a time to leave the prison. A trickle of visitors began to emerge onto the street.

For many of those who had been visiting relatives or friends this was just another Saturday afternoon. But some crept away with their heads bowed, while others clearly wanted to escape as quickly as possible. Mothers, fathers, wives, girlfriends, some carrying babies, all of them with a story to tell. And then she appeared, looking drained, tears streaming down her face. When Beth first saw him she froze, clearly horrified that she'd been found out.

William walked quickly toward her and took her in his arms.

"I love you," he said, "and I always will."

He felt her body slump, and he almost had to hold her up.

Several visitors walked past them as she continued to cling on to him, like a prisoner who had just been released.

"I'm so sorry," she said, not letting go of him. "I should have told you when we first met, but it became more difficult as each day passed. I didn't plan to fall in love with you. Can you ever forgive me?"

"There's nothing to forgive," said William, taking her hand. He opened the cab door for Beth before joining her in the back.

"Where to, guv?"

"Thirty-two Fulham Gardens," he said as Beth rested her head on his shoulder.

"When did you find out?"

"This morning."

"I'd understand if you wanted to move out."

"I'll say this once, Beth, and only once. You're stuck with me, so get used to it."

"But—"

"There are no buts."

"There is one but," she said quietly. "You have to understand that I'm in no doubt my father is innocent."

That's what they all say, William could hear SO Rose repeating. "It doesn't matter to me," he said, trying to reassure her. "I don't care either way."

"But it does matter to me," said Beth, "because I'm determined to clear his name if it's the last thing I do."

They sat in silence for some time before William said, "Can I ask one thing of you?"

"Anything. I've always assumed you'd leave me the moment you found out about my father. So anything."

"As you know, my father is one of the leading barristers at the Criminal Bar."

"And I foolishly fell in love with his son."

"If I were to ask him to review the case and give an unbiased opinion, would you be willing to accept his judgment?"

Beth didn't respond immediately, but after some thought she said, "That's the least I can do."

"And would you also be willing to move on if it's not what you wanted to hear?"

"That might be a little more difficult."

"Well, at least it's a start," said William. "If you'll come to lunch with my family tomorrow, you can tell my old man why you're so convinced your father is innocent."

"I'm not quite ready for that," said Beth, taking his hand. "The day after I've visited my father is almost worse. Sometimes I just cry all day, and can't wait for Monday when I can get back to work. One step at a time, please. When we get home, I'll tell you the whole story, but it might be some time before I can face your father's judgment."

"But you'll have to meet him eventually, whatever he decides, because my parents will want to meet the woman I'm going to marry."

Most proposals are followed by joy and celebration; Beth wept.

When the cab drew up outside their home, William got out and thanked the cabbie.

"My pleasure, guv, and I have to admit, that's the first time someone's proposed in the back of my cab."

He made William laugh for a second time.

William opened the front door and stood aside to let Beth in. The first thing she did was go straight to the study and take down all the postcards from the mantelpiece, tear them into bits, and drop them in the wastepaper basket. She then opened the bottom drawer of the desk, took out a photograph of her parents, and placed it on the mantelpiece.

"No more secrets," she said, as they went through to the kitchen. "In future, only the truth."

William nodded, leaned across the table, and took her hand as she began to tell him how and why her father had been convicted of murder and sentenced to life imprisonment.

He occasionally interrupted to ask her a question, and by the time they went to bed, he also wanted to believe that Arthur Rainsford just might be innocent. But he knew his father would be far more demanding and skeptical when considering the facts of the case than an inexperienced detective constable and a young woman who obviously adored her father unreservedly. They both agreed to abide by Sir Julian's judgment.

◄○►

On Sunday morning, after a sleepless night, William had far more questions than answers to consider as he prepared to face his father. When he left for the station after breakfast, neither he nor Beth was in any doubt about what was at stake.

Although William sat gazing out of the carriage window, he was unaware of the countryside rushing by. When he got off at Shoreham, he decided to walk the last couple of miles to Nettleford so he could compose his thoughts and go over what he planned to say, aware that he would be facing not just his father but one of the leading advocates in the land.

When the thatched cottage in which he had been brought up came into sight, he began to walk more slowly. He opened the front door, knowing it would be on the latch, and found his father sitting in his study by the fire, reading the *Observer*.

"Good to see you, my boy," he said, putting down the paper. "Have you found that Rembrandt yet?"

"Father, I've met the woman I'm going to marry."

"That's wonderful news. Your mother will be delighted. So why isn't the young lady joining us for lunch?"

"Because her father's serving a life sentence for murder."

◄○►

Sir Julian Warwick QC sat at the head of the table and listened attentively to his son as he told the family how his life had changed in the last twenty-four hours.

"I can't wait to meet her," said his mother. "She sounds very special."

Sir Julian didn't offer an opinion.

"Do you remember the case, Father?" asked Grace when William had come to the end of his story.

"I have a vague recollection of the trial, but no more than that. Rainsford condemned himself when he confessed to the crime in the presence of two senior police officers."

"But—" began William.

"However, I will read the court transcripts, and if I can see even a smidgen of doubt, I'll visit Rainsford in Pentonville and listen to his side of the story. But I have to warn you, William, that the DPP will not agree to a retrial unless there is fresh evidence to suggest a miscarriage of justice may have taken place. It's rare, but not unknown. So I'm glad to know that Beth has agreed to move on, if I consider her father's case not worth challenging."

"Thank you, Father. I couldn't have asked for more."

"If you visit Mr. Rainsford," said Grace, "can I come with you?"

"For what purpose, may I ask?"

"Because if you consider he might be innocent, and if new evidence were to come to light, and if—"

"If, if, if. Where is all this leading?"

"If you decide to take on the case, and it comes before the high court, you'll need a junior."

24

"I'll be in touch Ross," said the commander, when he heard a knock on the door. The three of them walked in and took their seats around the table in Hawksby's office for the Monday morning meeting. They all knew there was an elephant in the room, but the commander was determined to carry on as if it was business as usual.

"I've just heard that Kevin Carter has been seen back in Barnstaple," began Lamont, "and according to the local police, his house is up for sale."

"So Carter must have finally found out the truth," said William, "and it looks as if Faulkner has even covered his expenses."

"Perhaps it's time we had another chat with Lieutenant Monti," suggested Hawksby. "He must have had the professor's findings so we should start making preparations to arrest Carter."

"Nothing would give me greater pleasure," said Lamont, "than to go down to Barnstaple and arrest the bastard myself."

"And possibly also the man behind the whole scam," said William.

"Even better."

"Perhaps Monti even knows who that is," said Hawksby. "I'll call him now and put him on speaker phone so we can all hear what he has to say. If either of you have a point to make, don't interrupt me. Write your thoughts down and pass them across." He didn't wait for a response as he looked up the number and began to dial.

An unfamiliar ringing tone followed, and it was some time before the call was answered.

"Good morning, my name is Commander Hawksby—"

"Sorry, no speak English."

A long silence followed, but there was no purring sound to indicate he'd been cut off.

"Good morning. Captain Loretti speaking. How may I help you?"

"Good morning, captain, this is Commander Hawksby calling from Scotland Yard. I was hoping to have a word with Lieutenant Monti concerning a case we are both working on."

"Lieutenant Monti is no longer with us, sir. But I can tell you the matter you are referring to has been satisfactorily resolved."

"Resolved? But we agreed to wait until Monti had received a report from the professor at the Museum of Ancient Artifacts in Florence, when we would announce simultaneously that the Spanish cob coins were fakes, and the whole salvage operation was a scam."

"That is not my understanding of the situation," said the captain. "The professor from Florence verified an example of the coins as genuine, and as a result the Italian Naval Office has officially declared them treasure trove. It was well reported in the Italian press. And the good news, commander, is that Lieutenant Monti pulled off a bit of a coup for this department."

"What form did this coup take?" asked Hawksby, trying to remain calm.

"Following several days of tough negotiations, the Italian Naval Office agreed on a valuation of the rest of the coins that was well below the amount proposed by Mr. Carter's representative."

"How much?" spat out Hawksby.

"Six hundred thousand pounds, of which the Italian government only had to pay out three hundred thousand. So Lieutenant Monti's skillful negotiations saved the government some fifty thousand pounds."

"One coin?" whispered William, breaking the commander's orders.

"Lieutenant Monti sent only one coin to be examined by the professor?" asked Hawksby.

"Yes," said the captain. "The remainder were kept under lock and key in Rome. Monti considered it would be pointless and unnecessarily risky to send the entire casket to Florence." Lamont scribbled a few words on a scrap of paper and passed it to Hawksby.

"You said Lieutenant Monti is no longer with you . . ."

"That is correct, commander. He recently took early retirement."

"But when I last spoke to him, he mentioned the possibility of promotion."

"Yes, it was all very sudden," said Captain Loretti. "It seems his mother is suffering from cancer, and he felt that as her only child he ought to resign and return home to look after her. Quite a sacrifice, because, you're correct, he was just about to be promoted to captain and made head of the department."

Where is he? wrote William.

"Is there any way I can get in touch with him?" asked Hawksby.

"We have a forwarding address in Sicily where I think his family comes from."

Lamont threw his arms in the air. "I should have been born in Italy," he muttered as William wrote down another suggestion for the Hawk to consider.

"One more question, if I may," said Hawksby. "Can I ask who conducted the negotiations on behalf of Carter?"

"One moment please, commander, while I check."

William wrote down a name and waited for the captain to confirm it.

"Ah yes, here it is," said Loretti. "A lawyer from Lincoln's Inn, in London. A Mr. Booth Watson QC."

"Thank you, captain," said Hawksby, trying not to sound exasperated.

"My pleasure, commander. It is always a privilege to work alongside our colleagues in the Metropolitan Police."

Hawksby slammed the phone down as Lamont repeated the same four-letter word again and again.

"Why don't we go ahead and arrest Carter anyway?" said William calmly.

"And break off any relationship we still have with the Italian police? No, I don't think that would please the politicians in either country."

"So there's absolutely nothing we can do about it?" asked William.

"Except shoot Miles Faulkner, and hope there's a bullet left over for Booth Watson," said Lamont.

"Calm down, Bruce, we have no proof that Faulkner is involved. Let's take a deep breath and move on."

"Whatever you say, boss," said Lamont, "but there was one more question I would have liked you to ask." Hawksby indulged him with a nod. "How many people who work in the Italian Naval Office also took early retirement?" he said before storming out of the room.

William was about to follow when Hawksby said, "Don't forget your files, DC Warwick."

"But I didn't—" began William, as he turned around and saw two thick files lying on the table. He picked them up and left the room without another word. When he arrived back in his office he found Lamont punching a telephone directory.

"Faulkner or Carter?" asked William innocently.

"The system," barked Lamont. "That always gives the crooks an advantage."

William sat down at his desk and opened the first of the two files Hawksby had left on the table. He only had to turn a few pages to realize what a risk the commander was taking.

◄○►

"Where did you get these?" asked Grace after a cursory glance at the contents.

"I can't tell you," said William.

She continued turning the pages. "They look promising, but I'll have to read them more thoroughly when I get home this evening, and then brief my leader first thing in the morning."

"Does that mean Dad has agreed to visit Mr. Rainsford in Pentonville?"

"Yes. He spent the rest of the weekend reading the transcripts from the original trial, accompanied by ums, ahs, and even the occasional 'disgraceful.'"

"So does he think there might be a chance . . ."

"No, he does not," said Grace firmly. "However, he does think that he owes it to you to visit Mr. Rainsford before he offers his considered opinion."

"Can I come along?"

"Yes, but on one condition."

"And what might that be?"

"When Father begins to cross-examine Mr. Rainsford, you will not, under any circumstances, interrupt him. If you do, he will leave the meeting and withdraw from the case altogether."

"I still want to come."

"Then don't take his threat lightly."

"Will you be there too?"

"Yes, he's appointed me as his junior for the case, and given me the unenviable task of coming up with some fresh evidence that would make it possible for him to apply for a retrial."

"Anything so far?"

"Nothing, but it's early days. And if I'm going to read these files on DI Stern and DC Clarkson before midnight, I'd better get started."

"Will you let your friend Clare read them?"

"She's agreed to be the instructing solicitor on the case."

"That's good of her," said William. "Now we'll just have to wait to hear Dad's verdict."

"Just be thankful he's in your corner. Because if he thinks there's been a miscarriage of justice, he'll not only come out fighting like the heavyweight he is, but he'll go the whole fifteen rounds."

25

Sir Julian, Grace, and William each made their way to HMP Pentonville by different modes of transport: William by bus from Fulham—two changes; Grace by tube from Notting Hill—one change; and Sir Julian in a chauffeur-driven car from Shoreham in Kent.

They all met up in reception, where a prison officer signed them in.

"Rainsford's waiting for you," said the officer, before accompanying them to the interview room. Arthur Rainsford rose as they entered the glass cube and shook hands with his three visitors.

"I don't know how to thank you for your kindness, Sir Julian," he said. "I feel I already know your son because whenever Beth visits me, she talks of little else. Though I find it somewhat ironic that my daughter fell in love with a detective, as my experience of policemen hasn't been particularly happy."

"I think you'll find it was me who fell in love with her," said William, as the two men shook hands for the first time and took their seats around the table. "By the way, she sends her love, and is looking forward to seeing you on Saturday."

"Thank you," said Rainsford. "I'm looking forward to seeing her too."

Up until that moment Sir Julian hadn't spoken, although his eyes had never left the prisoner as he tried to make an assessment of the man, something he always did whenever he met a potential client for the first time. He knew from Rainsford's charge sheet that he was fifty-three years old, almost six feet, and had a broken nose from his days as a college boxer. He suspected that Rainsford's hair had turned gray since he'd been in prison. He looked fit, which suggested he spent his voluntary hour each afternoon in the gym rather than strolling around the yard smoking, and also that he avoided the usual prison diet of sausage, beans, and chips. He was softly spoken, clearly well educated, and certainly didn't look like a murderer. However, Sir Julian had learned over the years that murderers come in all shapes and sizes, some with first-class honors degrees, others who had left school at fourteen.

"I have, Mr. Rainsford—" began Sir Julian.

"Arthur, please."

"I have, Mr. Rainsford, read the transcript of your trial most carefully, examined the evidence presented by the Crown, considered your testimony from the witness box, and gone over your confession word for word. However, as this is the first time any of us have met you, I would like to hear your side of the story. Forgive me if I occasionally interrupt to ask you to clarify a point or ask a question."

"Of course, Sir Julian. I was born in Epsom, where my father was a GP, and from an early age he hoped I would follow in his footsteps. I did well enough at school to be offered a place to study medicine at University College Hospital, which pleased my father. But it didn't take me long to realize I wasn't cut out to be a doctor. So, much to his disappointment, I hung up my short white coat in exchange for a long black gown and transferred to the LSE to study economics, which I enjoyed from the opening lecture.

"After I'd graduated, I joined Barclays Bank as a trainee, but once again I quickly realized I wasn't by nature a corporate animal. So in the evenings I returned to the LSE and took a business degree, which was how I finally discovered my natural vocation. With too many letters after my name and too little income, I joined a merchant bank in the City."

"Which one?" asked Sir Julian.

"Kleinwort Benson. I began life in their small business division, and spent the next three years helping the bank's customers to expand their companies. Nothing gave me greater pleasure than to see them become larger businesses.

"I had two close friends at the time, Hamish Galbraith, an old school chum, and Gary Kirkland, whom I'd met at the LSE. Hamish joined John Lewis as a trainee manager after he left school. He had a natural flair with people, and the gift of getting the best out of them. Gary was far brighter than both of us, but spent most of his time as an undergraduate drinking and socializing. Frankly I was surprised he got a degree, let alone came out near the top of his year. He became an accountant in the City and enjoyed reading spreadsheets more than novels.

"One Friday night when we'd all had a little too much to drink, Hamish suggested we should set up our own business. I spent the rest of the weekend wondering if he could be right. After all, I'd spent the past three years advising others on how to expand their companies, so perhaps I was ready to set up one myself. I prepared the same detailed proposal I would have expected from any prospective client, with myself as the salesman, Hamish as the company's office manager, and Gary as the accountant. I then presented my thoughts to my would-be partners."

"With what result?" asked Sir Julian.

"They both naturally wanted to know what the company would do. I told them we should open a boutique investment business and take advantage of my knowledge of and contacts in the field of medicine. Some exciting discoveries were being made in that area at the time, which offered promising investment opportunities.

"It was another six months before the three of us had the courage to hand in our resignations, and I might not have done so even then if my boss at Kleinwort's hadn't encouraged me, and offered to put up the initial seed capital in exchange for fifty percent of the company."

Grace was busily taking notes; William wanted to ask several questions; while Sir Julian, sphinx-like, sat and listened impassively.

"We set up RGK Ltd. in 1961, and rented a couple of rooms in Marylebone, but could only afford one secretary between the three of us. I traveled around the country visiting doctors and hospitals, while also attending medical conferences. The company just about broke even during our first five years, but all that changed overnight when I invested some of our clients' money in a small pharmaceutical company not long before it developed beta blockers. The following year we made a fourteen percent profit for our backers, and suddenly we were flavor of the month, with potential investors as well as with researchers in need of capital.

"We celebrated our tenth anniversary by buying back our fifty percent shareholding from Kleinwort's and renting another floor in Marylebone."

William now had several questions he was desperate to ask, but one look at his sister reminded him that it would be unwise to go down that path.

"Over the next few years, Beth was the only thing that was growing faster than the company. Despite the economic uncertainties of the seventies, we still felt confident about the future. However, I didn't see the problem coming, even when it was staring me in the face. I knew Gary's marriage was in trouble, and shouldn't have been surprised when it ended in an expensive divorce. In the years that followed I saw so many women come and go that I couldn't always remember their names. But I didn't say anything, even when his behavior in the office caused one of our young secretaries to resign, while another threatened to sue the company and we ended up having to settle out of court.

"I was on the road five days a week drumming up business, so I didn't realize the full extent of the problem until the night of the office Christmas party, when Gary got drunk and made a pass at my secretary, who was married. She resigned the following day, and the company gave her a generous settlement after she agreed to sign a nondisclosure agreement.

"Hamish and I made it clear to Gary that if he stepped out of line again, he would have to resign. To be fair, we never had another complaint from that moment, and a couple of years later Gary announced that he was engaged to the love of his life, and was looking forward to getting married again, and finally settling down.

"His fiancée, Bridget, was attractive and bright, and gave every impression of being devoted to him. But it turned out that she was only interested in his money, and it didn't take her long to empty his bank account. She then broke off the engagement and went in search of her next victim, leaving Gary to pick up the pieces. Sadly, it wasn't too long before the women in the office began once again to complain about his behavior, even when he was sober. But when Beth told me after a leaving party that she now understood why he was known in the office as 'wandering hands,' I finally lost my temper and accepted that he had to go.

"I would have demanded his resignation the next day if I hadn't had an appointment in Coventry with a potential investor that had been in my diary for the past month. I called Hamish to let him know what I had in mind, and we agreed I should wait until I got back the following day, when we would issue Gary a joint ultimatum. Resign or be sacked.

"I had a fruitful meeting with my potential new client, and invited him to lunch afterward. Over coffee, he mentioned the sum that he was considering investing in RGK, which was even more than I had anticipated.

"But when I handed over my company credit card to pay for the meal, an embarrassed waiter returned a few minutes later and whispered that it had been declined. Not clever in front of a prospective investor. I paid with my personal card, but the damage had been done. I called my bank manager from the station and demanded an explanation. After all, the company had declared a profit of over a million pounds the previous year. He told me we'd exceeded our overdraft limit, and that he'd spoken to Mr. Kirkland about the situation several times.

"I immediately rang Gary and he denied that there was any problem. He suggested I drop by on my way home, and he would explain everything. As soon as I got off the train at Euston, I took a cab to the office.

"As I was opening the front door, a short, heavily built man, whom I thought I recognized, brushed past me and ran out into the street. I went up to Gary's office on the first floor and found him lying spreadeagled on the carpet.

"I rushed over to him, but I didn't need a medical degree to realize he was dead. His jaw had been broken, and there was a deep gash on the back of his skull. I was about to call the police when I heard a siren in the street outside, and moments later half a dozen policemen burst into the room to find me kneeling over the body. The next thing I knew one of them was reading me my rights."

"Did you say anything at the time?" asked Sir Julian.

"Only that they'd got the wrong man. I assumed the whole matter would quickly be cleared up. I was driven to the nearest police station, and left alone in a cell for a couple of hours. Eventually I was taken to an interview room where two detectives were waiting for me."

"Would that have been DI Stern and DC Clarkson?" asked Sir Julian.

"That's right. I told them exactly what had happened, but it was obvious they'd already made up their minds, and nothing was going to convince them otherwise. But they did let slip during the interview that they'd had a tip-off from an anonymous caller, which explained why the police had got there so quickly."

Grace made a note, and pushed it across the table to her father, who studied it carefully.

"And you pointed out during your trial that this was irrefutable proof that someone else must have killed your partner."

"Yes, I also suggested that the man who'd come running out of the building might have been the same man who phoned them, but they weren't interested."

"And then what happened?"

"Stern asked me if I was prepared to make a statement.

Of course I was, as I had nothing to hide. He wrote down my words, and I double-checked each page before signing it, not least because I could smell alcohol on his breath."

Grace made another note.

"You claimed during the trial that your original statement was three pages in length, whereas the version read out in court was only two. So I have to ask, Mr. Rainsford, did you sign all three pages?"

"Yes, I did. The first two with the initials AR, but I wrote my full name on the third page."

"Were the three pages numbered?"

"I can't remember."

"How convenient. When the police submitted your statement as evidence before the trial, there were only two pages, clearly numbered one and two, and on the bottom of the second page, two of two, was your full signature, along with those of DI Stern and DC Clarkson. How do you explain that?"

"The only explanation I can think of," said Rainsford, "is that someone must have removed the middle page and added the numbers later."

"The mystery man, perhaps?" said Sir Julian. "What happened next?"

"I appeared before a magistrate the following morning and my application for bail was refused. I was placed on remand and sent to Pentonville to await trial."

"Which took place five months later, while you remained in custody."

"Yes. But I was still confident the jury would accept that my statement had been three pages, and not two, because I was able to reproduce every word I'd written on the missing page."

"However, Mr. Justice Melrose would not allow you to submit your missing page as evidence. At the end of the trial, did you feel the judge summed up the case fairly, without bias or prejudice?"

"I did. His summation was fair and well balanced, which only made me more convinced that the jury would come down in my favor."

"But they didn't."

"No, they were out for four days, and even longer nights. On the fifth day, they found me guilty of murder by a majority of ten to two. The next morning, Mr. Justice Melrose sentenced me to life, with a recommendation that I should be eligible for parole after twelve years. I've now served two years of that sentence."

Grace made another note and underlined the word "twelve," before passing it to her father.

"Did you at any time consider changing your plea to guilty of manslaughter?" asked Sir Julian. "Struck him in the heat of the moment, never meant to kill him, will regret it for the rest of my life?"

"But I didn't strike him, Sir Julian. My solicitor made the same suggestion at the time, and told me he was confident if I agreed to change my plea I'd only get four years, and be out in two, but I turned him down."

"Why?"

"Because my solicitor, like you, didn't believe I was innocent."

"But you can't deny, Mr. Rainsford, that you lost your temper when you learned your daughter had been sexually harassed by Mr. Kirkland, and you became even more angry when you discovered that he had been embezzling money from the company to pay for his different women. So why should the jury believe that there were three pages in your statement and not two, and that the murder was committed by a mystery man who appeared out of nowhere and then conveniently disappeared into thin air, never to be seen again?"

"Because it's the truth, Sir Julian," said Rainsford. He put his elbows on the table and placed his head in his hands. "But of course I can understand why you don't believe me."

A long silence followed, while the other three waited for Sir Julian to pick up his Gladstone bag and disappear, also never to be seen again.

"But I do believe you, Arthur," he said quietly. "I am now in no doubt that you did not murder your partner."

Arthur looked up in disbelief to see the distinguished QC smiling at him.

"What finally convinced you, Father?" asked William, ignoring his sister's gimlet eye.

"Three things, completely unconnected, which, had the jury been made aware of at the time, might well have caused them to reach a different verdict." Sir Julian couldn't resist pacing up and down before he delivered his closing statement. "In all my years at the Bar, I have never known a murderer who wouldn't have settled for a plea of guilty to manslaughter and a reduced sentence."

"And the second reason?" asked Grace.

"The length of time before Arthur is eligible for parole."

"Twelve years," said William.

"Precisely. Because Mr. Justice Melrose is known in the trade as 'Life Means Life' Melrose. I checked his record last night, and he's presided over twenty-four murder trials during his time on the Crown Court bench when the defendant was found guilty. Arthur is the only one he gave a minimum term of twelve years. Why would 'Life Means Life' Melrose break the habit of a lifetime? Could it be that he also wasn't convinced Arthur was guilty?"

"And the third thing?" asked Grace.

"We have William to thank for that."

Once again, Sir Julian couldn't resist a brief perambulation around the room before sharing his thoughts. He pulled at the lapels of a gown he wasn't wearing before he spoke.

"You told me, William, that when you first mentioned Arthur's name to SO Rose, his immediate response was, 'If Rainsford's a murderer, I'm Jack the Ripper.' In my experience, a senior prison officer would never admit, even in private, that any prisoner just might be innocent."

"So does that mean you'll take the case, Father?" asked Grace.

"We already have, my dear. And with it, we take on the considerable task of uncovering fresh evidence to convince the DPP that they should order a retrial. Because if they don't, our personal opinions are irrelevant."

"Not quite, Sir Julian," said Arthur, "because I'm delighted that my future son-in-law knows I'm innocent."

26

The phone began to ring.

"Who would even consider calling us on Christmas Day?" demanded Sir Julian. "And just as I'm about to carve the turkey."

"Mea culpa," said William, "I'm afraid I might have told the office where I'd be."

"Then you'd better go and answer it while the rest of us enjoy our Christmas lunch. Beth, would you prefer a leg or breast?"

William quickly left for his father's study and picked up the ringing phone. "William Warwick."

"Christina Faulkner. Happy Christmas, William."

"Happy Christmas, Christina. Where are you calling from?"

"Monte Carlo."

"Unwrapping presents, no doubt."

"No, wrapping them up, actually, which is why I called. I need you to come and join me as soon as possible so I can give you your present, which I'm looking at now."

"I'll have to call my boss," said William, who would have happily left immediately. "And as long as he gives his blessing, I could fly over tomorrow afternoon."

"No later than that," said Christina, "because once I've finished packing, all sixty-nine crates will be loaded onto Miles's yacht."

"Will you also be on board?"

"No, that's not part of my plan. Once the *Christina*—named in happier times—has set sail for Southampton, I'll be flying back to Heathrow. I'll then be driven to Limpton Hall to wrap up some more of my presents, which have to be ready in time for the re-movers who will be turning up the following morning and taking them to Southampton, where they'll also be placed on board the *Christina*. It's all in the timing."

"Dare I ask what happens after that?"

"All will be revealed when I see you in Monte Carlo tomorrow. Give me a call when you know which flight you're on, and I'll send a car to pick you up."

"I'll phone you back once I've spoken to the commander. Good-bye, Christina, and happy Christmas." William put the phone down and returned to the dining room. How much he wanted to tell them, and Beth in particular, that by this time tomorrow he might be in possession of the Rembrandt. He sat down next to his fiancée, to find an empty plate in front of him.

"You missed the main course, my boy. But not to worry, I'm sure there'll be some pudding left over."

"Ignore him," said his mother. "We haven't even started yet. Joanna's been telling us what she's been up to in Arthur's absence."

William smiled at Beth's mother, as he helped himself to some brussel sprouts.

"When Arthur first went to prison," said Joanna, "we all assumed that the company would be wound up. But we quickly discovered that Hamish was made of sterner stuff when he continued to run the office as if Arthur was still out on the road.

"Meanwhile Arthur set up office in his cell at Pentonville, while I sat at his desk in Marylebone. I wrote to him every day, keeping him up to date."

"But what happened when someone made an appointment to see the chairman, only to find that he was in prison?" asked Grace.

"After a while I took his place and even began to travel around the country visiting the company's clients. I was pleasantly sur-prised by how few of them deserted us."

"Reputation is the shield of the righteous in difficult times," said Sir Julian.

"Who said that?" asked William.

"I did, you insolent child. But please continue, Joanna. You'd lost your accountant, and your bank must also have been apprehensive."

"Barclays did everything they could to help," said Joanna, "but it was Kleinwort Benson who came to our rescue and gave the investors the confidence to stick with us. And then, when we least expected it, we had a stroke of luck."

Everyone at the table stopped eating.

"Gary Kirkland hadn't written a will, and his son Hugh inherited everything, including his father's gift for figures, so he now sits in Gary's old office and accounts for every penny the company spends. And before you ask, unlike his father, he's happily married."

"So does that mean the company's back on track?" asked Grace.

"No, we're just about breaking even, but once Arthur returns, we should soon be showing a profit."

"No pressure then," said Sir Julian as the phone rang again. "Are we having our Christmas lunch in the BT Tower?" he asked, letting out an exaggerated sigh. "As it's bound to be for you, William, why don't you invite whoever it is to join us in the hope that we won't be interrupted again."

William scurried out of the room and returned to his father's study. He grabbed the phone, assuming it would be the commander. "William Warwick."

"Sorry to bother you on Christmas Day," said a voice that could only have hailed from New York, "but I need to speak to Ms. Grace Warwick on a personal matter."

"May I ask who's calling?"

"Leonard Abrahams."

"Please hold on, Mr. Abrahams, and I'll let her know you're on the phone."

William quickly returned to the dining room. "It's for you, Sis. Leonard Abrahams?"

"Would you tell whoever it is, Grace, that we were rather hoping to have one course at which the whole family are present."

"I think it might be the professor," said Grace.

"Then you'd better speak to him immediately," said Sir Julian, his tone suddenly changing.

Grace nodded and quickly left the room.

"Professor Abrahams, it's Grace Warwick. I'm sorry to have kept you waiting."

"No, Ms. Warwick, it is I who should apologize. I wouldn't have considered disturbing you on Christmas Day if it hadn't been urgent, but I thought you'd want to know that I'll be in London tomorrow."

"That's wonderful news. Where will you be staying?"

"Probably in an airport lounge. I only have a four-hour layover before my connecting flight for Warsaw, where I'll be visiting my dear mother. We Jews are cunning," the professor added. "We always know when you Gentiles are on holiday, and as long as we're back at our desks the day after Boxing Day, you don't even notice we've been away."

Grace laughed. "Have you had a chance to read the trial depositions I sent you?"

"I've only glanced through them. But I'll work on them more thoroughly during my flight, so by the time I reach Heathrow I should be able to give you a preliminary opinion."

"I'll book a room at the Airport Hilton, so we're not disturbed. What time should I expect you?"

"I'm on Pan Am flight 716 out of JFK, landing around ten twenty in the morning, your time."

"Then I'll be at the arrivals gate waiting for you."

"That's kind of you. But how will you recognize me?"

"Don't worry, I've read your book."

"It's a few years since that photo was taken," he said with a chuckle. "But I look forward to seeing you tomorrow, Ms. Warwick, and once again, I apologize for having disturbed you on Christmas Day."

"Don't give it a thought. I know my father will be delighted to hear your news."

Grace slipped back into the dining room and took her seat

without a word, although William noticed the nod that passed between the two lawyers.

"Allow me to warn all of you," said Sir Julian as Marjorie passed him the brandy butter, "that should anyone consider calling while Her Majesty is delivering her Christmas message to the nation at three o'clock, the phone will go unanswered, even if it's the Archbishop of Canterbury."

◄○►

William checked in at Heathrow just after nine the following morning. He didn't tell Beth where he was going, and she didn't ask. A ticket for Nice was waiting for him at the BA counter.

Much to his father's disapproval, he had called Scotland Yard only moments after the Queen's message had ended. The switchboard put him straight through to the commander's home.

When Hawksby heard William's news, he said, "Book yourself onto the first available flight to Nice. If Mrs. Faulkner is in possession of the Rembrandt, we can't afford to keep her waiting. Whatever happens, let me know immediately, no matter what time of the day or night, because I won't be getting much sleep until I find out."

William fastened his seatbelt as the plane taxied out onto the north runway.

◄○►

Grace was dropped off at Heathrow just after ten, and checked the arrivals board to find that Pan Am flight 716 was running twenty minutes late. She bought a copy of *The Guardian* and a cappuccino, sat down and waited.

When LANDED flicked up on the board next to flight 716, she took her place behind a barrier heaving with impatient greeters.

Professor Abrahams was among the first passengers to come through the gate, as his luggage was being transferred directly to a connecting flight for Warsaw. He came to a halt and scanned the crowd. When she spotted him, Grace was taken by surprise.

The photograph on the back of his book didn't reveal that he was barely five feet tall. But his massive domed forehead and thick pebble glasses made him instantly recognizable, even if the yellow tracksuit and the latest Nike trainers did come as something of a surprise.

"I always wear a tracksuit on a long-haul flight," he explained as they shook hands. "I got the idea from Joan Collins, but unlike her, I don't change back for the photographers before getting off the plane."

"I thought we'd walk across to the Hilton," said Grace. "It's not far, and as there's always a long queue for a taxi, we'll probably get there quicker."

"And save a few dollars," said the professor as they walked the short distance to the hotel, chatting about everything except the one subject that was on both of their minds. Grace had booked a suite for two hours, and the receptionist handed her the room key thinking they were an unusual couple to be booking a private room at that time in the morning.

As Grace made the professor a cup of steaming black coffee, he took a file out of his briefcase and placed it on the table between them. He began to turn the pages while giving her a running commentary, as if he were teaching a bright undergraduate attending one of his lectures on how his particular expertise might—he kept repeating the word "might"—be of assistance in the Rainsford case. Once he'd turned the last page, he dealt with all of Grace's queries with an assurance that didn't brook contradiction. By the time he'd answered her last question, Grace knew she'd found the right man.

Abrahams checked his watch and put the file back in his briefcase. "I ought to get moving if I'm going to make my flight," he said, as he rose from his chair. "Can't afford to be late for my mother. She's probably already at the airport waiting for me."

Grace accompanied Abrahams back to terminal two, and before he went through to the departures gate she thanked him once again and asked, "Can I tell my father that you'd be willing to appear as an expert witness, if there's a retrial?"

"I wouldn't have wasted your time if I hadn't been willing to do that, young lady. However, I still need to see Rainsford's original two-page statement that was presented as evidence in court before I'll know if I'd be wasting mine."

━◦━

Professor Abrahams boarded his plane for Warsaw just as William landed in Nice. As William only had hand luggage, he headed straight for passport control and was among the first to step out into the concourse, where he was greeted by a man holding up a placard reading WARWICK.

He sank into the back seat of a Bentley and tried to compose his thoughts before meeting up with Christina Faulkner again. However, the driver had other ideas.

By the time they reached the Villa Rosa, William knew the driver's views on everything from the Pompidou Center, designed by an Englishman, to the Common Market, which Britain should never have joined in the first place. However, he didn't once raise the only subject William would have liked to know more about: Mr. and Mrs. Faulkner.

A vast pair of wrought-iron gates swung open when the car was still a hundred yards from the entrance. They turned into a long drive lined with tall cypress trees on both sides, which ended in front of a handsome belle époque villa that made Limpton Hall look like a country cottage.

As William stepped out of the car, the front door opened and Christina emerged to greet him. He kissed her on both cheeks as if she were a French general. She took him by the hand and led him into a spacious hall that was crammed with wooden crates of different sizes. He only needed to look at the faded outlines on the walls to imagine what might have been there just the day before. He was beginning to understand why Christina needed her husband to be away for a month if she was to carry out her plan.

"Still one left to pack," she said as he followed her through to the drawing room, where a single framed canvas remained in its place above the mantelpiece.

William gazed in awe at a painting that even an amateur like himself instantly recognized as a work of genius. He took a Fitzmolean postcard out of his pocket and checked the right-hand corner of the canvas to confirm that Rembrandt's characteristic signature, RvR, was in place. Having done so, he returned his gaze to the six pompous Syndics dressed in their long black gowns with stiff white ruffled collars, holding wide-brimmed black hats as they luxuriated in their exalted position as member of Amsterdam society.

"I can see you like your Christmas present," said Christina.

--◄o►--

Grace phoned her father within minutes of arriving back at her flat in Notting Hill, and gave him a detailed report of her meeting with the professor.

"I do believe the time has come for me to call the Director of Public Prosecutions and make an appointment to see him before any of my colleagues return from their Christmas breaks," said Sir Julian. "I need to get a trial date penciled in to the court calendar as soon as possible."

"That might not be so easy," suggested Grace.

"There are always canceled slots that need to be filled. I'll just have to make sure my name is near the top of the list."

"But why should the DPP pick you rather than any of the other equally worthy applicants?"

"I'll tell you why, Grace, but not over the phone."

--◄o►--

William kept a close eye on the packers as the heavy brigade carefully lowered the Rembrandt into its custom-built crate before carrying it into the hall to join its companions.

Every one of the crates had a large square sticker attached to

it, declaring PROPERTY OF MRS. CHRISTINA FAULKNER. TO RE-
MAIN ON BOARD. The only exception was the Rembrandt, which
had an even larger circular sticker that read, PROPERTY OF THE
FITZMOLEAN MUSEUM, PRINCE ALBERT CRESCENT, LONDON
SW7. TO BE COLLECTED.

"Are you confident," said Christina, "that the commander will
be on the dockside waiting to welcome the *Christina's* distinguished passengers when they arrive in Southampton?"

"He'll be the first person on board the moment we dock, with
the cavalry not far behind," said William. "I'll call him tomorrow,
as soon as the paintings are all on board."

"He'll only be interested in one of them."

"What's going to happen to the rest?" asked William, although
he assumed Christina was unlikely to reveal their final destination.

"Next stop, New York, where they'll be joined by a remarkable
collection of modern American artists who are presently residing
in our Manhattan apartment."

"But by the time the yacht docks, your husband could be standing on the dockside waiting for you."

"No, I don't think so. After Melbourne Miles plans to fly to Sydney so he'll be among the first to see in the New Year, by which
time all his paintings will be hanging in their new home—my new
home."

William didn't waste his time asking her where that might be.

◄O►

Grace and her father spent the evening holed up in his study.

"The next thing Professor Abrahams needs to do," said Grace,
"is study Arthur's original two-page statement that was presented
in court. He did warn me that it could also prove that Arthur has
been lying and the jury got it right."

"If that turns out to be the case," said Sir Julian, "we'll say nothing to Joanna or Beth other than that we've been unable to come

up with any fresh evidence that would make it possible for us to apply for a retrial."

"And if Arthur has been telling the truth?"

"My next call will be to the DPP's office to request a retrial."

"You still haven't told me, Father, why the DPP would give priority to this case?"

"Desmond Pannel and I were at Oxford together. I was his campaign manager when he stood for president of the University Law Society, and you'd never believe who his main rival was. The president's job was a thankless task, but then Desmond is a man who has always enjoyed taking on thankless tasks, which is why he's ended up as DPP. And now, after thirty years, I intend to call in my marker."

◄○►

It wasn't long after he'd climbed into bed that William heard the door open. Suddenly he was wide awake. A sylph-like figure silhouetted in the moonlight glided across the room, slid under the blanket, and began kissing him on the back of his neck.

He didn't have long to consider what he should do next. Turn on the light and politely ask her to leave, was his first thought, or just get on with it but don't tell Beth, was his second. And then he wondered what Beth would say if he told her he'd rejected Christina's advances and sacrificed the Rembrandt. A one-night stand in exchange for a masterpiece. He wasn't in any doubt which she would expect him to do.

◄○►

Professor Abrahams made a second stopover in London on his way back to New York, and once again he was met at the arrivals gate by Grace. This time he was clinging on to what he described as his box of tricks.

The following morning Sir Julian and Grace accompanied him to a room in the basement of Scotland Yard where, in the presence of an independent witness, he spent the next few hours closely examining the two-page statement that had been submitted at Arthur's trial.

Sir Julian and Grace returned to chambers, where they anxiously awaited the outcome of the professor's findings. It was Grace who spotted him sauntering across Lincoln's Inn carrying his box of tricks in one hand and a bottle of champagne in the other. She leaped in the air and cheered.

After listening in silence to the professor's pronouncements, they both bombarded him with questions to which he always had an answer. Finally Sir Julian picked up the phone and dialed a private number. When the Director of Public Prosecutions came on the line, all he said was, "Desmond, I need a favor."

◄o►

A large removal van arrived outside the Villa Rosa at nine the following morning, and it took the heavy brigade nearly two hours to load all sixty-nine crates on board. They were then driven slowly, very slowly, down to the port, where it took another three hours to transfer them into the *Christina*'s hold. After he'd seen the door of the hold locked and bolted, William went ashore and called Commander Hawksby to let him know he'd be on the next flight home.

"No you won't," said Hawksby firmly. "Get back on that boat and don't let the Rembrandt out of your sight until you dock at Southampton."

"But shouldn't I be keeping an eye on Mrs. Faulkner?"

"No. You should be keeping an eye on six Syndics from Amsterdam, who mustn't be allowed to wander off again."

William didn't argue.

"When you dock tomorrow evening, I'll be on the quayside," said Hawksby, "along with a small army to make sure the painting is returned safely to the Fitzmolean."

Christina was disappointed that the commander had insisted

William remain on board, as she was rather hoping he would be keeping an eye on her. William leaned over the railing and waved to her as the yacht left the harbor. As soon as it was out of sight Christina told her driver to take her to the airport, so she could carry out the second part of her plan.

27

If it was all in the timing, as Christina Faulkner suggested to William, then she made one fatal error. She instructed her solicitor to issue a writ for divorce on December 22. The petition landed on Booth Watson's desk on the 24th.

Booth Watson wasn't surprised by the timing, as he assumed Mrs. Faulkner had chosen the date in a clumsy attempt to spoil his client's Christmas. He decided not to contact Miles until he returned to his chambers on December 28. After all, what difference would a few days make? He locked the petition in his safe and went home.

◄○►

Mike Harrison called Mrs. Faulkner from Melbourne on December 27, to report that her husband had spent the day in a hospitality box at the MCG, watching the second day of the Test match. After stumps, he'd gone to dinner with friends and picked up his room key from reception just after midnight.

"Was he alone?" asked Christina.

"No, he was with a young lady who works as a cocktail waitress in the hospitality suite. I have a photograph and a name."

"Thank you, Mike."

Harrison then called DCI Lamont at the Yard and repeated the same message before going to bed.

◄○►

Booth Watson returned to his chambers just after ten o'clock on the morning of the 28th, pleased that Christmas was over and he could get back to work. He read the divorce petition a second time, aware that the grounds were a real concern. Faulkner's wife had clearly been preparing the petition for some time, as several women were named. He decided to call his client and let him know the news of his impending divorce, although he suspected it would not come as much of a surprise.

He first phoned Limpton Hall, but there was no reply, so he assumed Makins must still be on holiday. If he'd made the call an hour later, Mrs. Faulkner would have answered. He next called the Faulkners' home in Monte Carlo, and a maid picked up the phone. Clearly English wasn't her first language.

"May I speak to Monsieur Faulkner?" he asked.

"No here."

"Do you know where he is?" asked Booth Watson, enunciating each word slowly.

"No. Young man say Australia."

Booth Watson wrote on his pad: *Australia/young man.*

"And is Mrs. Faulkner there?" he asked just as slowly.

"No, Madame fly home."

"Home?"

"Angleterre."

"Thank you," said Booth Watson. "Most helpful."

He wondered what Miles could possibly be doing in Australia, and in which city he might be. Reg Bates, the chambers' head clerk, came to his rescue.

"Has to be Melbourne, sir. He'll be watching the second Test."

Booth Watson had no interest in cricket, and simply instructed the head clerk to find his client.

Bates spent the rest of the morning calling all the leading hotels in Melbourne, and by the time Booth Watson had returned from lunch he found a yellow Post-it on his desk with the details. He immediately called the Sofitel and asked to be put through to Miles Faulkner's suite.

"Before I do, sir," said the voice on the other end of the line, "are you aware it's one thirty in the morning?"

"No, I wasn't," admitted Booth Watson. "I'll call back later."

After he'd hung up, he did some calculations, and decided he would try again when he got home that evening.

◄○►

Miles Faulkner was shaving when the phone rang in his suite, but he abandoned his razor when he heard Booth Watson's resonant tones. Whenever BW called it was rarely good news. Faulkner sat on the end of the bed and listened to what his lawyer had to say.

"Is there any reason I should hurry back, BW?" he asked after Booth Watson had informed him about the writ. "The Test match is finely balanced. I'd planned on flying up to Sydney to celebrate the New Year, so wouldn't be home before the third at the earliest."

"That shouldn't be a problem. We've got fourteen days to acknowledge receipt of the petition, so we can deal with it when you get back."

"Good. Then I'll call you in a couple of weeks' time. Anything else?"

"Yes, there was something. It seems your wife spent Christmas in Monte Carlo with a young man. By the time you return, I'll have his name and all the details. It might prove helpful when it comes to making a settlement in claim."

"Put a private detective onto it straight away," said Faulkner.

"I already have," said Booth Watson, "and you should assume your wife's done the same thing."

"Any good news?" asked Miles.

"I've handed over the Renoir to Standard Life, and they've transferred half a million to your account in the Cayman Islands."

"Half a million Christina won't be able to get her hands on."

"Enjoy the Test match, and call me the moment you're back."

Miles put the phone down and finished shaving. After the

cocktail waitress—whose name he couldn't remember—had left, he decided to find out if his wife was still in Monte Carlo.

The maid was able to go into far greater detail with her boss than she had with Booth Watson, but then Faulkner spoke fluent French. He asked when Madame had left for England, and she replied, "I'm not sure, sir. All I know is she followed the van down to the yacht."

"What van?" demanded Faulkner.

"The removal van that came to take away all your pictures."

Miles slammed the phone down, then immediately picked it back up again.

"I'm checking out," he told the receptionist on the front desk. "Get me on the first available flight to London, I don't care which airline."

"But Australia look like winning—" she began.

"Fuck Australia."

—◦—

Mike Harrison called Mrs. Faulkner's number in Monte Carlo and was also told by the maid, "Madame fly home." He next tried Limpton Hall, but there was no reply. He finally called the commander, who was at his desk.

"Faulkner's booked onto a Qantas flight to Heathrow that lands at two o'clock tomorrow afternoon. That wasn't part of his original plan."

"That's all I need," said Hawksby. "And I have no way of getting in touch with DC Warwick to warn him."

—◦—

When Christina Faulkner's plane touched down at Heathrow, she was picked up by her husband's chauffeur and driven to Limpton Hall, where she had a light supper before going to bed. After all, she had a busy day ahead of her.

—◦—

William was sitting in a deck chair sunning himself and enjoying a glass of Pinot Grigio when Faulkner's plane took off on its twenty-three-hour journey to London. He had a clear view of the entry to the hold, which no one had gone near for the past two days. But then why should they? The sun was shining, the sea was calm, and he didn't have a care in the world.

◄○►

At nine o'clock the following morning, a Bishop's Move removal van drew up outside the front door. The loaders took their time packing the sixty-nine artworks into crates before loading them onto the van. After a long lunch break they set off for South-ampton.

"Do not, under any circumstances, go more than thirty miles an hour," Christina instructed the driver. "We can't risk damaging any of the pictures."

"Whatever you say, madam," he replied, only too pleased to oblige, as it guaranteed that he and his men would clock up more overtime.

Christina enjoyed a leisurely lunch in a dining room surrounded by picture hooks. She set off for Southampton just after three, but then she wasn't in any hurry as the *Christina* wasn't due to dock until later that evening. She did hope Miles was enjoying his cricket match. She had been pleased to read in the *Mail* that morning how finely balanced the game was.

◄○►

Miles Faulkner cleared customs at Heathrow just after two o'clock. He had considered calling Limpton Hall from the first-class lounge at Melbourne airport and asking his driver to pick him up, but he decided against the idea as it might alert Christina to his unscheduled return.

He made a taxi driver happy when he asked "Where to, guv?" and received the reply, "Limpton in Hampshire. And you can double the fare if you make it in under an hour."

243

—◁o▷—

Mike Harrison had traveled on the same plane as Faulkner, but not in the same class. He didn't follow his mark out of the terminal, as he considered it was more important to contact Mrs. Faulkner and warn her that her husband was on his way to Limpton Hall. But there was no reply.

He then rang Scotland Yard, and asked to be put through to DCI Lamont.

"DS Roycroft," said a voice.

"Hi, Jackie, it's Mike Harrison. Can I have a word with Bruce?"

"He set off for Southampton with Commander Hawksby just over an hour ago, Mike."

"Thank you," said Harrison. "Good to know you're back, Jackie," he added.

"On probation, more like," said Jackie before putting down the phone.

Harrison made another taxi driver happy when he told him "Southampton."

—◁o▷—

It took well over an hour before Faulkner was dropped off at Limpton Hall, but then he knew the cabbie had no chance of getting there in under an hour.

"Hang about," he said as he jumped out of the cab. "I may not be long."

He ran up the steps and unlocked the front door. When he walked into the hall, he felt sick. No Constable, no Turner. She'd even removed the Henry Moore. He walked slowly around the house, horrified by the extent of her looting, to find only dark rectangles and squares where pictures had once hung, and empty stands where sculptures had proudly been displayed. But the final humiliation came when he entered the drawing room, and saw the one painting she'd left behind. Eddie Leigh's copy of the

Rembrandt was still hanging above the fireplace. If Christina had walked into the room at that moment, he would have happily strangled her. He ran back out of the house and shouted at the driver, "The front gates."

The taxi accelerated down the long drive, coming to a halt by the entrance gates. Faulkner leaped out and ran into the gate-house.

"Have you seen Mrs. Faulkner today?" he demanded.

"Yes, sir," the guard said, after checking his list of arrivals and departures. "She left just over an hour ago."

"Left for where?"

"No idea, sir."

"What about them," said Faulkner, placing a finger on the words *Bishop's Move, arrived 8:55 a.m., departed 2:04 p.m.* "Where were they going?"

"No idea, sir," repeated the hapless guard.

Faulkner grabbed the phone, and it took him two calls and a lot of threatening before an area manager reluctantly gave him the information he wanted. He leaped back in the taxi and said "Southampton," without bothering to look at the ticking meter. The cabbie couldn't believe his luck.

-◦-

The commander sat alone in the back of the lead car. They were followed by a Black Maria with six constables and a sergeant on board. Bringing up the rear was a Wolseley with DCI Lamont in the driving seat. Mob-handed was how Lamont had described the exercise, but the Hawk wasn't going to take any risks.

The little convoy kept to the inside lane of the motorway, and although they never once exceeded the speed limit, they still managed to reach the exit for Southampton docks with a couple of hours to spare.

Hawksby immediately reported to the harbor master, who confirmed that the MV *Christina* was due to dock at quay 29 around seven that evening. The commander then handed the harbor master a special warrant which authorized the removal of one specific crate from the yacht, without interference or inspection by customs and excise.

"Must be the Crown Jewels," said the harbor master, after he'd studied the warrant.

"Not far off," said Hawksby. "But all I can tell you is that it has to be handled with the utmost care, and its contents mustn't be exposed to sunlight."

"Sounds like Dracula."

"No, that's the present owner," said Hawksby.

"Can I help in any way?"

"It wouldn't do any harm to have a couple of your boys hanging around, just in case there's any trouble."

"Brains or brawn?"

"Two of each, if possible."

"Consider it done. They'll be with you half an hour before the *Christina* is due to dock. I think I'll come along myself," he said. "Sounds as if it might be interesting." Hawksby climbed back into his car, and the small convoy made its way across to quay 29 to await the arrival of the six Syndics who were resting peacefully in the hold of the *Christina*.

Everyone was in place and waiting impatiently when a Bentley appeared on the dockside and parked about fifty yards away.

"Who the hell—?" said Lamont.

"Has to be Mrs. Faulkner," said Hawksby. "Just ignore her. As long as the Rembrandt is handed over, it's none of our business what she does with the rest of her husband's art collection, although I hope for her sake she knows he's back in the country."

"Should we inform her?" asked Lamont.

"Also none of our business," said Hawksby.

"And what are they doing here?" asked Lamont as a large Bishop's Move van proceeded slowly along the dockside and came to a halt behind the Bentley.

"Not hard to guess what's inside," said Hawksby, as the driver climbed down from his cab and walked across to the Bentley.

Mrs. Faulkner wound down her window.

"What the hell are that lot doin' here?" the driver demanded, pointing at the three police vehicles.

"They're picking up a crate from my husband's yacht before returning it to its rightful owner in London. Once it's been handed over, they'll be on their way and you can start loading the paintings on board."

"What are the cops so interested in?"

"Six gentlemen from Amsterdam, who left the country several years ago without a visa."

"Very funny," said the driver, who returned to the van without another word.

Christina was winding the window back up when a black taxi appeared. Mike Harrison paid off the cabbie, and then quickly joined his client in the back of her Bentley, without acknowledging any of his former colleagues.

"I think I can see our Dutch friends," said Lamont, who had a pair of binoculars trained on the harbor entrance. He passed them to Hawksby.

"How long do you estimate before they're with us?" Hawksby asked the harbor master, while keeping his eyes focused on the *Christina*.

"Twenty minutes, thirty at the most."

"I've just spotted Warwick standing on the bridge," said Hawksby. "Do you suppose he's taken over?"

"Or been clapped in irons," said Lamont. "Either way, I'd better put the troops on standby."

The commander, the harbor master, DCI Lamont, a sergeant and six constables, Mrs. Faulkner, Mike Harrison, and the loaders from the removal van watched as the MV *Christina* drew closer and closer, until it finally came alongside and tied up at the dock. William was the first person to come running down the gangway.

"We're all set, sir. The crate should be unloaded in a few minutes."

"Then we'll—" began Hawksby as a second taxi raced past them and screeched to a halt beside the yacht. Faulkner leaped out, ran up the gangway, stopped, and exchanged a few words with the captain before they disappeared into the hold.

"Don't move," Hawksby said to William, who was champing to get back on board. "If our crate isn't unloaded, we've got him bang to rights."

"But—"

"Be patient, William. He's not going anywhere. Harbor master, if they were to make a run for it . . ."

"They wouldn't get as far as the harbor entrance before my men cut them off."

"So if they even consider unmooring," said Hawksby to William, "you have my permission to go back on board and arrest Faulkner."

"It doesn't look as if that's going to be necessary," said Lamont, as four of the crew emerged from the hold carrying a large crate. It took them some time to carry it across the deck, down the narrow gangway, and onto the dockside.

Hawksby took his time checking the label: PROPERTY OF THE FITZMOLEAN MUSEUM, PRINCE ALBERT CRESCENT, LONDON SW7. TO BE COLLECTED. He nodded, and four constables took the place of the four crewmen. "Put it in the back of the van," ordered Hawksby, "and don't let it out of your sight."

The four young constables lifted up the crate and, like crabs, began to edge their way slowly toward the Black Maria.

"OK, Bruce," said Hawksby. "I think you've earned the right to lead the convoy back to London. Warwick, you can join me. There's something I need to discuss with you."

William didn't move. He was still watching Miles Faulkner, who was standing on the bridge, looking smug as members of the crew began preparing for an imminent departure.

"Let's go, Warwick. We've got what we came for."

"I'm not so sure we have, sir."

"But we have our crate. You saw the label."

"Yes, I saw the label, but I'm not convinced we've got the right crate? Do you have the authority, sir, to open any crate on board?"

"No," said Hawksby. "We'd need a search warrant for that."

"But I have the authority," said the harbor master, heading toward the gangway, with William only a pace behind. Hawksby and Lamont were left to chase after them.

William went straight to the hold, to be faced with eighty crates of varying sizes. "One must have been relabeled," he announced.

"But which one?" asked Hawksby.

"Be my guest," said Faulkner as he strolled back into the hold, the captain following close behind. "But should you damage any of my priceless works, I can assure you the compensation bill will not be covered by your combined wages," he added with a smirk.

William took a closer look at Faulkner. If he'd expected a broken-nosed, muscle-bound, tattoo-covered thug, he could not have been more mistaken. Faulkner was tall, elegant, with a head of thick wavy fair hair and deep blue eyes. His warm smile explained why so many women had been so easily taken in. He wore a blazer and slacks, an open-necked white shirt and loafers, which gave him the look of an international playboy rather than a hardened criminal.

For the first time, William understood what the commander had meant when he said to wait until you meet the man.

"Perhaps you'd be wise to remember what happened the last time you raided one of my properties," said Faulkner. "I was able to supply you with receipts for every one of my artworks. And just in case you've forgotten, you thought you'd got the Rembrandt that time too."

William hesitated, as his eyes circled the hold, but he was none the wiser.

"So which one do you want opened, detective constable?" said Hawksby defiantly.

"This one," said William, walking across to a large crate and tapping it firmly.

"Are you absolutely convinced that's the right one?" said Faulkner.

"Yes," said William, more out of bravado than conviction.

"I see, commander, that a young rookie is now running your department," said Faulkner.

"Open it," said Hawksby.

The harbor master stepped forward and, assisted by two of his team, began to extract the nails one by one until they were finally able to prise the crate open. Once they'd removed several layers of covering, they were greeted by six Syndics from Amsterdam, who peered back at them.

"I've wanted to do this for years," said Hawksby. The commander stepped forward and told Faulkner he was under arrest, then read him his rights. Lamont thrust Faulkner's hands behind his back, handcuffed him, and frogmarched him off the yacht as four constables carried the second crate slowly down the gangway before placing it carefully in the back of the Black Maria next to its unidentified companion.

"How could you possibly have known which case the Rembrandt was in?" Lamont asked William once they were back on shore.

"I wasn't absolutely sure," admitted William, "but it was the only one that had a large circular impression where the original label must have been. Faulkner obviously switched the labels, but he didn't notice that the crate he chose was considerably larger than the one that contains the Rembrandt, or that a circular mark had been left on the Rembrandt's crate where the original label must have been ripped off."

"You might make a detective after all," said Hawksby.

"So what's in the other crate?" demanded Lamont.

"I've no idea," said William. "We'll only find out after it's been delivered to the Fitzmolean as the label clearly instructs us to do."

Mrs. Faulkner had remained in the Bentley observing the whole operation from a distance. She didn't move until she saw Miles had been arrested, when she leaped out of her car and ran towards the dockside shouting, "Stop them! Stop them!"

Mike Harrison was only a yard behind as they both watched the *Christina* heading out of the harbor toward the open sea.

"On what grounds?" Harrison asked once he'd caught up with her.

"They've still got my pictures on board."

"That would be quite hard to prove," said Harrison, "when the captain is probably only carrying out your husband's orders."

"Whose side are you on?" demanded Christina.

"Yours, Mrs. Faulkner, and once your husband is safely locked up, I feel sure you'll find a way of getting them all back."

"But he'll come after me," protested Christina.

"I don't think so," said Harrison.

"Right, lads," said Hawksby. "Time to return the Rembrandt to its rightful owner, along with whatever's in the other crate."

"Sorry to bother you," said a man who looked even more distressed than Mrs. Faulkner. "But that bloke you've just arrested owes me two hundred and seventy-four pounds for his cab fare."

"Which I fear you won't be seeing for some time," said Lamont. "I suggest you contact his lawyer, a Mr. Booth Watson QC at Lincoln's Inn. I'm sure he'll be happy to oblige you."

"A job well done, DC Warwick," said Hawksby, as William joined him in the back of his car, and the little convoy set off for London. "You can be proud of the role you played."

William didn't respond.

"What's the problem?" asked the commander. "We've arrested Faulkner, and got the Rembrandt back, plus a possible bonus in the other crate that we couldn't have expected. What more could you possibly ask for?"

"Something's not quite right," said William.

"Like what?"

"I don't know. But Faulkner was smiling when you arrested him."

28

"I think I know what's in the other crate," said William.

"But you're not going to tell me, are you?" said Beth.

"No. Just in case I'm wrong, and then you'll be disappointed."

"You do realize that the painting would have to be of Dutch or Flemish origin and pre-1800 before it could be considered by our hanging committee."

"If I'm right," said William, "that won't be a problem. And its provenance is every bit as impressive as the Rembrandt. In any case, thanks to you, I've been invited to the opening ceremony."

"Not me," said Beth. "It was the museum's director, Tim Knox, who invited you to the 'opening of the crates ceremony.' I can tell you, you wouldn't have been my first choice."

"Dare I ask?"

"Christina Faulkner, the woman who made it all possible, and whom I can't wait to meet and thank personally."

William didn't need reminding of the last occasion he'd seen Christina, and wondered if there would ever be a better opportunity to tell Beth exactly what had taken place that night in Monte Carlo.

"I might even bump into her on Saturday," continued Beth, "if she visits Belmarsh to console her husband."

"I don't think so," said William. "But my father and Grace are going to the prison this morning to give your father some important news."

"Good or bad?" asked Beth, sounding anxious.

"I've no idea. He wouldn't even tell my mother."

"I wish I could be there to hear the news," said Beth, "but we'd better get moving if we're not going to be late for the 'opening of the crates ceremony.' This is one of those days when I wish I could be in two places at once."

◄○►

"Good morning, Sir Julian. The prisoner is waiting for you in the interview room."

"Thank you, Mr. Rose." The leading silk and his junior followed the prison officer along a corridor that was becoming all too familiar.

When they reached the interview room Sir Julian shook hands with his client. "Good morning, Arthur."

"Good morning, Sir Julian," Arthur replied, before kissing Grace on both cheeks.

"Let me begin with some good news," said Sir Julian, sitting down and placing his Gladstone bag by his side. Arthur looked apprehensive. "Thanks to the expertise of Professor Leonard Abrahams, a forensic document analyst at Columbia University in New York, the DPP has agreed to support our application for leave to appeal against sentence, which is virtually a retrial."

"That's wonderful news," said Arthur.

"And even better," said Grace, "we've been given an early slot in the court calendar, so your appeal should be heard in a few weeks' time."

"How did you manage that?"

"Sometimes you get lucky," said Sir Julian.

"Especially if you and the DPP were at Oxf—"

"Behave yourself, Grace," said her father. "Although I must confess I've used up all my markers."

"I'm most grateful," said Arthur.

"It was worth playing the long game," said Sir Julian, without explanation. "However, as we only have an hour, Arthur, we must use the time constructively. First, I should tell you that I intend to call only three witnesses."

"Will I be one of them?" asked Arthur.

"No point," said Sir Julian. "Appeal hearings are held in front of three judges, not a jury, and you have nothing new to tell then. They will only be interested in any fresh evidence."

"So who will you be calling?"

"The two police officers who gave evidence at the original trial."

"But they're hardly likely to change their stories."

"You're probably right. However, William has received some information from an unimpeachable source that might make their original testimony look a little less credible. However, our principal witness will still be Professor Abrahams. Grace has been dealing directly with him, so she'll take you through the evidence he has compiled, and, more importantly, his conclusions."

Grace took a thick file out of her briefcase and placed it on the table.

"Let me begin . . ."

◄○►

"Let me begin," said Tim Knox, the director of the Fitzmolean Museum, as he faced a small gathering of friends and staff, "by welcoming you all to what my colleague Beth Rainsford has described as the 'opening of the crates ceremony.' Once the Rembrandt has been removed from its crate and returned to its rightful place, we will then open the second crate and discover what hidden treasure is inside."

Get on with it, William wanted to say.

Beth contented herself with, "I can't wait."

"When you're ready, Mark," said the director.

Mark Cranston, the keeper of paintings, stepped forward and slowly lifted the lid of the first crate as if he were a conjuror, to reveal a mass of small polystyrene chips that his team took some time clearing, only to discover that the painting was wrapped in several layers of muslin. Cranston delicately peeled each layer away until the long-lost masterpiece appeared.

The rapt audience gasped, and a moment later burst into spontaneous applause. The works manager and his crew carefully lifted up the canvas and gently lowered the painting into its frame, securing it with tiny clamps. A second round of applause broke out when the picture was hung on its waiting hooks to once again fill a space that had been unoccupied for seven years.

"Welcome home," said the director.

The assembled gathering gazed in awe at the six Syndics of the Clothmakers' Guild, who returned their admiration with disdain. It was some time before the keeper suggested that they should now open the other crate, although it was clear that some of the patrons were reluctant to be dragged away from their long-lost companions.

Eventually they all joined the director around the second crate, some more in hope than expectation. They waited in silence for the ceremony to be repeated. First the lid was lifted by the keeper, then the packing chips were removed, before the layers of muslin were finally peeled away to reveal that Rembrandt had a genuine rival.

A collective gasp went up as a magnificent depiction of Christ's descent from the cross by Peter Paul Rubens was revealed.

"How generous of Mr. Faulkner," said one of the patrons, while another ventured, "Two for the price of one. We are indeed blessed."

"Shall I hang it next to the Rembrandt?" asked the keeper.

"I'm afraid not," said the director. "In fact I must ask you to place it back in the crate and nail the lid down."

"Why?" demanded another of the patrons. "The label on the crate clearly states that the painting is the property of the Fitzmolean."

"It does indeed," said the director. "And I can't deny that this remarkable painting would have adorned our collection, and attracted art lovers from all over the world. But unfortunately, I received a letter this morning from a Mr. Booth Watson QC who pointed out that the labels on the two crates had obviously been switched by someone, but certainly not his client. Mr. Faulkner had always intended to return the Rembrandt, and is delighted to know that it is safely back in its rightful place. However, the Rubens, which has been in Mr. Faulkner's private collection for the past twenty years, must be returned to him immediately."

William now understood why Faulkner had been smiling when he was arrested, but still couldn't resist asking, "Where's he going to hang it? In his cell?"

"Of course, I immediately sought legal advice," said the director, ignoring the interruption, "and our solicitors confirmed that we have no choice but to accede to Mr. Booth Watson's demand."

"Did they give a reason?" asked the keeper.

"It was their opinion that if a dispute over ownership were to result in litigation, not only would we lose, but it would be extremely costly. For the time being, the painting will be placed in secure storage until the board makes a final decision, though I have no reason to believe they will disagree with our legal advisers and instruct me to return the Rubens to Mr. Faulkner."

Some of the patrons and guests continued to admire the Rubens, aware they would never see it again. William only turned away when the lid of the crate was finally nailed down. A cold shiver went down his spine when he turned to see Beth deep in conversation with Christina Faulkner. He wondered if Christina was telling her the truth about what had happened that night in Monte Carlo.

◄○►

Mr. Booth Watson didn't acknowledge Sir Julian as they passed each other in the corridor.

"No prizes for guessing whom he's about to have a consultation with," said Grace. "What's the speculation in the robing room?"

"Faulkner's looking at six years at least, possibly eight, but it doesn't help that the tabloids keep referring to him as a modern-day Raffles, rather than the common criminal he is."

"But it's the judge who'll decide the length of his sentence, not the press," said Grace.

"That's assuming the jury doesn't acquit him. You can be sure he'll have a well-honed story by the time he appears in the witness box, and will deliver it with conviction."

They left the prison at the same time as Booth Watson entered the interview room.

"Good morning, Miles," he said, slumping down into the chair opposite his client. "I do wish you'd stayed put in Melbourne and watched the rest of the Test match, as I recommended."

"But if I had," said Faulkner, "my entire art collection would now be on the other side of the world."

"Not if you'd allowed me to handle Warwick in Southampton before he got off the *Christina*."

"Who's Warwick?"

"The young detective who visited your wife in Monte Carlo, came to an arrangement with her, and then sealed the deal in bed later that night."

"Then you'll be able to run rings around Warwick when you get him in the witness box."

"If he ever gets into the witness box. He certainly wouldn't if I was advising the other side. I'd let an old pro like Hawksby take the stand, not Warwick. So for now we'll have to forget him and concentrate on your defense, which is frankly looking a bit frayed at the edges."

"What are they charging me with?"

Booth Watson extracted a sheet of paper from his briefcase. "'That you did knowingly and willfully steal a national treasure with no intention of returning it to its rightful owner.' And before you say anything, I should advise you that it would be difficult to claim that you'd never seen the Rembrandt before, as your wife will undoubtedly testify that it's been in your home in Monte Carlo for the past seven years. And the Crown is also certain to ask, if you didn't switch the labels on the crates, who did?"

"What's the bottom line?" asked Faulkner.

"Eight years at most, but more likely six, depending on which judge we get."

"Can you fix that, BW?"

"Not in England, Miles. But I've got a public relations team working on your image, and currently you're seen in the media as a cross between the Scarlet Pimpernel and Raffles. But unfortunately, it's not public opinion, but a jury, that will decide your fate."

"Have you got a get-out-of-jail-free card up your sleeve, BW?"

Booth Watson looked his client in the eye before saying, "Only if you're willing to make one hell of a sacrifice."

29

The press had a field day. A murder appeal at the Old Bailey and the return of a stolen national treasure both in the same week. Fleet Street couldn't decide which story to lead on that Monday morning.

The Guardian favored Arthur Rainsford and the possibility of a miscarriage of justice, while the *Daily Mail* was more interested in Miles Faulkner, asking its readers, "Raffles or Rasputin?"

The Sun put both of them on its front page and claimed an exclusive by revealing a link between the two men: DC William Warwick had arrested the master art thief, and was engaged to the daughter of the "Marylebone Murderer."

Several newspapers carried profiles of the distinguished defense barristers involved in the two cases, Sir Julian Warwick QC and Mr. Booth Watson QC. *The Times* hinted that they were not on good terms, while the *Mirror* claimed they were deadly enemies.

William's and Beth's loyalties were equally divided. They left the flat in Fulham together that morning but parted on the steps of the Royal Courts of Justice on the Strand to go their separate ways: William to court fourteen to follow the Faulkner trial, while Beth attended court twenty-two to support her father. They both rose as the judges entered their respective domains.

THE CROWN V. RAINSFORD

Three judges entered court twenty-two and took their places on the bench, Lord Justice Arnott presiding, while his two learned friends would be in attendance and on hand to discuss the finer points of the law.

Lord Justice Arnott settled in the center chair and rearranged his red robe while everyone in the courtroom resumed their seats. Sir Julian liked to believe that judges were like cricket umpires—impartial and fair—and although he and Lord Justice Arnott had crossed swords several times in the past, he'd never known him to be unjust.

"Sir Julian," said the judge, peering benevolently down from on high. "My colleagues and I have spent some considerable time going over the evidence from the original trial, at which the defendant was convicted of the murder of his business partner, Mr. Gary Kirkland. Our sole interest in these proceedings is the presentation of any fresh evidence that might suggest a miscarriage of justice took place on that occasion. I would therefore ask you, Sir Julian, to bear that in mind."

"I will indeed, m'lud," said Sir Julian, rising from his place. "However, it may be necessary from time to time to refer back to the original trial. But I will do everything in my power not to try Your Lordship's patience."

"I am obliged, Sir Julian," said Lord Justice Arnott, not sounding at all obliged. "Perhaps you would now proceed with your opening statement."

THE CROWN V. FAULKNER

In court fourteen, Mr. Booth Watson was coming to the end of his opening statement. Following Mr. Adrian Palmer QC's submission on behalf of the Crown, the jury could have been forgiven for thinking that Miles Faulkner was the devil incarnate, whereas when Mr. Booth Watson resumed his place, they might have been under the illusion that his client was one step away from being canonized.

"You may call your first witness, Mr. Palmer," said Mr. Justice Nourse, looking down from on high.

"We call Mrs. Christina Faulkner," said Palmer.

The moment the journalists seated in the press gallery set eyes on the striking woman as she entered the court, few of them were in any doubt whose picture would be dominating their front pages the following morning.

Dressed in a simple, well-cut gray Armani suit with a single string of pearls, Mrs. Faulkner stepped into the witness box as if she owned it, and delivered the oath in a quiet but assured manner.

Mr. Palmer rose from his place and smiled across at his principal witness.

"Mrs. Faulkner, you are the wife of the defendant, Mr. Miles Faulkner."

"I am at present, Mr. Palmer, but not for much longer, I hope," she said, as her husband glared down at her from the dock.

"Mrs. Faulkner," said the judge, "you will confine yourself to answering counsel's questions, and not offering opinions."

"I apologize, My Lord."

"How long have you been married to the defendant?" asked Palmer.

"Eleven years."

"And you have recently sued him for divorce on the grounds of adultery and mental cruelty."

"Is this relevant, Mr. Palmer?" asked the judge.

"Only to show, Your Honor, that the relationship between the two of them has irretrievably broken down."

"Then you have achieved your purpose, Mr. Palmer, so move on."

"As you wish, Your Honor: This trial, as you will know, Mrs. Faulkner, concerns the theft of *The Syndics of the Cloth-makers' Guild*, by Rembrandt, a work of art the value of which is incalculable, and is acknowledged by art aficionados to be a national treasure. So I must ask you when you first became aware of the painting."

"A little over seven years ago, when I saw it hanging in the drawing room of our home at Limpton Hall."

"A little over seven years ago," repeated Palmer, looking directly at the jury.

"That is correct, Mr. Palmer."

"And did your husband tell you how he had acquired such a magnificent work of art?"

"He was evasive to begin with, but when I pressed him, he told me he'd bought the picture from a friend who was in financial trouble."

"Did you ever meet this friend?"

"No, I did not."

"And when did you become aware that the painting had in fact been stolen from the Fitzmolean Museum?"

"A couple of weeks later when I saw it on the *News at Ten*."

"Did you tell your husband about that news report?"

"Certainly not. I was far too frightened, as I knew only too well how he would react."

"Understandably."

"Mr. Palmer," said the judge firmly.

"I apologize, Your Honor," said Palmer, with a slight bow, well aware that he had made his point. He turned back to the witness. "And when you could no longer bear the deception, you took it upon yourself to do something about it."

"Yes, I felt that if I did nothing, I would be condoning a crime. So when my husband was away in Australia last Christmas, I packed up the painting and sent it back to England on our yacht, with clear instructions that it should be returned to the Fitzmolean."

Booth Watson scribbled a note on the pad in front of him.

"But weren't you worried about the consequences of that decision when your husband returned?"

"Extremely worried, which is why I made plans to leave the country before he got back."

Booth Watson made a further note.

"Then why didn't you do so?"

"Because Miles somehow found out what I was planning, and took the next flight back to London to try and prevent me from giving back the painting to its rightful owner." She bowed her head shyly.

"And when did you next see your husband?"

"In Southampton, when he boarded our yacht, and was so desperate not to lose the Rembrandt, he switched the labels with one on another crate."

Booth Watson made a third note.

"But this attempt to fool the police failed."

"Thankfully yes, but only because a detective from Scotland Yard, who'd traveled to Southampton to collect the painting, became suspicious and insisted that another crate should be opened. That's when they discovered the missing Rembrandt."

The journalists' pencils didn't stop scribbling.

"And thanks to your courage and fortitude, Mrs. Faulkner, this national treasure once again hangs on the wall of the Fitzmolean Museum."

"It does indeed, Mr. Palmer, and I recently visited the museum to witness the masterpiece being rehung in its rightful place. It gave me great pleasure to see how many members of the public were, like me, enjoying the experience."

"Thank you, Mrs. Faulkner. No more questions, Your Honor."

Booth Watson looked across at the jury, who appeared to be on the point of bursting into applause when Mr. Palmer sat down.

"Mr. Booth Watson," said the judge, "do you wish to cross-examine this witness?"

"I most certainly do, Your Honor," said Booth Watson, heaving himself up from his place and smiling sweetly at the witness.

"Do remind me, Mrs. Faulkner, when it was you first saw the Rembrandt?"

"Seven years ago, at our home in the country."

"Then I'm bound to ask, what took you so long?"

"I'm not sure I know what you're getting at," said Christina.

"I think you know only too well what I'm getting at, Mrs. Faulkner. But let me spell it out for you. Quite simply, if you knew seven years ago that the painting had been stolen, why wait until now to inform the police?"

"I was waiting for the right opportunity."

"And that opportunity didn't arise for seven years?" said Booth Watson, sounding incredulous.

Christina hesitated, allowing Booth Watson to thrust the knife in deeper.

"I would suggest, Mrs. Faulkner, that the opportunity you were actually waiting for, was to steal your husband's entire art collection while he was safely on the other side of the world?"

"But I didn't plan . . ." She hesitated, giving Booth Watson the opportunity to twist the knife.

"I think you'd been planning this outrageous piece of grand larceny for some considerable time, Mrs. Faulkner, and simply used the Rembrandt as a ploy to give yourself a better chance of getting away with it."

A babble of whispered conversations broke out in the court, but Booth Watson waited patiently for silence to return, before he slowly extracted the knife.

"Did you, Mrs. Faulkner, while your husband was in Melbourne, have all the artworks at his home in Monte Carlo packed up and taken to the port, where they were placed in the hold of your husband's yacht?"

"But half of them would have been mine in any case," protested Christina.

"I'm well aware that you are suing your husband for divorce," said Booth Watson, "as my learned friend so subtly reminded us, but in this country, Mrs. Faulkner, it is traditional to let the courts decide what portion of a man's wealth should be allocated to his wife. Clearly you weren't willing to wait."

"But it was only about a third of the collection."

"Quite possibly, but after the yacht had set sail from Monte Carlo for Southampton with one-third of your husband's art collection on board, what did you do next?"

Christina bowed her head once again. William frowned.

"As you appear unwilling to answer my question, Mrs. Faulkner, allow me to remind you exactly what you did. You took the next flight back to London, traveled down to your country home, and once again set about removing every painting in the house."

One or two members of the jury gasped, while Booth Watson waited patiently for the witness to reply. When no reply was forthcoming, he turned a page of his notes and continued. "The following morning, a removal van turned up at the house, loaded the paintings, and, as instructed by you, took them to Southampton to await the arrival of your husband's yacht, so that they too could be placed on board. So, you've now got two-thirds of the collection," said Mr. Booth Watson, glowering at his victim, who could only stare back at him like a mesmerized rabbit caught in the headlights.

"And even that wasn't enough for you," Booth Watson continued, "because you then instructed the captain of the yacht that you would be coming aboard with the intention of sailing to New York so you could go straight to your husband's apartment on Fifth Avenue and relieve him of the rest of his fabled collection. Then, like the owl and the pussycat, you hoped to sail away for a year and a day in your beautiful pea-green boat, or to be more accurate, your husband's beautiful yacht."

"But none of this alters the fact that Miles stole the Rembrandt in the first place, and then switched the labels on the crates to try and prevent it being returned to the Fitzmolean."

William smiled.

The judge nodded sagely, causing Booth Watson, like a master helmsman, to change tack.

"Allow me to ask you a simple question, Mrs. Faulkner," he said, almost in a whisper. "Would you describe your husband as a clever man?"

"Clever, manipulative, and resourceful," came back the immediate reply.

"I'm therefore bound to ask you, Mrs. Faulkner, if he's such a clever, manipulative, and resourceful man, why would he have switched the label to another crate which contained a painting worth even more than the Rembrandt that the Crown are claiming he stole?" Booth Watson didn't give the witness a chance to reply before he added, "No, Mrs. Faulkner, it is you who is clever, manipulative, and resourceful, and that is what made it possible for you to almost get away with stealing one of the most valuable art collections on earth, while at the same time plotting to have my client sent to prison for a crime he did not commit. No further questions, Your Honor."

THE CROWN V. RAINSFORD

"Sir Julian, you may call your first witness."

"Thank you, m'lud. I call Mr. Barry Stern."

"Is this the detective inspector who was the Crown's principal witness at the original trial?" inquired the judge on behalf of his colleagues.

"Yes, m'lud. And I've had to subpoena him as he is no longer a police officer, and therefore must be considered a hostile witness."

"I hope you're going to produce some fresh evidence, Sir Julian, and not just take us all on a fishing trip."

"I believe I will, m'lud, but, like you, I am willing to stretch the legal boundaries a little if it means there's the slightest chance that an innocent man will finally be granted justice."

Lord Justice Arnott didn't look pleased, but satisfied himself with a frown as the courtroom door opened and a stocky man in his early fifties, with a crew cut, wearing jeans and a leather jacket, appeared. Stern took his place in the witness box and delivered the oath without once looking at the card the clerk held up. He then glared across at defense counsel like a boxer waiting for the bell to ring.

"How many years were you a serving police officer, Mr. Stern?"

"Twenty-eight. Best years of my life."

"Is that right?" said Sir Julian. "So why did you take early retirement, when you would have been entitled to a full pension after just another two years' service?"

"Wanted to go out at the top, didn't I?"

"By ending your career with a murder conviction? But before I come to that, I have to ask you, during the best years of your life, Mr. Stern, how many times were you suspended?"

"Is this line of questioning relevant, Sir Julian?" asked Lord Justice Arnott.

"It goes to the heart of the case, m'lud," said Sir Julian as he picked up the first of the two personnel files that William had come across. He ostentatiously opened the first to a page marked with a large red tab. "How many times?" he repeated.

"Three," said Stern, not looking quite as confident.

"And was the first offense for being drunk on duty?"

"I might have occasionally downed a couple of pints on a Friday night," admitted Stern.

"While you were on duty?"

"Only after we'd banged up a villain."

"And exactly how many times were you disciplined for being drunk on duty, having banged up a villain on a Friday night?"

"I think it was twice."

"Think again, Mr. Stern," said Sir Julian, giving the witness time to reconsider.

"It might have been three times."

"I think you'll find it was four, Mr. Stern. And how many other times were you drunk on duty, but not disciplined?"

"Never," said Stern, his voice rising. "Just those four times in twenty-eight years."

"And always on a Friday night?"

Stern looked puzzled.

"And the second time you were disciplined, could you tell the court what you were charged with on that occasion?"

"I don't recall. It was such a long time ago."

"Then let me remind you, Mr. Stern. You were caught having sexual intercourse with a prostitute while she was in a cell. Now do you remember?"

"I do. But she was—"

"She was what, Mr. Stern?"

Stern didn't respond.

"Then perhaps I should remind you what you said on that occasion." Sir Julian looked down at the file, while Stern remained silent. "'She was a right little scrubber, who got no more and certainly no less than she deserved.'"

A sudden burst of chattering followed, and Lord Justice Arnott waited for it to subside before asking, "Is that not hear-say, Sir Julian?"

"No, m'lud, I was simply reading Mr. Stern's testimony from the tribunal report."

The judge nodded gravely.

"Mr. Stern, you told the court just a few moments ago that you were only disciplined on three occasions, but that was the fifth occasion, and I haven't finished yet."

All three judges had their eyes fixed on the witness.

"I meant for three different offenses."

"So you don't always say what you mean."

Stern looked as if he was about to respond, but just clenched his fists.

"Then let's move on to the sixth incident, after which a full inquiry took place, and you were suspended for six months."

"On full pay, after which the charges were dropped."

"That's not entirely accurate, is it, Mr. Stern? You actually took early retirement only weeks before the inquiry was completed. And on that occasion, you were charged with stealing four thousand pounds from a prisoner while he was in custody."

"He was a drug dealer."

"Was he indeed?" said Sir Julian. "So you consider it's acceptable for a police officer to steal from a drug dealer?"

"I didn't say that. You're putting words in my mouth. In any case, he withdrew the allegation the following day."

"I'm sure he did. However—"

"I think we should move on, Sir Julian," interrupted Lord Justice Arnott, "to the role this officer played at Mr. Rainsford's trial."

"As you wish, m'lud," said Sir Julian, nodding to Grace, who handed him the second file. "At Mr. Rainsford's trial, Mr. Stern, would I be right in thinking you were the senior officer investigating the crime?"

"Yes, I was," said Stern, looking as if he thought he was back on safer ground.

"Did you, in the course of your investigations, ever consider trying to find the short, heavily built man my client repeatedly told you ran past him in the corridor of his office, on the night of the murder?"

"The mystery man, you mean?" said Stern. "Why bother, when he was nothing more than a figment of Rainsford's imagination."

"And you also made no attempt to trace the anonymous caller who reported Mr. Kirkland's death to the police."

"Isn't that what anonymous means?" said Stern, who laughed, but no one else did.

"Didn't it occur to you, Mr. Stern, that the anonymous call could only have come from someone who had actually witnessed the crime?"

"But Rainsford confessed. What more do you want?"

"I want justice," said Sir Julian. "And with that seemingly innocent remark, Mr. Stern, you have raised the crucial unanswered question in this case. Who is the honest broker—you, or Mr. Rainsford?"

"I am," said Stern, "as the jury concluded."

"Then you won't have any trouble convincing three judges, will you?"

Stern stared up at the bench, at three men who gave no clue what they were thinking.

Sir Julian allowed their lordships a moment before he continued, "Was Mr. Rainsford telling the truth when he said his original statement, which you took down, consisted of three pages, one of which subsequently went missing? Or are we to believe, as you stated under oath in the witness box during the trial, that there were only ever two pages?"

"There never was a middle page," said Stern.

"Middle page, Mr. Stern? I made no mention of a middle page."

"What's the difference?"

"The difference is that it shows you knew which page was missing. Let me ask, did you number the pages of Mr. Rainsford's statement?"

"Of course I did, one and two, and Rainsford signed them both. And what's more, DC Clarkson and me witnessed his signature."

"But when did DC Clarkson witness that statement, Mr. Stern?"

Stern hesitated before saying, "The following morning."

"Giving you more than enough time to remove the middle page."

"How many times do I have to tell you there was never a middle page."

"We only have your word for that, Mr. Stern."

"And DC Clarkson, who went on to be promoted, not to mention the jury who didn't seem to be in any doubt that your client was guilty."

"Some considerable doubt, I would suggest," said Sir Julian, cutting him short, "because they took four days to reach a verdict, and then only by a majority of ten to two."

"That was good enough for me," said Stern, his voice rising slightly.

"Of course it was," said Sir Julian, "because it allowed you to finish your career on a high, as you so elegantly put it, and walk away without having to face yet another inquiry."

Mr. Alun Llewellyn QC, who was appearing for the Crown,

rose reluctantly from the other end of the bench and said, "Can I remind my learned friend that it's his client who is on trial, and not Mr. Stern."

A smug look appeared on Stern's face.

"Were you sober when you arrested Arthur Rainsford at five thirty that Friday afternoon?" asked Sir Julian.

"Sober as a judge," said Stern, grinning at the three judges, none of whom returned the compliment.

"And also when you booked him in at six forty-two?" he said, checking his notes.

"As a judge," repeated Stern.

"And when you locked him up at six forty-nine, and left him alone in his cell for nearly two hours?"

"I wanted to give him enough time to think about what he was going to say, didn't I?" said Stern, smiling at the three judges.

"While giving yourself enough time to down a few pints, having banged up another villain on a Friday night."

Stern clenched his fists and stared defiantly at his adversary. "What if I did have a couple of pints? I was sober enough to—"

"Sober enough to take down Mr. Rainsford's statement at eight twenty-three."

"Yes, yes, yes," said Stern, his voice rising with every word. "How many times do I have to tell you?"

"And sober enough to remove the middle page of my client's statement later that night to ensure you retired on a high?"

"I never removed anything that night," Stern snapped back.

"Then the next morning perhaps?" said Sir Julian calmly. "I imagine you were sober enough to remove it the following morning."

"And I was sober enough the night before to make sure the bastard got no more and certainly no less than he deserved," shouted Stern, jabbing a finger in the direction of defense counsel.

A stony silence hung over the court, as everyone in the room stared at the witness.

"'And I was sober enough the night before to make sure the

bastard got no more and certainly no less than he deserved,'" repeated Sir Julian, returning Stern's stare. "No further questions, My Lords."

"You may step down, Mr. Stern," said Lord Justice Arnott wearily.

As Stern made his way out of the court, Sir Julian looked up at the three judges, who were deep in conversation. Grace interrupted his thoughts when she leaned across and said, "I have to leave you for a moment. I won't be long."

Sir Julian nodded as his junior made her way quickly out of the courtroom, down the wide marble staircase, and onto the street, where a posse of photographers were waiting for a "today" photo of Faulkner as he left the court. Their only chance of getting a picture of Arthur Rainsford would be if he left the court as a free man.

Grace watched them from a distance for some time, before selecting the one whose eyes were continually on the lookout for a front-page picture. She crossed the road and whispered to him, "Can I have a private word?"

The snapper peeled away from the rest of the group and listened to her request.

"Only too delighted to help," he said as Grace slipped him a five-pound note. "That won't be necessary, miss," he added, handing back the money. "Arthur Rainsford should never have gone to jail in the first place."

30

The following morning Sir Julian arrived at the Royal Courts of Justice an hour before the trial was due to recommence. A clerk accompanied him and Grace down to the cells in the basement, so they could consult with their client.

"You demolished Stern," said Arthur, shaking Sir Julian warmly by the hand. "If you'd represented me at my original trial, the verdict might well have gone the other way."

"It's kind of you to say so, Arthur, but while I may have landed the occasional blow, unfortunately I didn't knock Stern out. And the fact remains, we're in front of three high court judges, not a jury. Their lordships' decision will be based not on reasonable doubt but on far more demanding criteria, before they can consider overturning the jury's decision and declaring a miscarriage of justice. A great deal now depends on Professor Abrahams's testimony."

"I'm not altogether sure how the three venerable Solomons will react to the professor," said Grace.

"Nor am I," admitted Sir Julian. "But he's our best hope."

"You've still got Detective Sergeant Clarkson to cross-examine," Arthur reminded him.

"Stern's sidekick will only parrot what his master has already said. You can be sure he and Stern spent last night in a pub analyzing every one of my questions." Sir Julian checked his watch. "We'd better get going. Can't afford to keep their lordships waiting."

—◄O►—

"You ran rings around my wife yesterday, BW," said Faulkner, over breakfast at the Savoy.

"Thank you, Miles. But when Palmer cross-examines you, you'll still have to explain to the jury where the Rembrandt has been for the past seven years, how you got hold of it in the first place, and why you switched the labels on the crates. You'd better have some pretty convincing answers to all those questions, and several more besides, because Palmer will come at you all guns blazing."

"I'll be ready for him. And I've decided to make that sacrifice you recommended."

"Very prudent. But keep that particular card up your sleeve for the time being, and leave me to decide when you should play it."

"Understood, BW. So what happens next?"

"The Crown will put up Commander Hawksby, and he'll undoubtedly back up your wife's story. For him, she's the lesser of two evils."

"Then you'll have to demolish him."

"I don't intend to cross-examine him."

"Why not?" demanded Faulkner, as a waiter poured them more coffee.

"Hawksby's an old pro, and juries trust him, so we need the commander out of harm's way as quickly as possible."

"But that doesn't apply to the choirboy," said Faulkner.

"Agreed, but the Crown won't be letting him anywhere near the witness box. It would be too much of a risk."

"Then why don't we call him?"

"Also too much of a risk. Warwick's an unknown quantity, and barristers always like to know the answer before they ask a question. That way, they can't be taken by surprise. So frankly, Miles, I need you to be at your sparkling best, because the most important thing in the jury's minds when they're considering their verdict will be your credibility."

"No pressure," said Miles.

"You've been in tight spots before."

"Never this tight."

"That's why you have to be on the top of your game."

"And if I'm not?"

Booth Watson drained his coffee before replying, "You won't be having bacon and eggs at the Savoy again for some considerable time."

THE CROWN V. RAINSFORD

"My Lords, in the tradition of the English criminal bar, a leader may call upon his junior to conduct one of the examinations in chief during a trial. With Your Lordships' permission, I will invite my junior to examine the next witness."

"Permission granted, Sir Julian," responded Lord Justice Arnott after a brief consultation with his colleagues. He then gave Grace the warmest smile he'd managed throughout the trial.

Grace rose unsteadily to her feet, aware that not only was everyone staring at her, but Arthur Rainsford's fate now rested in her hands. All those years of study and training, not to mention the hours spent at the feet of her father as he interpreted the law and explained court procedure to her. Now he was passing on the baton, expecting her to run the final lap.

Sir Julian sat back, hoping it wasn't too obvious that he was just as nervous as his daughter. It didn't help Grace that her mother was seated between Beth and Joanna Rainsford at the back of the court, both leaning forward and looking like football fans eagerly awaiting the first goal.

Grace placed her file on the little stand her father had given her on the day she joined him in chambers. She opened it, looked down at the first page and her mind went blank.

"Are you ready to call the next witness, Ms. Warwick?" asked Lord Justice Arnott, sounding like a benevolent uncle.

"We call Professor Leonard Abrahams," said Grace, surprised by how self-assured her voice sounded, because her legs weren't experiencing the same confidence.

If the courtroom door hadn't opened and closed, observers might have been forgiven for wondering if the next witness had actually entered the room. Abrahams blinked, looked around, and finally spotted the witness box in the far corner of the court. When he reached it, he was surprised to find that there was no chair for him to sit in, and that he would be expected to remain standing throughout his cross-examination. *Typical of the British,* he thought.

The clerk held up a card, showing no surprise that the witness was wearing a short white lab coat and an open-necked green shirt. Abrahams placed one hand on the Bible—well, at least the Old Testament—before reading out the words, "I swear by Almighty God that the evidence I shall give shall be the truth, the whole truth and nothing but the truth," before adding, "so help me God."

He then peered around the courtroom, relieved to see that his little box of tricks had been set out on the floor between the witness box and the three judges, just as he'd requested.

His gaze finally settled on Grace, one of the brightest young women he'd come across in many years of teaching bright young women. He'd liked her from the moment they'd met at Heathrow, but it was only later that he'd come to respect her grasp of detail and her patient pursuit of the facts as well as her passionate belief in justice. He wondered if Sir Julian realized just how talented his daughter was.

"Professor Abrahams," said Grace, "I would like to begin by asking you about your background, in order that their lordships may appreciate the particular skills and expertise you bring to this case." He'd become so used to Grace calling him Len, that he was taken by surprise when she addressed him as professor. "What is your nationality, professor?"

"I'm an American, although I was born in Poland. I emigrated to the United States at the age of seventeen, when I won a scholarship to study physics at Columbia University in New York. I completed my doctorate at Brown, when I wrote my thesis on the use of ESDA in criminal cases."

"ESDA?" repeated Grace, for the benefit of everyone else in the court, other than the two of them.

"Electrostatic Detection Apparatus."

"And you have since written two major works on the subject, and recently been awarded the National Medal of Science."

"That is correct."

"In addition to which, you—"

"I think you have established, Ms. Warwick," interjected Lord Justice Arnott, "that the professor is preeminent in his field. Perhaps it's time for you to show us what relevance his expertise has in this particular case. I only hope," he added, turning to face the witness, "that my colleagues and I will be able to follow you, professor."

"Don't worry, Your Honor," said Abrahams. "I'll treat all three of you as if you were first-year students."

Sir Julian held his breath, while Grace stared anxiously at the judges, waiting for a stern rebuke, but none was forthcoming. Their lordships just smiled, when Lord Justice Arnott said, "That's most considerate of you, professor, and I hope you'll forgive me if I find it necessary to ask you the occasional question."

"Fire away at any time, Your Honor. And in answer to your first question, about the relevance of ESDA to this particular case, I have to admit, I wouldn't have considered taking on this assignment had it not given me an opportunity to visit my mother."

"Your mother lives in England?" asked Lord Justice Arnott.

"No, Your Honor, in Warsaw. But England's on the way."

"I've never thought of England as being on the way to anywhere," said the judge, "but please continue, professor."

"To do so, Your Honor, I must first explain why ESDA is now considered by the American Bar Association to be an important weapon in its armory. That wasn't always the case. The change took place quite recently, when a congressman whom I intensely dislike told the court during his trial for fraud that he had read every page of a sensitive military procurement document, and suspected that some pages had been added at a later date. I was able to prove he had lied to the court, which resulted in him not only having to resign from office, but also ending up in jail for a long time."

"But in this case, as I understand it," said Lord Justice Arnott, "you will be attempting to prove the exact opposite, namely that a sheet of paper was removed, not added."

"That is correct, Your Honor. And if you'll allow me to examine the evidence in your presence, I believe I will also be able to establish whether it was Arthur Rainsford or DI Stern who lied under oath. Because they can't both have been telling the truth." The professor now had everyone in the courtroom's close attention.

"Beyond reasonable doubt?" asked Arnott, raising an eyebrow.

"Scientists don't deal in doubt, Your Honor. It's either fact or fiction."

This silenced his lordship.

"But in order to prove my case, Your Honor, I will need your permission to leave the witness box and conduct an experiment."

The judge nodded. Professor Abrahams stepped down from the box and walked across to a machine that looked like a desktop photocopier. He pulled on a pair of latex gloves and turned to face the judges.

"Your Honor, may I suggest," said Grace, "that you and your colleagues join us so we can all follow the experiment more closely?"

Lord Justice Arnott nodded, and all three judges left the bench and descended into the well of the court, where they were joined by both counsel to form a ring around the ESDA.

"Pay attention," said Abrahams, as he always did when he was about to address the students at his lectures. "No one has suggested," he began, "that Mr. Rainsford didn't initial the first page of his statement that was later produced as evidence in court. The only dispute is whether there were three pages rather than two. And if I'm to prove that, I will require the original two-page statement."

"This has been agreed by both sides, My Lords," interjected Grace.

Arnott nodded to the clerk, who handed the original statement to Professor Abrahams.

"Now, I suspect," said Abrahams, "that we will all need to be reminded of the wording of the original statement. I repeat, there is no dispute concerning page one from either party." He began to read.

My name is Arthur Edward Rainsford. I am fifty-one years old and currently reside at 32 Fulham Gardens, London SW7. I am the sales director of a small finance company that specializes in investing in burgeoning pharmaceutical companies.

On May 5, 1983, I traveled to Coventry by train to meet a potential new investor. Following that meeting, we had lunch together. When the bill came, I presented my company credit card and was embarrassed when it was declined, as this was hardly the way to impress a potential client. I was extremely angry, and contacted our finance director, Gary Kirkland, to find out how this could have been possible. He assured me that there was nothing to worry about, and that it must simply be a banking error. He suggested that I drop by the office on my way home that evening, when he would go over the accounts with me. I later regretted that I had lost my temper—and I should never have

The professor put the first page down and picked up the second.

"This, as you know," he said to his attentive audience, "is the second page of the statement given in evidence, although Mr. Rainsford still maintains it is in fact the third page." He began to read again.

—struck him. I immediately realized when I saw the deep gash on the back of his head that he must have hit the edge

of the mantelpiece or the brass fender as he collapsed to the floor. The next thing I recall was hearing a siren, and a few moments later half a dozen policemen stormed into the room. One of them, a Detective Inspector Stern, arrested me, and later charged me with the murder of Gary Kirkland, one of my oldest friends. I will regret his death for the rest of my life.

Arthur Rainsford

I have read this statement in the presence of DI Stern and DC Clarkson.

Professor Abrahams stopped for a moment to make sure he still had the attention of his students. Satisfied, he continued. "I now want you to turn your attention to the ESDA machine—the Electrostatic Detection Apparatus. I'm about to place this second page on the ESDA's bronze plate. Are there any questions?"

No one spoke.

"Good. I will now cover the page with a sheet of Mylar film, before sealing it."

The professor took a small roller from his box of tricks, and proceeded to roll it backward and forward over the Mylar film until he was confident that he'd eliminated any air bubbles. Next, he took a thin metal device from his bag, explaining that it was a corona. It made a faint buzzing sound when he turned it on. He held it an inch above the plate and scanned it back and forth over the page several times.

"What's the corona doing?" asked Lord Justice Arnott.

"It's bombarding the Mylar film with positive charges, Your Honor, which will be attracted to any indentations on the page."

Once he'd completed the task, the professor switched off the corona and announced, "I am now ready to sprinkle some photocopy toner over the surface of the paper, after which we'll quickly discover if my experiment has served its purpose or has been a complete waste of time."

The attentive crowd, heads down, stared at the piece of paper as the professor lifted one side of the bronze plate, before sprinkling the page with minute, pepper-like black filings that ran down its surface and disappeared into a narrow trough at the bottom of the plate. Once he was satisfied the paper had been completely covered with filings, he lowered the bronze plate back in place, and peered down at his handiwork.

"Look at Arthur," whispered Grace.

Sir Julian glanced up at the defendant, who was still standing in the dock. Arthur didn't seem to be in any doubt about what the result would be, whereas Lord Justice Arnott and his two colleagues still appeared skeptical, and Mr. Llewellyn downright unconvinced.

Professor Abrahams bent over the machine and placed a sheet of sticky-backed plastic carefully on top of the Mylar film, then deftly peeled the film from the plate. Finally, he separated the sticky-backed plastic sheet from the film, and placing a blank sheet of white paper behind it, held it up for everyone to see.

No one could have failed to observe the unmistakable impressions on the missing page.

Mr. Llewellyn still looked unimpressed when Lord Justice Arnott said, "Perhaps you would be kind enough, professor, to read out the words that are indented on the page, as I have a feeling you may have done this before."

"On several occasions, Your Honor. But I should warn you that there are bound to be some gaps. But first may I remind you of the final sentence on the first page, before I move on to the disputed second page." The judge nodded. *"I later regretted that I had lost my temper with him, and I should never have . . ."* The professor took a large magnifying glass from his bag and studied the indented page closely before he continued.

"done so before I heard   side   story. On arrival back   Euston S   I took taxi to our," he hesitated, *"office in Marylebone. When I open   the door I saw heavily built ma   rush   ward me. I held op   the doo for him,*

*but   barged past me and   to   street. I didn't think
about   at   tim but ater realiz   he co have be   the
mur erer. I went s   up to Gary' offi on the   loor,
and fo   im pread   on t floor by the mant   piec . I
rush   across bu   it was   ready   late. Someon must ave"*

The professor turned to the third page of the statement and continued, *"struck him."* One or two of those standing around the machine burst into applause, while the others remained stony silent.

"Thank you, professor," said Lord Justice Arnott, before adding, "Ladies and gentlemen, would you please return to your seats."

Grace waited until everyone had settled before she rose from her place and said, "No more questions, My Lords," and collapsed onto the bench.

"Chapeau," her father whispered, touching his forehead with the fingers of his right hand.

"Mr. Llewellyn, do you wish to cross-examine this witness?" asked Lord Justice Arnott.

Professor Abrahams braced himself for the Crown's rebuttal.

"No, My Lords," said the Crown's chief advocate, barely moving from his place.

"We are in your debt, Professor Abrahams," said Lord Justice Arnott. "I'm only glad that your mother lives in Warsaw, and that you dropped by to see us on your way to visit her. You may step down."

"Thank you, Your Honor," said the professor, before leaving the stand and gathering up his box of tricks.

Grace wanted to hug him as he walked across the room and winked at Arthur, before leaving the court.

"Do you have any more witnesses, Sir Julian?" asked Lord Justice Arnott.

"Just one, My Lords. Detective Sergeant Clarkson, the other signatory to Mr. Rainsford's original statement. He has been subpoenaed to appear before your lordships at ten o'clock tomorrow morning."

"Then we will adjourn until then."

Sir Julian bowed, and remained standing until the three judges had gathered up their copious notes and departed.

"Do you think Clarkson will actually turn up tomorrow?" asked Grace.

"I wouldn't bet on it," replied her father.

31

THE CROWN V. FAULKNER

"Please state your name and occupation, for the record," said Mr. Booth Watson.

"Miles Adam Faulkner. I'm a farmer."

"Mr. Faulkner, the court has heard that you own an impressive art collection, as well as homes in New York and Monte Carlo, an estate in Hampshire, a yacht, and a private jet. How can that be possible if you're a farmer?"

"My dear father left me the farm in Limpton, along with three thousand acres."

William immediately scribbled a note and passed it across to the Crown's QC.

"That still doesn't explain your lavish lifestyle, or your ability to collect valuable works of art."

"The truth is that, despite my family having owned Limpton Hall for over four centuries, some years ago the government issued a compulsory purchase order on my land, as they wanted to build a six-lane motorway right through the middle of it, leaving me with the house and just a couple of hundred acres. I opposed the order and took them to court, but sadly lost on appeal. However, what the government ended up paying me in compensation allowed me to pursue my lifelong interest in art. And thanks to one or two shrewd investments in the stock market over the years, I have managed to build up a reasonable collection."

William made a second note.

"Which no doubt you intend to pass on to the next generation," said Booth Watson, looking down at a list of well-prepared questions.

"No, sir. I'm afraid that won't be possible."

"Why not?"

"Sadly my wife had no interest in having children, and as I do not want to break up the collection, I have decided to leave my entire estate to the nation."

Miles turned and smiled at the jury, just as Booth Watson had instructed him to. He was rewarded with one or two of them smiling back at him.

"Now I'd like to turn to one painting in particular, Mr. Faulkner, *The Syndics of the Clothmakers' Guild* by Rembrandt."

"Without question a masterpiece," said Faulkner. "I've admired it since the day I first saw it as a schoolboy when my mother took me to visit the Fitzmolean."

"The Crown would have us believe that you admired the painting so much, you stole it."

Miles laughed. "I admit," he said, looking at the jury once again, "that I'm an art lover, even an art junkie, but I am not, Mr. Booth Watson, an art thief."

"Then how do you explain your wife's claim, under oath, that you have been in possession of the Rembrandt for the past seven years?"

"She's quite right. I have owned *The Syndics* for seven years."

The jury were now staring at the defendant in disbelief.

"Are you admitting to the theft?" asked Booth Watson, feigning surprise. The jury too appeared to be confused, while Mr. Palmer QC looked suspicious. Only the judge remained impassive, while Faulkner just smiled.

"I'm not quite sure I understand what you are suggesting," continued Booth Watson, who understood exactly what his client was suggesting.

"I wonder, sir," said Faulkner, turning to the judge, "if I might be allowed to show the court the painting that has been hanging above the mantelpiece in the drawing room of my home in Hampshire for the past seven years, in order to prove my innocence?"

Now even Mr. Justice Nourse looked puzzled. He glanced across at Mr. Palmer, who shrugged his shoulders, so he turned his attention back to defense counsel.

"We wait with interest, Mr. Booth Watson, to find out what your client has in store for us."

"I am most grateful, Your Honor," said Booth Watson. He nodded to his junior, who had positioned herself by the entrance to the court. She opened the door and two heavily built men entered carrying a large crate, which they placed on the floor between the judge and the jury.

"My Lord," said Palmer, leaping to his feet, "the Crown was given no warning of this unscheduled charade by the defense, and I would ask you to dismiss it for what it is."

"And what might that be, Mr. Palmer?"

"Nothing more than a stunt to try to distract the jury."

"Then let's find out if it does, Mr. Palmer," said the judge. "Because I suspect the members of the jury are as curious as I am to discover what's inside the box."

Everyone's eyes remained fixed on the crate as the packers became unpackers. They first extracted the nails, followed by the polystyrene chips, and finally the muslin, to reveal a painting that left some gasping, others simply bemused.

"Mr. Faulkner, would you be kind enough to explain how it's possible that Rembrandt's *The Syndics of the Clothmakers' Guild* comes to be in this court," said Booth Watson, "and not, as your wife claimed earlier, hanging on a wall of the Fitzmolean Museum?"

"Don't panic, Mr. Booth Watson," said Faulkner to a man who never panicked. "The original is still hanging in the Fitzmolean. This is nothing more than an exceptional copy, which I purchased from a gallery in Notting Hill just over seven years ago, and have the receipt to prove it."

"So this," said Booth Watson, "is the painting your wife has been looking at for the past seven years, under the mistaken impression that it was the original?"

"I'm afraid so, sir, but then Christina has never shown any real interest in my collection, other than how much it was worth. Which in this case was five thousand pounds."

"Mr. Faulkner," said the judge, looking closely at the painting, "how can a layman like myself be sure this is a copy and not the original?"

"By looking at the bottom right-hand corner, My Lord. If this was the original, you would see Rembrandt's initials, RvR. He rarely left a painting unsigned. To be fair, that's something else my wife was unaware of."

"While I accept your explanation, Mr. Faulkner," said Booth Watson, "I am still at a loss to know how the original, now safely back in the Fitzmolean, came into your possession."

"To understand that, Mr. Booth Watson, you have to first accept that I am well known as a collector throughout the art world. Each year I receive hundreds of unsolicited catalogs for art exhibitions, as well as several requests to buy paintings, often from old families who do not want anyone to know that they are experiencing financial difficulties."

"Do you ever buy any of these works?"

"Very rarely. I'm far more likely to make my purchases from a respected dealer or an established auction house."

"But that still doesn't explain how the original Rembrandt came into your possession."

"A few weeks ago someone offered to sell me a painting that he claimed was a Rembrandt. As soon as he described the work, I knew it had to be the one stolen from the Fitzmolean."

"Why did you make that assumption?" asked the judge.

"It's almost unknown, My Lord, for a Rembrandt to come on the market. Almost all of his works are owned by national museums or galleries. Very few are still in private hands."

"So if you knew the painting was stolen," said Booth Watson, "why did you have anything to do with it?"

"I confess that I couldn't resist the challenge. However, when I was told I would have to travel to Naples to view the painting, I realized it had to be the Camorra who had stolen it. I should have walked away. But like a footballer who's convinced he's about to score the winning goal, I charged on."

Booth Watson had never cared much for that particular metaphor but ran with it. "And did you score the winning goal?"

"Yes and no," said Faulkner. "I flew to Naples, where I was met by a smartly dressed young lawyer accompanied by a couple of thugs who never once opened their mouths. I was then driven to a rundown part of town which is a no-go area, even for the police. I've never seen such poverty in my life. And the only pictures on the walls of the tenement blocks were either of the Virgin Mary or the pope. I was taken down a long flight of stone steps into a dimly lit basement, where there was a large painting propped up against the wall. I only needed one look, to know it was the real thing."

"What happened next?"

"The bargaining began, and it quickly became clear they wanted to be rid of the painting, so we settled on a hundred thousand dollars. I knew, and they knew, that it was worth a hundred times that amount, but they weren't exactly overwhelmed with potential buyers. I told them I would hand over the money the day the painting was returned to the Fitzmolean. They said they'd be in touch, but didn't even offer to drive me back to the airport. I had to walk some distance before I came across a taxi."

"And when you got back home, did you tell anyone about your experience?"

"I had to share what I'd been through with someone, so I foolishly told Christina. I never thought she'd take advantage of it, and even lie under oath."

"And the gentlemen you'd met in Italy didn't keep to their side of the bargain and return the picture to the Fitzmolean."

"The Camorra rarely stray beyond their own territory," said Faulkner. "I heard nothing for over a month, so I assumed the deal must be off."

The judge made a note.

"But it wasn't?"

"No. The two thugs who I'd met at the airport turned up at my home in Monte Carlo in the middle of the night with the painting, and demanded their hundred thousand dollars. One of them was brandishing a knife."

"You must have been terrified."

"I was. Especially when they told me they would first slit the throats of the six Syndics, one by one, and then mine if I didn't pay up."

The judge made another note.

"You had a hundred thousand dollars cash on hand?"

"Most people who want to sell me one of their family heirlooms, Mr. Booth Watson, don't expect to leave with a check."

"What did you do next?"

"The following morning I rang the captain of my yacht and told him that a large crate would shortly be arriving at the dockside. He was to take it to Southampton and personally deliver it to the Fitzmolean Museum in London."

"And, Your Honor," said Booth Watson, "if the Crown so wishes, I can call Captain Menegatti, who will confirm that those were indeed the instructions Mr. Faulkner gave him."

"I bet he will," muttered William, "if he wants to keep his job."

"You flew to Australia the following day, assuming that your orders would be carried out."

"Yes. I had hoped my wife would come with me, but she changed her mind at the last moment. It turned out she had an assignation with a younger man."

William clenched his fists to try and stop himself trembling.

"But then she was well aware I had tickets for the Boxing Day Test in Melbourne," continued Faulkner, "which meant I wouldn't be returning to England before the New Year."

"But you returned to England halfway through the match?"

"Yes, Captain Menegatti called me at my hotel in Melbourne to" tell me that my wife had turned up at the yacht, not with the single crate I'd told him about, but with my entire Monte Carlo collection. She then instructed him to take them all to Southampton, where she would meet up with him before going on to New York."

"How did you react?"

"I caught the next plane back to London, and it didn't take a twenty-three-hour flight to work out what she was up to. As soon as I landed at Heathrow, I took a taxi to my home in Hampshire, aware I didn't have a moment to lose."

"Why didn't you ask your driver to pick you up?" asked Booth Watson.

"Because it would have alerted Christina that I was back in the country, and that was the last thing I needed."

"And was your wife at home when you turned up?"

"No, she wasn't, and neither were my artworks, which I discovered were also on their way to Southampton. I only got there just in time to stop them being shipped off to New York."

"So you then boarded the yacht, and gave instructions for the artworks to be returned to your homes in Hampshire and Monte Carlo—"

"With one notable exception," interrupted Faulkner. "I had always intended to return the Rembrandt to the Fitzmolean whatever the consequences." Once again he turned to face the jury, this time giving them his "sincere look."

"But before you could do that, the police charged on board, arrested you, and accused you of having switched the labels on two of the crates so you could keep possession of the Rembrandt."

"That, Mr. Booth Watson, is a farcical suggestion, for three reasons. Firstly, I was only on board the yacht for a few minutes before I was arrested, so it's obvious my wife had already informed the police that the Rembrandt was still on board. Secondly, the label for the Fitzmolean must have been switched by her before the pictures were even loaded in Monte Carlo."

"But why would she switch the labels, and then tell the police that the Rembrandt was still on board?" asked Booth Watson, innocently.

"Because if I was arrested, there would be nothing to stop her sailing off to New York and stealing the rest of my collection, which she had clearly been planning to do while I was safely on the other side of the world."

"You said there was a third reason, Mr. Faulkner."

"Yes, there is, Mr. Booth Watson. Commander Hawksby was accompanied by two other police officers. They had obviously been briefed by my wife that the Rembrandt was on board. What would have been the point of switching the labels when the harbor master had the authority to open every one of the crates? No, what Christina planned was that I would be arrested, and at the same time I'd lose my Rubens. She not only switched the labels, but knew she would be depriving me of my favorite painting."

"At least the Rubens has been returned to its rightful owner, along with the rest of your collection."

William noticed that Booth Watson gave his client a slight nod.

"Yes, it has, Mr. Booth Watson. Tim Knox, the director of the Fitzmolean, accepted that a genuine mistake had been made and kindly returned the Rubens to my home at Limpton Hall. However, after a few days, I began to have second thoughts. As you will know, the Fitzmolean's collection of Dutch and Flemish paintings is second only to that of the Rijksmuseum in Amsterdam. I began to wonder if Rubens's *Christ's Descent from the Cross* had found its rightful home, and after much soul searching, I have decided to make a gift of the painting to the nation, so that others can have as much pleasure from it as I have had over the past thirty years."

Word perfect, thought Booth Watson, looking at the jury. He was now convinced that at least half of them were on his client's side.

"And finally, I must ask you, Mr. Faulkner, if, before this recent regrettable misunderstanding, you have ever been charged with a criminal offense?"

"No, sir, never. However, I must confess that when I was at art school, I once pinched a traffic policeman's helmet and wore it to the Chelsea Arts Club ball. I ended up spending a night in jail."

"Did you indeed, Mr. Faulkner? Let us hope you won't be spending any more nights in jail. No further questions, Your Honor."

◄○►

"What's your point?" asked Sir Julian as Grace laid out a set of large black-and-white photographs on the bench between them.

"The photos show Stern leaving the court after you'd cross-examined him."

"I can see that. But what do they prove, other than that he's enjoying the limelight?"

"Not for much longer, I suspect. Take a closer look, Dad, and you'll notice something Stern didn't want us to see."

"I'm still none the wiser," confessed her father after he'd taken a second look at the photographs.

"The leather jacket is Versace, and the shoes are Gucci loafers, top of the range."

"And the watch?" said Sir Julian, catching on.

"A Cartier Tank. And it's not a fake, unlike the man."

"Stern certainly couldn't afford those kinds of luxuries on a detective inspector's pension."

"And there's a bonus," said Grace, pointing to another couple of photos showing Stern climbing into an S-type Jaguar and driving away. "The car's registered in his name."

"I think it's time to apply to a judge in chambers, and find out if he'd be willing to allow us to inspect Stern's bank accounts."

◄○►

"Do you think the jury believed a word of that codswallop?" asked William, after Mr. Justice Nourse had called for a recess.

"I'm not sure," said Hawksby. "But it doesn't help that Mrs. Faulkner was so obviously planning to steal her husband's art collection. So the jury will have the unenviable task of deciding which one of them is the bigger liar. How are things progressing in court twenty-two?"

"I'm just on my way to see Beth and find out. By the way," he added, lowering his voice, "those files I left on the table in your office have proved most helpful."

◄○►

When William entered court twenty-two, the first thing he saw was Arthur Rainsford disappearing down the dock steps to the cells below, accompanied by a policeman.

"We're finished for the day," said Beth, as William sat down beside her. "So we may as well go home."

William thought about having a word with his father, but noticed he was deep in conversation with Grace, so he decided not to interrupt them. Beth took his hand but didn't say another word until they'd left the building and were out on the street.

"Your sister was forensic in her examination of Professor Abrahams," said Beth as they walked across the road.

"My father allowed Grace to examine the principal witness?" said William in disbelief.

"And Abrahams was so convincing that the Crown didn't even bother to cross-examine him."

"Once again I've underestimated the old man," said William. "But was Grace able to prove there was a missing page?"

"By the time Professor Abrahams had left the witness box, even the Crown's leader accepted there were three pages," said Beth as they joined a bus queue.

"That's good news. But what about the judges? After all, they're the only ones whose opinions really matter."

"There's no way of knowing. Like seasoned poker players, they reveal nothing."

"Who's next up to be demolished by my father?" asked William once they'd boarded the bus.

"Detective Sergeant Clarkson, Stern's former partner."

"He's a weaker character than Stern, so might well crack under pressure."

"How do you know that?"

"I wish you could have seen Hawksby when he was in the witness box," said William. "Even the judge was impressed."

Beth got the message and followed his lead. "But didn't Booth Watson give him a hard time?"

"No, he didn't even cross-examine him. He'd obviously decided there was nothing to be gained from it."

"And what was Faulkner like on the stand?"

"Impressive," admitted William, "if not altogether convincing. He looked a little over-rehearsed and kept putting the blame on his wife."

"Surely the jury won't like that."

"Booth Watson took Christina apart yesterday." William immediately regretted saying "Christina," and moved quickly on. "And Faulkner put the boot in today. He also made a promise that took us all by surprise, although I don't think he has any intention of keeping it."

"That he'd gift the Rubens to the Fitzmolean?"

"How did you know that?"

"I rang the gallery during the lunch recess, and Tim Knox told me that Booth Watson had phoned to tell him Faulkner would be donating the Rubens as soon as the trial was over."

"That sounds to me distinctly like a bribe," said William, as the bus came to a halt in the Fulham Road. "Surely the judge will be able to work that out?"

"Perhaps you should give Faulkner the benefit of the doubt for a change."

"I fear that's exactly what the jury might do. But it will take a lot more than that to convince me he hasn't been in possession of the Renbrandt for the past seven years."

"Do you think we'll ever be able to go a whole day without discussing either case?"

"That will depend on whether your father is released and Faulkner is locked up for a very long time."

"But what if it's the other way around?"

32

"I'm the bearer of glad tidings," said Booth Watson, as a waiter appeared by his side. "But let's order breakfast first."

"Just black coffee, toast, and marmalade for me," said Faulkner. "I've lost my appetite."

"I'll have the full English breakfast," said Booth Watson. He didn't speak again until the waiter was out of earshot. "I've had an approach from the other side. They're willing to drop the charge of intent to steal if you'll plead guilty to the lesser offense of knowingly receiving stolen goods."

"Bottom line?" asked Faulkner.

"If we accept their offer, you'll probably get a couple of years, which means you'd be released in ten months."

"How come?"

"As long as you behave yourself, you'd only serve half the sentence, with a further two months knocked off as it's your first offense. You'd be out in time for Christmas."

"Ten months in Belmarsh isn't my idea of a generous offer, and more important, it would give Christina enough time to steal my entire collection."

"That shouldn't be a problem," said Booth Watson, "because while you're away, I'll make sure Christina doesn't get anywhere near any of your properties."

Faulkner didn't look convinced. "And if I don't accept their offer?"

"If you're found guilty of both offenses, theft and receiving, the maximum sentence is eight years, along with a hefty fine."

"I don't give a damn about the fine. I have a feeling Palmer knows he's fighting a lost cause, and is hoping to save face. In any case, I think the jury's on my side. At least two of them smiled at me yesterday."

"Two's not enough," said Booth Watson, before pausing while a waiter refilled their coffee cups. "The foreman looks to me like a retired colonel or the headmaster of a prep school, who's likely to believe that the punishment should fit the crime."

"That's a risk I'm willing to take, BW. So you can tell Palmer to get lost. Feel like a glass of champagne?"

THE CROWN V. RAINSFORD

"Call Detective Sergeant Bob Clarkson," cried the clerk.

Grace didn't take her eyes off Clarkson as he walked across the courtroom and entered the witness box. He delivered the oath with none of the swagger Stern had displayed.

An honest, decent copper, who's easily led, and sometimes led astray, was one of the sentences Grace had highlighted after reading Clarkson's personnel file.

Sir Julian sat patiently through the Crown's cursory examination of Clarkson, which didn't throw up any surprises. But then he'd never thought it would.

"Do you wish to cross-examine this witness?" asked Lord Justice Arnott.

Sir Julian nodded as he rose from his place. He had always intended that Stern should regard him as the enemy, but not Clarkson.

"Detective Sergeant Clarkson," he began, his voice gentle and persuasive, "as a police officer you will know the consequences of committing perjury. So I want you to think most carefully before answering my questions."

Clarkson didn't respond.

"On the day Arthur Rainsford was arrested and charged with

the murder of his business partner, Mr. Gary Kirkland, were you present at the scene of the crime?"

"No, sir. I was back at the station."

"So you did not witness the arrest?"

"No, sir, I did not."

"But you were the junior officer who signed the statement Mr. Rainsford made later that evening."

"Yes, sir, I was."

"Did that statement, written by DI Stern and witnessed by you, consist of three pages or two?"

"Originally I thought it was three, but DI Stern assured me the following morning that it was only two, and I accepted his word."

That wasn't the answer Sir Julian had been anticipating. He paused for a moment, aware that his next five questions were redundant, before asking for confirmation of what he'd just heard.

"So you originally believed the statement was three pages and not two, as Mr. Stern claimed?"

"Yes, sir, and having studied yesterday's court report I accept Professor Abrahams's findings without question."

"But that would mean you also accept that Mr. Stern must have removed a page from the original statement?" said Sir Julian.

"Yes, I do, sir. And I regret not challenging him at the time."

"Did you challenge him about the possibility of there being a mystery man, the man who Mr. Rainsford stated ran past him as he entered the office block, and who he has always claimed could have been the murderer?"

"Yes, I did, but DI Stern said he was just a figment of Rainsford's imagination, and we should dismiss it for what it was worth."

"What about the anonymous telephone call informing the police of Mr. Kirkland's murder? Was that also a figment of Mr. Rainsford's imagination?"

"No, sir. We did receive a call from a man with a foreign accent, who told us he'd been passing the block at the time, when he heard the sound of two men shouting, followed by silence, and

JEFFREY ARCHER

moments later, a man came running out of the building onto the street, which was the reason he'd phoned the police immediately."

"Did he give you his name?"

"No, sir, but that's not uncommon in such cases."

"As recorded on the missing page of Mr. Rainsford's statement, the police arrived at RGK's offices only a few moments after he did."

"That's what a guilty man would say if he wanted to put the blame on someone else," said Clarkson. "So I didn't bother to follow it up, not least because chasing anonymous calls is a thankless task, and usually ends up being a complete waste of time."

"So you never discovered who the mystery man was?"

"Yes, I did, sir," said Clarkson.

Sir Julian was once again taken by surprise. He took a step into the unknown.

"Please tell the court in your own words, detective sergeant, how you found out who this mystery man was."

"A couple of days after Rainsford had been charged, a black cab driver turned up at the station and told us he'd seen the story on the evening news. He said he'd picked up Rainsford from Euston on the afternoon of the murder, and dropped him outside an office block on Marylebone High Street. He'd only just turned on his FOR HIRE sign when a man came rushing out of the building and asked to be taken to the Admiral Nelson pub in West Ham, but after he'd traveled about a hundred yards the man told the driver to stop. He got out, and ran into a nearby phone box. He returned a few minutes later when the cabbie continued on his journey to West Ham."

"Did he give you a description of the man?"

"May I refer to the notes I made at the time?" asked Clarkson, turning to the judges.

Lord Justice Arnott nodded and Clarkson opened a small black pocketbook and turned several pages before he continued. "The cabbie said he was around five eight, dark hair, and could have

300

done with losing a couple of stone. He also said that he'd put money on him being Greek or Turkish."

"What made him think that?" asked Sir Julian.

"The cabbie did his national service in Cyprus at the time of the uprising, and was fairly confident he recognized the accent."

"Did you report this conversation to DI Stern?"

"I did, and he wasn't best pleased. But he said he'd visit the Admiral Nelson and check the story out."

"And did he discover who the mystery man was?"

"Yes, he did. But he told me that the man had a cast-iron alibi. He'd been in the Admiral Nelson at the time of the murder, which the landlord confirmed, as did several other customers who'd also been in the pub at that time. In any case, Stern reminded me, we had a signed confession, so what more did I want?"

"So you didn't follow up that line of inquiry?"

"No, I didn't. After all, DI Stern was the senior officer on the case, and I was just a rookie constable not long out of probation, so there wasn't a lot I could do."

"And there's no paperwork to prove that DI stern visited the Admiral Nelson pub, or interviewed the so-called mystery man."

"DI Stern didn't care much for paperwork. Said he believed in nailing criminals not filing them."

"I understand you weren't called to give evidence at Mr. Rainsford's trial?"

"No, sir, I was not. And when Rainsford was convicted, I assumed DI Stern must have been right all along. That was until I read about Rainsford's appeal in the *Daily Mail*, and began to wish I'd interviewed Mr. Fortounis at the time, and not left—"

"Vasilis Fortounis?" said Arthur, leaping up from his chair in the dock.

"Yes, I'm pretty sure that was his name," said Clarkson.

"His daughter was Gary Kirkland's secretary," shouted Arthur.

"Sir Julian, restrain your client before I do," said Lord Justice Arnott firmly.

Arthur sat back down, but began waving frantically in Sir Julian's direction.

"I think this might be an appropriate time for a recess, Sir Julian, as it is clear that your client wishes to consult you. Shall we reconvene in an hour?"

THE CROWN V. FAULKNER

"Members of the jury," said Mr. Justice Nourse, "you have heard the arguments presented by both learned counsel, and it is now my responsibility to sum up this case dispassionately and without prejudice. It will be up to you, and you alone, to decide if Mr. Faulkner is guilty or not guilty on the three counts brought against him on behalf of the Crown.

"Let us consider each one in turn. Firstly, did Mr. Faulkner steal a painting by Rembrandt from the Fitzmolean Museum? Do you feel that the Crown produced sufficient evidence to prove its case beyond reasonable doubt? If not, you must find for the defendant. And secondly, if Mr. Faulkner was not directly involved in the theft, was he nevertheless a party to it? You must make your decision based solely on the facts presented in this courtroom."

Faulkner allowed himself a brief smile, while Booth Watson sat back in his place, arms folded, aware that the judge hadn't yet reached the least convincing piece of his client's evidence.

"Then there is the charge that Mr. Faulkner knowingly purchased the stolen painting, as claimed by his wife. Although Mr. Faulkner produced a copy of the Rembrandt, you must ask yourselves how long the original had been in his possession.

"Are you inclined to believe Mr. Faulkner's testimony that he visited Naples, and attempted to make a deal with the Camorra to purchase the painting for one hundred thousand dollars, with the sole purpose of returning it to the Fitzmolean? And do you think it likely that the Camorra initially turned his offer down, but turned up with the picture some time later at Mr. Faulkner's home in Monte Carlo, and demanded the hundred thousand dollars? This, despite the fact that Mr. Faulkner told us that in his experience," the judge glanced down at his notes, "the Camorra rarely stray beyond their own territory.

"And did you find it credible that one of these men, who never spoke to him when he was in Naples, threatened to cut the throats of the six Syndics, and then Mr. Faulkner's throat, if he didn't pay up? Or do you consider that might be one embellishment too many? Only you can decide who to believe—Mr. or Mrs. Faulkner—because they can't both be telling the truth. However, you must also ask yourselves if Mrs. Faulkner's evidence can be relied on, as she admitted quite openly that she was attempting to remove all of her husband's artworks from their homes in Monte Carlo and Limpton Hall, while he was in Australia, and I have no doubt she would have sailed on to New York to carry out the same exercise, had her husband not intervened. And finally, members of the jury, you must take into consideration the fact that the defendant has no previous criminal record.

"Members of the jury," he concluded, looking directly at the five men and seven women, "once you have considered all the evidence you must be sure of guilt beyond reasonable doubt before you can convict. If you are not sure, you must acquit. So please take your time. If, during your deliberations, you should require assistance on any matter concerning the law, do not hesitate to return to this courtroom, and I will do my best to answer your questions. The bailiff will now accompany you to the jury room, where you can begin your deliberations. Please take your time considering all the evidence before you reach your verdict."

THE CROWN V. RAINSFORD

"Sir Julian."

"My Lords. I am grateful to have been given the opportunity to consult with my client, and would request that the court recall

Mr. Stern, and also subpoena Mr. Vasilis Fortounis, as the defense would like an opportunity to question both of them under oath."

"I will grant your request, Sir Julian, and suggest that we adjourn until tomorrow morning, by which time I hope the bailiff will have been able to locate both of these gentlemen."

"Thank you, m'lud," said Sir Julian, trying to sound convinced.

All three judges rose from their places, bowed, and left the court.

"I can't wait for tomorrow," said Beth.

"Don't get your hopes up," said Grace, as she gathered her files. "Stern and Fortounis will be well aware of what happened in court this afternoon, and I don't suppose either of them is currently heading in the direction of the Strand."

THE CROWN V. FAULKNER

"You wish to seek my advice?" said Mr. Justice Nourse after the jury had filed back in and resumed their places.

"Yes, Your Honor," said the foreman of the jury, a distinguished-looking gentleman wearing a charcoal-gray double-breasted suit and a Cavalry tie. "We've been able to reach a verdict on the first and second counts, but are divided on the third, that of receiving stolen goods."

"Do you think it would be possible for you to deliver a majority verdict upon which at least ten of you are agreed?"

"I think so, Your Honor, if we were allowed a little more time."

"In that case we will take an early recess, and reconvene at ten o'clock tomorrow morning, to allow members of the jury time to sleep on it."

Everyone in the court rose and bowed. Mr. Justice Nourse returned the compliment before leaving his domain.

"Don't you sometimes wish you could skip twenty-four hours and find out what's going to happen?" said William.

"You won't when you've reached my age," replied Hawksby.

33

THE CROWN V. RAINSFORD

"Sir Julian, you may call your next witness."

"I am unable to do so, m'lud. Although subpoenas were issued yesterday as you directed, the court's bailiff has been unable to serve writs on either Mr. Stern or Mr. Fortounis."

"Then we will have to wait until they have been served," said the judge.

"That might not be for some time, m'lud."

"What makes you think that, Sir Julian?"

"I'm told that Mr. Fortounis returned to his home in Nicosia a few days before the trial opened, and has not been seen or heard of since."

"Who is the source of your information?"

"The proprietor of the Admiral Nelson public house in West Ham Grove, where he was a regular."

"And Mr. Stern?"

"It appears that he flew out of Birmingham airport late last night."

"Let me guess," said the judge, "also on a flight bound for Nicosia."

"And as he'd booked a one-way ticket, the bailiff may have some difficulty in enforcing your edict, for as I'm sure you are aware, m'lud, Britain has no extradition treaty with Cyprus."

"Then I shall issue a directive that Mr. Stern's assets will be seized, and that he will be arrested should he ever set foot in this country again. I suppose it's too much to hope that like Bolingbroke, banishment will prove an even harsher punishment for him than incarceration."

No one offered an opinion.

Mr. Llewellyn rose from his place. "May I approach the bench, My Lords?"

Lord Justice Arnott nodded. Mr. Llewellyn and Sir Julian walked to the front of the court to join their lordships. They spoke in hushed voices to the three judges for some time before Lord Justice Arnott raised a hand and began conferring with his colleagues.

"What are they talking about?" Beth whispered to Grace.

"I have no idea. But I suspect we're about to find out."

THE CROWN V. FAULKNER

"Will all parties involved in the Miles Faulkner case please go to court number fourteen," boomed out a voice over the tannoy, "as the jury is about to return."

Several people who'd been standing around in the lobby stopped chattering, while others stubbed out cigarettes before making their way quickly back to the courtroom. William joined Commander Hawksby, DCI Lamont, lawyers, journalists, and the simply curious, as the bailiff led his charges into court to resume their places in the jury box.

Once they had all settled, the clerk said, "Will the foreman please rise."

The foreman rose from his place at the end of the front row.

"Have you reached a verdict on all three counts?" asked Lord Justice Nourse.

"We have, Your Honor," replied the foreman.

The judge nodded to the clerk of the court.

"Mr. Foreman, do you find the defendant, Mr. Miles Faulkner, guilty or not guilty of the theft of a Rembrandt painting entitled *The Syndics of the Clothmakers' Guild* from the Fitzmolean Museum in London?"

"Not guilty, Your Honor."

Faulkner allowed himself a smile. Booth Watson showed no emotion. William frowned.

"And on the second count, that the defendant was an accomplice in that theft. How do you find the defendant, guilty or not guilty?"

"Not guilty."

Lamont cursed under his breath.

"And on the third count, namely that of receiving goods that he knew to be stolen, namely the said painting by Rembrandt, how do you find the defendant, guilty or not guilty?"

"By a majority of ten to two, Your Honor, we find the defendant guilty."

Loud chattering erupted in the well of the court, and several journalists rushed out to grab the nearest available phone and report the verdict to their news desks. The judge waited until the court had settled before turning to the prisoner.

"Will the defendant please rise," said the clerk.

A less confident figure rose slowly in the dock, stumbled forward, and gripped the railing to steady himself.

"Miles Faulkner," said the judge gravely. "You have been found guilty of receiving stolen goods, namely a work of art of national importance. Because of the seriousness of your crime, I wish to spend a few days considering what punishment is appropriate. I shall therefore delay passing sentence until next Tuesday morning at ten o'clock."

"What's he up to?" said Hawksby as Booth Watson heaved himself to his feet.

"My Lord, may I request that my client's bail be extended until that date?"

"I will allow that," said Mr. Justice Nourse, "on the condition that he hands in his passport to the court. And I am sure, Mr. Booth Watson, that you will spell out the consequences to your client should he fail to appear before me in this courtroom next Tuesday morning."

"I will indeed, Your Honor."

"Mr. Booth Watson and Mr. Palmer, would you be kind enough to join me in my chambers."

"What's he up to?" repeated the commander.

THE CROWN V. RAINSFORD

The courtroom was packed long before Lord Justice Arnott and his two colleagues made their entrance at ten o'clock the following morning.

Lord Justice Arnott placed a red folder on the bench in front of him and bowed to the court. He then took his place in the center chair, rearranged his long red gown, and adjusted his spectacles before opening the folder and turning to the first page.

The courtroom had fallen so silent that he had to look up to make sure they were all in attendance. He peered down at the expectant faces and then at the prisoner in the dock before delivering his final judgment. He felt sorry for Rainsford.

"I have in my life as a judge presided over many cases," Arnott began, "and in each one I have attempted to remain detached and emotionally uninvolved, so as to ensure that justice is not only done, but seen to be done.

"However, I fear that in this case, I did become emotionally involved. It became clear to me after hearing Mr. Stern's evidence, that an injustice might have been done. That feeling was reinforced when Professor Abrahams brought his expertise to bear on this case. I and my colleagues were finally persuaded of this during the cross-examination of Detective Sergeant Clarkson, whose frank and honest evidence was a credit to his profession.

"Although the real perpetrators of this crime may never be apprehended, I am in no doubt that Arthur Edward Rainsford was falsely charged with the murder of Gary Kirkland, his friend and business partner. I therefore order that the verdict of the original trial be overturned." A cheer went up, which only died down when the judge frowned, making it clear he hadn't finished. "A judgment of this type should never be taken lightly," he continued. "I do not consider the jury at the original trial is to blame for the verdict it reached, as they took a detective inspector's word at face value, and because of that man's duplicity, they were never allowed to consider the missing page from the statement Mr. Rainsford gave to the police on the evening of his arrest, with the result that a grave injustice was done to an innocent man. It gives me considerable pleasure not only to release the prisoner, but to make it clear that there never was, and never should have been, a stain on this man's character. Mr. Rainsford, you are free to leave the court."

Beth and Joanna Rainsford were among the first to leap in the air and applaud as the curtain finally came down. However, the gesture that Arthur would remember long after all the fury of battle had subsided came when Mr. Llewellyn left his place on the Crown's bench, walked across to the dock, and shook hands with the defendant. Arthur had to bend down to hear his words above the clamor of the crowd.

"For the first time in my life, sir," whispered Llewellyn, "I am delighted to lose a case."

◄○►

Mr. Justice Nourse took off his gown, discarded his wig, and was pouring himself a glass of malt whiskey when there was a knock on the door.

"Enter," he said. The door opened, and Booth Watson and Palmer joined him in his den.

"While I'm doing the honors, can I get you anything, BW, Adrian?"

"No, thank you, Martin," said Booth Watson as he took off his wig. "I know you won't believe this, but I'm still trying to lose weight."

"Adrian?"

"Yes, please, judge," said Palmer. "I'll join you in a malt if I may."

"Do sit down, both of you," said the judge as he handed prosecuting counsel his drink. He took a sip of whiskey, and waited for them both to settle before he spoke again. "I wanted a private word with you, BW, but I felt Adrian should be present so that no misunderstanding could arise at a later date."

Booth Watson raised an eyebrow, which he would never have considered doing in court.

"I'm curious to know if your client is serious about his intention to donate his Rubens to the Fitzmolean?"

"I have no reason to believe he isn't," said Booth Watson. "But if you feel it's important, I could certainly find out and let you know."

"No, no. I was simply curious. And while you're here, allow me to congratulate you both on the way you conducted your cases. I think you could fairly describe the result as a score draw."

"I don't think my client sees it that way," said Booth Watson.

"Perhaps he should have accepted my offer," said Palmer, draining his glass.

"Dare I ask?" said the judge.

"The Crown would have dropped the charge of theft if he'd pleaded guilty to receiving."

"So the jury got it right," said Nourse, before taking another sip. "The other half, Adrian?"

"Thank you, judge."

"And you, BW, are you sure I can't tempt you?"

"No, thank you, Martin. I have a consultation with my client in a few minutes' time, so I'd better be on my way."

"Yes, of course, BW, see you on Tuesday morning."

Booth Watson rose from his chair and turned to leave.

"And perhaps you could let me know if your client hands over the Rubens to the Fitzmolean, as he said he would under oath," he paused, "before Tuesday."

Booth Watson nodded, but didn't comment.

Palmer took another sip of whiskey and waited for the door to close before asking, "Did I just witness a subtle bit of arm twisting?"

"Certainly not," said the judge, raising his glass. "I have already decided Mr. Faulkner's fate, although I confess that should he show the slightest sign of remorse, there is one concession I just might be willing to consider. But then, on the other hand, I might not."

◄○►

"Why do you think he asked you that?" said Faulkner.

"Judges have been known to make concessions at the last moment, but only if they sense genuine remorse."

"How genuine?"

"If you were to hand over the Rubens to the Fitzmolean before Tuesday, I have reason to believe his lordship might consider that a genuine act of contrition."

"And what could I expect in return?"

"Nourse is far too shrewd to give anything more than the suggestion of a hint, but it's in his power to decide between the maximum tariff for the offense, of four years, or the minimum, of six months. There's even the possibility of a suspended sentence and a fine of ten thousand pounds—but it's only a possibility, so don't get your hopes up."

"As you know, BW, I don't give a damn about the fine. But if I had to spend even six weeks in jail, heaven knows what havoc Christina could cause in my absence."

"Does that mean you are willing to donate the Rubens to the Fitzmolean?"

"It means I'll think about it."

"Before Tuesday."

◄○►

Arthur fell asleep at ten o'clock, which was slightly embarrassing for the rest of the family as they were all enjoying a celebratory dinner at San Lorenzo, his favorite restaurant, where he was welcomed as if he'd never been away.

"Lights out at ten," he explained. "After nearly three years, it's not an easy habit to break."

"What's the first thing you'll do when you wake up tomorrow morning?" asked Grace.

"At six o'clock," said Arthur.

"Sausage, eggs, bacon, and beans?" suggested William.

"Scrambled egg that isn't out of a packet, and perhaps I'll allow myself a sliver of smoked salmon, some toast that isn't burned, and a cup of steaming hot coffee with milk that isn't powdered," responded Arthur.

"And after breakfast?"

"I shall take a long walk in the park before going shopping. I'll need a new suit if I'm to look smart when I return to work tomorrow morning."

"Why not take a break before going back to work," suggested Sir Julian. "Go on holiday."

"Absolutely not," said Arthur firmly. "I've already had a three year break. No, I intend to return to the office as soon as possible."

"Could you bear to put it off for one more day, Dad?" asked Beth. "You and Mum have been invited to the Fitzmolean tomorrow for the unveiling of the Rembrandt, and I expect every one of you to be present for my moment of triumph."

"*Your* moment of triumph?" said William.

Everyone laughed except Arthur, who had fallen asleep again.

◄◦►

Court number fourteen was packed long before ten in the forenoon, and, like a theater audience, they chatted among themselves as they waited for the curtain to rise.

Commander Hawksby, DCI Lamont, DS Roycroft, and DC Warwick were seated a couple of rows behind Mr. Adrian Palmer QC, the prosecuting counsel.

Mr. Booth Watson QC and his instructing solicitor, Mr. Mishcon, sat at the other end of the bench, discussing the coverage their client had received in the national press that morning. They agreed that it couldn't have been much better.

Miles Faulkner standing next to *Christ* adorned several front pages, along with the words Booth Watson had written and his client had repeated verbatim: *"Of course it's sad to part with one's favorite painting, not unlike losing an only child, but my Rubens couldn't have gone to a better home than the Fitzmolean."*

The press benches along one side of the courtroom were so crowded that several old-timers who'd been unable to find a seat were left standing behind their less illustrious colleagues. Once the sentence was delivered, they would race to the nearest available telephone and report the judge's decision to the duty editor.

The Evening Standard would be the first on the street, and it already had its front page headline set in type: FAULKNER SENT DOWN FOR X YEARS. Only the number needed to be filled in. The crime correspondent had submitted two stories the night before, and a sub-editor would decide which one would go to press.

From seven o'clock that morning, a queue of the simply curious and the morbid had begun to form outside the public entrance of the Royal Courts of Justice, and within minutes of a court official opening the door, every seat in the gallery had been taken. All of those present knew the curtain would rise as ten o'clock struck on the southwest tower of St. Paul's. Not that any of those cloistered in the court would be able to hear the cathedral chimes.

The moment Mr. Justice Nourse appeared, the chattering ceased, giving way to an air of expectation. The judge took his place in the high-backed red leather chair, looked down upon his kingdom, and surveyed his subjects, feigning no interest in the fact that he'd never seen his court so packed. He returned their bow, and placed two red folders on the bench.

William turned to look at Faulkner as he took his place in the dock. In a dark blue suit, white shirt, and Old Harrovian tie, he looked more like a city stockbroker on his way to work than a prisoner who was about to be dispatched to Belmarsh. He stood tall, almost proud, as he faced the judge, outwardly appearing calm and composed.

Mr. Justice Nourse opened the first red folder marked JUDG-MENT, and glanced across at the prisoner before he began to read his handwritten script.

"Mr. Faulkner, you have been found guilty of receiving stolen goods, and not some insubstantial bauble of little significance, but a national treasure of incalculable value, namely Rembrandt's *The Syndics of the Clothmakers' Guild.* I have no doubt that you were in possession of that unique work of art for some considerable time, probably for the seven years after it was stolen from the Fitzmolean Museum, and that you never had any intention of returning it to its rightful owner. Had your wife not dispatched the painting to England without your approval, it would probably still be hanging in your home in Monte Carlo."

Mr. Adrian Palmer allowed himself a wry smile on behalf of the Crown.

"You are not, Mr. Faulkner," continued the judge, "as some tabloids would have us believe, a gentleman thief who simply enjoys the thrill of the chase. Far from it. You are in fact nothing more than a common criminal, whose sole purpose was to rob a national institution of one of its finest treasures."

Booth Watson shifted uneasily in his seat.

The judge turned to the next page of his script, before pronouncing, "Miles Edward Faulkner, you will pay a fine of ten thousand pounds, the maximum I am permitted to impose, although I consider it to be woefully inadequate in this particular case." He closed the first red folder and shuffled uneasily in his seat. Faulkner had to agree with him that the amount was "woefully inadequate," and avoided a smirk at the thought of getting off so lightly.

The judge then opened the second folder and glanced at the first paragraph before he spoke again. "In addition to the fine, I sentence you to four years' imprisonment."

Faulkner visibly wilted as he stared up at the judge in disbelief.

The judge turned the page and looked down at a paragraph he had crossed out the night before, and rewritten that morning.

"However," he continued, "I am bound to admit that I was moved by your generosity in donating Rubens's *Christ's Descent from the Cross* to the Fitzmolean Museum. I accept that it must have been a considerable wrench for you, to have parted with the pride of your collection, and it would be remiss of me not to acknowledge this generous gesture as a genuine sign of remorse."

"He's going to waive the fine," whispered the commander, "which Faulkner won't give a damn about."

"Or perhaps reduce the sentence," said William, who couldn't decide whether to look at the judge or Faulkner.

Faulkner didn't flinch, desperately hoping to hear one word, and it wasn't "fine."

"Therefore, I have decided," continued the judge, "perhaps against my better judgment, to also show some magnanimity, and to suspend your sentence, with the clear direction that should you commit any other criminal offense, however minor, during the next four years, the full term of your prison sentence will automatically be reinstated."

Faulkner considered his generous gesture, as the judge had so kindly described it, to have been well worthwhile.

"You are therefore free to leave the court, Mr. Faulkner," said the judge, in a tone that suggested he was already regretting his decision.

William was livid, and didn't leave anyone nearby in any doubt about how he felt. Lamont was speechless, and Hawksby reflective. After all, Mr. Justice Nourse had said *any other criminal offense, however minor.*

When Beth heard the news later that afternoon, she simply said, "If I had to choose between Faulkner going to prison for four years or the Fitzmolean ending up with a priceless treasure, I wouldn't have to give it a second thought."

"I was rather hoping for the best of both worlds," said William. "The Fitzmolean would get the Rubens and Faulkner would spend the next four years languishing in Belmarsh."

"But which side would you have come down on if you were only given the choice between Faulkner spending four years in jail, or the Fitzmolean having the Rubens for life?"

"On the side of the Fitzmolean, of course," said William, trying to sound as if he meant it.

34

"Your Royal Highness, my lords, ladies, and gentlemen. My name is Tim Knox, and as the director of the Fitzmolean Museum, it is my pleasure to welcome you to the official unveiling of Rembrandt's masterpiece *The Syndics of the Clothmakers' Guild*. The Syndics, as you know, were taken from the museum just over seven years ago, and some thought they would never return. However, such was our confidence that they would eventually come home, we have never allowed another painting to hang in its place."

A spontaneous round of applause followed. The director waited for silence before he continued.

"I will now invite Her Royal Highness to unveil the lost masterpiece."

The Princess Royal stepped up to the microphone. "Before I do, Tim," she said, "can I remind you that my great-grandfather opened this museum over a hundred years ago. I trust that when I pull this cord, something my family have considerable experience in doing, there will be a Rembrandt on the other side and not a faded rectangle where *The Syndics* once hung." Everyone laughed. Princess Anne pulled the cord, and the red curtain parted to allow them all to admire the painting, some of them for the first time. William glanced at its bottom right-hand corner to make sure the RvR was in place before he joined in the applause.

"Thank you," said Knox. "But tonight, you are going to get two for the price of one, because you cannot have failed to notice that there is a second painting waiting to be unveiled. But for now, enjoy a glass of champagne and admire the Rembrandt, before we introduce you to our latest acquisition."

William didn't budge as he continued to admire the painting he'd first seen in Monte Carlo, and had wondered if he'd ever see again. He didn't notice the commander standing by his side until he broke into his thoughts.

"Congratulations, William," said Hawksby. "This has been a personal triumph for you."

"It was a team effort, sir," said William, reluctantly taking his eyes off the picture and turning to his boss.

"Balls. It would never have been returned to its rightful place if you hadn't joined the team. However, just to warn you, as soon as we get back to the Yard, I shall be reporting to the commissioner and taking all of the credit."

William smiled. "I'm delighted Jackie was invited this evening," he said, looking across the room to see her chatting to Beth. "She did so much of the spadework before I even arrived on the scene."

"I agree. And although she's been demoted, I'm pleased the department hasn't lost her altogether. But that has created a problem, because Art and Antiquities is only allowed one detective constable."

William accepted the rule that if you were the last to join a unit, and cutbacks had to be made, you'd be the first to leave. He just hoped he wasn't going back on the beat.

"I'm afraid, William, we'll have to move you to another department, but not before you've taken your sergeant's exam."

"But I'm not eligible to do that for at least another year, sir."

"I'm well aware of that, Warwick. That's why I'm putting you on the graduates' accelerated promotion scheme, which you tried so hard to avoid when you first joined the force."

William wanted to protest, but was well aware it was a battle he couldn't win. "And what department do you have in mind for me, sir?"

"I haven't decided between drugs, fraud, and murder."

"I've had enough of murder, sir, although I'll be eternally grateful for your help in ensuring my future father-in-law was released."

"Never mention that in public or private again," said Hawksby as Arthur drifted across to join them.

"I can't wait to see what's behind the other curtain," Arthur said. "Beth's been making such a fuss about it."

"And she's right to do so," said William, "but all I can say is you won't be disappointed."

Tim Knox tapped his champagne glass with a spoon several times before everyone had stopped talking and turned to face him.

"In the past," he said, "we have always considered *The Syndics* to be the star of our galaxy, but when this second curtain is opened, I wonder if you will consider that a genuine rival has joined the firmament."

Without another word, he pulled the cord to reveal Rubens's *Christ's Descent from the Cross*, to gasps, followed by thunderous applause.

"This amazing addition to our collection," he continued, once the ovation had subsided, "has been made possible by the incredible generosity of the well-known collector and philanthropist Mr. Miles Faulkner. As he is with us this evening, I ask you all to raise a glass and drink his health."

"Count me out," muttered William, despite the cries of "Hear, hear!" and the clinking of glasses.

"Count me in," said Beth, raising her glass, "while he's still got so many more rare gems on his walls that we'd be happy to see hanging in the Fitzmolean."

"I'd hang him first," said William.

"I think I'd better go and rescue my father," said Beth, "and take him home. It's getting close to his bedtime, and we mustn't forget that he's going back to work tomorrow."

William nodded. "I'll join you in a moment," he said, unable to tear himself away from the Rubens.

"I shall miss my favorite work of art," said a voice from behind him.

William swung around to see Faulkner also admiring the Rubens, but he refused to acknowledge him. That didn't stop Faulkner from saying, "Should you ever find yourself in New York, Constable Warwick, do give me a call, because I'd like to invite you around to my apartment on Fifth Avenue for a drink."

"Why would I want to do that?" said William, almost spitting out the words.

Faulkner leaned forward and whispered in his ear, "Because then I can show you the original."